KILLING MOLLY

A NOVEL BY

ERIC C. NOVACK

Elitist Publications 487 W Alexandrine, Third floor Detroit, MI
48202
www.elitistpublications.com

PRINTED IN THE UNITED STATES OF AMERICA
Printed at N.W. Coughlin & Company - Livonia, Michigan
www.nwcoughlin.com

This is a work of fiction. Any resemblance to actual persons, living
or dead, is purely coincidental.

Dedicated to

My parents
Ronald and Suzanne Novack

Alex Owen

and

Zack Papper

Special Thanks to

Holly Novack

Linda Lott

and

Captain Bob

AFTERWORD AS THE FOREWORD

I'm not exactly sure what this novel is about. I guess it could be considered a love story. You could even say it's a tale of human interaction. Or maybe it's just a satire. Whatever the case may be, this novel suffers from a horrible disease. I'll let you be the judge of what the affliction just might be.

IT'S JUST A STORY

It's a story about hope

Or lack thereof

It's a story about love

Or lack thereof

It's a story about faith

Or lack thereof

It's a story about...

Or lack thereof

The Elitists

MICKEY   late twenties, average in appearance, has sordid past, convicted felon. Currently on an eight month house arrest and probationary period, supervised by the state of Michigan. Employed by a wholesale tire company only a few miles from his parents' house, where he resides. His hobbies consist of reading and talking shit to his friends. He is currently single.

JEREMIAH   early twenties, tall and broad shouldered with long hair, grew up in the same neighborhood as Mickey. He has just returned from a year of voluntary service with the AmeriCorps and now works for his family, a manager of a soft-serve ice cream parlor. Jeremiah resides at the Hippie House in Ferndale, Michigan. His friends have also given him several nicknames: Miah, Mia, Jay (which he does not appreciate). Jeremiah's hobbies consist of hackie sack, disc golf, and talking shit to his friends. Jeremiah just ended a two year relationship with Molly.

BENEDICT   early twenties, average in height, has a stereotypical Jewish look. Resides in the Hippie House with Jeremiah. Benedict has just completed a bachelor's degree in philosophy. His hobbies consist of reading, instigating mischief, and talking shit to his friends while desperately trying to avoid spending time with them. He prefers to be called Ben and delivers pizza for a steady income. Benedict is also currently single.

THOMAS   early twenties, average in height, has a Greek look to him, which is uncanny, considering he's an Irish Jew. Currently resides at the Hippie House with Jeremiah and Benedict. He has plans to move to downtown Detroit in hopes of securing some sort of social life with the art crowd. Thomas has just completed his bachelor's degree in evolutionary science, but has gone back to school to become an EMT. He, as well, is currently single.

SANDIE   early twenties, average in height and build, currently working as an environmental activist for Greenpeace in Massachusetts. Received her bachelor's degree in science from the University of

Michigan, where she met and dated Thomas. She is also currently single.

PETER AND SIMONE   both in their early twenties, planning to marry in the near future and move to California. Peter and Simone attended high school with Benedict, Jeremiah and Thomas.

The Wannabe's

MARIE   late teens, supermodel pretty, works as a hair-stylist in Royal Oak, Michigan. Became friends with Mickey a few months before he was arrested. Marie's hobbies consist of reading and kick-boxing. She also practices witchcraft. Marie is currently dating a neo-Nazi named Brian.

TARA   mid-twenties, with a voluptuous body. Currently goes to school at Ferris State, which is located in the northern part of Michigan. She is currently involved with Cody, who has moved to Colorado in hopes of becoming a massage therapist. She also met Mickey before he was arrested.

CODY   mid-twenties, stereotypical hippie in appearance, moved to Colorado three months ago. Cody used to live in the Hippie House with Jeremiah and Thomas. He plans to return home for the Christmas holiday.

DARLA   mid-twenties, with an anorexic look to her. She used to live next-door to Mickey, before he got arrested. Frequently pops in on the residents of the Hippie House. She had become accustomed to it, as a place of refuge, when she dated Jerry.

JERRY   also referred to as the Pavement Hippie, moved to Florida after being kicked out of the Hippie House. Jerry used to live with Mickey, before Mick was arrested.

MARY BETH   early twenties, lives with Molly in Royal Oak. Slept with Thomas a couple times when Molly and Jeremiah were still together.

AND THEN THERE WAS MOLLY

MOLLY   mid-twenties, sordid past. Hobbies consist of reading and writing. Works as a waitress at a Mexican restaurant. Just got dumped by Jeremiah after a two year relationship, a year of it spent while Miah was in the AmeriCorps. Molly lives with Mary Beth in Royal Oak.

THE NIGHTMARE

I awoke suddenly. I was terrified. I must have been dreaming. My sheets were soaked with sweat. I couldn't tell you what the dream was about. I wouldn't remember. I shivered as the sweat chilled on my body. I wish I could remember what the dream was about. It gave me the feeling of......... I don't know. It's like being trapped somehow. No. No, it's worse. It's horrific. When I think about that feeling, my body shudders, almost as if I were buried alive. Or it might be how one would feel when they're eternally damned.

CHAPTER ONE

HATING GOLDMUND

"I hate Goldmund."

"What?!"

"Don't 'what' me!"

"God! You are such a fucking asshole."

"Goldmund! I hate Goldmund!"

"Okay. Who is Goldmund?"

"He's a character in *Narcissus and Goldmund*, by Hesse."

"Uh-huh?"

"Well, in the novel, he's a little prick that acts on all his urges, instead of his reasoning. He's like a kid that has no self-control. But what really pisses me off is that everybody loves the little prick. He's so beautiful. Every fucking town he travels to, women fawn over him like he's something special, when, in reality, he's a vacuum."

"Okay. So, you're jealous?"

"No."

"You are so fucking weird sometimes."

"Hmmm. Want some more coffee?"

"Yeah. Sure."

MICKEY   Marie left around nine; on the way out she muttered something about going to Brian's. I stayed in the garage for another hour or so. After downing two more cups of coffee that I retrieved from the kitchen, I headed to bed. While I lay unable to sleep, my mind began to wander. Here I am. Twenty-eight years old and living with my parents, yet again. Of course, the situation could be a hell of a lot worse. I could be serving twelve years in prison, instead of dealing with an anal mother and an emotionally dejected dad.

Where was I a year and a half ago? Selling drugs? No, that came later. I guess it was around that time I had come home to my apartment to find Anne getting plugged from both ends. Anne. What a bitch. I supported that cunt. I was patient with that slut. I even went as far as to get engaged to that pariah. You would think that's when I became so despondent. But I think that came a lot earlier in our relationship. Anne was always sucking the life out of everything we did. It was never good enough. The nice restaurants, the flowers, the constant understanding I spent on her. All went to waste. I'm tapped out when it comes to the matter of my heart. I don't have a heart. It's more like a black hole that I have caged up in my chest. I don't want to feel responsible for the poor bitch that might get sucked in.

Goldmund really pisses me off. I told Marie about my disgust for him today. I knew it would take some explaining, but I was sure she would understand. She didn't. It really all boils down to consumption. We're always eating, we're always smoking, we're always drinking, we're always fucking. I want to be an Indian. I remember stories of American Indians fasting for days. They could control their urges. I guess it's a culture thing, 'cause I smoke like a chimney and eat whatever is put in front of me. I'm like a horse. I'll eat and eat until I rip a hole in my stomach and die from some sort of toxic poisoning. I think most people would. We have no self-control. We're like primates, with less hair. I would drink like a fish, but my probation prohibits it.

My grandmother on my father's side died when I was fourteen. Right after the funeral, my parents took the family to Disney World. That's when I started having trouble sleeping. I was so afraid that I would die in my sleep. I wanted to face death when it came. I wanted to be fully conscious, so I could fight it. Fight death? Huh. I finally got over the whole thing and made it through my teenage years without a scratch. But that fear came back a few months ago. Now I just play games with death. I have a list of things I have to do before I descend into the netherworld. Sticking my dick in a girl's ass isn't one of them.

MARIE   When I got to Brian's I felt sick. I didn't want to tell him about the VD. But Mick may be right. He seemed pretty sure of himself on the subject. I know he's right. If Brian really truly does love me, he'll understand. I just don't know how to put it. "Brian? Sweetie? I got a little problem. Well, it's really more like an itch sometimes, or maybe just a flea or two playing house in my fucking pubic hair. But don't worry. The shampoo the doctor gave me should take care of it in a few weeks. And the warts only get inflamed once in awhile." Yeah. Sounds great. But Mick's right. I'm not a slut. I just feel like one.

MICKEY   Marie called rather late. I wasn't asleep, but there's no phone in my room. The whole thing created quite a stir in the house. My parents usually get all crazy about phone calls after ten. They say it's an invasion of their privacy that bugs them. Yeah. I'm sure it has nothing to do with my crazy sister that goes on drinking binges and ends up with some guy in a third world country every other week. After my parents finally calmed the fuck down and went back to bed, I was able to talk to Marie. She must have been in tears. She kept gasping for air. After an hour or so of blubbering on her part, she ended the conversation by thanking me and saying that she'll see me on Sunday. Thanking me? For what, I wonder. I sure as hell wasn't listening. While she was screeching like a rat in water, I had the phone on the desk so I could read *1984*. George Orwell. I told her no problem and hung up.

On Thursday, I called Marie when I got home from work. There's nothing like dealing with a depressed woman after a long day of changing tires for some rich SOB's wife. I never understood why a hundred-and-Coach-purse-pound woman drives a three ton SUV.

Anyway, Marie and I talked for about a half hour or so. I kind of felt sorry for her. It's just too damn bad that there are pricks like Brian out there. I guess the other night, when she went over to his house, she told him about her misfortune. He didn't even let her finish before he went on some tirade about how promiscuous she was. I, of course, offered to kick his ass in eight months, when I get off house arrest. That seemed to make her laugh. I'm not sure if it was the time restraint that made it so funny or the fact that she thinks of me as a pussy. No matter. Most women think guys who read more than their cell phone bills are weak. That's their hang-up.

MARIE　Even though Mick puts on this tough guy act, deep down he's a real sweetheart. He has a way with back-handed compliments that makes me smile. Especially when all I want to do is sulk. It's too bad he's on house arrest. He really doesn't deserve it. Well, maybe three felonies does deserve it. As soon as I got off the phone with Mick, I called my mom. My mom's a witch. I had her put a protection and prosperity spell on Mick and a curse of chaos and despair on Brian.

TARA　Somehow I started talking to Mick on a weekly basis. He seems a lot different. God! He used to be such an asshole. It must be the whole house arrest thing. Well, it really doesn't matter. I love hearing from him. He's so inquisitive about the most mundane shit. And we've got this word thing we play. We alternate weeks picking a word that isn't commonly used and then spend the whole week integrating it into our daily conversations. My roommates even got involved in our little game. So now every week when I get off the phone with Mick, I write the word up on the house bulletin board so they can play along. The word of the day is clothier, which is a maker or a retailer of clothing.

MICKEY　Clothier? What a stupid fucking word. This is why I should pick the word every week. Hell, I only play the game for some bullshit reason to call Tara. The pain one must endure to get down a girl's pants.

I wish I was a kid again. Being a kid was cool and I never got to really enjoy it. I remember how great it was not to feel any guilt. I could say the dumbest thing and never get in trouble for it. I was a kid and I was cute. People don't get mad at cute kids. I could say "I hate your guts" and people would laugh and say "isn't that cute?" They wouldn't even acknowledge that it might be true. Eventually you get to an age where your parents insist on instilling some sort of guilty conscience into you. No more speaking without thinking. You become devoid of the one ability that lets you be truly unique. I wonder what I would be like without a guilty conscience.

Marie came over on Sunday. As per usual, I try not to go too far from home. With me being on house arrest, I am completely paranoid about some big catastrophe happening that will prevent my successful return back home. The state only gives us criminals a couple of hours of freedom every Sunday. Marie took me to the book store and, after I found a novel that met my ten-page rule, I bought it. On the way into the store, I noticed how nice and friendly I was to people. I even opened the door for them as we went into the store. This must have been subconscious. Because I swear I had only ill will toward every patron in the place. Even on the way out I was charming and flirtatious to the cashier. Which was weird, because she was a rude bitch. The whole time she was ringing me up I just imagined myself slapping the arrogant little bitch across the face.

Eventually, Marie and I made it to Big Boy's for lunch. I had my usual Big Boy Classic and Marie had some salad thing. I brought up the whole Brian thing. We discussed it for awhile and then agreed that she could do better. I thought I might be able to discuss the whole guilty conscience thing. She seemed a little lost while I ranted on and one about how great it would be to punch someone full in the face and not feel ill about it. Marie always gets a kick out of my mindless noise pollution. Today was no different. She laughed and told me how crazy I was. Right around then I realized that Marie and I spend a lot of time together. She's great-looking, with her petite frame, nice hand-ful of breasts and has a great style. I started to think that I should be fucking her. We already talk like boyfriend and girlfriend. We should start doing other stuff too. It's been a year or so since Anne. I'm pretty sure I should start dating again. Hell, I have to have feelings for Marie. God knows I put up with enough of her shit. Then it was decided. Even if I didn't know I had feelings for her, I would still try to fuck her. What's love anyway? Nothing, I say. It's a delusion we force ourselves to believe in. To have some goal in our pathetic buy-everything-on-sale lives. That sounded really bleeding heart. I think I might have made myself sick. I can't be a liberal. I don't come from a rich family, and I think helping people is a posh thing to do.

MARIE   Mick and I were at lunch on Sunday. As usual, we went to Big Boy's, because God forbid we might get a flat and he would have to run home so not to miss his curfew. Really, I don't think they'll take him to jail for being late. During lunch, Mick ranted for an hour or more about not having a conscience. He insisted he would be able to kill someone and not feel bad about it. In fact, he went as far as to say that maybe murderers were right and that maybe we were wrong to judge them. He is so fucking weird sometimes I have to laugh at him. Then, out of the blue, he changed his tune and started hitting on me. What that was all about, I have no idea. Mick's like a brother to me. I mean, he's really not over the top in the looks department and he's way too depressing half the time. Oh, and the whole self-hate thing bugs the crap out of me. Besides, I'm still crazy about Brian.

The rest of the day Mick pulled the same shit. When we finally got back to his parents' house, he asked me to stay and watch a movie. I told him I couldn't 'cause I was going to my sister's. Which wasn't true, but there was no way in hell I was staying with him acting like a lost little puppy dog. I hate when men pull that shit. It doesn't seem real.

MICKEY   After Marie dropped me off, I called up Tara to give her the word of the day. She seemed all bubbly and happy, as usual. She babbled on for the next half an hour, while I read today's paper. I eventually had to end her conversation with herself by telling her I needed to get to bed. Really, my ear was hurting from the phone, so I made a mental note to put it on the desk the next time I talked to her.

In bed, while I attempted to sleep, I thought of all the stages people go through with each other until they end up in bed together. The introduction stage seems to be a little different each time. Sometimes you will be nervous and have difficulty speaking. Other times, you just find yourself bored, but still interested, in who this might be. Lately I have found that neither applies to me. I don't want to meet anyone and I don't feel nervous around anyone. I am a black hole. The second stage is the friend stage, where two potential fuck buddies feel each other out over dinners and numerous bullshit activities. Again, this would not apply to me, seeing as I don't even make it out of the first stage. But, if by some miracle I did, I would sure as hell not want to spend any time with anyone other than myself. The only thing a woman would have to offer me is a place to stick my dick. The third stage is moving the friendship you have developed into a romance. This depends largely on sexual attraction. So, if you're not fat and you chew with your mouth closed and don't say anything too stupid, you'll get your rocks off. Now many a time I have fancied the idea of getting past the first two stages and to the third right away. However, I know that the only time this is successful is when you have the face of a greek god and a chiseled body, or a big fat wallet. That's for guys. For girls, all they have to do is lay down and spread their legs. Then it just depends on how drunk the guy is, or how pretty the girl is. I think I may be in the second stage with Marie.

TARA   Mick seemed a little distracted today. He gave me the word of the week, which is charlatan. I looked it up, thinking it meant whore. Come to find out, it's some sort of showoff. That's Mick. He always has some book he wants to talk about or some movie he found interesting. Well, la-di-da. I had a rough day and needed to vent. So, I bitched for a half hour or so and was surprised that Mick didn't interrupt and just let me bitch the whole time. I really appreciated that. He can be real sweet once in a while.

MARIE   I called Mick to tell him I was on my way over. I was so

10

excited to see him. I couldn't wait to tell him about Jim. Jim and I met the other day. I was outside Brian's trailer screaming and throwing rocks at his door when Jim pulled up. He was so sweet. He asked me what was going on. I told him how Brian had dumped me and then started telling all my friends that I slept around and gave him AIDS. Jim invited me to go get coffee with him. We talked for hours. He pointed out how ridiculous I was being, wanting some sort of vengeance from a guy who was nothing more than an immature little boy. Right before I went home, Jim asked me out. I said sure. I figured it wouldn't hurt. Besides, Jim is Brian's best friend.

MICKEY   I have decided to express my feelings, or lack thereof, to Marie. I should be nervous, but I'm not. Marie just called and said she was on her way. I have chairs set up in the garage, where we usually sit. I have made coffee. I have reviewed a few of Kahlil Gibran's *Spiritual Sayings* to recite, if need be. You never know.

Marie has come and gone. When she first arrived, I couldn't help but notice how happy she was. I thought for sure I was on the right track with this love thing. She seemed so excited to see me. We talked for a little while about nothing of importance. After my third cup of coffee and fifth cigarette, I started in on the whole love thing. I told her how great it is to spend so much time with her. I told her how I find her attractive and all that crap. I even lied and said that she makes me a little nervous. Halfway through my proclamation of love, she began to cry. I was ecstatic. Yes. I got it right.

No. I got it wrong. She told me I was like a brother to her. And I was cute and all, but she didn't see me like that. So, what was she crying about? After she left, I went to bed thinking of the complete ass I must have made of myself. I should be embarrassed. But, I'm not. Maybe love is still out there for me. Maybe I still have a shot. Then, before I went to sleep, I jerked off fantasizing about Marie taking it in the ass.

MARIE   Goddamn it, Mickey. Why do you have to pull this shit on me? I was in a great mood. I wanted to tell you all about Jim. But nooooo! You had to make me feel like shit. You're always complaining about how nobody loves you. And then you pull this shit on me. How could you put me in this position? I didn't want to hurt you. You looked so depressed when I told you I thought of you like a brother. It's not fair. So I don't find you attractive. There should be rules against this sort of thing. A girl should have at least five guy friends who aren't gay, and won't fall in love with you, or lust after you, or even want to fuck you. Fuck you, Mick.

After I got home and calmed down, I felt really bad. I called Mick, but he was asleep. I didn't want this whole thing to ruin a great friendship. Mick has got to be the most dependable person I know. I want to still be able to count on him. A few minutes after I called Mick, the phone rang. I was sure it was Mick. To my elation, it was Jim. He wanted to grab a cup of joe. I couldn't refuse his beautiful blue eyes, so I said yes. I told him to come over my place and we could have coffee here. We had a couple cups while we watched a movie. We ended up making love and when I woke up the next morning, I found a rose on the pillow he slept on. I forgot about Mick.

MICKEY   My work has a black tie Christmas party every year in July. I was planning on taking Marie. But I haven't talked to her since I made an ass of myself. I'm not mad. I'm more dreading the whole pity thing. Girls always get this "I'm so sorry you're in love with me; I don't know what to say" face. I hate it. Just 'cause they think they have the upper hand and think I'm embarrassed by my actions. Well, I have no shame. I also hate girls that get mad at guys for being sensitive to their attitudes. I guess they're annoyed by men who care about their feelings. I'll make sure not to give a shit about a woman's feelings in the future. Which won't be hard, 'cause I could give two shits as it is. Well, I needed a date to the party, so I called Tara and asked her. She seemed excited about the whole thing and agreed to go. The best part about Tara going is that Marie is going to be pissed.

MARIE   Jim and I have been dating for almost two weeks now. I can't believe how attentive and nice he is. After he left one night, I sat around and smelled a shirt he'd left behind. God, I was in love. Then Mick called. We talked for five minutes or so. He seemed to be in a good mood. I told him what was up, and he told me what was up. Which included some party he had to go to and he was taking Tara. I asked if they were dating or something. He said no, but he needs someone to go. We made plans to have coffee the next day, on his Sunday free time. After he hung up, I sat on the couch, a little pissed off at him. I'm his best friend. I should be going to his stupid party. He doesn't even know Tara all that well. Fuck her. I got so annoyed with Mick that I called Jim. I told him to come over as soon as possible. He arrived in, like, two minutes. As soon as Jim walked in the door, I jumped him. We fucked all night. Fuck Mick.

MICKEY   I've come to the conclusion that I am a capitalist Buddhist. Christianity just doesn't seem to work for me anymore. So, I figured I would combine my capitalistic tendencies with the Buddhist philosophy. Then again, I could always revert and become an Irish Jew.

CHAPTER TWO

WHO? WHO?

"So, what's going on with you and Tara?"

"Hey, did I ever tell you about the owl?'

"No, but thanks for ignoring me."

"What?"

"Nothing. The owl?"

"When I was a kid there used to be this Tootsie Pop commercial on TV. It was about this kid who went around and asked all these animals if they knew how many licks it takes to get to the center of a Tootsie Pop. Finally, the kid comes across this owl. The owl takes the Tootsie Pop that the kid was carrying around and unwraps it. The owl takes two licks and then bites it. Then, that fucking owl tells the kid that it takes three licks to get to the center of a Tootsie Pop, when, in fact, it only took the bastard two licks and a bite. God, I hate that fucking owl."

"What's wrong with you? No, really. What the fuck is wrong with you?"

"That owl. That fucking owl."

"I'm going to go."

"Alright."

MICKEY   I spend so much of my time trying to figure out who I am. Funny how I know certain things I do that I hate. When I was a kid, I loved pineapple. I would eat it all the time. I would even drink pineapple juice. Eventually, I couldn't bear to eat it anymore. It's not like I began to hate pineapple, I just got bored with it. Now that I'm older, you would figure that I would grow out of such a stupid habit. Nope. I still find something I like and immerse myself in it until I get bored. How the hell am I ever going to have a lasting relationship if I can't even stick with the same breakfast cereal for more than a month? I don't even like cereal.

Tara called around eight. I could only talk for a few minutes, before Marie arrived. Tara seemed excited to be coming down this weekend for my company's Christmas party. After I hung up, I tried to fantasize a sexual encounter with her. I pictured kissing her passionately and undressing her slowly with the softest touch. This didn't arouse me at all. Then again, when I ripped down her panties and shoved my dick without lubrication into her ass, I was at full mast. The daydream was cut short by Marie's arrival.

Marie and I haven't talked in a couple weeks. We both seemed a little apprehensive. I broke the ice when I started talking about some commercial I had seen when I was a kid. She seemed to relax while I ranted on about the owl in the commercial. My thoughts drifted while I expressed my particular distaste for the owl. I don't think it's the owl I should be mad at. It's the kid. The owl is just a symbol of any situation he might run into. The kid is me, accepting the situation. If you told me I was ugly, I would accept the fact that I was. I should really be mad at the stupid kid, then. You're not ugly. You're just stupid. No confidence in himself, I guess. That's why I hate. I see myself in things I hate. With all this introspective crap going on in my head, I had stopped talking and was ignoring Marie. She was blabbing on and on about some guy she met. How wonderful he is. He even brought her a rose and he's so sweet. I don't know what that had to do with me, so I continued thinking about my hate.

MARIE   I went over to Mick's tonight. I was worried that he would

19

continue his pining for me. I was also curious if anything was going on with him and Tara. Mick and I were both a little quiet to each other. We sat in the garage, like always, and sipped coffee. I'm worried that Mick and I will never get back to the incredible friendship we had. He really means a lot to me. Even if he is a conceited asshole sometimes. I know he cares a lot more than he lets on. Mick finally started complaining about some commercial from his childhood. I think it was an attempt at breaking the ice. I figured I better tell him about Jim. The sooner the better. If he's going to mad at me, it may as well be while we're barely talking.

I left Mick's around ten. He was really offish the rest of the night. But I think he took the Jim news pretty well. I think he'll be okay. I'm just worried that I hurt him. Two months ago, if someone told me that Mick would be confessing his undying love to me, I would've laughed. But, now... he seems so dejected sometimes. And, what the hell was he talking about when he said that he was void of feelings? I hope he doesn't turn this whole rejection thing into some sort of reason to continue his woman bashing. I can see him now, telling people how I led him on. And those people will feel sorry for him. He's probably told Tara that I'm a manipulative, evil bitch. Great. Just great.

TARA   I left my house around two. I should get to Mick's around five. Just in time to change clothes. I'm kind of excited. This is so cool. Mick hasn't been out for months now. It was great to hear that his probation officer would let him go to his company's party. I brought my little black dress to wear. I want to look really good for Mick. Not for any other reason than for him to show me off to all his work buddies. It's go to be a little embarrassing for him sometimes. I mean, people look at you differently when you're a felon. The worst part of the whole thing is that Mick only got involved in the whole drug thing to bail out his friends. He really is a sweetheart. And, he is so obnoxious that you just have to laugh. I've seen him snub so many people. They'll just sit there all uncomfortable after he tells them off. Funny guy. I just hope he's not getting the wrong idea. He seems to be a little too attentive lately. He's a hopeless romantic. That's bad. He doesn't want love. He just wants to go through the motions. I just don't know when he's going through the motions. When I talked to him last week, it sounded like he tried to get with Marie. That girl is all high maintenance. I'm high maintenance, but Marie is a little over the top. She's young. I don't know why Mick was messing around with her. I'm sure it has something to do with his lack of mobility. He can't go out and meet anyone right now. Whatever. It doesn't matter. I'm going to look great. He's going to look suave. We will both turn heads at his Christmas party in July. What's with that, I wonder?

MICKEY Tara arrived around six. She changed into a hot little black dress that barely stopped her tits from popping out. There was valet parking and I made sure to tip the valet good. I also made sure to open every door for Tara. I have the feeling she's into me. Seeing as I have no feelings one way or the other, I thought for sure I better take advantage of the situation. I guess if I have a shot at love again, it might as well be with Tara. She's attractive, semi-intelligent and will probably take it in the ass. I wonder if she would make me coffee in the morning? Well, we got through dinner. It was horrible. I had some kind of fish concoction that tasted like fish. Tara had the beef dish that looked a hell of a lot better than my Tuna Helper. She offered to trade, and I refused. I was going to be a complete gentle-man. I even watched my tongue. The award ceremony lasted way too long. Tara and I made jokes about all the white trash and their hillbilly wives. I even stole some silverware off the table, while Tara grabbed a couple of the crystal highball glasses and put them in her purse. I thought it was cute. We seemed to be having a good time. I wasn't, but I'm pretty sure Tara was. After the dinner and awards ceremony, there was some ghetto gambling thing to do. Tara and I blew all the chips they gave us on roulette. I kept asking if she was alright. She, of course, said yes, and that she just wanted to make sure I was hav-ing a good time. We eventually left the party and headed home. Tara was getting tired and needed to take off as soon as she dropped me off. I had to be home at midnight. But, unlike Cinderella, there was no happy ending to this night. When Tara and I got back to my parents' house, she walked me to the door. We said some bullshit about how we both had a great time. The scene was perfect. Me, in my tux, and her nipples hard as rocks from the chill in the air. I kept thinking of the fantasy I had of her the other day. Then I went to kiss her. She backed up. What the...? I knew she was into me. She had to be. Otherwise, why was she here?

TARA   Oh, the pain. The horrible pain, the whole night. First of all, Mickey was so sweet and nice that I almost gagged. Then, I had to endure three hours of every redneck in this God-forsaken state. Third, Mickey kept trying to be all cute and mysterious, when he's none of those things. Fourth, when Mick and I were sitting at the table, he stole silverware. So, if he was going to be in poor taste, I decided to purse some of the nice crystal glasses. Then... then, he tried to kiss me. I didn't know what to say. I knew it was coming. The whole night he was acting like a lost puppy dog. But wait, Tara. It gets worse. Instead of you just telling him that you're not interested, you tell him you're not ready to get involved with anyone... you're still in love with Cody. Oh, but let's not forget that you're already dating Terrence... which no one knows about.... how could they? You want to make sure that Cody doesn't find out. God forbid people not think you're not still pining over Cody. FUCK!

MICKEY   At least there's still hope. This could be it. Maybe you're not as fucked up as you thought. Tara didn't reject you. She just wanted more time. That's good, I think. Maybe I'm not as without feeling as I once thought. Maybe I'm just so desensitized I just don't know when I'm in love. You know, I don't even know the real definition of love.

I woke up in a cold sweat last night. In it, the garage at work wasn't moving fast enough. The cars weren't coming in and out quickly enough. I was crazed. I started yelling and pushing the guys to move faster. I even threw a hammer at one of them. Wait. Maybe I wasn't dreaming. I think that might have been yesterday.

MARIE   Mick called. He seemed to be in a good mood. We talked about Jim. We talked about Tara. I think Mick might have a chance with her. But, I don't know what's going on with her and Cody. I know Mick called Cody to make sure it was okay to take Tara to that party. Cody didn't care. Although he did appreciate that Mick called and asked. Tara is so high maintenance. I just hope she doesn't hurt him.

TARA   Great. Nice. When I called Mick, he was so sweet that I felt vomit in the back of my throat. I really fucked up. Terrence had just left. We were making love all afternoon. And now I've got some love sick puppy dog to contend with. I should have known better. I should have just been honest with Mick. Mick's honest. He might exaggerate, but he sure as hell is bluntly honest. When I finally said goodbye to my delusional Romeo, I called Molly. She's the only one who knows about Terrence. She might have some advice. Molly and I have been friends for a few years. I met her when I was dating Cody and she was dating Miah. Makes sense, seeing as Cody and Miah are best friends. Molly and I stayed friends, even after all the break-up stuff between the four of us. Molly just broke up with Miah. He's a hopeless. Not a hopeless romantic. A hopeless. And Cody and I broke up when he moved to Colorado. But, we kind of stayed committed, even though we promised to tell each other if we found someone else. Well, I have apparently found a couple of someones. One I want, and one I don't want to hurt. Molly will know what to do. She's had this problem before. I'm sure she has. She's Molly, and everyone who's anyone loves Molly.

Molly proved to be useless on the subject of Mick. She hates him, which I never knew. I didn't even know she knew him. When I asked her about it, she blew up. "Mick," she said. "Miah's friend, Mick. I hate his guts." Of course, I had to ask why. I guess right before Mick got put on house arrest, Miah, Molly and Mick got breakfast. I think Marie may have been there, too. But seeing that Molly had never met Marie before then, she had no real definitive answer to whether it was her or not. Anyway, when they were having breakfast, Mick must have been his charming self 'cause Molly insists he was rude. She couldn't believe how much of an ass he was. Miah had talked Mick up to Molly before breakfast. So, she figured, if Miah really thought the world of him, he must have been a real sweetheart. Well, she found out what a sweetheart he is. I tried to tell Molly that's just the way Mick is with people he doesn't know. She didn't want to hear it. She just kept going on and on about what an asshole he was. She even kept repeating something he said. "You're not that pretty."

I had to laugh. I wanted so badly to tell he he was right. She really isn't.

MICKEY   When I was at work today, I got a phone call. I thought it was my mom. She probably wanted to remind me of something that had nothing to do with nothing. I do the same thing to her. The only problem is that we never seem to call each other at the right time. I'll call when she's engrossed in something other than wanting to hear my bullshit. And she'll call when I'm threatening somebody's life. So, seeing as I was in the middle of some unexplainable rage toward Tim, I let the phone call hold for three or four minutes. By the time I got to it, I was seething with anger toward all the guys in the garage. I had murder in my heart that day. The phone call ended up being from my probation officer. He wanted to let me know that my house arrest ended two days ago. I had to ask him to repeat what he just said. I was free. He told me to come in next week to get the tracking device taken off. I was free. I have been on house arrest for over eight months. I was free. But, then I thought about what he had said. Two days. You mean, I've been going home right after work for the past two days and not leaving until the next morning, just to go back to work? So what if I'd done that for eight months already? Those were my two days, that you took from me. I began to get angry about the whole thing. But, then I laughed. I was free.

Later that day, I drove and drove and drove, through every city that surroundes mine. Right after my PO called, I went and asked my boss if I could leave early. He agreed. I think he was happier for me then I was at the time. As I drove around, listening to the radio at full blast, I began to feel something. Happiness. Pure joy. Then, *ALIVE* by Pearl Jam came on the radio. And I cried. Tears flooded down my face. I cried for all the times I couldn't. I wouldn't let myself cry. I was not going to feel sorry for myself. I wasn't crying right then 'cause I was sad or upset. Those tears were the bittersweet tears of pure joy. I cried for another fifteen miles. I was free.

MARIE   Mick called. I have no idea what he was on, but he sure sounded happy. I have never known Mick to be happy, let alone sound happy. He asked me if I wanted to get coffee later tonight. I said sure. We made plans to meet at Big Boy around seven. He said he might be a little late. He was going to see a movie and wasn't sure what time it got out. After he hung up, it hit me. How the hell was he going to be able to go to a movie if he's on house arrest? And how the hell is he going to get coffee on a Tuesday if he's on house arrest? I smiled. I smiled and began to tear up a little. He was free.

TARA   Well, the shit is going to hit the fan. Mick is off house arrest. So, without thinking, I insisted he should get out of town and drive up to see me this weekend. What was I thinking? I was thinking of how nice it would be to see Mick. I was thinking how nice the drive all the way up here would be for a guy who just spent eight months in his parents' house, or in a garage changing tires. I wasn't thinking of his crush on me. I'll just have to deal with that when he gets up here.

MICKEY   The thrill of being free soon faded away. After I got home from driving the rest of my day away, I took a walk. While I was on foot, I couldn't shake the feeling that I was doing something I wasn't supposed to. I finally understood the word institutionalized. It was a fear that I was going somewhere that would endanger my well-being. I felt like turning around and running home to beg forgiveness of the electronic box that had recorded my whereabouts for the last eight months. But I didn't run home. I didn't turn around. I kept walking.

The first thing I wanted to do, other than take a long walk, was to go see a movie. As I waited in line at the movie theater, I had a rude awakening. Besides walking to places on my own, I wasn't really missing much. House arrest really wasn't that bad. When you're on house arrest, or even in jail, you get a sense of the freedoms that have been taken from you. But when you get out, you realize those freedoms you so much wanted, and dreamed about, weren't really there. We are not free. I can't tell the two kids in front of me that they are the biggest dumb-asses I have ever met. I had to listen to those two assholes while I waited to get my movie ticket. If we were truly free, I should be able to smack both of them upside the head. I bet I could even shove my foot up one of their assholes. I would love to try. But, I am not free. I left the theater without seeing the movie I wanted. I left the theater without seeing any movie. If I had stayed, I was afraid I would act out on one of the other movie-goers.

I was reading *Siddhartha* by Hermann Hesse when Marie showed up at Big Boy. I was also preoccupied with my waitress. Alice was her name. Marie sat down and asked for a coffee. Alice said sure, and smiled at me as she left. Marie must have noticed. I told Marie of my invite up north to see Tara. She seemed disinterested. She wanted to bitch about Brian. I thought she was going out with Jim now. She said that was correct, but it's weird because Brian and Jim are best friends. I said I understood. I guess Brian has been giving her shit every time they run into each other and Jim doesn't have the backbone to put Brian in his place. I told her I doubt they'll be friends much longer. Marie is a nice peice of ass and most guys will sacrifice friendship for a nice peice of ass any day. Alice finally came around with coffee. She slid me her number before she left to attend to another table. Marie laughed. I was aroused. Alice wasn't a nice peice of ass. She was more like a used peice of ass. I guess she seemed to be like Disney World. She has many wild rides, and many have ridden those rides. After Marie and I went our separate ways that night, I went home and jerked off.

ALICE   A cute guy came in this evening. He sat reading for a couple of hours. Every chance I got, I went over and flirted with him. He seemed real nice, and smart, too. He's not exactly the best looking guy, but he has a way about him that seems exciting. I asked him what he did. He said he was a bum. I asked him what he was reading. I really didn't care, but with these guys you have to pretend you're smart. Right before I was about to give him my number, his girlfriend walked in. Then again, I think she was just a friend. I eavesdropped on their conversation and they were discussing her boyfriend. So, when I went to give her a coffee, I slipped him my phone number on a napkin. It seems a little cliché, but it worked. He called around midnight the same night. I asked if he wanted to come over. He did. Before he showed up, I started doing shots. My goal is to get laid tonight. When he finally showed, twenty or maybe thirty minutes later, I was feeling pretty good. He sat down on the couch and we talked about all sorts of shit. I put on some music I thought he would like. I even showed him some naked pictures of me. Then, out of nowhere, he leaves. He didn't even say goodbye.

MICKEY   So, I figured what the hell and called the waitress around midnight. She asked me to come over, and I obliged. I always oblige. I stopped and got a pack of Camel Lights before I got there. When I did get there, she was trashed. I was aroused. I haven't gotten laid in a year or more. The last girl I fucked was Anne. Not even when I was dealing did I get any. Of course, like all dealers, you get women who will suck you off for a few hits of E. But, I never felt the need. Maybe Marie is right. I am a hopeless romantic. No matter. Tonight I had malicious intentions. I sat down on her black leather couch. She offered me a drink and I refused. I'm not usually a big drinker, but I don't even have a choice in this case. I may be off house arrest, but I'm still on probation.

Anyway, the slut named Alice and I talked for quite a while. She has got to be the dumbest bitch I've met in quite a few years. Well, next to Miah's ex-girlfriend. Alice eventually shows me naked pictures of herself. Not only were they just nude pictures, they were also pornographic. I was aroused. One of them even showed her getting fist-fucked in the ass. But, that is where the problem lies. The guy fist-fucking her is a notorious Russian mob guy I met when I was selling and such. In fact, I knew him well. I asked Alice about him. She said it was her boyfriend. I panicked. Not only am I in an apartment most likely rented by him, I'm about to have sex with one of his girls. When Alice went to use the little girl's room (most likely to snort some more coke), I high-tailed it out of there. Pussy or no pussy, I'm still on probation.

I'm still trying to figure out exactly what my probation officer does. The other day I asked him for help in finding a new job. He suggested that I check the want ads. I then asked for any information in regards to furthering my education. Kind of like state aid, I thought. My PO laughed at me. At that point I realized that my PO offers me no support whatsoever. But, I was on a roll, so I asked him if he knew of any program that could help me succeed in society. He told me to leave.

CHAPTER THREE

JESUS AND JIMMY

"Jesus was a lot like Jimmy Hoffa."

"How do you figure?"

"When it comes down to it, they were both union guys."

"I'm not really following."

"Jesus. Jesus' main shtick was to walk around and convince people that there was a better way. He preached and promised that everyone had an equal share and they all had the right to be treated better."

"Now, Jimmy did the same thing. But, unlike Jesus, Jimmy sold out to his Italian oppressors. Of course, the Dagos still killed him in the end... where are you going?"

"Away from you."

"Okay."

MICKEY   Tara goes to school at a small college upstate. It's a
three hour drive from my parents'. The drive itself, for anyone else,
I'm sure would have been boring. I, however, felt an exhilaration like
never before. Everything I drove past was new and exciting. The trees
seemed to have an unreal quality to them. I felt like an explorer, in the
midst of an adventure in a strange new world. My God! Everything
was so fucking beautiful. Even some kid picking his nose in the car
next to me brought me unimaginable glee. Without a doubt, I was like
a kid on Christmas morning. I eventually found myself lost in thought
over the whole experience. I figure everyone should be imprisoned,
somehow, at least four times in their lives. That way, we would all
have at least one or two months' worth of pure, unadulterated joy. The
windows down. The car racing along. The smell of the fall air. I was
in heaven.

On the drive, when the radio stations had faded out, I began to play
from the vast CD collection I'd brought with me. As my car was
humming along, I listened to Weezer, Alkaline Trio, Avail, Jimmy Eat
World, some EP by a local band called Avenue, Lucerio, Telegraph,
Face to Face, Jack Johnson, and that song by Cheap Trick that was
in the Diet Coke commercial. I really wanted that song, but I didn't
know who sang it. Marie found it on the internet for me. I remember
last Christmas, when Marie and I heard the song *Yellow*, by Coldplay,
every time we hung out together. Marie really liked that song, so I
went everywhere trying to find it. Every music store, I would walk
in and sing the song. The clerk, usually some fourteen-year-old girl
who didn't know anything but N'Sync music, would say she had no
idea what I was talking about. I eventually came across an indie music
store that specialized in Brit Pop. When I started singing the song
to this fifteen-year-old kid with a shaggy haircut, he started to laugh.
Then he said that he didn't know what song I was talking about, but
his co-worker might. So, I sang the song again. Well, his co-worker
also claimed not to have recognized the song. But he said that his boss
might know. Eventually, I drew a crowd. While I sang this stupid
song, all my onlookers chuckled and cackled. Come to find out, they
were playing a joke on me. They had all heard the song and finally
gave me a copy from the Brit Pop section of the store. They must have
felt kind of bad, because they gave it to me for free. I have no idea

why they felt bad. Maybe they thought I might have been embarrassed. They must not have known that I have no shame.

I eventually pulled off some desolate highway, that headed to the furthest reaches of hell, to come upon the small town that encompassed Tara's college. It was beautiful. Every house looked like it was built in the 1920s. There were no big retail stores, only small mom and pop establishments. A few people walked the streets, looking a little chilled in the fall air. I couldn't help but notice all the clothes they were wearing... wool jackets, knit sweaters, boots of every kind, and even scarves. I love scarves. I love fall and winter clothing. In the spring and summer, everybody dresses and looks the same to me. Fall and winter, you can really tell what kind of person someone is. They'll wear second-hand stuff from the Salvation Army if they have liberal tendencies. They'll wear Gap or Banana Republic if they come from conservative backgrounds. There will even be people that will wear the most absurd things, that are bulky and not aestetically pleasing. These people, I find, are usually the smartest of the bunch. They wear clothes for one purpose alone. To not get sick. I guess I would be a mix. But I know I sure as hell look pretty cool in my fall and winter garb.

I finally pulled up in front of Tara's apartment. It took me a little over four hours to get there. I stopped numerous times just to smell the flowers. Or the car exhaust fumes, to be more accurate. Funny that I didn't think about Tara the whole trip up. We talked a few times before I came up. Once to get directions, once to get the word of the day, and another to just shoot the shit. I'm pretty sure she wants to hook up this weekened. Just to be on the safe side, I took Monday off of work. I didn't know how long I would be staying. When I got up to the door, with a backpack that held a pair of jeans, two changes of underwear, and several pairs of clean socks, I knocked. Clean socks are very important. Nothing feels quite as good as clean socks, except maybe cleaning your ears with a Q-tip. Funny how that works. Some things that are manufactured seem to become a new word in our language. A Q-tip is really just a cotton swab. But, we have come to call all cotton swabs Q-tips. Same goes for facial tissue, which we all call Kleenex. Maybe it's just a bathroom thing.

I knocked on Tara's door two more times. I guess no one was home. I pulled out a book I had brought with me and sat on her front porch, to read while I waited. Michael Crichton's *Five Patients* entertained me long enough for Tara to eventually show up. She came walking up her front walk and gave me a big hug. I felt a little out of place when we embraced. I felt outside of myself.

TARA   I talked to Mick last night. I cut the conversation short when he started babbling on and on about how Jimmy Hoffa and Jesus shared some similarities. I'm sure it would be fascinating to some people, but I could care less. It's bad enough he's coming up here. I know he thinks something is going to develop between us. I don't want him to find out about Terrence. 'Cause then he's going to go and blab everything to Cody. Mick's like that. He cannot, for the life of him, keep a secret. He tried to explain it to me one time. He said something about how all secrets do is create unnecessary drama in our lives. And instead of using our brain capacity on that drama, we could use it for so many other stimulating things. I think that was pretty much it. I have no idea what the fuck he was talking about.

When I woke up at Terrence's, I freaked out. Mick was coming up today and I was sure he said something about one o'clock. It was already two-thirty. I woke Terrence up and told him I had to go and, besides, he was sleeping on my underwear. I ran out of his house and hopped in the car. When I got to my house, Mick was sitting on the front porch, reading and smoking. I walked up and gave him a big hug. He seemed a little rigid. He might have been mad. I apologized for being late and said something about being at the library. Like I even know where it is, in this God-forsaken shithole of a town. The only reason I'm here is the semi-decent film education they offer.

Mick and I went inside and I showed him around. I even showed him the word of the day board with the current word- multifarious- on it. I then offered him one of my multifarious beverages. He preferred to go out and get something. We went up to a small cafe downtown. He ate very little of his burger and only had a Sprite to drink. I had at least four thirty-ounce beers. I figured I might as well be drunk if I'm going to entertain his puppy dog ass all night. I suggested we go to one of my friends' party. He seemed uninterested, but agreed. Great. He probably wants to be alone with me. He's been doing his perfect gentleman routine all night. We drove over to Ed's house. There were about thirty or forty people there. I had four or five more beers while Mick just hung around me, not talking to anyone. He makes me sick. I eventually snuck away from his watchful eye. I ran into Ken. Ken and I snuck into the back bedroom. We made out for a few minutes, then I sucked him off. Ken and I then rejoined the party. I found out later that it wasn't Ken who came in my mouth, but some local high school freshman. After twenty minutes of looking for Mick, I found him outside talking to some hussy. I knew her. I had an art class with her. She's been around. So, I saved Mick from certain VD and suggested we head back to my place. He seemed upset, but said okay. He's probably mad at me for abandoning him.

Mick was going to sleep on the couch that night. I, however, felt like shit for treating him like dirt all night. So I suggested he sleep next to me in my bed. My roommates weren't home, so my reputation of being a prude would be intact. When we got to bed, we talked for a few minutes. I couldn't help but still feel a little bad for him. He seemed really nervous while we laid in bed, next to each other, talking. I figured if he was going to try something, I might as well give him a mercy fuck. I mean, for Christ's sake, he probably hasn't been laid in years. I fell asleep, thinking about how he must really believe in some stupid thing called love.

MICKEY   After I got my stuff stowed in Tara's apartment I suggested we go out to get something to eat. I was in no mood to be alone with her. And her roommates were gone for the weekend. Tara and I ended up eating at a quaint little cafe. I ordered their famous burger, which tasted like shit, and drank a Sprite while Tara polished off several beers. She seemed to get annoyed with me for not ordering myself a beer. I was hoping that I wouldn't have to explain, yet again, that I was on probation and that it wasn't worth the risk. I must seem like a square.

The atmosphere in the cafe inspired me to become philosophical. I tried to initiate a conversation with her that went beyond clothes, cars, and boys. She seemed disinterested in that idea. She seemed to prefer getting really drunk and talking about some guy named Terrence. Tara has mentioned him before. I figure she's fucking him and doesn't want to share that info. She must think I'd call and tell Cody. Which I would. Secrets between people are the dumbest thing I've ever heard of. Secrets do not create a mystery. They only create some sort of illusion about each other. And then when that illusion is broken, we find out that we are all selfish pigs. I know Tara is not an innocent. Please. She's a woman. That girl has probably already spread five different types of VD to seven different guys, this month alone. During dinner, I became aware of my complete and utter disinterest in Tara. But, then I had to rethink that. If I'm numb all the time, how do I know what I'm really feeling?

After dinner, Tara wanted to go to some stupid party. I agreed only to be cordial. I really wanted to go back to her place and get my shit. I wanted to get some shitty motel room on the outskirts of town and hole up in it all night, reading. Then, in the morning, I could go to the college library and rummage through the classics. I could even meet some girl, who is beautiful and smart, who would make me coffee in the morning without me asking. Instead, I found myself in the midst of a scene from the Bible. It was the night before God flooded the earth. And I was in the middle of Babylon. All these students must be really bored up here, or else just really short-sighted. The party was like an orgy. Half the girls were topless, while others were completely naked. Most of the men walked around with their dicks in their hands. Literally. There were a few people that remained clothed, Tara and I among them. After twenty minutes of being in this brothel, Tara gives me a look like I'm being a square. I'm sure that on any other night, I would have ripped off all of my clothes and stuck my dick in every orifice in the place. But tonight I felt above my human vices. I felt enlightened. Maybe I'm just becoming a snob? Maybe I am a square? Maybe I just don't want to get AIDS at such a young age? I think a disease like that is worth getting when you're seventy. I figure when I turn sixty-five and I'm retired, I will become an avid user of hookers and heroin. Until then, I'm going to play it safe. I could also be looking for that ever so elusive thing called love.

While I was watching all of these sins being committed, I thought about Rasputin. He was a pretty cool guy. He would say Mass to his congregation and then go fuck somebody's wife in back afterward. I think he truly believed that God gave us all our tastes and feeling toward the physical touch to act on. He really believed that God gave us our sexuality and sensuality to use on each other. I have to wonder, myself, if God really wanted us to see past all that and find what's really in each other's heart. I mean, tits and ass are just two-dimensional. A person's compassion and virtue are three.

While I was debating with Rasputin in my head over the virility of his life, Tara had snuck off somewhere. And then I caught him staring at me. I stared back, only to be polite. I couldn't completely make out his face. He was sitting in a chair in the corner and some dumb blonde bitch, who was completely naked and completely shaved, was grinding her ass against his crotch and blocking my view of him. Then his stare was gone 'cause the dumb hoe started writhing while she fingered herself. I couldn't help but notice that his hand was underneath her. It was dark in complexion, and he had long fingernails. I wasn't sure about his thumb, however, 'cause at present it was up the girl's ass.

THE DEVIL   I stared at him for several minutes before he noticed. When he did finally notice, he held my stare. This surprised me. Humans seldom surprise me. I find it rather exciting. I could see through him so easily. His struggle with his pathetic little soul. He is barely holding on to any remnant of virtue or hope. I'm sure I will be able to corrupt his soul with little, if any, difficulty. I do, however, imagine that I will need to engineer myself into his existence somehow. Look at the fool.

MICKEY   His stare. His stare was so cold. I couldn't shake it. I recalled a quick glimpse of his face as I headed outside to get some air. His face was flat, had this elf thing to it. No matter. I lit a cigarette and looked around to get my bearings. I was about to walk back to Tara's when this cute little blonde came up and asked me for a cigarette. I was happy to oblige her. We were about to start up a conversation of some sort when Tara came up behind me and hung her arm over my shoulders. Tara gave the blonde a territorial stare and insisted that we go back to her place. I didn't object, seeing as that was precisely where I didn't want to be. Tara drove very carefully on the way back to her place. At least she recognized she was drunk. I guess I should have driven, but I was too preoccupied with a fantasy about the blonde I had just left.

Tara and I shared her bed. I really didn't want to. I was hoping to sleep on the couch and quietly jerk off to the fantasy I had about the blonde. I found myself yet again drifting in thought. I was reliving my life the way I would if I could do it all over again. Eventually, in the fantasy, I was the most powerful and richest man in the world. I was internationally renowned for my kindness and my vision of a future that would equalize the social classes while I remained on top. It's an ego thing, I guess. Right before I fell asleep, I looked over to see some sort of dried white drool on Tara's lower lip. I only noticed it 'cause the moonlight from her window made it glimmer. I figured it was toothpaste.

I woke up around six. Tara was fast asleep and I wasn't going to wake her. I rummaged through her kitchen for coffee and filters. While I waited for it to brew, I packed my things. While I enjoyed a couple cups of coffee, I read the local paper. I have a fondness for small towns.

Somewhere in between the obituaries and the funnies, I had a flash-back of last night. I couldn't shake that guy's stare. Somehow I thought he might have been gay. Maybe the girl on his lap wasn't getting him off? Maybe to get a hard-on he had to fantasize about other guys? Just when I was considering the sixth sense of gaydar, Tara walked in. She poured herself some coffee and asked what my plans were. I informed her of my intent to get the hell out of here, and maybe make a quick stop at the library. I asked her where it was, but she didn't seem to know. While I finished my coffee, she began tell-ing me a story about some loser she knew that was in love with her. I guess this guy followed her around a lot. He wouldn't even interact with other people whenever they were together. He just had eyes for her. The arrogant little bitch is so transparent. She was obviously telling me this story in hopes that I would understand that she wasn't interested. I get it.

We finally said goodbye. She asked me to call her when I got home. I eventually called her the following week. I took my time driving home that afternoon. I had stopped by the library, like I wanted, only to find the fucking thing closed. I never understood why libraries and churches close. They are the two institutions that should always be accessible to the masses. When I got home, I slept for a few hours and then got up to call Marie. I wanted to tell her about the travesty that was my weekend. I also wanted to share the experience of the drive there and back. Marie wasn't home. She was probably out with Jim. And for the first time all I wanted, instead of a piece of ass, was a friend.

TARA   In the morning I noticed Mick was already up. I found him in the kitchen, drinking coffee and reading the paper. Go figure. I poured myself a cup, just to fit in. I never touch the stuff myself. When I looked around, I noticed that he had packed already. He said something about the library. He asked me where it was. I had no idea. This whole thing with Mick reminded me of Tom. So, I told him a story about how Tom would follow me around like a lost puppy and how he never wanted to meet anyone new. I felt awful about the whole thing. It was cute for awhile, but it's just too weird. Mick's nice and all, but I'm involved with Terrence.

After Mick left, I took a shower. I checked my e-mail and then I called Terrence. He told me about his night. He was watching some martial arts film when he got a call from the local police. I guess his brother got picked up for wandering around drunk. When his brother finally sobered up, he told Terrence about his awesome night. He told him how he got invited to a college party and how some girl pulled him into a back room and sucked his dick. The girl kept calling him Ken whenever she came up for air. I laughed. And then when I got off the phone with Terrence, I cried. How could I have been so stupid?

Luckily, his brother didn't recognize me when I "met" him a few weeks later. But Terrence always kids his little brother about the slut that sucked him dry.

MARY BETH   I couldn't wait to get home and tell Molly about Jamey. I walked into the apartment to find her still moping on the couch. She has been like that for days. Ever since her and Miah broke up. Miah, Mr. Wonderful. He's an ass, he doesn't have any money, and he isn't even ambitious. So, I turned off the crappy romantic comedy she was watching and pulled up a chair facing her. I told her all about my horrendous day. I even told her about running into a guy I fooled around with the other night. Even though I really slept with with him. I didn't want anybody to think I slept around. I then told her all about Jamey. I said, "you know what the first thing he said to me was?" I waited for a second, to give it a little drama. "I'm the DEVIL!!!"

CHAPTER FOUR

SELF-RIGHTEOUS

"You can still go to school!"

"NO... I... CAN'T."

"YES... YOU... CAN."

"Look. I cannot afford to go. The cost of living is too high. I can't pay for an apartment, and a car, and food, and some semblance of a social life and still go to fucking school!"

"Yes, you can."

"I'm sorry, I forgot who I was talking to."

"What's that supposed to mean?"

"You're a twenty-year-old woman. You live in this fantasy world where you think you can do whatever you want. It's probably your mother's fault. She probably tried to instill the idea of success over any adversity. It's some mass delusion that women suffer from. It most likely started after women's lib."

"GOD! I hate you!"

"That's okay... I could be wrong. We do live in a know-it-all society. No one's ever wrong. Everyone is always right. It's never their fault. Like the other day, on the phone. You said you'd meet me at ten o'clock, and then you show up at eleven. I call you on it and you start raising hell. You put the blame on me, and you even took it one step further. You told me that I wasn't listening. You were hoping that I would feel guilty, on top of feeling stupid, for making the mistake and then trying to blame it on you."

"You know...? No. You're right. You're always right. You're so fucking self-righteous."

"I always liked the phrase self-righteous. Look at all of it's components. Self... right...eous. Self is for the individual. Right is for being right. Eous is to show abundance. You're right. I am self-righteous."

"Did I say I liked you today?"

"Ah...? No."

"Good."

MICKEY   I've started to consider myself well-read. On Sunday, I finished *The Great Gatsby* and then started on another American classic, *Blackhawk Down*. Well, it's kind of an American classic. I found it informative and entertaining. And it complimented the movie rather well. I hear so many people complain that the movie is never as good as the book. Sometimes I agree, and sometimes I don't. I find myself enjoying both, and I will even go out of my way to rent a movie that was based on a book I have just read. Five months ago, I hated libraries. I thought they sold out, somehow. I didn't accept the renting, or borrowing, of movies and CDs. It took me awhile to realize that movies and CDs are just another book, that has a different way of representing itself. The sad part about all that is that I felt good about myself when I achieved this great enlightenment. How pathetic am I? I may be mentally retarded somehow. I may suffer from a learning disability, like my uncle. It could be a tumor, that slows my mental development. It could be due to my crooked face. Who the fuck knows?

Seeing as the weekend was a complete waste of my time, I decided on a little male bonding to liven up my spirits. I hadn't seen Miah in a few months. When I called him up, he seemed pleased to hear from me. I invited myself over to the Hippie House, offering to stop and pick up Chinese. He, of course, had to check with his fellow roommates, Tom and Ben. I met Tom right before I went on house arrest. He's a pretentious dickhead. I had only seen Ben once; and he, too, looked like a pretentious dickhead. Miah called me back within five minutes and said that tonight was a go. I left work around five. I went home, showered, and then drove out to Ferndale. I stopped at a shitty little Chinese place, that was a health inspector's dream come true, and ordered an ample amount for all four of us. While I waited, I insulted every chink in the place. I even threatened to call INS. It always amazes me when people don't recognize my nasty disposition toward them. They laugh and smile, and think I'm being funny... or cute... or even charming. Charming? Can they not see the murder in my heart? Can they not see the disgust in my face? Do they not notice the complete and utter contempt I have for them? It...

JEREMIAH   I struggled through the day. I don't want to be here.
I planned on leaving two months ago. No particular destination in
mind. I guess that a ranch would be a nice place to hole up. But, I
can't keep running. My pops made a good argument the other day. I
need some stability in my life, or even some sort of roots. I just... I
just don't want to be pushing ice cream to a bunch of slobs for the rest
of my life. The other morning, when I was getting my morning coffee
at White Castle (they've got great coffee), there were these two
degenerates eating lunch. I could appreciate them eating on the back
of their pick-up, but then they threw their trash on the pavement and
took off. The worst part about the whole thing is that there was a trash
can not five feet away from their lazy asses. Maybe it's the city. I
can't imagine folks in the country being so inconsiderate to our only
hope for a promising future.

Mick called around noon. I was a little surprised to hear from him.
He's good people, so I was looking forward to seeing him. We made
plans for tonight, but I had to check with the Jews first. Tom was
alright with Mick coming by. Benedict, on the other hand, seemed a
little apprehensive. I'm sure it had to do with all the stories I've told
him about Mick. Well, that, and the fact that Mick is a three-time
felon. Ben's got a thing about drug dealers. He just doesn't seem to
accept that all drug dealers aren't all bad. It's not like Mick was
running around selling to kids. Most of his clients were in their mid-
thirties and had respectable jobs, like lawyers and doctors. Hell, he
even had a mayor buying ganja from him. Ben is weird like that,
though. He's a by-the-book type of guy. I can appreciate that, but I
can also appreciate a tightly-packed bowl. Ha. I remember... I
remember when the po-po came to the house, right after they
apprehended Mick. I was on the porch, toking some great hydro, when
a cop came up the steps, showing a badge and a warrant. I had to
choke, and laugh. Luckily, the police had no interest in my little bowl
of wonders. They were only looking for Mick's stash. But it wasn't in
the house. Mick was too smart for that. Anyway, it will be great to see
him. I only hope that Ben can, at least, keep an open mind.

BENEDICT   Great. Just great. Some fucking degenerate that Jeremiah grew up with is coming over. I already had to deal with a bunch of white trash on the freeway today. I don't need to deal with a crack-dealing, homicidal maniac on a Monday night, a night that I specifically cherish. I want to spend my Monday night re-reading a timeless classic by Dostoevsky. But, instead, I have to entertain some mental cripple, who will probably reduce my own intellectual capacity by being in the same proximity.

Great. Just fucking great. My night already looked bleak, but now Tom wants to watch the oh-so-fake, and annoying, television show of wrestling. Let me recap. First, some degenerate that pushes crack to kids is coming over. Second, I am not able to relax and read a Russian classic. And last, but not least, I will spend my special evening watching Jeremiah's extended family hump each other. I am really glad that I have spent my entire life getting an incredible education just to waste it.

THOMAS   How horrific my life has become. Jeremiah, the hillbilly from hell... Ben, the recluse with no ambition... and, now, to make the nightmarish picture complete, Mick returns. The house in which I suffer has never seen a mop and bucket. My classes are for the mentally disabled and last, but certainly not least, I have not felt the touch of a woman in months. I need pussy, I say! I need pussy now! Goddamn it, now!

MICKEY   I arrived at the Hippie House just in time to see Jay beating the crap out of Tom. I found it amusing to see Jeremiah pop his head up and say hello, while continuing a choke hold that was stopping the flow of oxygen to Tom's lungs. I noticed Ben on the couch, cheering the carnage on. I went over and set the Chinese on the table, then sat down on the couch adjacent to Ben. We exchanged pleasantries and started to discuss what initiated Tom's would-be demise. Ben carefully explained, while still egging Miah on, that he had mentioned how the Pollacks suffered more than the Jews. It was ingenious. Jeremiah, being a Pol, has always considered himself

51

persecuted. And of course, Tom, being a Jew, is blinded by his complete and utter disgust for the Holocaust. I rather enjoyed it, and admired Ben's manipulation. It would be easy to get Tom and Miah at odds. They both suffer from some jealousy toward each other that developed long before I entered their lives. Ben and I talked for a few minutes and then proceeded to the kitchen. We served ourselves huge plates of MSG, and ate. Tom and Miah eventually noticed that dinner was served and dismounted each other. I think they both might be gay.

BENEDICT   What can I say? I was bored. Tom, Jeremiah and I were sitting in the living room, watching *Malcolm in the Middle*, while we waited for the crack dealer. After *Malcolm*, I found myself in need of amusement. So, I started a debate on whether the Jews or the Pols had endured more persecution. It took a whole thirty seconds for Jeremiah to start getting physical with Tom. They both have a certain amount of disdain for each other, which I exploit. I can get those two assholes to fight in under five minutes. I think it's a form of therapy. Why should I suffer alone? Roughly five minutes into it, the baby killer arrived. Mick. His name is Mick. I made sure not to insult him. I had it in the back of my head that he would pull an Uzi on me. He seemed pleased at the debacle I'd created. He even inquired about, and admired my handiwork. We went on to discuss our total dislike of Tom and then turned our conversation to the topic of self-hate. Mick proved to be quite inquisitive. I found myself talking about all the things I wanted to talk about, but had no one to direct them toward.

While we were eating, shortly after the neanderthal and the retard had joined us, we started discussing handicaps. All of us took it one step further and discussed our own personal choices for a handicap. Tom wanted to be blind, so he wouldn't have to look at fat people. Jeremiah wanted to be crippled so he could roll his wheelchair down a hill at full speed and scream "weeeeeeee!" Mickey had the oh-so-familiar, intellectual response , that you would get from any third-year ivy leaguer. He said he would be deaf. But, then, he said something remarkable. He changed his mind. In five seconds, he went from being deaf to having no memory, like the guy in *Memento*. I told him that would suck. He disagreed. Mick felt that having any memory would be like not having a consciousness. I put it in a hypothetical situation. I explained that if you could only remember the guilt over something you had done ten years ago, all you would do is relive that every twenty minutes or so. He threw back at me that living with that kind of guilt wasn't going to matter. In fact, he would most likely kill himself. And that it wouldn't be so bad. I like Mick, even if he sold crack to toddlers.

The rest of the night, while we sat around and watched Jeremiah's boyfriends grunt and hug each other, I kept thinking of our dinner conversation. Mick and I were like Robert DeNiro and Christopher Walken in *Deer Hunter*. We were playing Russian roulette, but the gun was unloaded.

THOMAS   I hate Ben. He, of course, manipulated Jeremiah into beating me again. Jeremiah is so stupid. I bet he rolls around on the floor licking his own balls. Well, the night was trite, as I thought it would be. Mick and Ben made stupid conversation about nothing. I think they're both gay. They were laughing and giggling like little girls all night. I have rug-burns on my knees and, of course, the numbing that only comes from Jeremiah's special choke hold. What a fucking buffoon. I hate my life. I hate my friends.

JEREMIAH   It surprised me to see that Mick and Ben hit it off, like they did. Overall, it was a fun night. Although I wish Tom would keep his fucking mouth shut. "The Jews have suffered more than any other race". I don't know about them, but Tom will. He's so gay it's not even funny. It's just sad that he has to hide in the closet. I never thought that I would see the day that I was friends with a gay Jew that wants to be black. Anyway, I really had a good time. For once. Even Mick did. And then out of the blue. Ben suggested that we do the same thing next week. Go figure.

MARIE   I called Mick around ten. His mom seemed annoyed, and said that he was out in Ferndale. So I left a message and started working on a new hairstyle. I'm only three credits shy of graduating, with a degree in cosmetology. I usually use the school's dummy heads with wigs, so that I'm able to shape and cut it any way that I want to. But, I didn't bring one home so I was using Jim. Halfway through his haircut, Mick called. I asked about Ferndale and he gave me the impression that he had a good time. I also asked about Tara. He seemed disinterested in the topic. Mick's kind of like that. He finds someone he likes and becomes obsessed with them. He changes himself to fit their idea of the perfect companion. But, eventually, you notice the vacancy in his eyes. He really doesn't care about you. He only hopes he does. Anne really fucked him up. Or I guess he could've been that way before he found her with multiple partners, in their bed. Anyway, I hung up with Mick a little after we discussed the possibility of going to the Renaissance Festival, in Holly.

When I finished Jim's hair, we made love and went to bed. I kept thinking about Mick. I was worried about him. I was worried that he would never be able to have a normal relationship again. I was worried that he would waste so much time looking for something that he was incapable of feeling. I asked Mick once, what he thought love was. He said it was like a disease. Then, he said that love was defined as an unselfish concern for others. And that he only hopes that he'll find that in himself one day. I spent the rest of the night watching Jim sleep, and hoping that I had discovered what Mick was so desperately looking for.

TARA   I finally called Mick. I was a little worried about how he would treat me after the whole weekend thing. Surprisingly, he was really cool. He even gave me the word of the day, which is benevolent. We talked for twenty minutes or so about Jeremiah and Tom. I was really glad that Mick was getting out a little more socially. This whole looking-for-love thing was really starting to get on my nerves. I mean, Mick's a great guy, but c'mon. You have to give a shit about someone before you love them. Mick doesn't even give a shit about his sisters, let alone his friends. I could call him right now and tell him that I never wanted to see his pathetic ass again, and he wouldn't give two shits. How the hell is any girl going to take him seriously if he won't even get jealous? Christ! It's called passion, you stupid prick!

While I was talking to Mick, about whether America is a country or an empire, I told him about Terrence. I knew it was a mistake, but I had to tell someone. I know he's just going to call Cody and tell him. I had talked to Molly earlier today. We had talked about the Terrence situation also. She made me feel better about it. So, Mick knows now and he seems happy for me. Even though I know Mick is incapable of being happy for anyone, including himself. He swore up and down that he wouldn't tell Cody. He kept saying it was my business. I know that the little shit called Cody as soon as he hung up.

CODY   I had called Mick, to see what he knew about the whole Tara thing. He didn't even mention it. Figures. Everybody gives him a bad rap, but he's probably the most honorable one in the bunch. Molly, my little secret lover woman, phoned me earlier to tell me about Tara's deceit. It really pisses me off that the cunt couldn't just call me and tell me that she was fucking somebody else. We already discussed seeing other people. All she had to do was call and tell me. To make it even worse, her relationship with this guy has been going on for months. I talk to that bitch every night. And every night, she says "I love you" and "I miss you" and that I am the only one for her. Her new boyfriend's probably got his face in her twat while she's confessing her undying love. I figure that I won't let on that I know and see how long she'll keep this lie going. Thank God for Molly, my secret lover woman. Her and I have been friends ever since her and Jeremiah were going out. I guess I should be mad at Mick, but he really doesn't owe me anything. Hell, I barely know him. I asked Molly how he was doing, seeing as she and Tara are friends and I know Mick had just gone up for a visit. Well, Molly went on this torrid rant, about how she hated the cock-sucker. I guess she only met him once and he insulted her. I tried to explain that that was Mick's shtick, but she didn't want to hear it. She's got a crush on him, if you ask me. The only time a woman gets mad at a guy is when she wants to fuck him. But, then again, if that were true Mick would be knee-deep in telephone numbers. Which he's not.

MICKEY   Jerry called from Florida. Cody called from Colorado.
Jerry wanted to catch up. I informed him that nothing has changed,
except that I had discovered something special in myself. Hate.
Unconditional hate. He agreed that it would appear that nothing had
changed, and also let me in on a little secret. He said that this hate
thing was not a new talent of mine. I said that I knew that, and then
repeated that I had just discovered it. Eventually, we ended up
discussing what we always discuss... hookers. Jerry wants to get a
hooker one day. But not for any other reason than to throw lunchmeat
at her, and maybe some pop cans. Of course, the hooker has to pretend
to like it. Otherwise, the whole thing would seem demeaning or
something. I like talking to Jerry every once nd a while. He makes
me feel good about myself.

I'm still bothered by the concept of secrets. I don't know why people
are obsessed with having secrets. A secret limits our brain capacity.
I would rather think about things to throw at hookers then waste all
that time and thought on a fucking secret. I never thought of it that
way until I read something that Thoreau wrote. Now, there's a wack-
job. Henry David Thoreau wrote a book called *Walden*. It was a story
about him, living an existance secluded from the rest of humanity. But
here's the wacky part. I found out, in *An Underground Education*, that
good old Henry would go to his mom's every day for lunch. When he
wrote *Walden*, he was living only five miles from his mother, in some
cabin by a pond. And, to top it off, the bastard had barbeques every
weekend for his friends and family. I guess seclusion for some is not
the same for others. Maybe for Thoreau, being secluded only meant
to be without human interaction for only a matter of hours at a time.
I wonder how long I could go. How often do I need to toot my own
horn? Am I really complacent? Or am I in need of some sort of
recognition? I think that's what love is all about. Gloating.

THE DEVIL   I finally started making progress, in the inevitable
achievement of my goal. Mary Beth and I have started a sordid relationship. I find the manipulation of women an easy task. Women have
always succumbed to my charms. Let's just say that Eve took little, if
any, persuasion. But I am not here for the women. I am here for him.

JEREMIAH   Mick called and said that he was going to get Chinese. I'm really getting into the whole Monday night thing. I would, of course, never tell the guys that. I wouldn't want them to think I was a stable human being. I like having that control over them. I like to tell them that I don't know if I'll be around for dinner. Of course, they ask why and I tell them it's none of their damn business. That really gets their goat. Then they'll interrogate me for an hour or so. I like the attention.

Molly and I had coffee today. We sat and stared at each other for an hour or two without saying a word. We have really been trying to make a truce. I don't want to tell her what I really think, and she doesn't want to tell me the truth either. The whole scene was pretty uncomfortable. Thank God, Mary Beth showed up with her new boy-friend, Jamey. All four of us discussed child abuse for a bit, and then I headed out. I don't think Molly and I can be friends. I need a reason to be upset with her. Then, I won't have to see her or talk to her. I can hide.

BENEDICT   Jeremiah came home in a bad mood. I have no doubt that it has something to do with Molly. Everyone seems to hate Molly. I don't know why, she's not that bad. I'd fuck her, but Jeremiah fucked that up. He always dates cute girls. Which, of course, makes those girls off-limits. It's a guy thing. In fact, that's the reason Tom and him fight all the time. Some girl, in school, caused them both to make a pact and I think one of them broke it or something. Some territorial, pissing ground thing, I think. It's stupid. They're stupid.

CHAPTER FIVE

AND THE ELITISTS SHALL INHERIT THE EARTH

"My sex life is kind of like the Bible."

"How do you figure?"

"Well, for one, it's by far the greatest story ever told. It also has incestuous fantasies in it. And, when it comes down to it, you really don't know if it's true. Yeah. I think I should have been a priest."

"Listen to me. No! Look at me. Listen. Listen. Okay, you're stupid."

"Oh. Hurt my feelings, did ya? Tear."

"I don't like you very much."

"Why? 'Cause your sex life's like the New Testament? Very few women and mostly guys...?"

"I hate you."

"Yeah. I get that a lot."

MICKEY   I've been spending my last couple Monday nights at the Hippie House. I bring the Chinese food over around seven. We eat and converse, until eight, then we watch wrestling. Ben suggested that they buy the Chinese next time. I don't care either way. I still live at home, and they have to pay for rent and such. I guess it makes me feel important, to be needed or wanted, to provide for other people. Well, not just any people. My friends. Last Monday, we decided to dub our new ritual "Family Night." It seemed appropriate. It's just like any family, where a few people with unrelated lives get together and suffer through a meal, and talk about unimportant crap. We even sit around and insult each other like any other family. As far as Ben, Tom and Miah are as friends, well, they're the best. They're completely unsupportive of everything I do. Yeah, they qualify as the healthiest relationships I've ever been in.

Tonight is yet another Family Night. However, Ben and I decided to meet up at a coffeehouse in downtown Ferndale before the usual ritualistic crap. I think we discussed this possibility last week, while Miah and Tom beat each other senseless over whose brother seemed more homosexual. I learned a lot about Benedict. He has aspirations of being in politics, although he seems to be in a rut right now. He wears his disappointment with himself on his sleeve. I can only hope that he'll find some way to reach his goals.

Ben is what you would call good people. He has an amazing eye for detail and is one of those people that dots every I and crosses every T. I think he would make an excellent leader. I wouldn't want one of those happy-go-lucky guys that always insist on entertaining you with some cliché story from their past life. I would want a guy like Ben. A pain in the ass, who makes sure we're all doing what the fuck we're supposed to be doing.

Ben and I also discussed his relationship with Tom. Tom and he have been friends since grade school. Ben seemed a little frustrated with Tom still being in his life. Which is understandable, I guess. Tom's kind of like a used car salesman. The Tom conversation lead into the Russian author conversation. I have never read anything by a Russian author, and Ben was more than happy to recommend a few. He went on to talk about his favorite book, *The Brother Karamazov*, by Dostoevsky. The whole time we exchanged pointless ideas that we had conjured up in our heads; we insulted each other, as well. Oh, and made fun of retarded and deaf people. We also made fun of cripples, Jews, blacks, white trash, gays, Jeremiah, Tom, Chinese people (which we called Mexicans) and last, but not least, women. Ben and I share mutual ground on the subject of women. We hate them. We hate their manipulations, their lack of self-control, and most of all, we hate them because they don't love us. Ben and I also found common ground on the subject of each other. Not only do we both hate each other, we hate ourselves. I think I hate him more than I hate him hating me. We finished our coffees, bought the Chinese and headed to the Hippie House to perform our first joint effort. To have Jeremiah beat the living shit out of Tom.

TARA   I left a message with Mickey's mom for him to give me a call. I need to talk to him about maybe going bowling with me later. I came home for the holiday vacation ten hours ago and I'm already going stir-crazy. I miss Terrence. Mick doesn't really make a suitable replacement, but it will be nice to have him being all sweet and cutesy to me, thinking he might get a piece of ass. Anyway, if he doesn't call me back, maybe I'll catch up with Molly at her work and get a few free margaritas.

BENEDICT   Mick and I grabbed coffee before Family Night. When we got back to the house, we told Jeremiah that Tom was talking shit about Tommy "The Machine Gun" Morrison. We gave Jeremiah the idea that Tom had said that the oh-so-shitty boxer had gotten AIDS from sucking dick and taking it in the ass. Jeremiah was livid. He loves Tommy "The Impotent Gun."

When Tom finally came home from class, he didn't make it but two steps in the door before Jeremiah jumped on him and began beating the fuck out of him. Mick and I sat on the couch adjacent to the door, reveling in our handiwork. Tom is only half the size of Miah, so he was quickly subdued. After a good ten minutes of pounding on Tom,

Miah decided to use choke holds and arm bars on him. It was great. I haven't been this happy in so long. I had trouble controlling my glee. I bit down, hard, one of the chopsticks I was using to eat. Mick had the same problem, trying to control his enthusiam. He bit down on his knuckle to stifle his laughter. We knew if Jeremiah realized that we were manipulating him, he would stop Tom's suffering. Neither of us had any intention of letting that happen.

After Family Night, I thought about Mick's education, compared to mine. I thought about how that son-of-a-bitch is making twenty-eight grand a year, while I'm barely making ten. I thought about the chip we both have on our shoulder toward people who seem to be lucky in life. That's all life is. Luck. And Mick sure as hell doesn't have any. He's told me all these stories that seem so unreal that you have to believe them. He talks about his teenage years, when he was some kind of degenerate vandal that hung out with a bunch of low-lifes that called themselves the Hick Posse. And, then... then, the whole Clawson Mob thing, which ended up getting him five years of probation. The shit he tells me, you would think they would've given him life in prison. If I had been his judge, I would have, but I wouldn't have known all of the circumstances. I wouldn't have known about his despair and anger, toward everything and everyone. I wouldn't have known about his frustration toward a system that is set up to make men like him fail. Between affirmative action, women's lib, corporate corruption and the little guy getting ahead, guys like Mick are destined for their nightmares, not their dreams. I keep telling him not to give up, but I don't let on that I'm afraid of living the same kind of life, in the same kind of shoes. Lately, it seems like I can't get ahead.

I spent the rest of the night dwelling on my own failure. I spent the rest of the night hating Mick for being a failure. I spent the rest of the night...

THOMAS   AHHHH! I hate Mick. I hate Ben. They're fucking dickheads. They lied to this retarded hillbilly just to have me beaten. I can't do this anymore. I can't live in this type of environment anymore. I have to escape. GODDAMN! Ben is such a fucking miserable fuck. He justs sits there and laughs. Some fucking friend. He's such a loser. And Mick, that fucking degenerate, I wish the judge would've sent him to prison for years. He would've been somebody's bitch, that's for sure. AHHHH! I can't feel my arm. I CAN'T FEEL MY ARM! YOU FUCKER! YOU BROKE MY FUCKING ARM!

JEREMIAH   OOOOOOO! OOOOOO! My name's Tom, and I'm a little cry-baby. I just love any excuse to beat the shit out of Tom. Benedict always gives me one. Now Mick seems to have joined the team. I like it. Oh! Ha! I think I might have broken his arm. Aha!

MICKEY   I got home from Family Night really late. I would've tried to be quiet coming into the house, but why? My mom is always up, in the family room. I think she may be an insomniac. I woke her up as soon as I walked in. She seemed annoyed. I couldn't blame her; she must have been worried. I should move out again, seeing as I'm off house arrest. But, I like the security. I worry about having panic attacks.

The other day, I couldn't shake the feeling that I was going to shove my fist down my throat. I would break my teeth, and crack the bone while I did it. I would eventually chew off my own arm, at the bicep. I really felt like I might do it. It felt like I couldn't control it. I get the same feeling in the car sometimes when the cars are inching along, and I just want to go. I can feel myself slamming down on the gas and ramming the car ahead of me. I would use that shitty movie, *Falling Down*, as an example to explain the feeling. But, that movie was about a pussy losing it. Not a man. If I was that guy, I would have beat the guy to death in the party store, smacked the kid in the fast food restaurant and shot half the fuckers in there. In fact, I never would have gotten out of the car. I would've kept ramming it into other cars on the freeway until I was forced to get out. Then, I would start beating anything and anyone with my fists until the cops came and shot me dead. That's losing it.

As far back as I can remember, my parents have always found a reason to fight on Christmas. It was weird to wake up on Christmas morning, run down the stairs to open your gifts and get your stockings, only to have your parents start insulting each other halfway through. I always figured they got that way 'cause of the money they spent.

Relationships, nowadays, are always ruined by money. My parents were no different. Except that the money was just a reason to fight when, really, us kids were the cause. My sisters and I were such little brats. My parents spoiled us early on. They wanted to give us everything they never had. But they forgot to include respect, dignity and responsibility.

I need to move out. I also need to go to school. I realize that now, after spending time with educated fucks like Tom and Ben. They have a way about them that makes them better than us common folk. I think Shaw called them "supermen." I want to be one. I want to know things other people don't. I want a reason to be liked. I want a reason to like me.

MARIE   I called Mick, to let him know that I talked to Jerry. He's doing really good down in Florida. He's working for his father and seems to be interested in some little tramp down there. Jerry and I reminisced about the past. We mostly talked about the Ghetto Penthouse. That's the name Mick gave his apartment when he was selling drugs. He used to have so many people crash there that you could walk across the entire place without ever touching the floor. Mick used to come home and kick people that were asleep on the floor, in the head, just for fun. Jerry and I laughed about all that. I guess I miss those days. But, everyone, at some point, has to grow up. I guess.

I wanted to continue my stroll down Memory Lane, but Mick seemed disinterested in the topic. He seemed almost remorseful. I can't figure him out sometimes. So, I changed the topic to Jim. I told Mick all about the date Jim took me on the other night. Shortly after that, he said he had to go. I really wish Mick could find somebody. He seems so lonely.

TARA   Last night, I went and met up with Molly. After she got off, we went and got trashed with a bunch of people she works with, at a bar down the street from her job. Last call segweyed to Sean's house (one of the guys Molly works with). Several other people had joined us, to have an orgy. I woke up the next morning to see Molly on the couch, with two guys wrapped around her. One of them must have woken up a little before me. He had already started penetrating Molly, while she was still asleep. I found my panties, and left.

I called Mick right after I got up from sleeping the day away. I wanted to go bowling and I needed someone to make me feel good about myself. We made plans to meet up at a bowling alley on my side of town. Right after I hung up, Molly called. She asked what I was up to tonight. I told her that I was going bowling with Mick. She gave a heavy sigh and said that she was getting off work soon, and that she wanted to hang out. I told her to meet us at the bowling alley. She started giving me crap about Mick being there. I told her not to come, then. She said that she would, but that she wasn't putting up with any of his shit. Whatever.

MICKEY   I talked to Jerry this afternoon when I got off work. He seemed to be doing fair, except that he sounded a little bored. He informed me of Darla's upcoming visit. I was surprised he was still fucking around with that bitch. Pussy's pussy, I guess. I discussed the idea of writing a book about the whole Clawson Mob thing, and maybe a play about the Ghetto Penthouse. He chuckled, and said that he didn't really see the need for another novel about a bunch of drug addicts, sitting around doing drugs while talking stupid. Then, he reminded me of all the felonies I had committed and had not, as of yet, been charged with. I saw his point, but started writing it anyway. I guess it might be a form of therapy for me, or maybe just a distraction.

Tara called right after I got off the phone with Jerry. She asked if I wanted to go bowling. I wasn't really interested, but I figured what the hell. I had been reading a John LeCarr book for the last couple days, and I was getting a little burned out on all the slang he uses. Tara also mentioned that Molly was coming. I really don't remember who the hell Molly was, so I said sure. I was hoping Molly would be really cute, and be able to provide sufficient visual aid, so I could fantasize about her tonight. I really wanted to jerk off when I got home later on.

On my way to the bowling alley, I kept thinking about the word love. Everyone seems to use it way too often in their vocabulary. Women shopping, for instance, always say "I love this" and "I love that." When, in actuality, they mean "I want this," and "I want that." Also, everyone has a tendency to love several people at the same time. I always thought that love only involved one other person. I wasn't thinking about the love for your family, or even your love for God. I was thinking more along the lines of man-and-wife type shit.

Women seem to cheapen, or even ruin, the word love. They're such an impulsive sex. I don't think they should be allowed to use the word. I truly doubt they even fall in love. But I know that theory is total poppycock because of my complete disdain toward the opposite sex. I can never think clearly when it comes to matters of the heart.

I finally made it to the bowling alley. When I walked in, I noticed lots of high school girls bowling there, with their pre-pubescent boyfriends. I felt sorry for the bastards. They had no idea what was coming. Those girls were going to eat them alive. I reflected on my first serious girlfriend, the Antichrist. When I had discovered the disease-spreading whore cheating on me, I was livid. When I confronted her, she looked me dead in the eye and told me that if I didn't like it, tough shit. Then, she said not to give her that hurt look, and that I had a choice. I could leave, or I could stay and be her friend. I stayed. I still have no idea why. I thought maybe it was 'cause I wanted to show her how much pain I would endure for the sake of love. Maybe I was hoping that she would realize her mistakes and beg for my forgiveness. Maybe I had no backbone and was just a complete sack of shit. Or maybe, just maybe, I didn't know that women were evil. I mean, evil, heartless, demonic, scandalous creatures that have no other purpose than to create suffering in this world. I should have fucking left.

When I was deep in thought about demonic creatures, Tara came up behind me and grabbed my ass. I was hoping it was someone that I didn't know and turned around, only to be disappointed. We headed over to the bar to get a pitcher of beer, and a Coke for me. I went to get a lane for us while she downed two and a half pints. After only a few minutes of waiting for Molly we started bowling . Tara didn't think she would show. I inquired why. Tara explained that I had insulted Molly before, and that she wasn't comfortable being around me. I couldn't even remember meeting her before. Tara looked at me like I was a complete dumb-ass and said that Molly used to go out with Miah. I must have seemed shocked by that statement 'cause Tara enunciated the name Jeremiah. Hell if I knew. I was always thought Miah was gay. I figured he was just in the closet and scared to tell his brothers. Which is weird, 'cause Miah's brothers seem to be screaming homosexuals themselves. Anyway, I told Tara that it finally registered who Molly was, but I still had no fucking clue. Tara and I were five frames into our third game when Molly showed up. I should have left.

TARA   Well, Miss Fancy Pants finally showed up, wearing her work uniform. Her tight little white blouse, with her tight little black pants, that complimented her tight little white ass. AHHHH! Mick and I had been there for an hour or two already. I was about to call it a night. I had polished off three pitchers, while listening to Mick go on and on about Jimmy Hoffa and Jesus Christ. For the love of God, he would not shut the fuck up. I hate when he gets all smart and shit.

Anyway, Molly comes strolling in, and I could not hide my joy. I ran over and hugged the little slut. I introduced her to Mick, and he did his whole I-don't-give-a-fuck routine. So I excused Little Miss Tart, and myself, to the ladies' room. I had to talk to her, in private, about last night. We headed toward the bathrooms, but sat on some benches just out of Mick's sight. I asked Molly if she remembers who I fucked, and if they used protection. She didn't seem to know what the fuck I was talking about. She kept glancing over toward Mick. He was bowling by himself. Mick's weird like that. I think the word for him is complacent. Which is really a turn-off, if you ask me. Women like drama. Women like to be used and abused. Fuck, I know eventually I'm going to have to marry some guy, but I'm going to get fucked two ways from Sunday, until then.

Molly kept looking over toward Mick, while I tried to explain what had transpired the night before. We sat sharing a beer. I finally gave up on the whole thing when I noticed Molly smiling at Mick's obnoxious ass. She found him cute, and I found him dull. No. No. Safe.

MARY BETH   Molly went out with Tara tonight. I guess they were going bowling. Yeah, right. They're probably going to fuck the guy they kept talking about over the phone. I think his name was Mick. Jamey was in a really good mood tonight and took me to a nice place for dinner. I told him what I thought Molly, the little slut, was up to. He seemed disinterested.

We eventually got back to my place. Jamey is usually rough in bed, but he took the cake tonight. He fucked me so hard that he bruised the insides of my thighs. Oh, and I think my asshole will need stitches after he shoved his fist in it. I really didn't mind him being so rough. I love him. And I know that he loves me.

After he fell asleep, I thought about us girls and why we do that. We do the whole never tell our little-secrets-from-behind-closed-doors thing. It really depends on the guy, to determine how far you'll go sexually. I mean, all the women I know, over twenty, take it in the ass and give head. Hell, I've got one friend who will let her man shit on her. But we'll turn around and be virgins the next day. I guess we have to do it. The harder we make it, the more we get out of it.

THE DEVIL   "Jamey, don't, it hurts." "Jamey, I'm not like that." "AHHHH! Jamey, please, don't!" What a fucking dumb bitch. All women are dumb bitches, and the quicker Mick realizes that, the quicker I can have his fucking soul.

CHAPTER SIX

GOOD MORNING SUNSHINE

"What's your favorite color?"

"What's your favorite color?"

"Grey."

"Blue."

"Why grey?"

"Why blue?"

"Because blue reminds me of the sky, which reminds me of the earth, which reminds me that we live on a huge planet, which reminds me that I will not have to live in this God-forsaken place my entire life."

"Hmmm..."

"Why grey?"

"Because it reminds me of an overcast sky, which I will never be able to get out from under."

"Okay. That's morbid as hell."

"You asked."

"You started it."

"This is true."

"What's your favorite food?"

"What's your favorite food?"

MICKEY   I can't explain this. I'm not sure I even want to. Molly and I talked and talked and talked, the entire night. The only time we stopped was for a bathroom break or when one of us had to bowl their frame. Halfway through the second game, I decided Molly needed a nickname. I dubbed her "Gutter Girl", on account of her constantly sending the ball down the lane in the gutter. It was cute. I thought that I should be equally as cute and granny-style each of my frames. Listen to me. Cute. It's not fucking cute. The entire night I have been second-guessing myself on the things I have said to her. God knows what she must think of me. Why the fuck should I even care? I sure as hell can't fuck her. Molly and Miah went out for at least a year. If I did anything with her, it would be like spitting in Miah's face. Not that he doesn't deserve it or anything. What to do...? I tried to get my mind off it, and Molly, by imposing some sort of conversation on Tara. But, Tara was far too inebriated to hold a conversation on anything but Terrence. She loves him, she needs him, she misses him. She needs to shut the fuck up and help me out. Molly is scaring the hell out of me.

Seeing that Tara was going to be no help, I decided to suck it up and weather the storm. So, Molly and I talked and talked and talked. We talked about art, which I know nothing about, but still proclaim myself as a consummate critic, promising to divulge what sucks and what doesn't. We talked about Molly. She comes from a broken home, and her innermost fear is that she will live in Clawson, her hometown, for the rest of her life. We talked about Christians in the twentieth century, compared to Jews in the twentieth century. We talked about Molly's middle name which I think, is Luella. I quickly changed it to Lou, hoping she would assume I was being cute, and not realize that I was afraid to mispronounce it. Oh, how cute. I've known this dumb bitch for two hours and I've already given her two nicknames. God help me.

Eventually, Tara, Molly and I grew tired of the bowling alley scene. We decided to go our separate ways. As we walked to the door, I noticed Molly turning to go to the far end of the building, which had doors leading to the parking lot. Unfortunately, I couldn't follow her to try and secure some sort of later date. Tara was drunk as a skunk, and I'd already volunteered to drive her home. I stood at the doors a second longer, to see if Molly would turn. She did, and waved. She might have been waving to both Tara and I, or maybe just Tara. But, in my screwed up little head, I hoped she was waving to just me.

TARA   OH...MY...GOD!   What was the fuck was that all about? Molly flirted with Mick the entire night. And Mick, being so fucking gullible, became quickly infatuated with her. What a hussy. I invite her out and show her a good time, and she has the gall to hone in on my in-case-of-emergency-break-glass dick. Well, fuck her. I knew I had to defend myself. I knew I would have to come up with a plan that would ensure the bitch went home alone. I got drunk. Really drunk. I even flirted with Mick a bit. Not that he noticed. He was way too wrapped up in his conversation with little Miss Fancy Pants. I don't even know what they were talking about. I think it had to do with the church or something. Like she's ever been to a church. If she ever dared to walk into one, I'm sure she would be struck dead by some higher power. Not that I believe in any of that crap. I'm an atheist. Or is it agnostic?

Later, while the two love birds were still cooing to each other, I started missing Terrence. I missed him so much I decided to drink another pitcher, just in case I needed it. Without Terrence around, I would probably have to fuck Mick. God forbid. Fucking him would be like fucking the Pope or something. Somewhere between my second and fourth glass, from my fifth pitcher, I blacked the fuck out.

MARY BETH   Well, Molly came home in a disgustingly good mood. I asked her what would get her in such an elated state. She said nothing, as usual. Oh, right. I forgot. Her life is so incredible that she needs to keep it secret. God forbid we would find out, and be jealous. Please. She goes out every night after work and gets obliterated; then finds a guy, preferably with a big dick, and goes home with him. The next morning, she wakes up and runs away from whoever she might have been with, and pretends like it never happened. I tell this to Jamey all the time. He doesn't seem interested. But guys have a way of hiding what they really feel. I think Jamey wants to fuck her. In fact, I know he does. It's not really his fault either. If Molly would put on some fucking clothes once in a while, and stopped flirting with him every chance she gets, maybe Jamey could concentrate completely on me.

THE DEVIL   I stayed awake til I heard Molly come in. I wanted to get the scoop on how things had gone with him. Mary Beth was in the living room at the time, attempting to study things that her mind was not suited for. She interrogated Molly as soon as she walked in, but Molly didn't divulge a single detail. However, I knew what transpired and I was pleased. Very, very pleased. After that, I fell fast asleep and only woke to fuck Mary Beth when she came to bed. Somewhere between her mouth and her asshole, I devised a devilish idea to kill time while I waited for his soul. I decided to fuck with Mary Beth a little bit. I decided to fuck Molly.

BENEDICT   Mick came over to see what was up. I told him the usual, not a damn thing. I asked how he had been. He said good. Good? That can't be right. I wonder why he would lie. I wondered why he would lie to me. Was he trying to make me feel worse? I already feel bad, as it is. I know that I am a despicable human being. I know I'm a piece of shit. I know Mick is no better than me. That's what's so great about our friendship. He makes me feel not so alone. But now he comes over with a spring in his step and announces to the heavens that he's doing good. Good! Fuck him, I say! Fuck him!

MARIE   When I called Mick to say hello and catch up, his mother informed me that he had gone bowling with Tara. I was not only surprised Mick had gone bowling, but to have gone with Tara seemed a little weird. I left a message with his mom and then went to the Denny's down the street from my place. I really wanted to talk to Mickey about Jim. I think I may be using him. But, then again, I think I may really love him. I know Mick seems like the wrong person to ask about love, but he really does know his shit when it comes to people. I guess I just was hoping for his opinion on the whole thing.

79

MICKEY   I couldn't shake the feeling Molly has given me. It was like... it was like a warm hug. I could have sat in my car the whole night outside of Tara's house, thinking about Molly. Thankfully, I quickly recovered some sort of self-control and drove to the Hippie House. I wanted to share my good spirits. Ben was sitting on the couch, being miserable, when I got there. I think I cheered him up, however. I was about to head for home when Tom came strolling in. He suggested a cup of coffee over at the diner on Nine Mile.

At the diner, I questioned Tom on his thoughts about me going back to school. He seemed very supportive. In fact, he was really impressed that I had graduated high school. On a normal day, I would've broken one of his fingers for being so facetious, but today was his lucky day. Today was a special day. All my food tasted better, which isn't saying much... my cigarette seemed somehow stronger, maybe 'cause I bought lights instead of ultralights... and the coffee tasted simply divine. I was in a good mood. I decided to attend the community college next semester. Now, I just had to rid myself of Molly.

THOMAS   Mick's not really that bad of a guy. He's always seemed a little... I don't know... violent? Instead, I find him semi-intelligent and witty. I encouraged him to attend community college while we ate some putrid type of eggs benedict. I even inquired into some of Mick's past. It seems like I was racking up the good karma points today.

Mick and I got back to the house around five a.m. I went right to bed, and he said he was heading home. Around six, I woke up to Jeremiah screaming at the top of his lungs. No doubt the dumb bastard got drunk again, and was probably starting shit with our neighbors. I don't know if it was my conversation with Mick, or Jeremiah's screaming, that made me decide to move out of the house.

The next morning, I informed Ben and Miah that I was planning on leaving the next month. I simply told them that it was time for me to move on. Ben didn't care. In fact, he seemed rather happy about the whole thing. Jeremiah said something in hillbilly, and seeing as I'm not fluent in that language, I could only assume that it was some sort of recognition toward the situation.

I phoned Shelley that afternoon and asked if she still had a room available at her place. She said she did, and asked if I could move in right away. No problem. That night, I moved all of my stuff down-town, into Shelley's apartment, which was now my apartment. I don't know if I'll miss the house. I do know I won't miss Benedict, or Jeremiah. I figure they can always get Mick to move in. He said something about finding a place to live. If that happens, I might be inclined to say God help him, but it's probably Ben and Miah that I should really be worried about.

JERRY   This must be what hell is like. I've been living in Florida for the better part of a year, and I still can't get used to all of the conservative people in this state. You would almost think that's it's some sort of mass hysteria that has plagued the whole state, making them believe that being an uptight asshole is somehow right. I finally heard from Mickey this afternoon. We didn't talk much. He said he'd decided to take classes at the community college. Great. Mickey being given higher learning. Just what the world needs- a highly-educated criminal mind. I have no idea what's going on with him. Before you know it, he'll call me and tell me that he's in love. Ha. Mickey also talked about Tara and Molly. He said that they'd all hung out the other night. Of course, I questioned him about the Molly part. Last I heard, she hated his guts.

MICKEY   I called my district manager today and informed him of my plans to cut down to part time, in order to go to school. He asked me to reconsider, and to take time to think about it before I made such a big decision. I said that I had, and wished to be demoted as soon as possible. He wasn't pleased, but he wished me luck and said he would make the arrangements as soon as possible.

The following week, I called my district manager again. I asked him to transfer me to the Centerline store. He asked if there were problems in my current position, and I told him no. I just wanted to move out, to Ferndale. Tom was moving out of the Hippie House, and Miah asked me to move in. I couldn't pass up the chance to live there. I would only be paying two hundred a month, in rent and bills combined. The district manager, again, seemed reluctant to allow me to make such a drastic decision but, to keep me happy, he agreed to the transfer and said that he would make it effective on the first of the month.

Things are changing quick. I've registered for winter classes at the community college. I'm not going to bite off more than I can chew, so I only took two classes, a philosophy and political science. I got transferred and I'm moving into the Hippie House, and all this happens next month. Now I'm just chomping at the bit, waiting. I figured while I wait I might as well see what's going on with Tara. I called her up at school. She had gone back as soon as the holidays were over. She said that her birthday was coming up, and asked if I wanted to come up for the weekend. I said sure. She seemed excited about it. Then she asked me to call Molly, to see if she wanted to ride up with me. I said, "excuse me?" "Why not call Molly and ask her to ride up with you?" she asked me. Molly? I didn't want to do that. Molly had already jeopardized my mental stability once, and that was enough. Tara pushed the issue, and asked me to at least call her. I caved in. I called her.

Molly's voice strikes me as if it were summer rain, splashing down on the burning asphalt. It's soothing. I'm a snake under her spell. I hate it. I don't ever want to be a beggar again. I don't want to be giving, or attentive, again. I feel like a fool when I do. And Molly makes me want to play the fool. Molly makes me feel the fool. And all that fucking cunt has to do to make me this pathetic wreck of a human being, is say hello.

I barely made it through the conversation with Molly. As soon as she realized it was me, she said "good morning, Sunshine." I'm not sure if she was making fun of my cynical nature or what. My palms were sweating the entire time, and I felt the room closing in each minute that I was on the phone with her. I made plans with her, to get a cup of coffee tomorrow. We're going to meet at the Café D in Royal Oak, which is just north of Ferndale. As soon as we had made the plans, I slammed the phone down. I knew I was just seconds away from oblivion.

MARY BETH   Molly was on the phone when Jamey and I got home. I waited in my bedroom until she was off the phone. I really needed to talk to her. She had left me an obnoxious note on the kitchen table this morning. It said that she wanted to discuss Jamie's presence in the apartment. I didn't want to upset Jamey with this information, so I left him in my room while I went to talk to her, as soon as I heard her hang up the phone.

That arrogant bitch. I told Jamey what she said as soon as I got in my room. She said that Jamey walked in on her in the bathroom, while she was taking a shower. She said that she doesn't see why he has to be here all the time. Well, well, well. I knew she was jealous of my relationship, but I had no idea. It's not my fault that she can't keep a man for more than a night. Maybe if she didn't fuck them right away, they would stick around for a few weeks. And, excuse me, but this is my apartment, too, and Jamey is my boyfriend. It's not like she doesn't have some loser sleep over every other night. Maybe she's contracted syphilis and it's starting to affect her brain. 'Cause there is no way that Jamey would try anything with a whore like her. But I didn't say any of that. I just told her that Jamey might be open to chipping in some rent. She seemed receptive to my suggestion. Figures. You can always buy a whore.

THE DEVIL   When we got back to the apartment, Molly was on the phone with Mick. I was curious, but I went into Mary Beth's room immediately. I already knew they were making plans. Molly, Molly, Molly. How important you are to me. You will be the reason that Mick gives in to his lust and anger. You will be the reason that he will make so many suffer. I need you, Molly, even if I can't have you myself. I was surprised by her rejection last night. I approached her in the shower. I joined her. She looked stunned, as if I had done something completely out of character. I moved closer to her and began to massage her breasts. Just when I moved closer, to kiss her neck, she said no. I looked into her eyes, and saw a strength in them I had not expected. Again, she said no. I smiled at her and left her in the shower, attempting to cleanse herself of her past indiscretions. This might work out better than I had planned.

BENEDICT   God is not merciful. I thought he might have been, when Thomas said he was moving out. But then Miah told me today that Mick was taking his place. God has forsaken me. I must have been a real bastard in my past life, to deserve such punishment. You would think being friends with these assholes would be redemption enough. Ach!

MICKEY   My parents were pleased as punch that I was moving out, although my dad seemed a little skeptical of the whole thing. I don't think he liked the idea of me cutting down to part time and moving out. My dad is a good man, and truly believes you need financial security to make it through life. In some ways, he's right and in others, I think he may have missed the boat. I think you need some sort of love to make it through life. But I have no experience in the notion of love to back my theory up. Sure, I thought I was in love once. But I know better now. So, maybe my father is right. Then again, I think there is something divine in this world other than a new car, a pair of Nikes, and a prostitute that most men would call a wife.

I couldn't sleep. I was really worried about tomorrow. I didn't know what to expect. Molly seems safe, in some ways. She dated Miah, for God's sake. She's probably a virgin. That would be bad. Miah's like a fucking saint. And I'm... I'm like the devil. I know I'm not a good man. I know that. I don't deserve anyone like Molly. Maybe I don't deserve anything.

While my mind whirled around and around about Molly, I began to have a panic attack. I kept thinking I could shove my entire arm through my mouth to my stomach. I could imagine my teeth cracking from the pressure, the bone being forced down the back of my throat. I could imagine the blood running down my face. I could feel my finger floating around in my stomach, then starting to squeeze the inner wall of it. I could almost hear my moans, as my elbow rested on my lower jaw.

I took a three mile walk to rid myself of the panic. I walked and walked and walked. When I got home, I collapsed in my bed from exhaustion. Before I fell asleep, I looked at my clock. It was around five o'clock. Twelve hours. Twelve hours until I see her. Twelve hours until I share a table with her. Twelve hours until I spill coffee on myself and she smiles at me, for being a klutz. That smile is to be feared. It reminds me that life is not all that bad. That smile reminds me of all the beautiful things I haven't seen in this world. That smile. God help me. God help her.

I woke up this morning in a panicked state. I couldn't go through with it. I couldn't see her. I called her as soon as I got in to work. I knew she worked late, so I didn't expect her to pick up at seven in the morning. I planned on cancelling our kind-of sort-of date. I figured there was no way she was going to answer the phone. She did, and the first words that she uttered to me, from her half-sleeping state, were "Good morning, Sunshine."

CHAPTER SEVEN

UGLY HOMELESS HATE

"I'm going to become an art critic."

"Yeah?"

"Yep."

"Don't you have to go to school or something for that?"

Yeah, but that's just a waste of time. I know what's good, and what's not. And I'm very critical of what's not."

"I didn't think you even liked art."

"I don't. I hate it. That's why I would be so good at critizing it. Of course, I'll end up hating all of it. Then, I'll be able to berate all of the artists for their lack of vision. Hopefully, then, they'll all kill themselves due to their own ineptitude."

"Ah... I see."

"Aren't writers considered artists?"

"No. Writers aren't usually women in their early twenties who think they know everything."

"That's not true. You ever read *Prozac Nation*?"

"Yeah, and I burned it."

MICKEY I didn't have time to go home and shower before I met up with Molly. I walked into the Café D, in Royal Oak, a little nervous and insecure. I made sure to bring my book. I wanted to make sure I had the appearance of being an intellectual. I've been to the Café D many times. I walked in, said hello to Desmond, the owner, and ordered a house coffee. The nice part of Café D is the service. Desmond brings the coffee out to you, after you've seated yourself at the table of your choice. Most cafes make their patrons stand there like fucking idiots, and then expect a fucking tip. A tip for doing nothing at all. It's almost insulting, if you think about it. The person who serves you is usually some snot-nosed suburban kid, making six bucks an hour. This kid's only job is to pour coffee into a mug, hand it to you, and get a tip... for what? For looking stupid? Needless to say, I don't tip.

Molly hadn't shown up by my second cup of coffee. I didn't really mind. I was pretty engrossed in H.G. Wells' *The Time Machine*. This particular edition also had *War of the Worlds* in it, which I found rather enjoyable. Nothing like a good story that involves some alien force helping us out, by killing off stupid people before they have an opportunity to reproduce. There were four cigarette butts in the ashtray on the table. I figured I'd been at the Café D a little over an hour, waiting for Molly. I decided to switch seats. I have no idea why. I ended up moving to the only couch in the cafe. It always seemed a little out of place, and I'd never sat on it before. I found it rather comfortable and, strangely enough, familiar. Five minutes later, Molly walked in.

Molly set her purse, and a travel guide book of Nepal, on the table that sits in front of the couch. I looked up and did a foolish thing. I made eye contact. I had made this mistake at the bowling alley, as well. She said that she was going to get coffee, that she'd be right back. When she returned, mug in hand, she mentioned that she had never sat on the couch in here. She said that she always thought it looked a little out of place. I had pretended to go back to reading, but I really wasn't. I had lost the ability to read as soon as she walked in. I wanted her to think that her arrival made no difference to me. She picked up her book and began reading, when she realized I wasn't going to stop due

91

to her arrival. Of course, proper etiquette would dictate that I put my book down and give her my undivided attention. I, however, will not be the beggar. I will not be the attentive one. I will not.

I couldn't take it anymore, so I put my book down and asked Molly how she was doing. Good, she said... great, in fact. I asked if she had plans to travel to Nepal. She giggled and said no, but that she liked to read about the places that she hopes to go, someday. This simple question and answer thing lead into a non-stop conversation that lasted two hours.

It was getting late. I told Molly that I had to go home and attempt to get some sleep. Before I left, we discussed our plans to meet up on Friday. I told her that I would drive up to Tara's, and she said that she would let me. Which is a good thing. I hate to relinquish control. If I always drive, I will not be subjected to staying some place, or going some place, I don't belong or want to be.

The day after I saw Molly to make traveling plans, I called her from work. It was around ten a.m. When she answered the phone, the first words out of her mouth were "good morning, Sunshine." I wanted to hate that. Instead, I found the whole thing rather cute. Molly and I then spent a little while playing cutesy on the phone. I spent most of the time berating the guys I work with, while half paying attention to her. I think she found the whole thing rather amusing. I wasn't trying to be. I just can't do two things at once.

BENEDICT   Mickey and I are going to meet up to have coffee, before Family Night. I kind of like this time with him. Mickey just makes me feel good... good about myself. He is such a pathetic piece of shit that one cannot help but feel better about their own wretched life.

Mickey was waiting for me at the Java Hutt, which is smack dab in the middle of Ferndale. I think it's becoming our favorite haunt. I know Mickey spends a lot of time here, reading and doing a little writing. He probably does it just to meet women. Women control his life.

Mickey's whole existence revolves around finding The One. The one woman who will leave the last Coke in the fridge for him, the one woman that will take it in the ass to please her man, the one woman that will make him coffee while she's wearing one of his old shirts. These are his criteria, not mine. I just want a woman who will sleep with me once a month.

I went up to the counter and asked for a house coffee. I take mine black, unlike that fucking pussy over there, reading Ellis' *The Informers*. The girl behind the counter poured me a hot cup of house, from the air pot, and handed it to me. I stood there like a buffoon, waiting for her to ring me up. She had turned her back on me and was cleaning the countertop. She turned again, to see me waving a couple of dollars in front of my severly annoyed face. She said there was no charge, 'cause Mick had already paid for my it. I hate that. I like paying for my shit. I don't want to feel like I owe anybody. I must have stood there a second too long, because then she wanted to make sure that I was Mick's friend, the child molester. I stood there, in shock from the statement, which again must have been for a little too long. She followed up the insult by asking if I was, or was not, the guy who served time in prison for molesting a ten-year-old boy. I smiled and walked away. When I sat down, in the seat adjacent to Mick, he smiled like the devil. I told him I hated him and then opened my book on the Roman Empire. As I read about Pontius Pilot during the time of Christ, I couldn't help but smile, knowing that Mickey- in some weird way- was my best friend.

I enjoy Mickey's company the best out of all my friends. Mickey and I rarely talk, and if we do, it'll be about something worthwhile. About twenty minutes had gone by, since I first sat down, when a homeless guy came into the cafe to solicit change. Maybe he wasn't home-less. It doesn't matter. The worst part about living in Ferndale is the assholes who beg for change. They all come up here from Detroit to work or something, and before they take the bus back to the city, they panhandle. Most of these dickheads wear better clothes than I do. The guy came up to Mick and I, told us some stupid lie about needing bus fare. Of course, Mick gave him almost a buck in change. I just stared at him, thinking of how arrogant this guy was being. How dare he come in here and disturb my downtime? Does he not know that I work all day, that I do not appreciate him making me feel guilty about not being sympathetic to his plight? Besides, you can't trust these people. They could have a job paying six figures, and do this for the extra cash. It's sad that I have to live this way. It's sad that this guy is making my life tense, because I can't trust him enough to be compassionate. I wanted to pick up my ceramic coffee mug and beat him until he was dead, dead, dead.

We decide to change our entertainment on Family Night. Instead of watching wrestling, we played *Axis and Allies*, a World War II strategic battlefield game. Kind of like *Risk*. I had never played it before, but I guess Jeremiah and Mick grew up with it. We changed the rules a little bit, so that instead of being against each other, we made it a free-for-all with secret diplomacy. We played this fucking thing for twelve hours. I decided that if I ever had to play this game again, I wasn't going to be an active player. I was going to be the U.N.

During our third helping of Chinese food, Mick and I got into a huge debate on hate. I tried to convey my message... that hate was not a good thing, that we should keep with the idea of tolerance. I hid my true feelings, which were to support hate and make laws that would force people to settle their differences in a huge Colliseum, like Rome had. It would be great. I changed my tune about tolerance during the debate and told Mick about my idea about the Colliseum. He said it kind of sounded like a movie he saw once. I think the name of it was *Series Seven*.

THOMAS   Jeremiah, Mick, Ben and I decided to play a board game, instead of watching Miah's relatives hump for Family Night. The game lasted twelve hours. I was eliminated from play within two. They all ganged up on me. I hate them. I decided to exact my revenge by starting an argument. I remembered Mick talking a lot about C.S. Lewis' *Screwtape Letters* around that time. Mick mentioned that, in his copy, the preface had some quote by Lewis, saying that to hate someone only means that you've become disillusioned. The whole thing sounded absurd, and I didn't believe Mick to be accurate in his information. So, after I got eliminated, I brought it up again. Mick, who always wants to prattle on about his own vast knowledge of nothing, began to discuss it with Ben.

Ben had a different take. Ben knows a lot of stuff and has very serious convictions. When he debates, it's like talking to a brick wall. He only wants to win. He will only change his mind, or waiver in his opinion, when he reads or hears an opinion from someone he considers more educated, or more knowledgeable in the field, than himself. Mick is, by far, not one of those people.

Mick and Ben argued the point for over two hours. It finally ended when I made the mistake of calling Miah a faggot. Miah jumped from his chair and put me in some horrible headlock. Ben and Mick stopped fighting to enjoy the predicament I had gotten myself into. I hate them.

JEREMIAH   It was a good Family Night. We ate Chinese and played a board game. Mick and Ben argued about something. They both wanted to be right, and wanted the other one to give in, so it lasted probably two hours. I finally got sick of hearing them bitch at each other, so as soon as Tom said something, I put him in a headlock. I held it until he lost circulation in the majority of his body. I also gave him several nuggies which will, hopefully, result in premature hair loss.

I heard, through the grapevine, that Mick's hanging out with Molly. I would say something, but it's not my business. The last time her and I got together, we ended up having a huge fight. She made me feel worthless, and I made her feel insufficient. I don't want Mick dating her, but if he does, I won't make a big deal about it. Mick might be a prick... ha. I made a rhyme. Anyway, he might be a total asshole most of the time but, deep down, he's good people. No matter what he might think of himself, the guy always ends up doing the right thing.

MARY BETH Molly has been bouncing around the house all day. It's really starting to get on my nerves. I guess she's all excited to go on this trip up north, to see Tara. Ever since she met this guy, Mick, all she does is talk about him. She even started reading some book he recommended, by Hemingway. Lately, she's been coming home right after work. Which is weird, 'cause usually she'll stay out all night, fucking some chotch. Molly taught me the word, chotch. When she first used it, I was, like, what the fuck? She told me that it's the perfect word for someone who's shallow. It has to be a masculine word, 'cause girls are far from shallow. We're future mothers.

I tried to tell Jamey how annoying Molly has been lately. He just ignores me whenever I bring it up. As long as I'm sucking his dick, or fucking his brains out, he could care less about my problems. So the other night, I figured I would teach him a lesson, and not put out. He got pissed and left. I went running after him. I caught up to him at his car, crying my eyes out and begging for another chance. He kissed me, passionately, and said that it was okay. We went back up to my room. That night, he tied me up and fist-fucked me. It hurt so fucking bad, but I want to make him happy.

THE DEVIL I'm growing tired of waiting. I know that I must have patience, but if I have to put up with Mary Beth's incessant whining much longer, I'm afraid I'll have to leave. God, that woman is always singing the same tune. Me, me, me. Mickey and Molly will be going up north soon. I have no doubt that they will begin some sort of romantic relationship soon. I'm worried about Molly though. I didn't think Mickey would influence her as much as he has. I think he is giving her something called hope. Which is some barbaric human idea that life is worth living, and that everything will work out in the end. This is the ideology I wanted Molly to give Mick, not the other way around. I guess it doesn't really matter, as long as Mick gets the same stupid idea from her. Molly will not let me down in the end. She will do what is in her nature, and run. Run, far and fast. She is too scared to accompany Mickey on his journey. Molly only thinks that she wants to experience what he is going to experience. She really only wants to find a place, like so many others, and hide.

Mickey is unlike so many humans. He truly wants to believe. He wants to believe that there is something better. He wants to believe that the human race hasn't forgotten God's humble love. It's not a facade either. I hear lots of humans say that they feel compassion toward their brethren, but, deep down, it's a hollow belief... a hollow idea they have about themselves, in order to rationalize their shallow ideologies. Ha. Listen to me. It almost makes me sound like I'm a fan. But I will not subscribe to Mick's blind ideology. I will not stomach such an out-of-date belief in humanity. I will remove any reason to hope from his life and, in turn, he will remove any semblance of faith he has in my ENEMY.

TARA   I had just gotten off the phone with Mick when Molly called. They both told me the 411 on their arrival time. I am beginning to get a little worried. Terrence and I have been spending a lot of time together and I think he will be around the entire weekend, when Mick and Molly are here. I know they both know about Terrence, but I'm still feeling guilty over it 'cause of Cody. About ten minutes after I got off the phone with Mick, the phone rang. I thought it was Mick, calling back to give me the word of the day. It was Cody.

Cody knew about Terrence somehow. At first, he said that he was calling to wish me a happy birthday, but then he started fishing for any info on a new love interest in my life. I denied everything and anyone, and he called me a fucking liar. Then he reminded me of our whole deal when he left. He said I should have told him. He told me that it wasn't fair for me to lead him on that way. I began to cry. He continued to scold me, and I continued to cry. He eventually slammed down the phone on me. I cried for hours. I stopped at only one point, to remember when Mick had watched me break down, in his parents' garage, over Cody's move out of state. I cried in front of Mick, confessing my undying love to Cody. He just sat and watched. Then, he teared up himself, and said that he was amazed at the concept of loving someone loving another so much. When he said that, I had cried even harder. Now, when I think of that...

It has to be Mickey who told Cody about Terrence. Then again, it could be that little bitch, Molly. She was always too cutesy with him. Her and Cody used to pretend that they were secret lovers, and that she only dated Miah so that they could be close to each other. I hated that.

CODY   I called Mickey earlier today. I wanted to hear his take on what to do about Tara's betrayal. Tara and I had promised to keep each other informed of any new developments in the love department. I would have told her if I found someone. Obviously, she didn't tell me. She wanted to hide it and, to make matters worse, she would sit there on the other end of the telephone and lie. She would confess her undying love to me every time we talked. She would swear that there was no one else when I hadn't even asked. I hate that lying, two-timing bitch. I want her to pay. So, I called the only man I know who can make someone suffer from their own guilt.

Mickey suggested that I send her flowers and call to wish her a happy birthday. During the conversation, I should make her lie a couple times. He said to ask her if she's found someone else, to ask if she truly loves me and no one else. He even suggested that I drop the name Terrence, just for fun. He told me to introduce a story, about a fictional Terrence that so happens to be a friend of mine, in Colorado. I swear, Mick is evil. He also told me to make sure that I am very, very pissed off when I drop the bomb.

I ordered flowers, by phone, from some florist down the street from Tara. However, the florist said that they would be unable to deliver the flowers until tomorrow. I called Mick, after I ordered them, and told him my problem. He said not to worry, that it would work even better. She would get the flowers the next day, which would result in her feeling ashamed, and possibly making her cry again. He also said that if she thinks I'm trying to apologize for the day before, she'll end up calling me. Then, I could yell at her again. It started to get really confusing, but Mickey told me to trust him. Which I did.

I called Tara and told her off yesterday. Today, she called and thanked me for the flowers and begged for forgiveness. She said that she has been crying since yesterday, and that the flowers just made it that much more unbearable. I called her a lying whore and told her that she should never call me again. She became hysterical, so I slammed down the phone on her, again. Mick was right about the whole thing. It went down exactly how he said it would. I felt like shit for it. Mick was right about that, too. He said I would.

MICKEY   I have a problem. My face is crooked. When I used to work in a store that sold video cameras, I would always be freaked out to see my face on TV, as I walked by. I never realized how ugly I am. I also think I may be a little retarded. I think I have always been slow. I think people might feel bad, if they pointed out either my face, or my lack of mental capacity. I think my parents pay people to be my friends. They might even call newly associated friends of mine, and workplaces, to tell them not to mention my physical ugliness or my retardation.

I have never told anyone of these insecurities of mine. I keep them to myself. I have never told anyone that I am constantly thinking about my crooked face or my own stupidity. I never mention that I feel like that guy in the Bible, carrying around the lamp during the day. I don't even remember if that's a real story, or something I made up in my head.

I have never told anyone this. I have never wanted to tell anyone. And, when I think about this crap, I usually try to forget it as quickly as I can. But, now, it's different. Now, I have someone to call. Now, I know there is someone who wants to know, or at least pretends to care, about all this insecure crap that goes through my head. Now, as soon as I think of something, or even anything, I pick up the phone. I dial the number like I've known it my entire life. And the first thing I hear when the line is picked up, the only thing that makes it worthwhile is "good morning, Sunshine."

CHAPTER EIGHT

BARREL OF MONKEYS

"I'm always paranoid."

"Really? I'm not, but I do try to keep a look out for any bad omens."

"What?"

"Bad omens. You know, like a sign to warn you of upcoming events in your life. There are always bad signs and good signs... Don't laugh at me."

"You're so stupid."

"Hey. Just because I believe in something that you do not particularly subscribe to is no reason to laugh at me, or call me stupid."

"Have you been reading those cult books? Like *The Celestine Prophecy* and *The Alchemist*?"

"I'm not talking to you."

"Oh. Well, those books are a bunch of crap. You ever notice that the main characters always succeed, in their life-challenging task, by the end of the book?"

"Yeah. That's called hope. I wouldn't expect a cynic, like you, to understand."

"Understand? Yeah, well, I do understand. I undestand that the authors of that crap live in a two-dimensional world. They subscribe as you would put it to a destiny where everything works out in the end."

"If you want it to, it will."

"Tell that to all the Jews murdered during the Holocaust. Tell that to all the starving people aound the world, that haven't seen an ounce of

food in days. Hell, go ahead and tell it to all those people that suffered so needlessly in the World Trade Center."

"I think you're missing the point."

"Yeah, you might be right. I should go through life with blinders on, write some self-centered, arrogant, naive novel about hope. But you'll only appreciate the message if you can afford the twenty bucks to buy it."

"Are you always like this?"

"And, to top it off, I wouldn't want to forget to write the novel really poorly, in hopes that Fitzgerald, Hemingway, and Clemens will roll over in their graves."

"Why would they roll over in their graves?"

"They would feel so much humiliation that they would roll over, in order to avoid having to face the public."

"Is that what that expression means?"

"I don't know. I just made it up."

"Maybe we should talk about something less controversial."

"What would you like to talk about?"

"I ran over a squirrel once. I thought the bad karma would haunt me for the rest of my life. But, the next day, I..."

"Wait a minute. Karma? You believe in karma? You have to be a fool to believe in karma. You might think the good you're doing will outweigh the bad, but there is no way in hell that will ever happen. Human beings are evil, selfish, wasteful creatures and if you think you do more good in a day than bad, you've got another thing coming.

Karma? What idiot got you into the whole karma thing?

"My mother."

"Oh, well, I'm sorry your mother is a moron."

"I hate you."

"I know."

"You're the devil."

"So you keep telling me."

"Anyway, the day after I ran over the squirrel, I helped..."

MICKEY   Molly and I went shopping together, the day before we were supposed to go up north, for Tara's birthday weekend. We wanted to find a suitable gift for Tara. I recommended a pet store, where we could aquire a muzzel. Molly had another idea. She wanted to find something a little more contemporary. We ended up at Pier One. We ended up settling on a set of wine glasses for our mutual, alcoholic friend. One glass could hold a whole liter of wine. I took this as an omen for the upcoming weekend.

While Molly and I discussed the purchase, I glanced over toward the register and noticed one of the salesgirls smiling in our direction. I couldn't imagine that she was smiling at me, so I assumed she must have been checking Molly out. Molly's pretty hot. Okay, she's really hot. Not like supermodel hot. More like you're-the-girl-of-my-dreams hot. Molly's about five four, a hundred and five pounds, size B cup, and a nice full ass. She has a really sexy strut when she walks, and one of those innocent smiles, to go along with her devilish blue eyes. But the best physical feature I can see is her ears. They're elf ears. Tiny, thin, cute, with nice full lobes that any guy would want to suckle. I have issues.

I took Molly to dinner in Birmingham, one of the richest cities in the state. We shared a pizza at Max and Erma's, then decided to see a movie. *Monster's Ball* was playing at the old Birmingham Theater. The show didn't start for another half and hour, so we stopped in at the Java Hutt next door and grabbed a couple of coffees, to go. I kept thinking about the salesgirl at Pier One. I still wasn't sure why she had smiled at Molly and me. I noticed a younger woman, also smiling at Molly and I while we walked the streets, huddled together, sipping our coffee, waiting for our movie to start. Were we being that cute? Could Molly and I have given the appearance of a couple in love, to these nosey should-mind-their-own-business, smiling women?

We sat on a bench, a few blocks from the theater, to finish our coffees. We still had another thirty minutes to kill. I finally asked her what she thought her favorite physical feature was. She said that most men love her back. That's not what I asked, but I let it go. She asked me what I find so attractive in her appearance. I smiled, and said her ears. We started to talk about nothing in particular. Twenty-nine minute later, I noticed that we were about to miss our movie, so we ran to the theater as fast as our pack-a-day smoking habit would allow. We made it into some seats in the third row, just in time for opening credits. I looked around, and noticed an old couple to our left. The old woman was smiling at us. She had nice ears.

MARIE   I called Mick five times today. He wasn't home, every time I called. I needed some moral support, and my boyfriend's isn't enough. No boyfriend's support means shit to a girl. Women already have their boyfriends in their back pockets. Would the King of Egypt ask a slave what his take was on building the pyramids?

Mick finally called back around midnight. I asked him, right away, when he was planning on moving into the Hippie House. He said next weekend. Good. I was worried he already had and I had been calling all day, which probably pissed his mom off. He said it did. I told Mick about my dilemma with my ex, Brian. Mick didn't even give me a chance to tell him what the asshole said before he cut me off, to tell me about Molly. I said, "Who? Molly?" He told me all about her, that she and Miah used to date, and I thought "Oh, God. Here we go again."

Mick finally stopped talking, only to take a breath and then continued, on a completely different train of thought. He said that he doesn't believe love has anything to do with sex. He had some funny notion that sex was just an activity. I told him that was a bunch of bullshit. I had to know where this was coming from, so I inquired on what brought Mick to this conclusion. He, of course, said Molly. I guess he jerks off every night. I said "every night?". He said "every night." I asked him how long this has been going on, and he said since he was fourteen. I said "every night?" and he said "every night."

So Mick thinks that his lack of sexual attraction toward Molly is due to his excessive jerking off habit. I told him to stop jerking off, and see how Molly makes his little buddy feel. He said he can't, and I asked why the fuck not? He said that it's the only way he can get to sleep, and, besides, there's another issue on top of that. When he jerks off, he only fantasizes about two scenarios. One is him fucking his ex-girlfriend, Anne, in the ass while she begs for him to stop. The second is a template scenario. It could be of many different women, but they are all made to feel cheap while Mick does degrading things to them.

I told Mick that he had a lot of issues and baggage from what Anne did to him. He said he knows, but he doesn't know if he'll ever get over it. He doesn't remember how to love. I told him he probably never loved her. Mick didn't say anything for a minute. Then, he said maybe he was incapable of love and hung up the phone.

I cried for Mick that night. No, that's not true. I cried for myself that night. Mick doesn't realize that he exudes love. He does things unconsciously every second of every day, for people other than himself. A lot of people have said that they hate being around Mick. I always ask why, even though I already know the answer. 'Cause he's an asshole, they all say. But what they're really saying is that we...

MICKEY   I picked Molly up from work. We had planned on leaving directly from there, and heading up north. She met me out in front of the Mexican-style shithole she works in. Molly was dressed in a white shirt and black, ass-hugging pants. She said she was going to sleep the whole way. I said no problem. When we got on the highway, we were engrossed in a conversation about southern belles. I have always felt that southern women would make much better wives than northern ones. Molly agreed. She was born in Clawson, Michigan, which is five miles north of Ferndale. But I guess Molly spent a substantial part of her childhood in Texas. Her parents had divorced early on, and her father lives down in Texas. Her mother kept a home in Clawson.

Molly lives with a girl named Mary Beth, who slept with Thomas a couple of times last summer. She and Mary Beth share an apartment in Royal Oak. Molly also mentioned that Mary Beth's boyfriend, Jamey, might start paying rent as well, seeing as he stays over every night. Molly also told me about her daughter. She got pregnant when she was still in high school, and had given her daughter up for adoption. I inquired about the father, and found out that his name was Anthony, who happened to be her first boyfriend. Of course, I had to know why her and Anthony had never made a go of it. I wanted to know why they hadn't gotten married, or at least kept their baby girl and raised her themselves. Molly said she was too young, besides her nightmare has always been marrying her high school sweetheart and living the rest of her life in the God-forsaken town of Clawson.

I told Molly that I was a three-time felon. I had sold drugs, did some embezzlement, and even a little B and E. I didn't tell her about the other sins I had committed. I was afraid that I would scare her away from me. I know she already must be weirded out by my crooked face. She asked me when most of this had occurred. I told her about my old apartment, the Ghetto Penthouse, where I let a bunch of drug-gie raver kids hang out. That's how I met Tara, as a matter of fact. I told her how a few of us began a small criminal organization, dubbed the Clawson Mob. She wanted to know if the Ghetto Penthouse was in Clawson. I told her no. It was in Troy, west of there. So, why did we end up naming our little band of criminals the Clawson Mob when none of us lived in Clawson? Well, we all ate at a restaurant in Clawson and thought that it fit, in some weird, David Lynch way.

Molly and I ended up talking the entire ride. I became aware of the vortex that was around us whenever we were together. Time stood still for us. I wanted to live in this vortex. We pulled up in front of Tara's apartment building as it began to snow. Before Molly got out of the car, she looked me in the eye and asked if it had ever been like this before. I said I didn't know, I had never been to Tara's in the winter before. Molly said that wasn't what she meant. I said that I know.

TARA Terrence and I made love all day. I needed to... I needed to after all the shit Cody said to me yesterday. I didn't think that Cody could made me feel any more like shit than he had, but then I got a bouquet of flowers from him this morning. No doubt it was to rub salt in the wound, which it did. Terrence and I were still in bed when Molly and Mickey arrived.

M and M had brought a birthday gift with them. I opened it right away, and was thrilled at how beautiful the wine glasses were. They even bought a bottle of wine to fill them up. Terrence, Molly and I sat around and drank the full bottle while catching up. Mickey didn't partake in the alcoholic beverage. He has this weird thing about drinking. I've never known him to drink. I think it could be a control issue or something with him.

I wanted to go bowling. We left my apartment and went to the only alley in town. We bowled a few games and polished off a couple of pitchers. Mickey drank Sprite. I decided to go over a friend of mine's house after that. But, out of nowhere, Mickey and Molly said they wanted to go get something to eat. I didn't want to and if I didn't, Terrence didn't. I was a little pissed when Molly and Mick went their own way and said they'd meet us back at my place. Okay, I was more than a little pissed: this was my birthday weekend. And they were sneaking off to go play kissy-face. I would've never guessed that those two would hook up.

Terrence and I went over to my friend's house. I wanted to buy some coke, and his is the only place in town. We sat and did a couple of lines with him, bought an eight ball. I was sure Molly would want some. Of course, Mick doesn't do drugs. He'll only sell them. I swear, drug dealers are the scummiest people on the planet.

When Terrence and I returned to my place, we found the two love birds cooing over each other while they shared a cup of coffee. It almost made me physically ill. All four of us went upstairs. M and M had stopped to pick up another bottle of wine. While the three alcoholics of the group drank it, the non-alcoholic still participated in our conversation. I like that about Mick. He is never boring, no matter where you go. I do, however, hate when he argues a point with me. Terrence doesn't do that. I've trained him well. Halfway through the bottle of wine, I grabbed Molly and pulled her into the bathroom. I asked her what the fuck was going on with Mick. She denied that anything had transpired. Right. Molly is such a fucking whore. She's probably already sucked his dick, at least twice, since they met. While I listened to Molly lie through her teeth, I cut a couple lines of coke for

us. I knew I couldn't do this in front of Mick. He would freak out.
Not like he's against drugs, he just doesn't want anything to do with
them. He told me a couple weeks ago that he has to be really careful.
I guess he's on a suspended sentence. Serves him right for dealing.

Anyway, I offered Molly the first line. That little bitch turned it down.
I did both lines and asked if she was sure. While I cut up two more
lines from the eight ball, I asked her how Sean was. Sean is Molly's
go-to guy. Her fuck buddy, if you will. She said that she ended it
with him last week. What? That guy was totally hot, even if he was a
chotch. I assumed she had a new fuck buddy, and I asked who might
that be? The lying bitch denied having anyone to give head to. I was
like, please. That girl cannot go without dick for more than ten days.
When she was going out with Jeremiah, and he was gone doing his
service for the AmeriCorps, she had to have slept with six or seven
guys. I offered her the rolled-up dollar bill, to do a line. She didn't
want to at first, but I said it was my birthday. She inhaled both lines
like a pro. We did two more before we went back and joined the boys,
in the living room.

That night, M and M shared the pull-out couch in the living room
while Terrence and I did the rest of the eight ball and fucked like
rabbits. Before we all went to bed, we made plans to have breakfast
at the corner diner and then go shopping in Big Rapids, which is just
a half an hour away, and then maybe go to the new Chuck E. Cheese's
that just opened up near the mall in Grand Blanc.

The next morning, M and M were already long gone. I went back
to bed a little pissed. Terrence asked if I was okay, and I told him to
leave for a little while. He left, and I cried. I called him an hour later
and asked him to come back over. He came back right around the time
that M and M showed up. I asked them what the fuck happened. They
said they waited til ten and didn't want to wake me. I had slept til one.
Big deal. It was my birthday. It was going on six now.

Molly, Terrence and I shared a bottle of wine, that I had stashed in the
kitchen cabinet and then the four of us went to Chuck E. Cheese's.
As soon as we got in the door, M and M disappeared. Terrence and I

114

ordered pizza, and the customary one glass of beer for adults. I got Mickey one, planning to drink it myself. I was a little pissed that I was out of coke. Terrence and I played some games, and eventually went up and got our food. Out of nowhere, Mickey showed up. Molly came along only a few seconds later. We sat and ate, drank our beer. Mick gave his to little Miss Innocent. M and M had been playing games as well and they had acquired a few tickets, which they intended to redeem before they left. Terrence and I did the same. When we left, Terrence and I picked out some stickers from the prize counter. M and M got some stupid game called *Barrel of Monkeys*. The whole ride back to my place, the two love-sick puppies kept giggling over their *Barrel of Monkeys*.

We stopped at a liquor store and bought a huge jug of wine. The four of us sat at my place again, and talked. Mickey and Terrence both liked Weezer and they wouldn't shut up about it. Molly and I snuck into my bedroom and talked about Cody. I cried a little. Molly hugged me, and said that it would be okay. I wanted to bash her face in for telling him, and I told her so. She tried to deny it, at first, but then said that she thought it would be for the best. She thinks secrets cause too much damage among friends. I had to laugh. She was starting to sound like Mick.

I had originally planned on M and M staying the entire weekend. But after the second night, I asked them to leave. I was getting really sick of their lovey-dovey shit... they spent a couple of hours taking turns reading from a book Mick brought with him. It really was making me physically ill.

They thanked me for my hospitality when they left. I was glad to see them go. As soon as they pulled away, I told Terrence to go and get us more coke. When he came back, we did a few lines and fucked. I had trouble reaching climax the second time we did it. I kept thinking about the looks Mick and Molly shared between each other. Cody and I used to look at each other like that. After Terrence had cum, I asked him to leave. I didn't want him to see me cry.

MICKEY   On the way home from Tara's, Molly and I inadvertently slipped into our vortex again. I noticed that a lot of our conversations revolve around religion. Or, more importantly, about the lack of religion in the world. We both agree that the Jewish community benefits from having a strong belief in organized religion. Christian communities used to reap the same type of benefits. The members of the community would share, and share alike; both the prosperous, as well as the not-so-prosperous, times. Somewhere down the line, Christianity got perverted. I am personally not a strong believer in organized religion, but I do believe in God. Or maybe I just fear him.

I dropped Molly off at her apartment around four in the afternoon. I drove back to my parents' and started packing my stuff, to make it easier next weekend, when I move into the Hippie House. Around six, I finished packing. I really haven't been big on owning things since Anne and I broke up. My books are the only thing of value to me. I don't own a couch, or even a bed, for that matter. They're too much responsibility.

I was sitting in my parents' study, finishing the last few pages of *The Prophet*, by Kahlil Gibran. Molly and I read most of it this weekend, together. I wanted to call her to see if she wanted to grab dinner. I couldn't. I wouldn't. No matter how much I missed her, or wanted to spend time with her, I was not going to let myself be the beggar. The phone rang. It was Molly. She wanted to get dinner. I told her that the weird thing was, I wanted to call her, too, but I didn't want to seem like the sick, stalker type. She said she wouldn't mind if I was.

THE DEVIL   Molly was only home for a few minutes before she started to get antsy. I could tell she wanted to see him. How pathetic humans are, when they're enamoured with each other. It's as if they can't breathe without the other one close by. She finally called him a few hours later, to see about having dinner.

I had begun to worry a little, during their trip up north. Molly was starting to show signs of becoming someone I had not expected. Mickey was obviously influencing some sort of good nature, or moral code, in her. But, I've relaxed. Molly will not disappoint me. She's a runner. She will never be content with a pure love. She needs the corruption. She needs the drama. She's a woman.

I'll let this little love affair continue for a while longer, before I pull the rug out from under them. Mickey will be destroyed. This will be the final nail in his coffin, so to speak. He will commit his last sin. He has begun to acquire some virtues. That is why I must strike soon. He is in limbo. If I play my cards right, he will commit the most horrific sin of them all, and having done so, he will have corrupted his soul beyond repair. A soul which is rare to find, in this barbaric-heathenistic world the humans have created. I just need him to take that one final step. I need him to kill Molly.

CHAPTER NINE

HETERO LIFE PARTNER

"Lesbian women always look pissed off, even when they're in a relationship with another woman. You'll see them walking down the street, holding each other's hand, but they won't be smiling. Or even looking happy, for that matter."

"I know what you're talking about. I don't think two women could ever make each other happy. They'd spend so much time criticizing and being envious of each other, how could they ever give each other any sort of positive feedback?"

"I just think they need dick."

"Could be true. They do buy a lot of toys that are just a fill-in for a big, fat dick."

"Yeah, and look at gay men. They always seem happy with each other."

"I liked your pun, by the way."

"What pun?"

"Fill-in."

"Oh."

"I just think they need dick."

"Will you stop saying that?"

"Dick. Dick. Dick."

"Yes, we know all you think about is dick."

"I think he's just trying to tell us that he's a dick."

"Well, he's not. He's more like a stupid peice of crap."

"Can shit be stupid? I mean, does it have an intellect?"

"I want dick."

MICKEY   I met Molly at the Café D. You would think we would be sick of each other, after spending the entire weekend together. No dice. Dare I say, my heart leapt when I saw her sitting on our couch. Yes, "our couch". We shared a smile, as I walked toward our table. I set down my book and gave a nod to Desmond. He asked if I wanted a coffee, and I asked if he was kidding. I sat down beside Molly. We were still sharing that stupid smile. I knew I was in trouble. I was infatuated with this girl. I found myself thinking that maybe, even, I was in love with this girl. What the fuck am I thinking? My heart? Love? This was getting out of hand. Am I destined to become the beggar? Am I going to become the fool? And, besides that, even if I had a chance with this woman, what could I possibly say to Miah to make it okay?

My mind began to take off, into a fantasy about our future together. Molly would find me irresistible and want to love me for who I am. We would marry and properly raise two children after I made my fortune, in who knows what. My fantasy was getting out of hand when Desmond came over with my coffee. I thanked him and, finally, turned to Molly and said hello. We talked about our trip and about how eerie it was that we still wanted to be together.   Molly asked what I was reading. It was *The Communist Manifesto*, by Karl Marx. I had picked it up at Borders the other day. I had also got *The Catcher in the Rye*, by Salinger, at the same time. I paid for both books by credit card. No doubt I would be blacklisted by the federal government from here on out.

Karl kind of pisses me off, and I know a lot of people who would agree. Here's a guy who has no idea what it's like to live poor. I can't believe that the lower classes bought into his shit about living in the same, sad state. If he thought he was roughing at the time, I wonder how he would've felt waiting in line for five days to get a loaf of bread. Then again, I never met the man personally, so he could have been pretty down-to-earth. You wouldn't think so though, 'cause in the *Manifesto*, he starts talking crazy. I think it's around page ten.

I told Molly all of this, and more. She started to shift the conversation. I think she wanted to talk about art. After two cups of coffee each, I suggested that we go get something to eat, at the Mongolian Barbecue. She agreed, but only after another cigarette and the final sips of her coffee.

We were two minutes from departure when Peter and Simone walked in. They're very good friends of Jeremiah. I met them, briefly, once. I assumed Molly knew them well. She had to, after dating Jeremiah for so long. They took a seat by the window as I mentioned to Molly that they were here. She panicked a little, not sure if they would make a big deal about her and I being together. I didn't understand at first, but then I realized that Jeremiah has this weird thing about his friends dating, or hanging out, with his exes. I decided to face the issue head-on and approached their table to say hello. I stood there, feeling awkward, for a second as I asked what was up. They immediately started talking about their plans to move to Arizona. I guess Peter's getting a job out there or something. They finally shut the fuck up long enough for me to take my leave. I did, however, ask them to come join Molly and I, over near the couch. When I went back, she asked me what I'd talked to Peter and Simone about. I told her I had no idea. I couldn't figure out why Molly didn't go over to them and say hello. Miah dated her for at least two years, they had to have had some sort of double date with Peter and Simone. Maybe she just didn't like them. I was personally kind of uncomfortable around them. They make you feel immature for your age. Here they are, high school sweethearts, both graduated from Ivy League schools, with decent white-collar jobs, sharing an apartment in the good part of the state. They seemed like *Body Snatchers*, or something like that, to me. Molly and I were about to leave when they came over to our table.

They stood there, and talked on and on about Arizona. I couldn't wait for them to leave. While Molly chit-chatted with them, I went and got us another cup of coffee. I came back in time to hear Molly ask Simone if she was wearing a new coat. Simone seemed a little taken aback, and said no. The whole thing was getting too weird for me. I insisted that they join us, instead of hovering over our table. Then, I excused myself and went to the bathroom. I took a few minutes to sober myself up from the caffeine high, dancing around and clapping my hands. When I went back out to join Molly, our new-found friends

126

were still hovering over the table. When I got back to the table, Peter and Simone said goodbye and went back to their table, near the front of the Café D. I sat next to Molly and began to laugh. I was, like, what the fuck? She cursed me for not sticking around. She was really embarrassed about the whole jacket thing. She told me that she'd only met Simone and Peter once before. Once before? I told her that I was under the impression that she knew them rather well. Quite well, in fact. Molly and I began to laugh and laugh and laugh about the whole stupid thing. And when it wasn't funny anymore, we laughed out of the fear that they would think we were laughing at them. Which, in fact, we were. We laughed like two lovers playing in a field. We finally left, to grab a bite to eat, making sure to avoid any further contact with Peter and Simone.

On the way to dinner, Molly and I discussed the rush of our secret relationship, which wasn't really a relationship. I kept thinking about the ass-whopping I was going to get from Miah, when he found out that I was getting fresh with one of his exes. Was I getting fresh? Hell yes I was, and I was loving it. I needed this. This was my life, my love, my hope, my faith... all riding on this one chance, with this one girl. Like it or not, I was in love. But... did this woman love me, or was she playing me for a fool? All I want, and all I've ever wanted, was to be loved in the same way that I love. Unconditionally. My parents have always had conditions, for the love they bestowed on me.

I used to leave a Coke in the fridge for Anne when we lived together. It was the last Coke. And everyday, I would come home to find that Coke gone. All I wanted was to come home and find that Coke still there. Hell, I would've even settled for a brand-new six pack. The three years Anne and I lived together, never once did I come home to crack open an ice-cold Coca Cola.

BENEDICT   Mickey moved in last week. He really isn't that bad. He spends a lot of his nights out. I think he may be seeing someone. He cut down on his work schedule at the tire place so that he can take some classes at the community college in Royal Oak. I still hate the bastard. Thomas stopped in, to whine like a little bitch, today. His

car has already been broken into twice. The first time, they shattered
his driver's window and yanked out his stereo. The second time, they
broke his passenger's window and ripped out his climate control.
Why? I have no idea. I relished in the fact that I continually tell him
"I told you so." He should have never moved to Detroit. He's already
becoming a racist. Every time he refers to a problem with his car, or
the area he lives in, he says "those people." I try to remind him that
"those" are his "people." I mean, c'mon. He's a gay Jewish guy that
wants to be black.

I've been doing a lot of soul searching lately. I think I may join the
army. I can't find a job that will enable me to use my degree. The
army is the only way for me to get enough civil service experience to
get into the Diplomatic Corps. I've been considering this for some
time. I cannot continue this lifestyle much longer. I work a shit job,
delivering pizzas. I throw the pizzas that I have to deliver on top of
the diploma that cost me a hundred thousand dollars, now student
loans. When I'm not working, I sit at home reading or playing the *X-
Box*. God help me, 'cause I can't help myself. I have to join the army.
The only thing holding me back from getting on with my life is fear.
My fear of failing. That fear, however, is becoming a thing of the past.
I don't consider myself a failure when I'm around Mick. In fact, I feel
pretty good about myself.

Mick and I caught coffee today again, before Family Night. I told him
of my plan to join the army. He seemed supportive, but also skeptical.
I think his reservations had to do with his fear of my success. I asked
him who he was dating. He said Molly. I said "Miah's Molly?" and
he replied with a nod. What a fucking moron. Miah's going to kill
him. I knew the answer before I asked, but I asked it anyway. Was
he spending the night at her house? Is that why he's only home two
or three nights a week? "Of course," he said. I reassured him, that I
would miss him when he was dead. Miah will surely see to that.

Miah, on the other hand, was acting weird himself. Like Mick, he was
spending only a couple nights a week at home. I really shouldn't complain, seeing as I hate them both. Miah also seems rather light-hearted

and, dare I say, normal lately. I could only assume that he, too, had found himself a piece of ass.

THOMAS   I'm so stupid. How could I have made such an error in judgement? These people have no self-control. All they do is steal and do drugs. I hate them. I hate them for breaking into my car. I hate them for selling crack, or ass, down the street from me. I hate them for making me hate them. I never thought of myself as a racist, but there comes a time when we must choose to live like human beings or like animals.

I explained all of this to Mick the other day. We caught a cup of coffee. He told me his idea for a book. It was a lame story that dealt with a bunch of drug-addicted suburban kids who went down to Detroit to party in a condemned warehouse, just so they could have stories to tell their grandkids. I told Mick it was stupid. I also told him about my newly-found racism. He said that it was good to recognize one's hate. It was important to become disillusioned with other people. He believes, in the end, that we will understand each other better through hate. I hated him. And, I understood.

I told him that I knew about him and Molly. I asked if they fucked yet, and he denied it. He seemed a little worried about Jeremiah finding out. We discussed the whole code-among-friends thing that Miah supposedly lives by. Then, I let Mick in on a little secret. I told him that Miah had been dating an ex of mine, for the past couple weeks. I want Mick to be on an equal playing field.

SANDIE   I had only been back in town for a few weeks when I met up with Jeremiah. He still looked good. He has a boyish way about him, and it doesn't hurt that he has a great body. We were first introduced a couple years ago, when I was dating Thomas. When Thomas and I broke up, Jeremiah and I remained friends. We got pretty close. I think we were about to get involved when he up and disappeared. A week later, I ran into Thomas and asked about Miah. He laughed and told me to forget about that closet-case. So, I did. A year later, when

I came home from college on holiday, I saw Miah at the mall. I asked him what had happened, way back when. He told me that it wasn't right. I think he was referring to the fact that Thomas and I had dated. I'm not sure. Guys are weird like that. They never want to know who you've dated. Just because I had a guy's dick in my mouth doesn't mean I'm still in love with him.

Well, I guess Miah's had a change of heart. We've been hanging out every day this month. And, we've been involved. My only complaint is that we only fool around after we've had a few too many. I don't think that would be considered a healthy thing for a new relationship.

Somewhere in this whirlwind, I met Miah's roommate, Mick. Mick and I get along quite well. I even told him about my relationship with Miah. He had heard about it already. I was stunned. Miah and I have been trying to keep it quiet. We didn't want Thomas to find out... re-open the whole wound thing. Mick said that he didn't see the big deal. In fact, I found out, Thomas already knew. I have no idea how he found out, but he knew. I panicked. Mick told me not to have secrets of that kind, that all they do is slow down the inevitable. I told him to practice what he preached. He didn't know that I knew that he and Molly were seeing each other. I found out from Jeremiah.

MICKEY   I must say, I'm a little lost right now. I work thirty hours a week, go to school another fifteen, spend at least five hours on homework and Mondays with my roommates, and every other waking hour in the presence of Molly. I've only known the bitch a month, and I already sleep at her house five out of the seven nights a week. We have never kissed. We have never even hugged for that matter, unless you call snuggling in the same bed hugging. When we're not acting like a couple of spoons, we'll share meals at shitty diners... see movies of actual content... talk... read books with some degree of intellect... shop for thing we don't need... drink numerous cups of coffee, while we make eyes at each other. I'm exhausted. Molly and I have different work schedules. I work and go to school during the day. She works at night and sleeps all day like a fucking vampire. Needless to say, I get the least amount of sleep between the two of us.

Molly shares her apartment with a loud-mouth, annoying, in-the-closet whore, named Mary Beth. I can't stand her. Mary Beth's boyfriend, however, is pretty cool. There's something off about Jamey, though. I think I've met him before. It's not necessarily his face that gives me the feeling of déjá vu. I think it's his hands. He's got really long nails and they have a very dark complexion. Then again, it could be a genetic thing that all American Indians have. Jamey and I talk a lot about "his people." He tells me how wonderful they are, that they have a belief in nature. I agree with him. I like their beliefs. To use, and waste, and rape the land they live on until it is uninhabitable and then move on to another piece of land, and do the same thing. Thank God we wiped that perverse and incompetent culture off the face of the earth. If everyone was an A.I., we would all be stricken with venereal disease, walking around in a climate that reeks of human excrement and piss. It's called a toilet, you backwards, bone-wearing, buffalo wasting, not-burying-your-dead-in-order-to-not-spread-diease assholes.

Somehow, Jamey and I got into a competition over who is the better boyfriend. I think it started when I came over to Molly's and made us dinner. He, in turn, made dinner the following week. His was much better than mine. I'm not a cook. I was just trying to impress upon Molly that I would do anything to win her heart. The following week, the VCR went kaput and I went out that night and bought one at a going-out-of-business sale, and gave it to the girls as a present. The following day, Jamey went out and bought Mary Beth a pair of diamond earrings. There was no way I was going to buy some bitch diamond earrings. I did enough of that when Anne and I were together, but I still had to retaliate. I went out and bought the movie that the VCR ate when it died. It just happened to be Molly's favorite movie of all time.... *Some Like It Hot*, starring Marilyn Monroe. The next day, when I gave Molly the movie, Jamey simply pointed out that a real man would've bought the movie when he bought the VCR. I agreed, and pointed out that it wasn't really a gift for Molly but a luxury for myself. He didn't seem to understand what I was implying.

Molly and I have found our own little code to speak in. We even have a song. It's by Mad Happy. The chorus goes something like "good

131

morning, Sunshine... good morning, Strychnine." We definitely have some sort of perverse way to show each other affection. The other night, she informed me that men found her the prettiest when she slept. I had to disagree. I find her much prettier when she's awake. I don't think that "pretty" has anything to do with physical beauty. I think it has to do with the whole package. What Molly has on the inside far outweighs what God has given her on the outside. Natural beauty is only skin-deep, they say. In her case, that's not true.

Today is going to be a bad day for Molly. Five years ago, on this day, she gave up her only child for adoption. I'm not a woman, but I still know that this is a big fucking deal. I decided to surprise her. Yesterday, I heard on the radio that Ani DiFranco was going to be doing a concert, this Friday in Ann Arbor. I went to the florist and ordered a huge bouquet of irises, her favorite flower. I included the tickets, and a note, in the card. It simply said, "You're smiling. Aren't you?" The flowers and the card were going to be delivered to her work that afternoon. Around ten o'clock that morning, I called her and made a bet. I bet that I could make her smile when I wasn't around. She said that I already did.

THE DEVIL   Boy, do I love Mick! He has got to be the most arrogant asshole I have ever corrupted. He has this thing about getting the whole picture when he's debating. The shit that came out of his mouth about the American Indians was fucking hilarious. It was all true, and I think that's why it was so hilarious. It was bluntly honest. Humans aren't like that anymore. They spend so much time hiding their true feelings that the false becomes what they believe is true.

Ah, well. No matter. I think the honeymoon period is over. They're madly in love with each other. I was hoping to see Molly in poor spirits today. Usually, it's an unbelievably bad day for her, but Mick- that fucking prick- did this incredibly sincere thing for her and now she's bouncing around like a superball flung from a slingshot. She came home like this, with a huge bouquet of flowers. I have had enough myself. I plan on pulling the rug out from under them, starting tomorrow.

MARY BETH   I cried all night last night. Jamey doesn't seem to care about the way I feel anymore. I love him so much. The past couple of weeks he has been so giving and caring. It's like he was competing with Mick on who could give their lover more. But today we went to the mall and I saw a beautiful sapphire ring. I told my little devil that I wanted it. He replied only with a look at first, so I figured he was being playful. In reply to his look, I began to beg and whine. He said nothing. When we left the mall, without the ring, I began to cry a little. On the drive home, he asked me why I was so upset. I told him I knew that I knew that he didn't love me anymore. He said he never did. I wondered if it that was it then. He ignored me. When we got home, he told me to go to bed. So, I did.

BENEDICT   For the first time in our friendship, Mickey and I discussed our pathetic little love lives. I told him about Asia, the girl I dated and fell in love with during college. Asia and I complimented each other rather well, but the whole love thing scared the crap out of me, so I ran. And she, in turn, ran straight into another man's arms for comfort.

I knew I fucked up the second it happened. I didn't want Mick to make the same mistake that I had. I even went as far as to tell him that it was too bad that Jeremiah and Molly had ever dated. Their past was bringing a shadow over Molly and Mick. Mick told me that the only thing missing between them was physical contact. He didn't exactly say it like that. Mick is far too blunt for that. I suggested he make a move. Take her out for once, to a really nice dinner and do all that old-fashioned shit you see in the movies. I even told him to try for the kiss at the door, though it seemed they'd been dating for a few weeks. Poor bastard. Mick is really falling for this girl. I only hope he can handle the fall if it doesn't pan out.

MICKEY   Ben and I grabbed coffee at the Java Hutt in Ferndale. We discussed Molly and I, for the first time. He had some surprising thoughts about us. Even though he said that seeing her and I together made him violently ill, he gave me a plan to remedy my reservations about Molly. Tomorrow, I will attempt to put the plan into effect.

I chickened out. Well, I kind of fucked it up, actually. I had made
plans to have dinner with Molly, by double booked on accident. I
was also supposed to have dinner with Jim and Marie, so Molly and
I ended up going out to Ann Arbor to have dinner with them, instead
of having it alone. We ate at a Thai place somewhere on Michigan
Avenue. I hate Thai food. It tastes like Chinese, but has some sort
of seasoning that makes your shit burn your ass crack for two days.
During dinner, we all talked about nothing and seemed to have a pretty
good time. On the way out to our respective cars, Marie pulled me to
the side and said she was in love with me. I was shocked. I told Marie
that I had feelings for Molly. She corrected the miscommunication
immediately and said, "no, stupid. Molly is in love with you." I
wasn't sure how to answer that, so I didn't.

Seeing I fucked up the night before, I made plans to have dinner alone
with her on Thursday. We went down to the Renaissance Center, in
Detroit. There's a great eatery on the west side of the building, overlooking the Detroit River. We had an expensive, but delicious, meal.
The entire night I was a perfect gentleman. I even turned down her
offer to spend the night on the ride home. I did, however walk her to
the door. Then, I went in for the kiss. It proved to be nothing. Molly
did not kiss me back. She said goodnight and went inside.

I was stunned, to say the least. She acted like it never happened. I
walked back to my car. I was halfway home when I turned around to
go back to Molly's. The whole thing was bullshit. Why would she
act like that? We had to be in love. Isn't this what love is? And, she
looked so fucking hot in the dress she wore to dinner. I had to keep
adjusting my dick during our meal. Five minutes later, I was in front
of her door again. I knocked lightly at first. Then I grew impatient
and almost kicked the door down. I was nervous. Molly opened the
door and, as she did, I heard Mary Beth's recognition of the
situation. She said that I was back for more. Molly stood in the
doorway, wearing the sweats she likes to wear to bed. I wanted to kiss
her, but instead I asked what this was. She said "what?" I said "this."
She said "I don't know."

I drove home with my tail between my legs that night. I didn't know what to make of it. I didn't want to know, or need to know. I just knew that I had to hold on to it. The past few months have been the only time I can remember feeling like this. If this isn't love... It has to be.

I have always wanted to be loved. I know none of my past girlfriends ever truly loved me. And maybe I never truly loved them. I think love is when you can't do without, or be without. I don't remember ever having a girl jump me, seduce me, love me. It seems shallow, I guess, to use sex as the basis of measuring love. But that's all I seem to understand. I have never had a faithful girlfriend. Getting a blow job was always like pulling teeth. I guess I just want a girl to give me head without me begging for it. I think that's what love is. I'm afraid that I've already fucked up our chances. I have already become the beggar. I have already become the fool. Now, I am so infatuated with Molly that I can't leave her side. This has always been my problem and it always will. But, then again, maybe she's just scared to love. I'm a rather complacent individual. Maybe she thinks I don't care about her. Well, I'm in for the long haul, sweetheart. The long fucking haul.

THE DEVIL   Oh, poor little Mickey. He just wants his cock sucked so bad. Fucking typical human male need. They actually think that love is represented by how much of their cum their stupid little slut girlfriend swallows. Oh, but Mick... too bad you don't know. Tick-tock, tick-tock. Last night, Molly had already sucked a cock.

JEREMIAH   I stopped by Molly's work, to talk to her about Mick. I don't think she realizes how impulsive, and fragile, he can be. I had a few beers at the bar, while I waited for Molly to get off. She didn't have time to talk while she was working, so I opted to wait. We decided to grab a drink down the street when she got off. I guess we had a few too many, 'cause I woke up at her place, still drunk and hardly clothed. This was bad. I looked at the alarm clock next to her bed. Six a.m. I slid past Molly's naked self, and headed for the door.

CHAPTER TEN

SAINT MAKES YOU CRY,
DEVIL MAKES YOU SMILE

"No, you're right. Movies don't give you a chance to talk. I prefer going to a concert, or some bar with live music. Like Baker's. That way, if he turns out to be a jackass, I'll still be able to sit back and listen to music."

"You actually think about stuff like that? Women think?"

"Ah, yeah. What? You don't worry about how a first date turns out?"

"No, I..."

"No, no. You're right. Women don't think about that stuff. We just walk around in a daze, waiting for some man to come along and lead us to our next destination."

"No. I... I just... I was surprised that you thought about that stuff. I didn't think... women think."

"Oh, my God! Could you possibly be a bigger asshole?"

"That's not what I..."

"Newsflash, dickhead. We actually do worry about meeting guys like you. I hate you!"

"I know."

MARY BETH Thank God. Molly has gone back to being her virtueless self. She was really beginning to get on my nerves. "Oh, Mick is so wonderful" and "I'm really enjoying this book" and "oh, I do love to listen to the rain against my window" blah, blah, blah. I would never have thought Jeremiah would be back. But I'm glad he showed up, even if it was only for one night. I couldn't help but feel bad for Mickey. He took the little bitch to a really nice restaurant the other night. He had no clue that she was thinking of Jeremiah the whole time. She must have called him thirty times that day, and he never answered his phone. She was so pissed that night. She kept asking me to go and buy her some coke. I kept telling her that Mick was going to be here before I could get my hands on some. And besides that, the little tramp doesn't deserve any help from me. I know she wants to fuck Jamey.

The past week, I haven't seen Mickey around and all Molly does is bitch about what an asshole Jeremiah is. This morning, just to fuck with her, I asked how Miah was doing. She just gave me a cold stare. Poor little bitch. I told Jamey what fun I was having, messing around with her. For the first time in a week, he smiled and told me I was beautiful. I waited for Molly to leave for work, and then I fucked my boyfriend.

MICKEY I figured I would give Molly some space after the other night. So, with my new-found free time, I read a couple of books, quit my job at the tire store, got a job at a carwash, then a second job as a bartender. I finally made it over to the community college and dropped all my classes. I haven't been going anyway.

The tire store proved to be too much stress. I needed something different. I needed less responsibility. So, I got a job at a carwash, drying cars. I don't do anything but dry cars. I make, like, seven dollars and hour plus tips. I wasn't really worried about the pay cut I had given myself. My rent at the Hippie House is only two hundred dollars a month, plus utilities. My first day at the car wash we had maybe ten cars. So I read. I almost finished my book by Mario Puzo by the end of my shift. Needless to say, I love my job. My second day at the carwash was slow again. This time, my boss felt that we should clean, instead of doing absolutely nothing. He came down to the drying end of the carwash and asked if I would clean the display windows. I told him to fuck himself and he apologized for interrupting my reading. That was it. I love my job.

My third day at the carwash was, yet again, uneventful. I was beginning to worry about money. I guess I had been counting on tips. No cars, no tips. I decided to supplement my income. When I got off work, I took a drive up to Troy, to see Mary Beth's boyfriend. He had mentioned a job opening at his work. Jamey works in a Carribean-themed shithole bar. I got a job that day. I was destined to be one of their illustrious bartenders.

Ben and I went and grabbed breakfast this morning. We talked about the usual melodrama. But I really enjoyed our conversation about midgets. I hatched a theory the other night, when I had gotten a cup of coffee with Marie. I told her at the time, and reiterated the same thing to Ben at breakfast. Midgets must get laid a lot. All a midget has to do is go up to any woman, raise his hands as if pleading to God, and say "look at me!" Now, if he says this with enough angst, he's sure to get laid at least two out of five times. Women pity-fuck a lot. Ben disagreed. We argued, and then he proved his point by saying "look at me!"

Molly and I finally started talking on the phone again. It only took five minutes of hellos and how are you doings to agree to meet at the Café D. When I got there, she was already on our couch. That surprised me. She kind of freaked me out by being so nice to me. I had thought for sure I had blown it completely the other night. What did I know? She could have been on her period, for that matter. We both consumed several cups of coffee and spoke out of turn the entire night. Molly and I were acting like we were high school friends that hadn't seen each other in five years. I guess ten days is a lifetime to us. Molly agreed with my assessment, when she heard all that I'd been up to. She even told me I looked happy. I was. I was with her.

After coffee, we decided to grab a bite to eat at Tom's Oyster Bar. It was pretty good. Molly had a couple of cocktails with her dinner, I had a Sprite. After dinner, I suggested we take a drive. I always like to drive on dates. It gives you the sense that you're going somewhere, accomplishing something, but really all you're doing is depleting the ozone. Luckily, Molly likes to take drives as well. We were halfway to Port Huron when Molly told me that she'd missed me. I began to cry, and told her that I loved her. She didn't say anything except "I know."

Ben, Thomas and I decided to have Family Night without Miah. Miah has this game he likes to play. It's called "Look at me. I'm not going to answer you when you ask me a question 'cause that way I can have a lot of attention and still be an asshole at the same time." We played *Axis and Allies* after Chinese. Thomas spent most of his night bitching about "those people." Ben and I just kept antagonizing him, pointing out that it was he who moved to Detroit, not the other way around. I love pissing Tom off.

Ben and I began a discussion on fantasy life while we played the game. I always slip into some type of fantasy. I'll be driving and some dickhead will go flying by, doing a hundred miles an hour. I, of course, am jealous and can't help but think of all the times I get pulled over for disobeying the speed limit. I start getting mad, watching this guy cruising along and not getting pulled over. And, then, my fantasy starts. I follow this guy until he pulls over or stops for some reason. I get out of the car and shoot him in the face. Or maybe I beat him to death with a crowbar.

Another fantasy of mine happens when I see a homeless guy asking for change. I, personally, like homeless people. I think they know a secret to life that those who participate in society don't. But I can't help fantasizing that I tell the homeless guy to fuck off, when he approaches me for change.

The funny thing was that Ben and I had so many hateful feelings inside us, that our conversation about fantasy could've gone on all night, but Jeremiah came home. Miah came in and started bitching at us for not waiting for him. Thomas, Ben and I just rolled our eyes at each other.

143

Jeremiah had only been home for five minutes when Molly walked in. Miah and Molly looked at each other for a long moment. Miah didn't say anything, and Molly turned and ran back out the door. I was in shock.

I totally forgot that I talked to Molly. I told her it was okay to come over 'cause Miah wasn't going to be there. Well, that's what he told us. I didn't think it would be a big deal anyway. Molly and Miah broke up almost a year ago. You wouldn't think that they would both hold grudges this long.

Miah looked around right after Molly left, called us all a bunch of faggots, laughed to himself, and went downstairs. I failed to join in when Ben and Thomas began to laugh. What I really wanted to do was run after her, not sit here and pretend that the whole thing was funny somehow. I wanted to catch her before she went into some crazy hysteria and drove her car into a brick wall. That's what women do. But, I couldn't leave the table right then. I couldn't tell Thomas and Ben that I was going after her. I didn't want them to know how much I love her.

Marie called me exactly five minutes after Molly had bolted. Marie's phone call gave me the excuse I needed to leave. I told Thomas and Ben that Marie had gotten into an accident and needed my help. They were both concerned about Marie's well-being. I said that she was just shaken up. I grabbed my coat and ran out of the house. I drove like a bat out of hell to Molly's. She wasn't home.

I drove around for at least three hours looking for Molly. I wanted to be there for her. I wanted to hold her, to console her. I wanted to feel her warm tears soaking into my shirt. I wanted to be the hero. But I couldn't. How could I be a fucking hero when I can't even find the bitch? How can I ride in on my white horse and save the fucking day when the useless whore won't even answer her phone?

I stopped at a gas station and filled up before I headed home. On my way back to the Hippie House, I changed my mind and decided to drive by Molly's, just one more time. She wasn't there. I decided to wait in her apartment's parking lot until she showed up. It must have been around three a.m. when I fell asleep.

MARY BETH   Jamey and I went to his best friend's birthday party last night. The party turned out to be a total sausage fest. There I was, sitting on some ragged couch, with fifteen guys checking out my cup size. I started doing tequila shots, hoping that it would take away the boredom. On my third shot with a beer as a chaser, I asked Jamey if we could leave. He looked at me real hard and told me to do another shot. One of his friends broke out an eight-ball of coke and cut up several lines. He was pretty cool 'cause he let me do a few of the lines. Some other guy gave me a pill of E, which I took from the palm of his hand with my tongue. I kept doing shot after shot, in between the lines of coke and the pill. A couple other guys showed up with a nitrous tank and passed around balloons to everyone.

Around my twelfth shot, my fifth line, another pill of E, a couple balloons and three bumps of K that someone else had offered me, I began to lose consciousness. Jamey smacked me in the face a couple of times, to sober me up. I asked him to leave me alone while I leaned on him for support. He told me to take my clothes off, which I did with his help and, I think, a couple of his friends. I guess I should've been embarrassed, but I had been in a couple of orgies before. Jamey smacked me again, and told me to suck his dick. I did. I eventually fucked and sucked the entire party. I kept hearing the front door open and close. It sounded like more people showed up as the night when on. I finally passed out while I was giving head to... I think a dog, and taking two guys in the ass at the same time. Around five, I felt Jamey smack me in the face and tell me to get dressed. I didn't want to, but he got a little rough and I know better than to really piss him off. I asked him if I could go to the bathroom before we left. He said to make it quick.

While I peed, I started to cry. I hurt so bad. I don't know if any of the guys used protection or not. What the fuck was I doing? Jamey pounded on the bathroom door and told me to hurry up. I dried my tears the best I could and wiped myself, only to notice semen all over the tissue. It made me vomit. My puke looked like... maybe cum. There was a lot. Jamey started pounding on the door and told me to hurry up. I rinsed my mouth and opened the door, to see him pissed off. We left in a hurry. I asked him why such the rush? He told me to mind my own business. I started to cry on the way home. He asked why I was crying. I said I didn't like myself too much. He said he liked me just fine. I love him so much.

THE DEVIL   Things were going as planned with Mickey, so I decided to take the night off and corrupt a few souls. I almost forgot how easy it is to corrupt a soul. Mickey's has proven to be quite the choir. After a fun-filled night of perverse sexual acts and the spreading of many different venereal diseases, Mary Beth and I came home to find Mickey sleeping in our parking lot. I was elated. This was going to be so much better than I had once thought. Molly arrived home at eleven a.m. I had sat in the living room, expecting her, while Mary Beth cried herself to sleep. I asked Molly how her night was. She said fine, and went to her room to cry. Oh, I knew it was fine all right. Molly had gone out last night, with a bunch of what she would call chotches. She ended up at Sean's house again, and participated in a four-way. I knew she wouldn't change. The funny thing is that Molly will never know that Mickey searched for her the entire night. Molly will never know that his dumb ass waited in the parking lot until ten a.m. He wanted to be the white knight so bad. I guess what's even funnier is that Mickey will never know that Molly was out contracting herpes while he dreamt of being the hero.

MICKEY   I have been accused, on several occasions, of being a hypochondriac. I think this perception of me comes from my con-stant paranoia. I don't see the big deal in thinking that the cookies might be poisoned, or that I might have an aneurism at any time. I do, however, fear that I may have developed a new ailment, Molly Stress. Yes, Molly Stress may be the one disease that will put me in the grave. I ended up sleeping in my car til ten in the morning, and then drove home a little discouraged. I had to work at the carwash at three in the afternoon. Ben was reading *The New York Times* when I walked in the door at the Hippie House. I sat down and enjoyed a cigarette while he and I discussed the difference in writing quality between *The Detroit News* and *The New York Times*. We both agreed that it wasn't surprising that the *Times* would be better written, seeing as it had a circulation in the millions. Besides, most of metropolitan Detroit is illiterate anyway. I took a shower and went to work.

I called Molly several times during the day. She never answered her phone, so I left a series of really obnoxious messages every time that I called. I've been known to leave twenty minutes of prattle on a voicemail. Most of my friends tell me not to, which is why I do it. Fuck phones anyway. We carry them around like leashes. Whatever happened to peace and fucking quiet? Why the fuck do we need to talk to each other so much? Whatever happened to "absence makes the heart grow fonder"? I don't know. When I was selling drugs, my phone used to ring every fifteen minutes. I bet there's a lot of demons getting their wings.

I got out of work around nine, and changed to go to my second job. But I didn't feel like it. I like bartending and all, but all the cokeheads I work with kind of piss me off. In the bar industry, ninety-nine percent of all the workers- waiters, bussers, cooks, bartenders, and managers- have a hardcore drug problem. They're all about two steps away from Betty Ford, if you ask me. I didn't want to deal with any of that tonight, so I called in. This was my second week on the job, and I had already called in five times. My boss at the bar always says "no problem." Most likely 'cause he's getting head before the bar opens, from a fifteen-year-old hostess.

I left Molly six messages during the day. She finally called me back. She had one major fucking attitude. No doubt from Jeremiah's inconsiderate behavior last night. We decided to get coffee and a late breakfast, at the IHOP on Woodward. Molly and I eat frequently at the IHOP. It's open twenty-four hours and she usually works until two in the morning. When I arrived, she was already there. She even made my cup of coffee just the way I like it. I told her she looked a little rundown, but still fucking beautiful nonetheless. She gave me a half-smile. I asked what had happened to her last night. She said she took a drive to clear her head and then went over a friend's house and had a few drinks, slept there until she had a hangover. I told her how concerned I was about her. She said she understood. I then told her the most important thing I could share with anyone. "A saint will make you cry, while the devil makes you smile," I said. She didn't seem to understand at first, so I explained. Jeremiah, in this case, is the saint. He always does the right thing, and says the right thing. He's like Johnny Walker, or *Captain America*. She nodded as it began to sink in. She asked if Miah was the saint, who the fuck was the devil? Me," I replied. Molly couldn't help but show me all her pearly whites.

TARA   I was talking to an old friend of mine that works downtown. He said that Molly had started coming back around again. Which translates to her doing coke and fucking a different guy every night. Normally I wouldn't give a shit, but I know Mick. He's a little naive. I know everyone thinks he's apathetic, but he's really not. I've seen the way he looks at her. God, this is going to get so messy. I just hope Molly will realize what's going on and have the decency to do the right thing. I should've never introduced Mick to her. But, I guess it's his own damn fault for being so easily swayed by his heart. The heart is a terrible thing, Mick. I just hope everyone is right and you don't have one anymore.

BENEDICT   Mick came home in a bad mood again. He kind of freaks me out sometimes. Most people see Mick as this real laidback, nice-guy type. What they don't see is his lack of self-control. The guy is always consuming something. Now, that's a tell-tale sign for me, that says that he cannot control his urges. No wonder he's always bitching about Goldmund. I even hear him jerking off. I can't help it, his room is directly over mine and I know he's not dating anyone but Molly. She's sure as shit not giving it up, especially in this house. For Christ's sake, he used to sell dugs. I've met people who have told me stories about Mick. Like the one time a runner of his didn't have the money he owed him, so Mick repeatedly smacked this kid across the face, in a crowded restaurant. The storyteller went on to say that Mick bent the kid over his knee, and spanked his bare ass in that same restaurant. The guy has a screw loose, if you ask me. I like him. I like him a lot. I wonder what I could get him to do to Thomas.

THOMAS   Mick and I got lunch at the Cass Café. He's the only one that has come down to Detroit to see my new apartment. We talked during lunch mostly about his crooked face and my lack of sincerity toward women. Mick seems to think that I spend too much time thinking about what I'm going to do before I do it. He believes that this will only hinder my life, while I think that it will only protect me from making mistakes in my life. Mick completely countered my statement by saying that life was a mistake.

CHAPTER ELEVEN

SOME THINGS ARE BETTER LEFT UNSAID

"Why do you insist on doing that? I don't appreciate it! You always have some snide remark toward me, or my clothes, or my life! Why don't you try something new for a change, and give me a compliment or two instead of the usual insult?"

"I... I didn't mean anything by it. I was just pla-"

"Playing, I know. You're always playing around, or kidding! Well, guess what, asshole? I don't think it's funny!"

"Then, why are you smiling?"

"FUCK YOU!"

MICKEY Six months ago, I found myself searching for any sort of emotion in myself other than anger or hate. Now I find myself in complete emotional disarray. Molly has done this to me. I can honestly say that before I met Molly, I was in control of my own emotional domain. After Anne and I had gone our separate ways, I made the decision not to put myself in an emotionally unstable place ever again. It was working beautifully. All the women I would subsequently date would only have one, shared complaint about me. They said that they were afraid of my ability to be detached. They could easily imagine me walking away from them without a tear in my eye. I was not upset by their assessment. Why would I be? It was true. But those days are blissfully in the past. I know I have lost that ability, to free myself from emotional carnage. I cannot imagine myself walking away from Molly. I know it would be too painful. I doubt if anyone was lost in a vast desert, like I was, that they could bring themselves to walk away from the oasis that they had stumbled upon. I just hope that the oasis I am living in now is not a mirage.

Molly and I have seemed to rekindle our romance. I was concerned after the half-assed kiss. But we got back on the horse of friend-ship relatively quickly. And now we seem to have fallen back into an imaginary bed together. I wanted to take her out to a nice dinner again. We made plans to go to Como's in Ferndale. She picked the place. I would've chosen something fancy, in another attempt to show her how much I care. The restaurant choice did leave me a little weary on the subject of us. But when I picked up Molly, I was not concerned with the issue anymore. She looked incredible. On the way to dinner, I imagined myself caressing her legs and rubbing her pussy while she exuded an erotic type of passion from my tender touch. I've been doing a lot of that lately. Benedict and I share this same trait. We always find ourselves discussing our imaginary lives, rather than our real ones. Between us, we have fucked seven hundred and forty-two girls, beaten to death at least seventy obnoxious drivers, and shot a whopping two or three thousand in the face. I, however, am the only one who has nuked a few cities.

Molly ordered a pasta dish at dinner. I always enjoy watching her eat. She does it with such grace. God, I make myself sick. We spent at least five minutes between each bite, discussing absolutely nothing. I find that Molly and I can make the most mundane things interesting. I inquired of her after dinner, if we should rent a movie tonight and curl up on her couch. She said sure. I then asked about us. She immediately got a rigid look on her face. As I was thinking how much I loved to hear her voice, she said she was seeing some guy named Sean.

I got up from my seat uncertain of my intentions. I found myself with a handful of her hair. I smashed her face into the table repeatedly. I ripped her head all the way back, to see her bloodied face and her eyes roll back in an unconscious state. I sucked a ton of saliva onto the top of my tongue and then spat it across her stupid whore face. I smashed her head against the table one more time for good measure, and then walked out of the restaurant without paying the check.

Molly kept repeating my name until I came to. She asked if I was alright. I said no. She asked if I wanted to get going. I said yes.

On the way back to Molly's, I couldn't bear to look at her. I was enraged with jealousy. Here I've been, feeding her, caring for her, even secretly loving her, and some other asshole was getting to wet his dick inside her. I used to have that same jealousy toward Anne. After the fact, I always figured that I let Anne sleep around as long as she kept me sexually happy. But this was Molly, and it was far different. I didn't want to share Molly with anyone. No one deserved to ejaculate inside her but me, and I wasn't even sure if I wanted to. I'm sure I would fuck Molly all the time if I stopped jacking off every night. But now I don't even have that option. She's spreading her legs for Sean. Probably some good-looking drug addict with a big dick.

I pulled into Molly's parking lot not sure what to say to her. I decided to ask about Sean. She said he was great and he was exactly what she would hope for in a boyfriend. I convulsed with anger.

I reached over and grabbed her by the eye socket. She screamed in pain as soon as I did. Her eyeball hung out while I pulled her face closer to mine. I bit into her cheek and ripped the flesh from her face. I spit it against the window. She kept screaming, begging me to stop.

156

Then I smashed her head against the passenger window until she stopped her incessant begging. Her body lay limp while I held her head up, my thumb still jammed into the bitch's eye socket.

She asked if I was coming in. I told her no, that it wasn't right. I pulled out of her parking lot heartbroken. I had searched so long for this... this... this thing Molly had given me and now I've lost it, in the blink of an eye. When I got home, I imagined myself raping Molly over and over again. I ended up climaxing for several minutes. I had never experienced anything like that before. I laid in my cum afterward, smoking. I swore to myself that I would never see Molly again. Two days later, she phoned me and I picked up. We made plans to have coffee the following night.

I was not going to give up hope. I knew, deep-down, that Molly and I should be together. Before I met her for coffee, I kept replaying things I would say or do to impress upon her that all other men were jerk-offs compared to me. I imagined a life with her like I'm sure Gatsby had imagined with Daisy.

When I walked into the Café D, I noticed Molly already seated on our couch. My hopes grew by leaps and bounds with each step I took toward her. She seemed happy to see me. Why wouldn't she be? We made chit-chat for five or ten minutes, exchanged our usual "I miss you"s. Of course, then I asked about Stephen. She corrected me with a giggle, and said that his name was Sean. She said it was over with him, that he was just a passing fling. My mind exploded with glorious music.

After coffee, we grabbed a movie from the local video store. I slept over at Molly's that night. The next morning, I ran out to get coffee and bagels while she slept. When I came back, I woke her gently. She, of course, said "good morning, Sunshine." In return, I said "good morning, Strychnine."

Molly called and asked if I wanted to go up north with her. I was thrilled with the prospect of spending a week alone with her, so of course I agreed to go. It took us several hours to get to her parents' cabin. On the way, we fell back into our normal routine of non-stop talking. I always refer to this as the vortex. I drifted in thought a few times, however. I couldn't help but think about the whole Sean thing, again and again. He was gone, but the idea of him was still there. I know Molly must be thinking of me romantically now, to have invited me on this weekend trip. She also keeps hinting at the idea of us dating. She keeps telling me how much her mother adores me, and how she insists that Molly start dating me. I found this very flattering, and then fantasized about a menage-a-trois with Molly and her mother. Her mother's hot.

It was around midnight when we arrived at the cabin. Molly was not sure how long we would stay. The cabin was musty so we opened all the windows. I guess her grandparents have a cabin next door. We walked over to see them in the afternoon. I found the whole thing eerie. At this point, I was certain Molly and I would be starting an intimate relationship during this weekend trip. I figured she had some plan to seduce me. She must have detected my slight disinterest building. Little did she know, I would wait forever. I have known for some time that if she was unaware of our future together, I might have to bide my time until she was ready to accept it.

Molly and I took advantage of all the flea markets in the area. I found several classic novels, in hardcover, for a pittance. She found a few books herself. I enjoyed the excursion very much. Watching Molly interact with people always brings me joy. We ended up eating at a shitty little family diner in what northern Michigan people consider a town. I read the local paper while we drank several cups of coffee after our tasteless meal. I couldn't help but smile on the inside while I skimmed the engagement section of the paper. This town was so small that they actually wrote stories on couples being engaged. I imagined Molly and I would wed in a small town like that. The paper would carry the story with a glowing picture of us, holding each other with smiles from ear to ear.

On the way back to the cabin, we stopped for refreshments and snacks. We also rented several movies. I didn't think we would have time to watch them, but Molly disagreed. She didn't think we had anything

158

other to do then read or watch or movies in this God-forsaken place. She must have been scared to initiate intimacy with me. I'll have to make the first move, yet again.

It was evening when we got back to the cabin. Molly was tired, so she wanted to take a nap. She plopped down on the only bed in the place, while I put away our newly-bought groceries. The time has come to make a move. I laid next to her and started rubbing her shoulders. She jumped up, and told me not to touch her.

Molly frequently gets like this. She has always had some aversion to physical contact with me. I apologized and said that I merely thought she was looking for my attention. She began to pace the cabin, repeating that this was a mistake. It was all a mistake, she said. I told her not to be afraid to love someone that was going to love you back. She gave me a look of utter disgust. She began to rant and rave, about how I was incapable of love and she was incapable of loving me.

I was then suspicious of the reason we had come up to the cabin. If not to begin some sort of love affair, then what? She told me of her need to get away from her life; Jamey, Mary Beth, Sean, Anthony, Mike, Dave, and now Justin. At this point, she just lost me. I thought Sean was over. I did understand the need to get away from Jamey and Mary Beth. They were, by far, the most sado-masochistic couple I had ever seen. And I didn't see what her high school boyfriend, Anthony, had to do with anything. And who the fuck was Mike? And who the fuck was Dave? And who the fuck was Justin? She told me to forget it, to just leave her alone for awhile.

The cabin sat on the edge of a lake. A beautiful lake. The entire area looked like it was touched by the hand of God. I'm sure most of the world looked like that, before Man had decided to put his hands on it. I walked the length of the pier, behind the cabin, for what seemed like an eternity. Eventually Molly came walking up the pier from the cabin, wrapped in one of my sweaters. I got that sweater in Ann Arbor, on one of our excursions into the vortex. I remember, right after buying the sweater, Molly and I walked hand in hand around the city and I couldn't help but notice a girl smile at us. That happened a

159

Eric C. Novack

lot, the whole smiling at Molly and I thing. People must recognize others in love.

Molly walked up close to me and said she was sorry. I said it was okay. I figured she needed more time. I have plenty of that. She then told me about this guy, Justin, she had started to fuck.

I grabbed her by the shoulder and head-butted her until she was un-conscious. I then began to rip all her limbs from her body. This must have stirred her awake, 'cause she started to scream in agony. With all her limbs off, she kept screaming and screaming. I wanted her to stop, so I picked up her right arm, or maybe it was her left, and started to beat her cock-sucking face with it. Eventually, her eyes rolled back and all was silent. I removed my sweater from her bloody carcass. I didn't think the bitch deserved to wear it. I pushed all her limbs into the lake with my feet. I then picked up her torso, with the head still attached, and threw it into the lake as well. I watched her torn, life-less body float down to the next pier. As I hoped, the current had taken the fucking whore out of my sight. I enjoyed a few cigarettes while I watched it float away.

The next morning, I woke up to watch Molly sleep. I made the coffee we had gotten last night. After she had told me about Justin, I let myself fall into fantasy again. We eventually retreated to the cabin to watch the movies we had rented. She woke around ten or eleven. We shared a pot of coffee and then left for home.

Molly and I kept going on like this for months. We would continue to be on the verge of a moviesque relationship, and then she would tell me about some new guy she had decided to fuck. I would become withdrawn for a couple of days. I must've fantasized about killing the bitch a hundred times. But I was not going to be dissuaded. I knew I just had to bide my time.

I did seek counsel from Benedict, Thomas and Jamey from time to time. I was always intrigued by what they had to offer on the topic. Ben usually said we were made for each other, and then one day he changed his tune and said my life would lead in a different direction

160

altogether. Thomas just kept asking if I had fucked the bitch yet. And Jamey, he seemed to want to pour salt on the wound. He would antagonize me into a state of total despair. He always brought up things I was ashamed of, like how I would snuggle with Molly and not get any, or how I would give her all my attention while she was distracted by her love affairs. He even went as far as to say that I was a different person with her. He had observed that I didn't seem as stupid around her. I guess it's possible that Molly makes me better in some ways. I had just chalked it all up to my disinterest in everything else but Molly. I even took Jeremiah's new girlfriend's advice. Sandie had a Benedict-type of look at the whole thing. But it wasn't as in-depth as his. She was pre-occupied with her own turbulent relationship with Miah.

And, so it went, Molly and I would be as cute as a couple of kids during recess when we were together, but we would never venture into the "show me yours and I'll show you mine" stage. That is, until she gave me a definitive reason to give up all hope. Hope is for children.

Molly called me around five, and told me that she went to the doctor. She had been feeling ill for some time now. The doctor told her she had to get rid of her cat. I got her the cat during one of my many attempts to win her over. She asked me if I would take the cat, or if I knew someone that would. She knew I hated cats, so I refrained from telling her that I wouldn't, but I would ask around to see if someone else would. She thanked me and said she had to go. No problem. I always like being the hero, especially for Molly.

Ten minutes later, she called me back and said that she lied. I had to laugh; Molly and I had become masters at calling each other up to tell each other something and then calling back and changing our story. I thought it was kind of nice actually. We could never lie to each other. Well, the new story was a doozy. She said she was pregnant. My heart stopped beating. Like the day it started, it stopped just as quick. She said she couldn't explain right now, but she's get coffee with me later.

The next day, Molly and I met up at the Café D. I was not surprised to find her on the couch, but I was not thrilled like I usually would be either. She was drinking water and not smoking. She gave me a teary-eyed smile and said hello. I got a coffee and lit a Camel Light. I asked her to tell me the story of the dead rabbit. So, she cleared her throat and gave me the story of it's demise.

Several months ago, Molly had begun to "date" Anthony again. Well, she got knocked up again. I hated to ask my next question, but I had to. Was she sure it was his? She gave me a look of death, and said yes. It couldn't be mine, seeing as I had never stuck my dick in her, but let's face it, Molly has gotten around. Most women only tell other people about half the guys they fuck. This all had to do with men calling them whores. And that has to do with men being jealous of other men.

Molly then told me about her and Anthony's plans to marry. That was it. It was over. The girl of my dreams was going to marry another man, and have his child. I don't think waiting for Molly is going to work out. This was my enlightenment. Marie was right. Women do rule my life. I know now that I will never be with one. I should have been a priest. Molly and I chit-chatted for an hour or more, then I said that I'd walk the baby machine to her car. On the way, I saw a women's clothing store that sold maternity clothes. I imagined punching the pregnant mannequins in the fucking stomach. I have no idea why I said what I had just thought to Molly. I have no idea why I asked if she thought it was funny. She looked at me and said, in disgust, that I needed some serious help.

On the way back to the Hippie House, I kept thinking about what my mother always told me when I was young. Whenever I was really upset and on the verge of killing myself, she would simply hold me in her warm embrace and remind me that it always looks better in the morning.

CHAPTER TWELVE

COFFEE WITH LUCIFER

"Yeah, yeah... I would keep fucking her and fucking her and fucking her, and she would be begging me to stop, but I wouldn't."

"Ah, that's rape."

(Laughter, which will continue for more than five minutes.)

"He said... he said 'ah, that's rape'."

("Again laughter, accompanied by little prods of humor on the same subject, continues for another ten minutes.)

"You know, I had this dream once about killing three or four women. There I was, sitting in my parents' bedroom, covered with the girls' blood. I could even hear the sirens of the police coming. But the funny thing was, when I woke up, I wasn't afraid of what I had done. I was afraid of getting in trouble for it."

(No laughter.)

THOMAS   Benedict and I went out last night to get a drink together. He has decided to join the army. I knew he was sick of being in limbo, but the army! The dumb ass will probably get shot by friendly fire. Not that I really care if he gets killed or not. It would just be an inconvenience for me, if anything. I'll have to take a few days off to comfort his family and go to his stupid funereal. I hate funerals. They're always so dull. I usually have to stifle a laugh or two during the service. Figures Ben would do something to hog the spotlight, yet again.

During drinks, Ben and I discussed his decision. He kept trying to explain the boredom he struggles through on a daily basis. He was leaving in two glorious days, and somehow felt that I would care about this or something. He even expressed his concern about Mickey with me. Mickey?! Fuck Mickey! That son-of-a-bitch needs to be put away. Prison would be a sufficient place for the likes of him. That fuck tried to kill me the other night. I was joking with him about Molly while a group of us were walking down to Nine Mile to eat at Como's. He went nuts and picked me up and carried me into Woodward's oncoming traffic. Peter and Simone kept telling him to stop fucking around. Jeremiah and Sandie just sat there and laughed, and Ben...! Ben cheered the fucking lunatic on. After Mick came to his senses and let me go, Ben said it was too bad that we both hadn't perished.

Ben left for the army today. Sad thing is, I actually think I'll miss him. I mean, who else am I going to have a decent conversation with? Mickey?!

SANDIE   I've been spending a lot of time with all the guys lately. Mickey calls us all "elitists". Ben left for the army a few days ago. I was really surprised that a guy like that would join the army. I think of Ben as an intellectual. He just doesn't seem the type to shoot at people. I decided to take Ben's room at the Hippie House. I was sick of lying to my parents every day. Three or four months ago, I had started weaving a huge web of deceit over my plans for the future. The lies were starting to catch up with me, so I thought it best to get the hell out.

Jeremiah and I were getting pretty hot and heavy, until the carpet got pulled out from under us. We had discussed going public with our relationship, but Miah freaked out on me. Mick thinks Miah doesn't want to be known as the guy that fucked his friend's ex-girlfriend. Mick suggested that I talk to Thomas about it, and then Thomas could talk to Miah about it. Personally, I think the whole thing is more trouble than it's worth.

I never really talked to Thomas about Jeremiah and I. Miah and I just keep playing this game with each other, instead. The truth of the matter is... I like the game. It creates drama in my life. Mickey says that people have to have some sort of turbulence, otherwise God would have given us tails to chase around all day. I think it was his way of calling me a drama queen.

PETER   Simone and I have been spending a lot more time with Jeremiah and his friends. I only have a few reservations about hanging out with them. Mickey is a three-time felon who always says the worst things, at the worst possible times. Ben picks a fight with Simone every chance he gets. Miah and Sandie need to start going to AA. Thomas needs to accept his sexual preference. Besides all that, they're a lot of fun.

The other night, Ben and Mickey literally crawled out of the bar on their hands and knees. I had to help Jeremiah to the car. There was no way he was going to be able to stand on his own. Sandie was not in much better shape, but she insisted on driving herself home while Ben and Mickey recommended the use of a cab. Luckily, I had decided to stop drinking early on. It only took Sandie two glasses of beer and a shot to end up in a fist fight with some regular at the bar. I stopped drinking when I assessed the situation. I knew there wouldn't be any-one sober if I hadn't. I guess I could've asked Simone to be the DD, but she's always the DD. Plus, she has such a good time getting into drunken discussions with Ben that I would feel like a total heel.

This is what my social life has become. I babysit a bunch of immature assholes that refuse to grow up and become functional members of society. This is exactly what I told Mickey the other day. He said I sounded jealous.

DARLA   I ended up calling Mickey the other day. I just broke up with my boyfriend and I was feeling quite lonely. Mick's good for that. He has the quality to make you feel good about yourself. I think it's because he's such a piece of shit. We made plans to get coffee. When I got out of there, he had changed his mind about coffee and instead suggested that we go to the bar with his friend, Jamey. I had no problem with this at all. I needed a good drink.

His friend Jamey was real sweet. I was definitely hoping to fuck him later on. He kept ordering shots. I was completely taken by surprise, to see Mickey drink as much as he did. I had never seen Mickey drink before tonight. According to him, he's been doing a lot of that lately. By last call, I could barely stand. I was fading in and out of consciousness, somehow we made it back to Mickey's house. I woke up the next morning with my pants and panties off. I was definitely fucked last night. I just wasn't sure by who. When I could finally bring myself to move my head enough to look around, I saw Mickey lying next to me, naked from the waist down.

Mickey and I have started a fuck-buddy relationship. I go over to his place whenever I want dick. I hope he's not getting attached. I don't want to have a relationship with him. He treats me like shit, and has no interest in me other than getting me drunk and fucking me. The other night, I came over to find him hanging with Jamey and two girls. I went immediately into his bedroom and got into some pajamas. Mickey came in fifteen minutes later, wanting to fuck. I wasn't up to it. So he left me there. This really pissed me off. I finally fell asleep, waiting for him to come back, just to be woken up by one of the girls bitching about something. I went out there and told her to shut the fuck up. Three months later, I found out from Jamey what she'd been bitching about. Mickey had just got done fucking her on the living room floor and then asked her to leave. What an asshole!

Mickey told me not to call him anymore. I think he might be mad at me for fucking Cody when I went out to see him in Colorado. Or he could have heard about Jeff, or Matt, or Louis, or JR. The last time we talked, he said he stopped drinking again. I told him of my uncertainty in men. Then, he told me something I will never forget. Mickey said that I didn't have an uncertainty in men, I had an uncertainty in myself.

THE DEVIL   I am rarely disappointed in human behavior. I didn't expect Mickey to be such a rarity. This little cocksucker has proven to be quite the project. I have thrown every temptation I could think of at him. I have given him women, booze, an avenue to release his rage, and I have even given him love. I then took it all away, expecting him to completely give up on God. But his inner being, his soul if you will, is stubborn.

I have checked in on him, from time to time, only to get enraged at what he has become. The last time I had coffee with him, he dared to ask me if I believed in God. It took all of my being not to slap the smug son-of-a-bitch across the face. Do I believe in God?! As if that weren't enough, he then reassured me that whatever the case may be, it wouldn't really matter 'cause God believed in me. Fucking prick!

TARA   I ran into Mick the other day. Weird thing was I was kind of hoping to see him. I hadn't talked to him since he called and told me about Molly. He asked me how Terrence was, and he asked me if I was happy. I told him I wasn't sure how to answer that. He smiled and said we should all be able to answer that question the same.

I couldn't get that conversation I had with Mick out of my head. I don't know why, but I ended up calling Cody to say hello. He was glad I did.

CODY   Work and school began to give me a reason to question my choices. They created a seed of doubt within myself. I knew I was on the verge of some sort of depression. I couldn't think of any way to pull myself out of it. I even asked some of my friends what their take on it was. They offered me nothing except a kind word and a drink at the local tavern. The other day, I remembered that Ben always said that Mick always makes him feel better about himself. I always thought it was just some sort of joke that developed between them. But, I was desperate so I called Mick. He asked how I was, and I told him. Twenty minutes later, I finally asked him how we was. He said he must have been good, 'cause he woke up breathing.

MARY BETH   Jamey and I broke up several months ago. I see him from time to time. Moly moved out when she got pregnant. She even married Anthony. She seems happy. I started dating a decent guy who buys me lots of presents. Just like Jamey did. I think this guy might be the one. I ran into Mick the other day, at a booty bar, of all places. That surprised me, to say the least. A booty bar never seemed like his thing. He asked me how I was doing. I said I was wonderful. I asked him if he saw Jamey from time to time. And the dick gave me a cold stare and asked why I would care. I told him I didn't. Mickey just smiled at me and said good, 'cause Jamey sure as hell didn't.

SIMONE   I started losing my hair. I went to the doctor and they said it was stress-related. I found that easy to believe. Peter and I discussed the financial ramifications of the possibility of me quitting my job. We both felt it would jeopardize our nest egg. That night, we went out with Jeremiah, Ben, Sandie, Thomas, and Mickey. Mickey, Thomas and Ben kept talking about how they enjoy menial jobs that pay them shit. Mickey works at a car wash, Ben works as a security guard, and Thomas is doing what he has always wanted to. I was becoming envious of them as I sat in the midst of their discussion. I finally told Mickey that I was envious of them. He said that that was not entirely true. To be envious, one would have a hatred toward another... while jealousy is just a person's longing for what another person possesses. Mickey continued by saying that a person could never rid themselves of envy, but they could at least do something about their jealousy. I kept nodding and smiling while Mick tried to explain this to me, even though I had no idea what he was talking about. A week later, the day I quit my job, I understood what Mick was trying to say.

Eric C. Novack

JEREMIAH   Mick and I got into a huge fight the other night. I was sick of his constant sarcasm, so I punched him in his fucking face. I was drunk, so I don't really remember what happened next. In the morning, he apologized for what he had said. I told him it was no big deal, seeing as I didn't remember what had transpired. He said that was exactly what the problem was last night.

MARIE   For months now, I have been making Jim's life a living hell. Ever since I read *How to be Good* by Nick Hornsby, I have been unhappy in our relationship. Mick doesn't think it's the book that created my discontent. He thinks it has to do with my disinterest in everything that surrounds me. Discontentment, he says, is what life is all about. It sounds pessimistic, if you ask me.

JERRY   I called Mick to tell him the news. I told him about my engagement, and how I was going to live down here until my fiance graduated college. He was thrilled, and then he asked how my painting was coming. I told him I hadn't painted in months. He said that was too bad. Fucking prick.

BENEDICT   Two more weeks left of basic. I've received numerous letters from my parents and Mick. Thomas has also written me a few times. They all make home sound so good... I have contemplated going AWOL a few times. But I know better. Home is a place of uncertainty for me. It is a place to hide and waste away. Mick's letters remind me of that.

MICKEY   A friend once told me a story, about two men that met by chance on a sidewalk. One of the men was homeless and spent his whole day begging for change, dressed in what appeared to be rags. The second man had just come from his corner office, where he worked his typical nine-to-five, dressed in a five hundred dollar suit. When the two men crossed paths, they stopped and stared at each other for a moment. Then, one of the men said to the other (it doesn't really

172

matter who said what to whom), "do you believe in God?" And the other man replied (again, it doesn't matter who said what) "given the choice, yes. I do. Yes, I do."

To this day, I have no idea why I am so fond of that story. I'm not sure exactly what it is supposed to convey. Could it be that it is better to believe than not to believe? Or is it simply to remind us that we are all the same in God's eyes? It makes no difference to me. I just enjoy telling the story.

Molly and I had lunch a few months back. This would be the last time. She was glowing. Most likely due to her pregnancy and her newly-aquired husband. We spent most of our lunch talking over her future plans. They seemed dull to me. While she rattled off a story about Anthony, I fell deep into thought. I knew that it wouldn't be right to tell her that I loved her. I also knew it wouldn't be right to stick a butter knife into her left eye. But, then again, who am I to say what is right?

T H E   C O M P L E T E

Guidebook to Yosemite

N A T I O N A L   P A R K

by Steven P. Medley

Revised
Fifth
Edition
2004

YOSEMITE
ASSOCIATION

Yosemite National Park
California

W9-AXY-899

*"On the whole, Yosemite is incomparably
the most wonderful feature on our continent."*
– A. D. Richardson

For Jane and the boys

"From the discovery of Yosemite to the present day the wonders of this region of sublimity have been a source of inspiration to visitors, but none have been able to describe it to the satisfaction of those who followed after them."—Lafayette Bunnell

"You've got a good point Lafayette, but here goes anyway. . ."—SPM

Yosemite Association
P.O. Box 230
El Portal, California 95318

YOSEMITE
ASSOCIATION

The Yosemite Association initiates and supports interpretive, educational, research, scientific, and environmental programs in Yosemite National Park, in cooperation with the National Park Service. Authorized by Congress, the Association provides services and direct financial support in order to promote park stewardship and enrich the visitor experience.

To learn more about our activities and other publications, or for information about membership, please write to the address above or call (209) 379-2646. Our web site address is: www.yosemite.org

Original book design by Jon Goodchild.

Revised book design and maps by Reineck & Reineck, San Francisco.

Illustrations by Bob Johnson.

Interior photographs courtesy of the National Park Service in Yosemite.

Front cover photograph by Jeff Grandy.

Printed in Singapore.

Help Make This a Better Guidebook!

We are eager to hear your reactions to this book, and welcome your suggestions for additions or changes. Please send your commits, criticisms, and ideas to the Yosemite Association at the address above, or e-mail to: info@yosemite.org

Further Reading

To purchase any of the books mentioned in this guidebook, visit the Yosemite Store Online at www.yosemitestore.com, or call (209) 379-2648.

Acknowledgments

Thanks to everyone who helped in the production of this book, including Pat Wight, Penny Otwell, Holly Warner, Anne Steed, Laurel Rematore, Beth Pratt, Mary Vocelka, Ann Gushue, Jim Snyder, Linda Eade, Len McKenzie, Dean Shenk, Marla LaCass, Laurel Boyers, Craig Bates, N. King Huber, Jan van Wagtendonk, Peter Browning, Jim Alinder, Bill Neill, Mike Osborne, Mono Lake Committee, Keith Walklet, Nancy Lusignan, Kris Fister, Bob Jones, Tori Keith, Yosemite Concession Services, Jack and Gay Reineck, and Norma Craig.

Caveat

Given the rapidity with which things change, the accuracy and completeness of the contents of this book cannot be guaranteed. The publisher and author assume no legal responsibility for the appreciation or depreciation of the value of any premises, commercial or otherwise, by reason of their inclusion in, or exclusion from this book. Further, the names of businesses mentioned here are provided as a service to readers and not as an endorsement or guarantee.

Guidebook Update

This guidebook is regularly updated on the Internet at:
www.yosemite.org/member/update.htm

CONTENTS

Major Features of Yosemite Valley

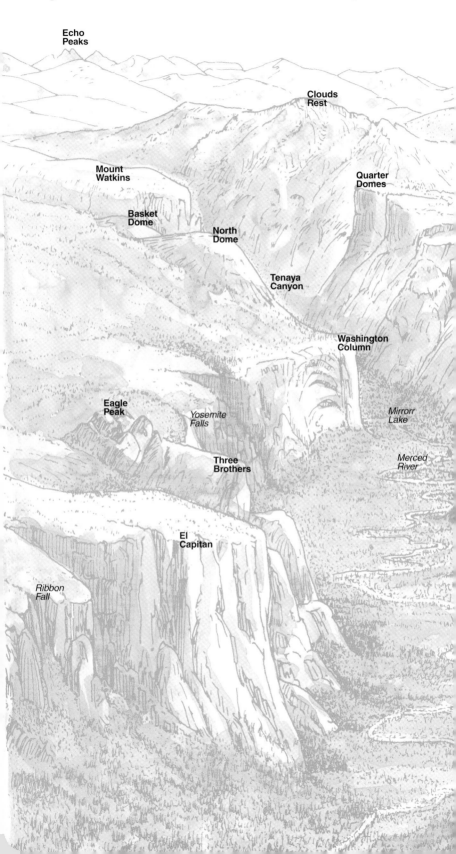

Mount
Florence

Half
Dome

Cacade
Cliffs

Little
Yosemite

Liberty
Cap

Sentinel
Dome

Mount
Broderick

Glacier
Point

Sentinel
Rock

Taft
Point

Cathedral
Spires

Cathedral
Rocks

Dewey
Point

Leaning
Tower

*Bridalveil
Fall*

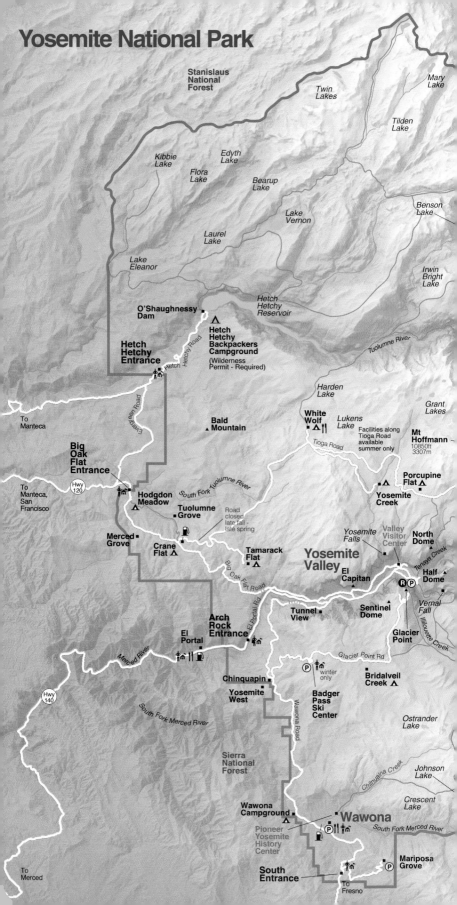

Yosemite National Park

Stanislaus
National
Forest

Mary
Lake

Twin
Lakes

Tilden
Lake

Kibbie
Lake

Edyth
Lake

Flora
Lake

Bearup
Lake

Benson
Lake

Lake
Vernon

Laurel
Lake

Irwin
Bright
Lake

Lake
Eleanor

Hetch
Hetchy
Reservoir

Tuolumne River

O'Shaughnessy
Dam

Hetch
Hetchy
Entrance

Hetch Hetchy Road

△ Hetch
Hetchy
Backpackers
Campground

(Wilderness
Permit - Required)

Harden
Lake

Grant
Lakes

To
Manteca

Evergreen Road

Bald
▲ Mountain

White
Wolf

Lukens
Lake

Facilities along
Tioga Road
available
summer only

Mt
Hoffmann
10850ft
3307m

Tioga Road

Big
Oak
Flat
Entrance

To
Manteca,
San
Francisco

Hwy
120

Hodgdon
Meadow

△

South Fork Tuolumne River

Tuolumne
Grove

Road
closed
late fall -
late spring

Porcupine
Flat △

△

Yosemite
Creek

Merced
Grove

Crane
Flat △

Tamarack
Flat
△

Big Oak Flat Road

Yosemite Valley

Yosemite
Falls

Valley
Visitor
Center

North
Dome

Tenaya Creek

Yosemite
Valley

El
Capitan

Half
Dome

R P

Vernal
Fall

Arch
Rock
Entrance

El Portal Rd

Tunnel
View

Sentinel
Dome

Illilouette Creek

El Portal

Merced River

Glacier
Point

Glacier Point Rd

Hwy
140

P winter
only

Chinquapin

Yosemite
West

Bridalveil
Creek △

Badger
Pass
Ski
Center

Ostrander
Lake

South Fork Merced River

Wawona Road

Sierra
National
Forest

Chilnualna Creek

Johnson
Lake

Crescent
Lake

Wawona
Campground
△

Wawona

Pioneer
Yosemite
History
Center

P

South Fork Merced River

Mariposa
Grove

P

To
Merced

South
Entrance

To
Fresno

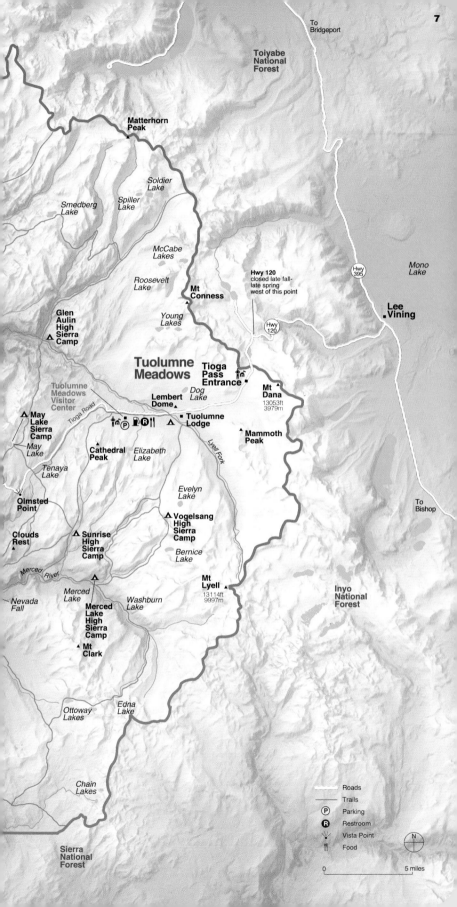

To
Bridgeport

**Toiyabe
National
Forest**

*Mono
Lake*

**Matterhorn
Peak**

*Soldier
Lake*

*Smedberg
Lake*

*Spiller
Lake*

*McCabe
Lakes*

*Roosevelt
Lake*

**Mt
Conness**

Hwy 120
closed late fall–
late spring
west of this point

Hwy
395

**Lee
Vining**

*Young
Lakes*

**Glen
Aulin
High
Sierra
Camp**

Hwy
120

**Tuolumne
Meadows**

**Tioga
Pass
Entrance**

Tuolumne
Meadows
Visitor
Center

**Lembert
Dome**

*Dog
Lake*

**Mt
Dana**
13053ft
3979m

Tioga Road

**Tuolumne
Lodge**

**May
Lake
Sierra
Camp**

*May
Lake*

**Cathedral
Peak**

*Elizabeth
Lake*

Lyell Fork

**Mammoth
Peak**

*Tenaya
Lake*

*Evelyn
Lake*

**Olmsted
Point**

**Vogelsang
High
Sierra
Camp**

**Clouds
Rest**

**Sunrise
High
Sierra
Camp**

*Bernice
Lake*

Merced River

**Mt
Lyell**
13114ft
9997m

**Inyo
National
Forest**

*Nevada
Fall*

*Merced
Lake*

**Merced
Lake
High
Sierra
Camp**

*Washburn
Lake*

To
Bishop

**Mt
Clark**

*Ottoway
Lakes*

*Edna
Lake*

*Chain
Lakes*

**Sierra
National
Forest**

Roads

Trails

P   Parking

R   Restroom

Vista Point

Food

N

0   5 miles

Yosemite by the Numbers

Yosemite National Park
Established October 1, 1890

Size: 748,542 acres, or 1,169 square miles; 94% of the park is designated wilderness.

Address: P.O. Box 577, Yosemite National Park, CA 95389

Campsites: 1,445 individual sites parkwide

Overnight Accommodations: 1,729 units

Paved Roads: 360 miles

Developed Trails: 800 miles

Wildlife Species (approximate):
  Amphibians & Reptiles - 40
  Birds - 242
  Fish - 11
  Mammals - 77

Flora Species:
  Flowering Plants- 1,400
  Trees - 37

Highest Peak: Mt Lyell, 13,114 ft.

Geographic Center of the Park:
Mt Hoffmann

Highest Paved Pass in the Sierra:
Tioga Pass, 9,945 ft.

Major Park Lakes: 318
  With Fish - 127
  Without Fish – 191

Rivers & Streams: 880 miles

Park Speed Limit: 45 mph (unless otherwise posted)

Yosemite's Ten Highest Peaks
1. Mt Lyell - 13,114 ft.
2. Mt Dana - 13,053 ft.
3. Kuna Peak - 13,003 ft.
4. Rodgers Peak - 12,978 ft.
5. Mt Maclure - 12,960 ft.
6. Mt Gibbs - 12,764 ft.
7. Mt Conness - 12,590 ft.
8. Mt Florence - 12,561 ft.
9. Simmons Peak - 12,503 ft.
10. Excelsior Mountain - 12,446 ft.

Park Visitation
1855 - 42
1899 - 4,500
1922 - 100,506
1940 - 506,781
1954 - 1,008,031
1995 - 4,101,928
2000 - 3,550,065

Entrance Fees
Private Noncommercial Vehicles: $20

Bus Passengers, Bicyclists, and Persons on Foot or Horseback: $10

Annual Yosemite Pass: $40

National Parks Pass *(good at all national parks for one year from purchase date):* $50

Golden Eagle Hologram for National Parks Pass *(covers entrance fees at other federal sites:* $15

Golden Age Pass *(a lifetime pass for US citizens 62 years and older):* one-time issuance fee $10

Golden Access Pass *(for blind or permanently disabled U.S. citizens or permanent residents):* ......Free

TDD Phones
These allow the hearing impaired with their own TDDs to call the park directly.
National Park
Service Information ....(209) 372-4726
Room Reservations ....(559) 255-8345
Camping Reservations ....(888) 530-9796

Important Yosemite Phone Numbers
Unless otherwise noted, all phone numbers in this book are for the (209) area code.

Camping Reservations 1-800-436-7275
(International Callers) ......(301) 772-1257

Dental Clinic 372-4200

High Sierra Camp
Reservations ....(559) 253-5674

Lost and Found 379-1002

Medical Clinic 372-4637

National Park Service 372-0265

Park Information (recorded) 372-0200

Room Reservations ....(559) 252-4848

Visitor Center, Big Oak Flat 379-1899

Visitor Center,
Tuolumne Meadows 372-0263

Visitor Center,
Yosemite Valley 372-0299

Wawona Ranger Station 375-1416
                              or 375-9520

Weather & Road Information 372-0200

Wilderness Reservations 372-0740

Yosemite Bookstore 379-2648

If You Have Only One Day in Yosemite

Three things only are well done in haste: flying from the plague, escaping quarrels, and catching flies. — H. G. Bohn

I f by some horrible twist of your itinerary you find yourself with but a single day in Yosemite National Park, you will be sorely cheated. The park is so large and so studded with fascinating features that usually three or four days are required to really "do the place justice." But take heart for there are some remarkable highlights that can be enjoyed in a day, many of them centered in Yosemite Valley.

Yosemite Valley

While Yosemite Valley's seven square miles comprise but a tiny fraction of the park's total area, they are jam-packed with spectacular scenic beauty. First of all, get out of your car (follow signs to day-use parking at Camp 6 near Yosemite Village) and board a free Yosemite Valley Shuttle Bus. Buses stop at practically every point of interest in the eastern end of Yosemite Valley, and they are the only means (besides bicycle or on foot) to enter the areas there that are closed to automobile traffic. Listed below are several activities that can be enjoyed in a day from stops along the Shuttle Bus route. See page 27 for more Free Shuttle Bus information.

Valley Visitor Center: Here is a logical starting point for your visit. See page 26. Park information, an orientation film, exhibits, and books are all available here. If time allows, take in the Yosemite Museum Gallery, the Indian Cultural Exhibit, and walk through the Indian Village behind the center. (15 minutes to 1 hour)

Lower Yosemite Fall: Walk from the bus stop to the base of Lower Yosemite Fall— about a quarter of a mile. See page 32. Be prepared to get wet in spring when runoff is at its peak; in any season you'll be impressed by the imposing height of one of the world's most famous falls. (30 minutes to 1 hour)

Happy Isles: This is the trailhead for hikes to Vernal and Nevada Falls, Half Dome, and other high country destinations (except in winter). See page 32. Walk to the Vernal Fall bridge (seven-tenths of a mile) for a breathtaking view of this beautiful cataract, or continue on to the top of the fall (if you've got the energy). This route is known as the Mist Trail for reasons that will be obvious. During the summer, the Nature Center at Happy Isles offers exhibits and books. (1 to 3 hours)

Mirror Lake: From the shuttle bus stop (not accessible in winter), Mirror Lake is a half-mile walk up a slight grade. See page 32. While the lake no longer offers the mirror-like surface for which it was named (it's filling up with silt), one of the best views of Half Dome is had from its banks. The hike around the lake is easy and rewarding. (1 to 2 hours)

When you've seen and done all you want by shuttle bus, you will need your car to finish up in Yosemite Valley. For a thoroughly entertaining treatment of the remaining sights, an audio CD program entitled *Yosemite Audio Guides: Yosemite Valley Tour* is available for sale at the Visitor Center and heartily recommended. The tour consists of ten stops and, besides descriptions of the scenery, features discussions of geology, Native American culture, history, and park management. The CD is exceptionally well-produced. Using it, you will require from 2 to 4 hours for your tour depending on how much exploring you do at each stop.

If you don't use the CD, there are at least two more Yosemite Valley points to visit:

Bridalveil Fall: Follow road signs to the Wawona Road (to Wawona and Fresno). Immediately after turning on to the Wawona Road, turn left into the Bridalveil Fall parking lot. The short trail leads to the base of the fall where a sheet of water floats downward 620 feet to the valley floor. (15 to 45 minutes)

Bridalveil Fall

Tunnel View: Turn left back onto the Wawona Road and drive approximately three miles to Tunnel View turnout, which is just below the entrance to the Wawona Tunnel. Before you is the classic panoramic view of Yosemite Valley that greeted the first visitors here. (10 to 30 minutes)

Glacier Point

A 32-mile drive from Yosemite Valley, Glacier Point is unquestionably a "must see" for visitors with limited time. Within 200 yards of the parking lot is the top of the sheer southern wall of Yosemite Valley. Not only does the valley lie 3,200 feet below you, but also the entire park is revealed with astounding vistas in every direction. Most of Yosemite's major peaks are identified, and exhibits explain the geologic processes that created this amazing landscape. There is probably no better view of Yosemite Valley and the surrounding high country that can be reached by automobile. The road to Glacier Point is closed in winter. See page 46 for more information. (1 hour for the drive from Yosemite Valley, and 30 minutes to 1 hour at Glacier Point)

Mariposa Grove of Big Trees

If you have already seen Yosemite Valley and Glacier Point and you've still got time (hard to believe!), the Mariposa Grove of Big Trees is located near the park's south entrance from Highway 41. See page 48. This magnificent stand of sequoias is Yosemite's largest and includes trees thousands of years old. A tram system transports visitors into the grove for a fee (from May to October), or you may enter on foot (the hike into the upper grove area is fairly rigorous, however). A small museum is open during the summer (the tram stops there), and famous trees like the Grizzly Giant and the fallen Tunnel Tree should not be missed. (2 to 3 hours)

Tuolumne Meadows and the Tioga Road

Open in summer only, the Tioga Road bisects the park and leads through Tuolumne Meadows, a beautiful subalpine meadow surrounded by soaring granite crags and polished domes. See page 65. If your trip takes you out of the park to the east, the Tioga Road is lined with scenery and exhibits describing it. See page 60. Be sure to stop at Olmsted Point for its remarkable view of Tenaya Canyon and the back side of Half Dome, and of Tenaya Lake, the deep-blue, icy-cold waters of which form Yosemite's largest natural lake. (Allow 2 to $2^1/_2$ hours for the trip from Yosemite Valley to Tioga Pass)

Just Passing Through?

If it happens that you are simply driving through Yosemite (a regrettable situation), be sure to pick up a copy of the *Yosemite Road Guide* that will provide an added dimension to your drive. It is keyed to markers along park roads and describes the sights, gives historical information, and is full of data about Yosemite's plants and animals.

Lodging in Yosemite

*M*ost overnight accommodations in Yosemite are operated by Delaware North Company Parks & Resorts at Yosemite (DNC), a contractor of the National Park Service and the park's chief concessioner. There is a single reservation system for all DNC lodging units. Whenever a Yosemite hotel or motel is not part of the DNC reservation system, that fact will be noted in this guidebook.

Reservations may be made by phone, over the Internet, or through the mail. The DNC reservation number is (559) 252-4848. Because thousands of calls are made to this number each day, you may not get through when you phone. Be persistent, let the phone ring, and try, try again.

Better yet, use the Internet. A percentage of the concessioner's lodging units are available only through its web site. If you've got a credit card, visit www.yosemitepark.com to request your reservation online.

If you're still not successful, try sending your reservation request in writing. Fill out the form provided below and mail it to: Yosemite Reservations, 5410 E. Home, Fresno, CA 93722. Be sure to indicate acceptable alternatives, as competition for popular dates is heavy.

Nine Tips for Getting a Yosemite Reservation

1 Public reservations for Yosemite lodging open exactly 366 days in advance. Call (559) 252-4848 immediately upon the opening of the Yosemite Reservations office (8 a.m. Pacific time) exactly 366 days before your intended arrival.

2 Choose to visit in Yosemite's off season, particularly the months of November, January, February, and March. You're sure to be accommodated if you elect to come during the week. There's a special winter reservation number: (559) 454-2000.

3 If you want to stay over a weekend, plan your arrival for a Monday, Tuesday, Wednesday, or Thursday. You can reserve up to seven nights in a row in any given stay. Often, lodging facilities are fully reserved for weekends more than 366 days in advance by people arriving earlier in the week.

4 Be flexible and have several arrival dates in mind. If your first option is not available, one of the others may be.

5 If you're willing to stay in a tent cabin at Curry Village, request it. Tent cabins are in the least demand and can usually be reserved up to two weeks before arrival. And when you arrive, you can always try to upgrade to a room with bath (but there are no guarantees here).

6 Call Yosemite Reservations on Saturday or Sunday. The office receives the fewest numbers of calls on weekends. Don't call at lunch. Everybody tries to call then.

7 Take advantage of the fact that some lodging units can only be reserved online. Visit www.yosemitepark.com if you're not having success over the phone.

8 Call 30 days, 15 days, or 7 days in advance of your arrival. These are common times when rooms held by previous reservations are cancelled. You may get lucky.

9 If you arrive in Yosemite without a reservation, stop by the front desk of any lodging facility between 10 a.m. and 4 p.m. and place your name on the waiting list. Persons with reservations that are held without a deposit must confirm or arrive by 4 p.m. If they don't, their reservations are cancelled automatically. If you are present at 4 p.m. you may pick up a cancelled reservation or you may not.

Reservations for Lodging

Reservations Request Form (please print)

Name
_____

Address
_____

City _____ State _____ Zip _____

Number in Party _____ Children _____ Ages _____

Preferred accommodation _____

Date of Arrival _____ Date of Departure _____

Number of Nights _____

2nd Choice, if preference is unavailable _____

Mail to: **Yosemite Reservations** 5410 East Home, Fresno, CA 93727

Camping in Yosemite National Park

Yosemite National Park offers visitors almost 1,500 campsites in its multiple campgrounds. If you're planning to camp, be sure to secure an authorized spot because camping is allowed only in designated campsites. Even if you've got a "self-contained" recreational vehicle, you are not permitted to pull off to the side of the road for the night. Neither should you erect your tent or throw down a sleeping bag wherever you stop; the rangers will send you packing. The impact on the park resources of such haphazard camping is too great.

Fortunately, there's a way to ensure that you'll have a Yosemite camping spot when you arrive. The majority of park campsites can be reserved through a campground reservation system administered by National Park Reservation System (NPRS). Throughout this guidebook, campgrounds with sites that can be reserved through NPRS are indicated.

How to Reserve Your Campsite

Campground reservations are available in one-month blocks up to five months in advance. They can be made on the 15th of each month for this one month "window" through NPRS. For example, on March 15, dates from August 15 through September 14 become available for reservation, and on April 15, dates from September 15 through October 14 are reservable.

You may reserve campsites through NPRS in three ways: by mail, over the Internet, and using the telephone. For telephone reservations, you should call (800) 436-7275. The number for international callers is (301) 722-1257. Phone reservations may be made between 7 a.m. and 7 p.m. Pacific time.

The system allows callers to choose from a full month of starting dates for their camping trip. This should do away with the previous arrangement where multiple phone calls had to be made if certain dates weren't available. Be sure to pick a number of possible start dates for your trip and you should be able to secure a reservation.

Online camping reservations can be made at reservations.nps.gov, but you may reserve only one campsite at a time using this system. This Internet service is only available between 7 a.m. and 7 p.m. Pacific time. Another web site, www.yosemitesites.com, provides helpful information about how many sites are available in each campground and still reservable.

To reserve by mail, fill out a copy of the form provided here and send it to: NPRS, P.O. Box 1600, Cumberland, MD 21502. You should time the mailing of your request so that it is received no sooner than two weeks before the 15th of the month that your desired camping arrival date goes on sale. Written requests will not be processed until the 15th of the month (at the same time that telephone requests are taken).

For additional information about park campgrounds, refer to the following pages:
Yosemite Valley, page 34
South of Yosemite Valley, page 51
North of Yosemite Valley, page 68

Camping in US Forest Service Areas Adjacent to Yosemite

The US Forest Service operates a variety of campgrounds near Yosemite. Many of them are operated on a first-come, first-served basis; some sites may be reserved in advance. For additional information, call the appropriate USFS district office.

Inyo National Forest
Eastern Sierra, Highways 120 & 395
Mono Lake Ranger Station
(760) 647-3044

Sierra National Forest
Western Sierra, Highways 140 & 41
Bass Lake Ranger District
Oakhurst Ranger Station
(559) 683-4636

Mariposa Ranger Station
(209) 966-3638

Stanislaus National Forest
Western Sierra, Highway 120
Groveland Ranger Station
(209) 962-7825

Camping in Yosemite National Park

Valleywide stay limit: 7 days
High country stay limit: 14 days
30 day stay limit per calendar year

Campground/general location	number of sites or spaces	daily fee: per site=/s per person=/p	RV space	tent space	tap water	stream water (boil)	flush toilets	pit toilets	tables	fire pits or grills	pets allowed	dump station	parking	showers nearby	laundry nearby	groceries	swimming	fishing	horseback riding	camping season (approximate)	
North Pines Yosemite Valley	84	$18/s	●	●	●		●		●	●	●	●	●	●	●	●	●	●	●	Apr-Sept	NPRS
Upper Pines Yosemite Valley	238	$18/s	●	●	●		●		●	●	●	●	●	●	●	●	●	●	●	all year	NPRS
Lower Pines Yosemite Valley	60	$18/s	●	●	●		●		●	●	●	●	●	●	●	●	●	●	●	Mar-Oct	NPRS
Sunnyside-Walk In Yosemite Valley	35	$5/p		●	●		●		●	●			●	●	●	●	●	●	●	all year	First come basis. Limited parking.
Backpackers Walk-In Yosemite Valley	25	$5/p		●	●		●		●	●				●	●	●	●	●	●	May-Oct	First come basis. No vehicles. Two night max.
Wawona Wawona Road in Wawona	93	$18/s	●	●	●		●		●	●	●	●	●				●	●	●		NPRS from May-Sept. ($18/s); first come basis from Oct-April ($12/s)
Bridalveil Creek Glacier Point Road	110	$12/s	●	●	●			●	●	●	●	●	●					●	●	July-Sept	First come basis
Hogdon Meadow off Big Oak Flat Road near entrance	105	$18/s	●	●	●		●		●	●	●	●	●					●		all year	NPRS from May-Sept ($18/s); first come basis from Oct-April ($12/s)
Hetch Hetchy Backpacker Hetch Hetchy Road	19	$5/p $50/s		●	●		●		●	●			●					●	●	Apr-Nov	First come basis. Two group sites, two stock use sites. Wilderness users only. No RV.
Crane Flat Big Oak Flat Road nr Tioga Road turnoff	166	$18/s	●	●	●		●		●	●	●	●	●			●				June-Sept	NPRS
Tamarack Flat Tioga Road	52	$8/s	●	●		●		●	●	●			●					●		June-Sept	First come basis. No RV.
White Wolf Tioga Road	74	$12/s	●	●	●		●		●	●			●	●				●	●	July-Sept	First come basis. No RVs over 27 feet.
Yosemite Creek Tioga Road	75	$8/s		●		●		●	●	●			●					●		July-Sept	First come basis. No RV.
Porcupine Flat Tioga Road	52	$8/s	●	●		●		●	●	●			●					●		July-Sept	First come basis. Limited RV.
Tuolumne Meadows Tioga Road	304	$18/s	●	●	●		●		●	●	●	●	●	●		●		●	●	July-Sept	NPRS advanced reservations for half of campground; same-day reservations for rest. 25 walk-in sites with no vehicles, $5/p.

NPRS: reservations required. **NO RV:** access road not suitable for trailers or large RVs.

Campsite Reservation Request

Please include middle initial in your name:

Name:

Address:

Zip: _____ Telephone: _____

No. of Persons: _____ Pets(s) ☐ Yes ☐ No

National Park Reservation Service
P.O. Box 1600, Cumberland, MD 21501

If necessary, will you accept fewer nights? ☐ Yes ☐ No

Specific campsites cannot be reserved.
Campsites are assigned upon arrival.

Be sure you complete all sections and enclose full payment.
Incomplete or incorrect forms will be returned.

Type of camping equipment:

Check ✓   ♿

#	Equipment	#
1	One tent or no equipment	17
2	Two tents	18
3	Large tent (over 9' x 12')	19
4	Tent trailer, total length?:	20
5	Van or bus with side tent	21
6	Pickup/camper thru 21'	22
7	Pickup/camper thru 24'	23
8	Motorhome thru 24'	24
9	Motorhome thru 27'	25
10	Motorhome over 27' (ft)	26
11	Trailer thru 15'	27
12	Trailer thru 18'	28
13	Trailer thru 21'	29
14	Trailer thru 24'	30
15	Trailer thru 27'	31
16	Trailer over 27' (ft)	32

Golden Access or Golden Age Passport
Serial No. if applicable

Not Golden eagle Passport or Park Pass

Charges: The daily campsite charge is required for each period and/or campsite, up to the stay limit.

No. of nights _____ @ _____ * = _____

No. of nights _____ @ _____ * = _____

No. of nights _____ @ _____ * = _____   **Total:**

*50% reduction for Golden Access or Golden Age Passport

☐ Check/MO ☐ Discover ☐ MasterCard ☐ Visa

Card No.: _____ Exp: _____

Cardholder: _____ Telephone _____

Signature: _____

Make payable to NPS and mail to:
NPRS, P.O. Box 1600, Cumberland, MD 21501

Name of Park	Campground	First Choice Arrival Dates	Nights	Second Choice Arrival Dates	Nights	Third Choice Arrival Dates	Nights	Official Use

So How's the Weather?

"There is really no such thing as bad weather, only different kinds of good weather." —John Ruskin

Yosemite's climate is as mild as its cliffs are steep. The months of April through October feature warm daytime temperatures and cool nights. Even winter is relatively benign with average maximum temperatures in Yosemite Valley (4,000 feet) in the high 40s and 50s. Of course weather is significantly affected by elevation, and with a topography ranging from 2,000 to 13,000 feet in height, Yosemite can experience amazing climatic variations on any given day!

Precipitation averages 35 to 40 inches of moisture annually, with the greatest bulk of that falling between December and March. Snowfall in Yosemite Valley averages 29 inches, but rarely accumulates to a depth of over two feet. At 7,000 foot Badger Pass, there is adequate snow pack to support a downhill ski area, and cross-country skiing is popular throughout the higher regions of the park. As temperatures warm in the spring, increasing runoff swells rivers and creeks producing a grand display of surging waterfalls. There is negligible precipitation during the summer months, and many of the park's waterfalls literally dry up.

Yosemite Valley in Winter

The first falls of snow in the Sierra generally occur in November, but they do not come to stay; they are but fleeting messengers, and having announced the approach of winter, are soon put to flight by the lingering god of the tropics, who still tries to maintain supremacy over his rival of the Arctic Zone. But it is his final effort to keep back the legions of the north. By the end of December snow hides from sight all but the forms of the mountains, covering them with a vast winding sheet. Only the mighty trees toss from their wind-shaken branches the white deposit, which ofttimes with its unyielding weight snaps their great boughs.

Owing to the retreat of the sun southward, and the immense height of the walls of the Yosemite, there is a considerable difference between the climate on the north and south side of the valley during the winter. While on the south wall the sun never shines during this season, and a chilling shadow is constantly cast over that portion of the valley, the rays of the winter sun fall upon the surface of the northern elevation almost at right angles with its plane. As a consequence, the weather on that side is mellow and mild, and in sheltered nooks among the warm rocks flowers are observed to bloom every month in the year.

From *Foley's Yosemite Souvenir & Guide* for 1913 by D. J. Foley.

Yosemite Valley Weather Data

	Jan	Feb	Mar	Apr	May	June	July	Aug	Sept	Oct	Nov	Dec
Rainfall* in inches	6.2	6.1	5.2	3.0	1.3	0.7	0.4	0.3	0.9	2.1	5.5	5.6
Max. Temp.	49	55	59	65	73	82	90	90	87	74	58	48°F
Min. Temp.	26	28	31	35	42	48	54	53	47	39	31	26°F

*37.2 inches annually

	January	April	July	October
Hours of Sunshine	3:57	7:38	9:34	6:45
Chances of a Sunny Day	39%	70%	97%	81%
Afternoon Temperatures	48°	66°	90°	75°
Relative Humidity	86%	69%	50%	64%
Chances of a Dry Day	74%	80%	97%	94%
Total Precipitation	6.8"	3.3"	0.4"	1.5"
Snowfall	25.4"	4.5"	–	0.2"

Comment: High country conditions are significantly cooler and much snowier during the winter months.

Online Weather Forecast

For the latest weather conditions for the Sierra Nevada from Yosemite to Kings Canyon, visit the following web site: http://www.wrh.noaa.gov/afos/SplitData/SFO/ZFP/ZFPCAZ096

Backpacking in Yosemite

*B*ecause there are some 800 miles of trail in Yosemite ranging through some of the most stunning scenery in the world, backpacking is a popular activity in the park. It allows its practitioners a true wilderness experience, and is really the only way large areas of Yosemite can be reached.

But successful, minimum impact backpacking requires good physical health, knowledge of backpacking techniques, proper equipment, and a respect for the natural world. Uninformed backcountry users can cause great harm to the wilderness and not even know it. What follows are basic tips for back packers, wilderness regulations, and sources for further information.

Get A Wilderness Permit

Free wilderness permits are required year-round for all overnight stays in Yosemite's backcountry. To avoid overcrowding and reduce impacts to wilderness areas, Yosemite limits the number of people who may begin overnight hikes from each trailhead each day. At least 40% of each trailhead quota is available on a first-come, first-served basis the day of, or one day prior to, the beginning of your trip.

These permits may be obtained at any of the following locations in the park: the Wilderness Center in Yosemite Valley (just east of the Visitor Center), Tuolumne Meadows Permit Kiosk (just off the Tioga Road on the road to Tuolumne Lodge), Wawona Information Center (see page 42), Big Oak Flat Visitor Center (see page 57), and Hetch Hetchy Entrance Station for those using Hetch Hetchy trails (see Page 57).

Wilderness permit reservations can now be made year-round, from up to twenty-four weeks to two days in advance. Those desiring a reservation can visit the Wilderness Center in Yosemite Valley, mail in a reservation request, visit the Wilderness Reservation web site at www.yosemitesecure.org/wildpermit/, or call the center at (209) 372-0740. A $5 per person, non-refundable fee is charged for reservations. Fees may be paid by check (payable to "Yosemite Association") or with a major credit card including expiration date.

The following information is needed to process a wilderness permit or reservation: name, address, daytime phone; number of people in group; method of travel (i.e., ski, snowshoe, foot, horse); starting and ending dates of hike; the entry and exit trailhead you use; your primary destination; number of pack stock (if applicable); alternative dates or trailheads if your first choice isn't available. Mail requests should be sent to Wilderness Center, PO Box 545, Yosemite, CA 95389.

Permits may be picked up no more than 24 hours prior to trailhead departure. Reservations are especially recommended for hikes leaving from Tuolumne Meadows or with destinations of Little Yosemite Valley, Half Dome, or Merced Lake, and for any hikers planning a Saturday night stay.

Wilderness Regulations

Group Size: Maximum group size in the Yosemite Wilderness is 15 people on trails and 8 people maximum for any off-trail travel.

Campsite Location: Please use existing campsites at least 100 feet from lakeshores and streams to minimize pollution and vegetation impact. Camp four trail-miles from Tuolumne Meadows, Yosemite Valley, Glacier Point, White Wolf, Hetch Hetchy, and Wawona, and at least one trail-mile from any road.

Human Waste: Bury human waste six inches deep in a small hole at least 100 feet from any lake, stream, or camp area. Toilet paper should be burned or packed out.

Garbage: Pack out all garbage (no exceptions). Do not bury garbage, scatter organic waste, or leave foil in campfire sites.

Fires: Use gas stoves rather than wood fires. Wood fires are not permitted above 9,600 feet due to firewood scarcity. Use only existing fire rings and dead and down wood in areas below 9,600 feet.

Pets: Dogs and other pets are not allowed in the Yosemite wilderness.

Soap: Putting soap, including bio-degradable soap, or any form of pollutant into lakes or streams is prohibited. Discard wash and rinse water at least 100 feet from water sources.

Firearms: Firearms are not permitted in the wilderness.

Route Planning Information

Space considerations prevent a listing of even some of the thousands of trips that can be made into the Yosemite wilderness. But never fear, there are many resources available to help with your route planning task. You can obtain maps or any of the trail guides listed on page 17 from the Yosemite Association, at the Wilderness Center, at one of the Visitor Center bookstores, through the Yosemite Bookstore online at www.yosemitestore.com, or through the mail by writing PO Box 230, El Portal, CA 95318, or calling (209) 379-2648.

Wilderness Tips

Visit the Wilderness Center: At the Wilderness Center, just east of the Visitor Center on the pedestrian mall in Yosemite Valley, detailed information is available about the park's wilderness, there are educational displays, a trip planning sect-ion is provided, and guidebooks, maps, and backpacker supplies are offered for sale. For additional information, visit the NPS wilderness information web site at www.nps.gov/yose/wilderness.

Key Phone Numbers:
Wilderness permit reservations
(209) 372-0740

Current wilderness conditions
(209) 372-0307

For more information about making reservation or obtaining a permit call (209) 372-0310.

Treat the Water: Unfortunately, microscopic organisms known as *Giardia lamblia* (see page 92) are present in wilderness lakes, rivers, and streams. They can cause illness (sometimes quite severe), so you should not drink from these sources withhout first treating the water. Your options are to boil it for three minutes, to use a chemical disinfectant like iodine or chlorine (less effective than boiling), or to use a Giardia-rated water filter available from outdoor equipment stores, at the Wilderness Center, or from the Yosemite Store online at www.yosemitestore.com.

Get Acclimatized: Many wilderness trips begin at elevations much higher than you may be accustomed to and then go even higher. It's a good idea to arrive a day early to let your body adapt to the thinner air. Don't over-exert, and drink plenty of fluids to avoid altitude sickness.

Bear-Proof Your Campsite
Yosemite's black bears are clever and very persistent. If you fail to set up your camp and store your food properly, your whole trip can be ruined. Always follow these six steps:

1. Use the food storage boxes at your trailhead for keeping any food that you will not be taking on your backpack trip. Never leave food or food-related supplies in vehicles left overnight at trailheads.

2. Store your food in a bear-resistant food storage container. Weighing just 2.9 pounds and holding from 5 to 7 days worth of food for one person, the canisters are strongly encouraged by the National Park Service, and required above 9,600 feet. They are for sale and rent at the Wilderness Center, the Curry Village Mountain Shop, and the Village Sports

Shop in Yosemite Valley, at the Crane Flat Store, at the Tuolumne Reservation Cabin and the Mountaineering School in Tuolumne Meadows, at the Wawona Information Station and the Wawona Store, at the Big Oak Flat Information Station, and at the Hetch Hetchy Information Station.

3. Hang your food and anything with an odor as instructed by the NPS if you don't use a canister. Hang pots and pans from food bags as an alarm. Sleep 20 to 30 feet from where you hang items so you can hear the bear and scare it away as quickly as possible.

4. If a bear approaches your camp, act immediately to scare it away. Yell and make as much noise as possible. Throw small rocks no larger than golf balls at the bear. Make noise and chase the bear. Multiple people chasing a bear increases effectiveness.

5. Always maintain a distance. Do not advance on a bear that appears to feel threatened or cornered by you. Do not attempt to retrieve food or gear from a bear until the item is abandoned.

6. Food taken by bears is your responsibility. Please clean up and report all bear damage to a ranger. Improper food storage can result in the killing of conditioned bears, personal injury, and property loss. Please do your part to keep Yosemite's bears wild.

Further Reading
Yosemite National Park: A Natural History Guide to Yosemite and Its Trails by Jeffrey P. Schaffer. Berkeley: Wilderness Press, 1989.

High Sierra Hiking Guides for Hetch Hetchy, Tuolumne Meadows, and *Yosemite* by various authors. Berkeley: Wilderness Press, various dates.

Guide to the John Muir Trail by Thomas Winnett. Berkeley: Wilderness Press, 1984.

Yosemite Climbing

Because of its granite landscape, Yosemite is mecca for rock climbers from all over the United States and the world. Yosemite Valley has been the location of so many climbing developments and innovations that it has become the yardstick against which all other climbing areas are measured. In every season of the year, climbers can be seen clinging to rock faces or hanging by their hands and feet from upward-leading cracks.

Passionate rock climbers populate a world foreign to most "normal" people, and have developed a subculture with customs, clothing, language, and tools of its own. In Yosemite, that world revolves around Camp Four (known on signs and maps as Sunnyside Campground). Across Northside Drive from Yosemite Lodge, Camp Four is the climbers' permanent temporary home. Many of the hard core climbers move to Tuolumne Meadows during the summer.

Not that long ago, climbers utilized many artificial techniques to accomplish their climbs. These included drilling holes in the rock and inserting permanent metal bolts, chiseling holds in the rocks, and hammering in steel "pitons" that damaged the rock and might not be removable. Such steps made certain routes climbable that might not otherwise be.

Today, a less destructive and harmful climbing ethic has developed. Bolts are placed much less often, chiseling is frowned upon, and high-tech devices like "chocks," "friends," and "cams" (that are inserted into cracks and removed easily) provide protection for modern climbers. It's known as clean climbing, and it's a matter of high priority for climbers who wish to protect and preserve a natural, non-artificial climbing environment.

One interesting aspect of the climbing subculture is its system of naming and rating climbing routes. The first climber to successfully undertake a new path up a section of rock (a "first ascent") is entitled to name that route. That climber, and those who come after, attempt to rate the difficulty of climbing that route. The Yosemite Decimal System is used for this purpose and is an elaborate scale with ratings from 5.0 to 5.13 with grades from "a" to "d" at each level signifying different degrees of difficulty to the climbing community.

Climbs range from short routes of 50 feet or less (a pitch) to multi-day ascents of Yosemite's biggest walls (like El Capitan), which are made up of many pitches. A number of practitioners of the sport are now engaged in what is known as "free soloing." Not recommended for other than the finest, most skilled climbers, free soloing is the climbing of rocks without the assistance and protection of a climbing partner. Generally, no ropes are used, no climbing devices are attached to the rock, and no one will be there to catch you if you fall. Most of Yosemite's largest rock landmarks have been "free soloed" in less than a day.

The technology of climbing has advanced considerably over the past several decades. Special ropes made from synthetic fibers are used, and they stretch to absorb the weight of a falling climber. Their strength under pressure has also increased. Shoes covered with sticky rubber that adheres to practically any surface are now commonly used. And the devices mentioned above like cams and friends made from high-strength alloys have expanded climbing opportunities as well.

But good equipment or not, climbers must still have the skill and strength to climb the rocks. The mastery that has been achieved by many "rock jocks" is astounding, and routes that many once considered unclimbable are now accomplished almost daily. New routes are being explored and climbed, and other climbing firsts, like paraplegic Mark Wellman's 1989 ascent of El Capitan, continue to occur.

Rock climbing is not recommended for the casual park visitor. If you would like to learn more about the sport, consider taking a lesson from the Yosemite Mountaineering School either in Yosemite Valley (call 372-8344) or in Tuolumne Meadows (summer only call 372-8435). Without proper equipment and without proper technique, you could severely injure yourself or die.

Ten Very Curious Names for Yosemite Climbing Routes
Agricultural Maneuvers in the Dark (5.8)
Chairman Ted Scraps the Time Machine (5.10a)
Colony of Slippermen (5.11d)
Dope Smoking Moron (5.11)
Gerbil Launcher (5.10d)
God Told Me to Skin You Alive (5.11a)
Public Enema Number One (5.11c)
Stand and Quiver (5.11a)
Tooth or Consequences (5.11b)
Vegetal Extraction (5.10)

A Ranger is a Ranger is a....

Oh, the ranger's life is full of joys,
And they're all good, jolly, care-free boys,
And in wealth they are sure to roll and reek,
For a ranger can live on one meal a week.
—Anonymous

Yosemite National Park is administered by the US National Park Service (NPS), an agency of the Department of the Interior established in 1916. As a bureaucracy based loosely on a military model, the NPS is characterized by a complex ordering of job ranks and by its distinctive field uniforms. The green pants, gray shirt, and universally recognized "Smokey the Bear" hat have become the trademark of the park ranger. The key descriptor here is "park" as park rangers differ from forest rangers. Forest rangers work for the US Forest Service, a branch of the US Department of Agriculture, in national forests throughout the country. While the job duties of park and forest rangers are often similar in their respective situations, park rangers work in parks and monuments, and forest rangers work in _____ (you fill in the blank!).

Now that you're able to recognize that the person in the flat-brimmed hat before you is a park ranger working in a national park, things start to get a bit more complicated. The National Park Service is divided into any number of departments ranging from visitor protection to interpretation to maintenance to resources management to administration. To confuse things, employees of the different divisions all wear roughly the same uniform. The traditional park ranger is employed by the Division of Visitor Protection, with duties that include law enforcement, traffic regulation, search and rescue, emergency medical treat-ment, and many others. In order to work as a traditional (or "real") park ranger, one must take special training and earn a law enforcement commission.

Park interpreters (interpretive rangers, formerly called naturalists) are responsible for the educational program at

Yosemite, and give walks, talks, and programs. They, too, are "real" rangers, but they generally have not been commissioned and do not perform law enforcement functions. Their uniforms are identical to those of protection rangers (except they don't carry guns and handcuffs).

Identical, too, are the outfits of the various park administrators like the Superintendent (the park's chief administrative officer), Deputy Superintendent, Chief Ranger, and other division chiefs. An easy way to distinguish these management types is by their skin pallor. They attend so many government meetings they almost never see the sun.

Things get a little more confusing with certain maintenance, fire, and resource management workers. They've got the green pants, ditto the gray shirt, but instead of the funny hat, they wear dark green baseball caps with the NPS arrowhead insignia. These employees are not technically rangers, but their roles at Yosemite are equally significant and their contributions considerable.

Most people don't realize that the National Park Service has "exclusive jurisdiction" over Yosemite National Park. That means that state, county, and local agencies do not operate and provide almost no traditional services here. In Yosemite there are no highway patrol officers, no sheriff's officers, no state or municipal firefighters, no state courts, and no incorporated local government. These services fall to the National Park Service, which very ably manages the park.

PARK RANGER

Please remember while you're in the park that if you need help of any kind (from emergency assistance to information), all uniformed NPS personnel are there to be of service.

Q: Who was Yosemite's first ranger?

A: Archie O. Leonard, hired in 1898, was the original "civilian" park ranger in the park. Government-hired rangers began in 1914, and the National Park Service was created in 1916.

Yosemite in Winter

*M*any have the impression that when the first day of winter arrives in Yosemite, the whole place closes up tight until spring. They are mistaken, however; the park and its residents do not hibernate. Yosemite only "closes" when deep snowfall makes it impossible to plow access roads (which is almost never).

There are notable park changes in winter, but most of them add to the unique qualities of this special season. Much of Yosemite wears a covering of snow, and once-thundering waterfalls quiet themselves in frozen dormancy. The Tioga and Glacier Point Roads close, and visitor activities center on such winter sports as skiing and skating.

Weekdays in winter are perfect for experiencing Yosemite in a less crowded, more serene environment. Yosemite Valley daytime temperatures can be surprisingly mild, and winter walks are some of the best. The biggest reward of all, however, is the sheer beauty and grandeur of a transfigured Yosemite and its surrounding high country.

The major routes to the park remain open throughout the year. The roadway least affected by the weather is Highway 140 which leads from Merced via Mariposa and through the Arch Rock Entrance to the park. Highways 120 (from the west) and 41 are also excellent routes, but they are more often subject to closure from heavy snowfall, and many times require the use of tire chains. The roads in Yosemite Valley are plowed throughout the winter.

Winter driving in Yosemite requires special precautions. Because roads are regularly covered with ice and snow, driving speeds should be reduced. Always carry tire chains in your vehicle and obey the chain requirement signs. Watch out for snowplows, and never stop in the roadway (find a pullout where traffic can safely pass).

Skiing and Snowboarding

Both cross-country types and downhillers will discover ski and snowboard opportunities in Yosemite. California's oldest operating ski area, Badger Pass, is located at 7,300 feet about 45 minutes from Yosemite Valley on the Glacier Point Road. It's primarily a "family" oriented operation with nine runs and lots of ski lifts. Badger is an ideal place to learn to ski, and a ski school is available to enable that process. Free shuttle buses to Badger Pass are provided during the winter from lodging facilities in Yosemite Valley (and from other points on busy weekends). Call (209) 372-1446 for information about Badger Pass and the shuttle.

Several miles of both groomed and ungroomed trails for cross-country skiers also originate at Badger Pass. Tracks are laid out the Glacier Point Road all the way to Glacier Point, and skating lanes are also provided. Well-signed trails lead into the wilderness and out to the south rim of Yosemite Valley. The cross-country ski school at Badger offers classes, individualized instruction, and guided tours. Phone (209) 372-8444 for details.

A variety of services is available at the Badger Pass Ski Lodge. Snowboard and ski rentals (both downhill and cross-country), ski repair, child care, and food and beverage service are all offered. There's also a locker room and restrooms. The National Park Service staffs a ranger station primarily as a first aid facility in the A-frame building at Badger. The phone number is (209) 372- 0409.

Another popular cross-country ski area is Crane Flat located at the intersection of the Big Oak Flat and Tioga Roads, seventeen miles from Yosemite Valley. There are no services provided here, but the meadows and forests are full of trails for skiers and snowshoers both.

Snowshoeing

You can showshoe on your own wherever there's adequate snow (at Badger Pass, Crane Flat, or the Mariposa Big Trees, for example), or enjoy a ranger-led showshoe walk where the snowshoes are provided. Walks are presented several days a week from in front of the A-frame at Badger Pass, and reservations are required. Check *Yosemite Today* or call (209) 372-0299.

Merced River in winter, Yosemite Valley

Ice Skating

A large outdoor ice rink is operated daily in Yosemite Valley at Curry Village (weather permitting) from November through March. It features a smooth, refrigerated skating surface, rental skates, a warming hut with lockers, a fire pit, and snack stand. For hours and rates call (209) 372-8341.

Snow Play

Provisions have been made for individuals and families with a passion for sledding, tobogganing, inner-tubing, and snow play generally. The designated area for these activities in Yosemite is at the Crane Flat Campground on the Big Oak Flat Road near its intersection with the Tioga Road. Another good snow play area is found just south of the park on Highway 41 at Goat Meadow in the Sierra National Forest. Supervise children well, and be careful. Many snow play related injuries occur every year.

Camping

There are four campgrounds in Yosemite that are open for use during winter. In Yosemite Valley, both Upper Pines Campground (see page 35) and Sunnyside Walk-In Campground (see page 35) have been winterized. The Wawona Campground (see page 51) is the winter camping area south of the valley, and in the north end of the park, it's Hodgdon Meadow Campground (see page 68). Reservations are required for Upper Pines Campground (follow the procedure detailed on page 12), while all others are first-come, first-served.

Backcountry Ski Huts

For the intrepid wilderness skier, two different huts are operated in Yosemite's backcountry. Nine miles from Badger Pass to the south of the Glacier Point Road is the Ostrander Lake Ski Hut. Set on the banks of a deeply frozen lake and below scenic Horse Ridge, the hut can accommodate up to 25 skiers overnight. There are beds with mattresses, cooking facilities, toilets, a wood stove, and water. Run by the Yosemite Association, the Ostrander Ski Hut is so popular that reservations are required. Call (209) 372-0740 for details, or write Ostrander, PO Box 545, Yosemite NP, CA 95389.

The second hut is located at Glacier Point and is reached by skiing the ten miles out from Badger Pass to the end of the Glacier Point Road. It is operated by DNC, which also requires reservations. Beds and meals are provided, and a guide will accompany you and do the cooking. To learn more about the Glacier Point Hut call (209) 372-8444.

Junior Snow Rangers

The National Park Service offers a winter version of the Junior Ranger program (see page 23). By attending various ranger programs and completing a series of requirements, children can earn Junior Snow Ranger certificates and patches. Check the *Yosemite Today* or stop by a visitor center for details.

The Bracebridge Dinner

Perhaps Yosemite's most long-standing winter tradition is the Bracebridge Dinner. A multi-course Christmas feast is presented at the Ahwahnee Hotel in the context of a colorful pageant based loosely on Washington Irving's Sketch Book account of a typical Yorkshire Christmas dinner in the manor of Squire Bracebridge. The music, costumes, food, and drama combine for an unforgettable experience. Tickets for the event (held multiple times) are in great demand, and reservations for the dinner are much sought after. For more information or to reserve tickets to Bracebridge, call (559) 252-4848. For the 2004 dinners, tickets were $300 per person (including taxes and gratuity), and reservations were accepted beginning February 2.

Cross-country skiing

Where in the Park Can I Find....???

Where can I find a public shower?

In Yosemite Valley, there are showers at Curry Village (open all year) and at Housekeeping Camp (closed in winter). The Tuolumne Meadows Lodge has public showers in summer only with very restricted hours. There are no public showers in Wawona. All showers require a fee.

Where can I find a public laundromat?

The only park laundromat is at Housekeeping Camp in Yosemite Valley (open spring through autumn).

Where can I find a post office?

In Yosemite Valley, the main post office is in Yosemite Village (near the Visitor Center), and there are branch offices at Curry Village (seasonal) and Yosemite Lodge (open all year). There is a year-round post office in the Wawona Store, and a summer-only post office in Tuolumne Meadows at the grocery store there.

Where can I find an ATM (automated teller machine)?

In Yosemite Valley, there are ATMs in Yosemite Village inside the Village Store and to the south of the store at the Art Activity Center, at Yosemite Lodge inside the main registration area, and at Curry Village inside the gift/grocery store. In Wawona, the ATM is inside the Wawona Store, and at Tuolumne Meadows, it's inside the grocery store.

Where can I find a babysitter?

Limited babysitting is available for registered guests at Yosemite Lodge and The Ahwahnee in Yosemite Valley. Call the front desk or see the concierge for additional information.

Where can I find a dog kennel?

The only park kennel is in Yosemite Valley at the Yosemite Concession Services stables. Dogs must be gentle, over 10 pounds, and have proof of shots and a license. Call 372-8348 for more information.

Where can I find a storage locker?

The only lockers in the park are in Yosemite Valley. They are coin-operated and located at Curry Village on the west side of the registration office.

Where can I find a copy machine or a fax machine?

In Yosemite Valley, contact the front desk of Yosemite Lodge, Curry Village, or The Ahwahnee. A fee is charged for these services.

Where can I find a good time?

If you're not enjoying yourself in Yosemite with all it has to offer, you need to see your therapist.

Where can I find a cup of coffee?

In Yosemite Valley, visit the Food Court at Yosemite Lodge, Degnan's Deli in the village, and the Coffee Corner at Curry Village. There's also good coffee at The Ahwahnee dining room and bar.

Steps on the Mist Trail

What Can I Do with my Children?

*T*hough just being in Yosemite should be enough to keep young people occupied and engaged, there are lots of activities and programs that will enhance their visit to the park. During your stay, be sure to check the *Yosemite Today* newspaper for scheduled events that are specially designed for kids.

Take a Hike
With just about every park locale offering flat to moderate walking, a family hike is a great way to burn youthful energy and to reach undeveloped, uncrowded spots with remarkable views and natural beauty. Take a picnic and make a day of it! See pages 30, 32, 45, 47, 59, 62, and 67 for hiking ideas.

Enjoy a Bike Ride
The best park bicycle riding is in Yosemite Valley, which features miles of bike trails. Bring your own, or rent bicycles at Yosemite Lodge or Curry Village. See page 29 for details. Don't forget your helmets.

Visit Happy Isles
The Nature Center at Happy Isles in Yosemite Valley is devoted to kids, with wildlife exhibits, nightlife display, and a number of other presentations. There are books for sale, and "Explorer Packs" on a variety of topics can be checked out. They include activities for children designed to help them learn more about the natural world they live in. See page 30.

Help Them Become Junior Rangers
There are two self-guided "junior ranger" programs for kids in Yosemite. Children 3 through 6 can become "Little Cubs" and earn a button by completing the activities set out in *The Little Cub Handbook*, available at visitor centers throughout the park. *The Junior Ranger Handbook* is for those aged 7 to 13, and completion of the program allows them to become Junior Rangers and receive a certificate and patch. Any questions? Check with a ranger for more information.

Explore the Indian Gallery and Garden
Within the Yosemite Museum in Yosemite Valley, a room has been dedicated to the culture of the local Native American people. Besides a number of educational displays, there is often someone demonstrating basketmaking or some other traditional art of the Miwok people. Behind the museum is a garden area that includes exhibits about the local Indians, and reproductions of several historic structures they might have used.

Take in a Campfire Program
What better way to finish off a day than attending a traditional campfire program? During the summer, there are usually such programs offered by rangers in campgrounds throughout the park, and there is also a fee-based "Old-Fashioned Campfire" at Happy Isles in Yosemite Valley in spring, summer, and fall. Check the *Yosemite Today* newspaper for schedules.

WINTER ACTIVITIES FOR KIDS

Engage in Snow Play
Grab your sleds, toboggans, and inner tubes and head to the snow play areas at the Crane Flat Campground or just outside the South Entrance at Goat Meadow on Highway 41. Relatively gentle and clear slopes have been identified for hours of slipping and sliding.

Go Skiing or Snowboarding
The ski area at Badger Pass is perfect for families, with nine runs, multiple lifts, and lessons offered by a first-rate ski school. Rental equipment is available for snowboarding and downhill and cross-country skiing. See page 20.

Visit the Skating Rink
From November through March when weather allows, an outdoor ice rink operates at Curry Village beneath the shadow of Glacier Point. You can rent ice skates, and there's a warming hut, lockers, a fire pit, and a snack bar. The phone number is 372-8341.

Snowshoe with a Ranger
Snowshoe walks are offered at Badger Pass by National Park Service rangers for adults and children 10 years and older. Rental snowshoes are available. Check the *Yosemite Today* newspaper for schedules.

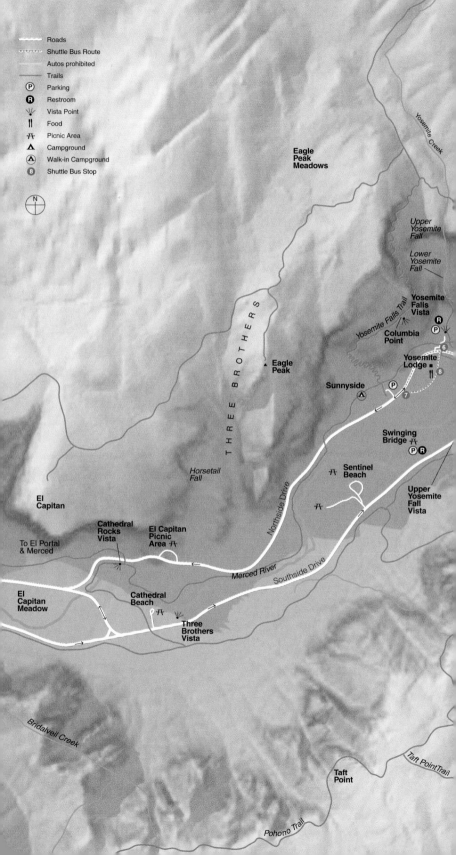

Yosemite Valley

Roads
Shuttle Bus Route
Autos prohibited
Trails
Ⓟ Parking
Ⓡ Restroom
Vista Point
Food
Picnic Area
Campground
Walk-in Campground
8 Shuttle Bus Stop

N

Eagle
Peak
Meadows

Yosemite Creek

Upper
Yosemite
Fall

Lower
Yosemite
Fall

THREE BROTHERS

Eagle Peak

Yosemite Falls Trail

Yosemite
Falls
Vista
Ⓡ
Ⓟ

Columbia
Point

6

Yosemite
Lodge
8

Sunnyside

Ⓟ
7

Horsetail
Fall

Swinging
Bridge
Ⓟ Ⓡ

El
Capitan

Sentinel
Beach

Upper
Yosemite
Fall
Vista

Northside Drive

Cathedral
Rocks
Vista

El Capitan
Picnic
Area

To El Portal
& Merced

Merced River

Southside Drive

El
Capitan
Meadow

Cathedral
Beach

Three
Brothers
Vista

Bridalveil Creek

Taft Point Trail

Taft
Point

Pohono Trail

Yosemite Valley is truly the heart of the park. With its granite monoliths, towering waterfalls, and pastoral meadows, the valley is unique in the world for its remarkable scenery. Its seven square miles make up only a small fraction of the park's entire area, but 75 to 80 percent of the visitors to Yosemite spend their time there.

Not surprisingly, this popularity results in crowded conditions on popular weekends and during the summer. Campgrounds fill, concessioner accommodations become completely reserved, and day users clog valley roads and parking lots. Efforts have been made to reduce the congestion caused by such heavy use, and some improvements have resulted.

Among them are a one-way road system, the closure of roads to automobile traffic in the east end of the valley, development of an extensive network of bicycle paths, and the implementation of a shuttle bus system that links most developed areas in eastern Yosemite Valley.

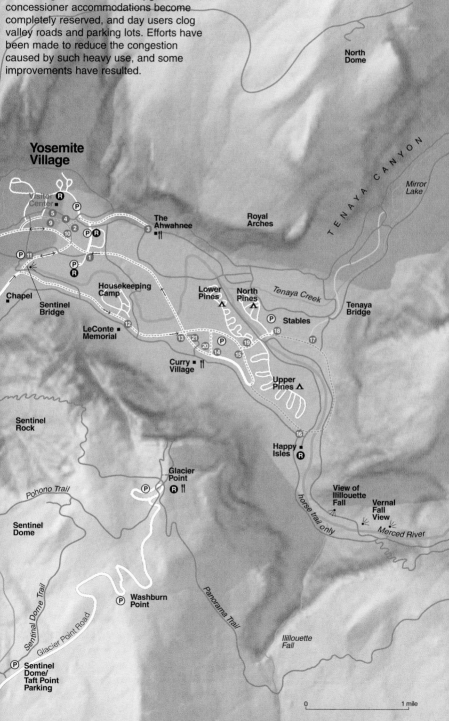

Can You Find the Visitor Center?

"At Yosemite the visitor's center is almost impossible to find. By the time I found it I knew my way around and didn't need it anymore." — Bill Bryson

Lots of visitors come to believe, after hours of searching, that the Yosemite Valley Visitor Center has been purposely hidden from them. In many national parks, the first place you are directed by prominent signs is the parking lot right smack in front of the Visitor Center. Not so in Yosemite Valley. Here you must either possess a doctorate in nuclear physics or have experience as a Green Beret to make your way to "Information Central."

It really is worth taking the time to find the Visitor Center because it's the ideal place to start your visit. There you will find an impressive orientation film program, interesting exhibits, information services provided by knowledgeable rangers, and a complete bookstore. Near the Visitor Center are an Indian Cultural Exhibit and Indian Garden, plus a Museum Gallery with new exhibits hung regularly.

Until 1971, a large paved parking lot at the center's front door was accessible to automobiles. But given the tremendous congestion that was occurring in the Yosemite Village area and the desire on the part of the National Park Service to begin to eliminate private vehicles from the valley, a decision was made to close the parking area and develop a pedestrian mall. The Visitor Center, for very good reasons, suddenly became unreachable by car.

But don't despair, you can still get to the Visitor Center by shuttle bus, on bicycle, or on foot. Here's how to manage it from selected valley locations.

From Day Visitor Parking (Camp 6):
Park your car here and board one of the free "express" shuttle buses headed to the Yosemite Valley Visitor Center (bus stop #1). The bus stops in front of the Visitor Center (its only stop), then returns to the Day Visitor Parking area. If you'd rather walk, there's a map available at the information station there that will guide you. It's about a one-third mile hike.

From the Pines Campgrounds:
Jump on a shuttle bus at the stop nearest to you (bus stops #15, #16, and #21 are all close), and disembark at Yosemite

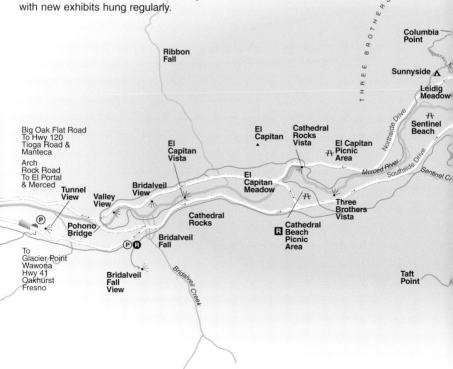

Village (bus stop #2). The Visitor Center is 200 yards to the west up the mall.

From Housekeeping Camp: The shuttle bus stops right in front of the entrance to the camp {bus stop #13). Take it and get off at Yosemite Village (bus stop #2). Walk 200 yards to the west up the pedestrian mall to the Visitor Center.

From the Ahwahnee Hotel: It's about a fifteen minute walk along the Ahwahnee Meadow and past the Church Bowl to the Visitor Center. Or take the free shuttle bus from in front of the hotel (bus stop #3) and get off at the Visitor Center (bus stop #5).

From Yosemite Lodge: Catch the free shuttle bus in front of the lodge registration area (bus stop #8). It will drop you off a few yards from the Visitor Center's front door (bus stop #9). The walk from Yosemite Lodge to the Visitor Center is less than a mile, it's flat and easy, and affords lots of good views along the way.

From the Parking Area behind the Village Store: Walk around or through the Village Store to the pedestrian mall on the other side of it. Turn to your right and walk approximately 200 yards up the mall to the Visitor Center.

These directions should make it clear that the key to finding the Visitor Center is locating the Yosemite Village pedestrian mall. The center is located at the mall's west end. If you're on your bicycle, bike trails are well marked, and signs will direct you to Yosemite Village and the Visitor Center.

Free Shuttle Bus Rides

The easiest way to get around in Yosemite Valley (and to get out of your car and avoid traffic) is to ride, free of charge, the Yosemite Valley shuttle bus system. With stops at just about all locations in the eastern end of the valley, the buses run every ten minutes or so (somewhat less frequently in the winter) and access areas such as Happy Isles and Mirror Lake that are closed to private automobiles. All the shuttle bus stops are indicated on the map below. In winter, shuttle service is discontinued to several stops.

Q: Where was the original Visitor Center (park headquarters) located in Yosemite Valley?

A: In old Yosemite Village, across from the present-day Yosemite Chapel just west of Sentinel Bridge.

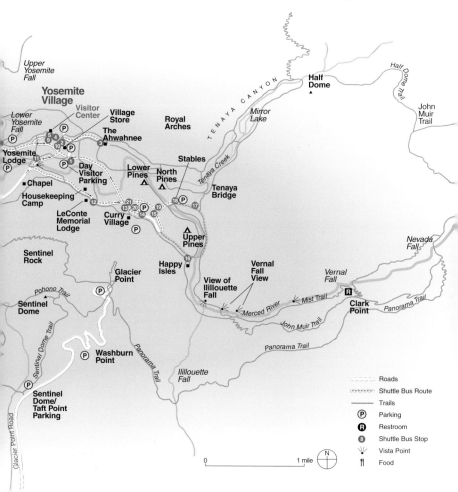

Best Bets in Yosemite Valley

The view from Glacier Point. From the railing at Glacier Point, you are lord (or lady) of all the Yosemite you survey. The view is unforgettable. See page 39.

John Muir in person. Noted actor Lee Stetson regularly portrays John Muir in dramatic presentations in Yosemite Valley. It's Yosemite Theater at its best. See page 31.

A browse through The Ansel Adams Gallery. This classy shop has been a leading Yosemite establishment since 1902. If you're a photographer, consider this your headquarters in the park. See page 22.

The hike to Vernal Fall. An amazingly popular trip, but for good reason. The walk is essential Yosemite: rock, light, and water at their most spectacular. See page 33.

A seat at Bracebridge Dinner. This lavish Christmas pageant is held annually at the Ahwahnee Hotel and features much delicious food, seasonal music, elaborate costumes, and festive decorations. See page 21.

Breakfast at The Ahwahnee. It's a delight anytime of the year to start your day with a casual yet luxurious breakfast in The Ahwahnee's grand dining room. See page 37.

The panorama from Tunnel View. This classic Yosemite viewpoint never ceases to take one's breath. From this spot the valley's geologic origin couldn't be more evident. See page 39.

A visit to the Visitor Center Bookstore. Nowhere else in the universe has such a complete collection of books and other materials related to Yosemite and the Sierra Nevada been assembled in one place. See page 26.

Lower Yosemite Fall in springtime. When the snows of the Yosemite high country begin to thaw, the results are a revitalized Yosemite Falls. Liquid thunder! See page 32.

Vernal Fall

Activities in the Valley

Once you have spent some time at the Visitor Center (page 26), there are unlimited possibilities for visitor enjoyment. Most of them involve seeing and learning about the amazing sights that Yosemite Valley has to offer.

Enjoy an Interpretive Program

Throughout the year, park interpretive rangers and others present a wide variety of programs, walks, demonstrations, campfires, slideshows, films, and talks. There is usually no charge for these activities, which occasionally do require reservations. Consult the *Yosemite Today* for the daily schedule for these programs.

Visit Yosemite Valley's Eastern End

The free shuttle bus route takes visitors to the area of Yosemite Valley that is no longer accessible by private automobile. Such locations as Happy Isles (the trailhead for the hikes to Vernal and Nevada Falls and Half Dome) and Mirror Lake can only be reached by the shuttle bus or on bicycle and foot. Excellent views of many landmarks including Glacier Point, Half Dome, Tenaya Canyon, and Washington Column are afforded from stops along the way. This section of the shuttle bus route is closed in winter.

Make a Circle Tour of the Entire Valley

To reach much of Yosemite Valley to the west of Yosemite Village you must still use your car. Many of the park's most famous spots such as El Capitan, Bridalveil Fall, Tunnel View, Cathedral Rocks, and Sentinel Rock are in west valley locations. At least two resources are available for a "self-guided" circle tour. If you've got a CD player in your car, try the *Yosemite Valley Tour – A Yosemite Audio Guide* by Bob Roney.

This audio tour is available for sale at the Visitor Center and other park stores, and is a comprehensive look at all aspects of the valley – from geology to Native Americans to history to plants and animals. The sixty-minute CD provides explicit directions to the ten stops on the tour that will take you from 2 to 4 hours.

An alternative is to use *The Yosemite Road Guide,* a well-written book that is keyed to roadside markers throughout Yosemite Valley and the rest of the park. You must develop your own route using the guide, but it's packed with interesting information and facts that will enhance your tour.

If you would rather be free of your car and not drive, DNC offers a two-hour guided tour in an open-air tram that visits most of the picturesque spots in Yosemite Valley. Check at the front desks of the various lodging facilities or behind the Village Store for tour details and prices.

Take a Bicycle Ride

Whether you've brought your bicycle or not, you can still see Yosemite Valley on two wheels. Bicycle rentals (with helmet) can be arranged all year at Yosemite Lodge (372-1208) and summer only at Curry Village (372-8319). More than eight miles of paved bicycle paths separate bicycle traffic from autos, and bicycling is especially good on the closed sections of roadway in the valley's east end.

Try to avoid bicycling on busy valley roads that are often flooded with automobiles. As a rule, distracted, sight-seeing drivers are not particularly attentive to bicyclists. Apart from that, there are some fairly strict rules for bicycle use in the valley:

- Bicyclists should stay on paved bike paths and highways.
- No riding on trails and into meadows. Erosion and vegetation damage will result otherwise.
- Mountain and all terrain bicycles are permitted, but not allowed on unpaved surfaces in Yosemite Valley. Check at the Visitor Center for appropriate mountain bike routes.
- Ride to the right in single file.

Catch a Fish

There are lots of trout in Yosemite Valley, but the Merced River is heavily fished. Stocking of trout is no longer done, and resident lunkers have developed a wariness of people and their multifarious fishing devices. Nevertheless, nice fish are caught every season by anglers of every skill level.

Fishing in Yosemite is allowed in streams and rivers from the last Saturday in April to November 15. Fishing is allowed year-round in park lakes and reservoirs. On the

Merced River in Yosemite Valley, only catch-and-release fishing is allowed for rainbow trout. No natural or organic bait may be used, only artificial lures and flies with barbless hooks. The limit is 5 per day with 10 in possession. California fishing licenses are required (16 years and over) and may be purchased at the Village Sports Shop and at the Wawona Store.

On the Merced River just outside the park between the boundary and downstream to the Foresta Bridge, fishing is allowed all year but only to persons using artificial lures with barbless hooks, with a minimum size limit of 12 inches total length and a maximum daily bag limit of 2. Consult the California Fish and Game Regulations for further Yosemite fishing rules.

Paint a Picture

Free outdoor art classes are available during most parts of the year at the Yosemite Art Center. Artists working in many different media offer hands-on learning experiences to interested students regardless of skill level. Located on the Village Mall south of the Village Store near Shuttle Stop #2, the Yosemite Art Center is co-sponsored by the National Park Service, the Yosemite Association, and DNC Parks & Resorts at Yosemite. Class sessions are four hours in length and are scheduled from early spring through October, and during holiday periods.

Ride 'Em Cowboy

Horseback rides are offered (for those with hardened backsides) by DNC Parks & Resorts at Yosemite from their stables in the east end of Yosemite Valley (bus stop #18). Guided trips in two-hour, half-day, and full-day lengths are given to such destinations as Nevada Fall and Glacier Point. For reservations and information call 372-8348 between 7:30 a.m. and 5 p.m.

GetYour Head Wet

If you'd like to swim, the Merced River provides miles of beaches and numerous refreshing swimming holes during the summer months (it's too cold and fast-flowing in the spring). Or try out Mirror Lake and Tenaya Creek. If you must swim in a heated pool, in summer there's one at Yosemite Lodge and another at Curry Village. A small pool is available for guests only at the Ahwahnee Hotel.

Indulge the Kids

The Nature Center at Happy Isles (near Shuttle Stop #16) is a great spot for parents and their children, open from early spring until October (check the *Yosemite Today*). You can purchase workbooks for the Junior Ranger and Little Cub programs, and there are exhibits of park animals, a children's corner, a night display, and much more. Kids can check out, free of charge, an "Explorer Pack" – a convenient-to-carry daypack filled with guide books and activities for the whole family. There are packs available on different topics including "Small Wonders," "Tree Trivia," and "Rocking in Yosemite."

Go for a Hike

There's a price to be paid for Yosemite Valley's towering cliffs and sheer walls. Practically every hike leading out of Yosemite Valley is straight up and strenuous! But the valley floor offers many enjoyable walks over flat terrain, and no matter what your hiking ability, you can find a trail to suit you. Several Yosemite Valley floor trails are wheelchair accessible.

When you hike be sure to wear sturdy, comfortable shoes and clothes that allow freedom of movement. Carry a flashlight and raingear. Rain (or snow) is a possibility in every season. Don't forget plenty of water (drinking from streams and rivers is not advised), and lunch and snacks. Dogs on leash are allowed on trails on the floor of Yosemite Valley, but nowhere else.

Take in the Yosemite Theater
Throughout the year, dramatic and musical performances are offered by the Yosemite Theater program. Designed to supplement the interpretive activities of the NPS, Yosemite Theater is sponsored by DNC Parks & Resorts at Yosemite. Modest fees are charged for the various presentations. Best known of the theater programs are Lee Stetson's one-man stage productions in which he portrays John Muir. There's a program for every taste including musical campfire programs and slide and film presentations. Tickets for the performances may be purchased at the door, or check at DNC activities desks.

Hear a Lecture
Each summer the Sierra Club operates the LeConte Memorial Lodge, an educational center and library located across from Housekeeping Camp at shuttle bus stop #12. The lodge was built by the Club in 1903 in honor of Joseph LeConte, eminent University of California geologist. Berkeley architect John White designed the Tudor-style, rough-hewn granite building. Most evenings, special lectures are presented here free of charge to interested visitors and Sierra Club members. Consult the *Yosemite Today* or visit the LeConte Lodge for a schedule.

Saunter in the Cemetery
Fascinating insights into Yosemite's history can be gained from a visit to the Yosemite Cemetery located across the street just west of the Yosemite Museum. Several significant figures from the park's past are buried here including a number of Native Americans. First laid out in the 1870s, the cemetery houses the graves of such persons as James Mason Hutchings, Galen Clark, James Lamon, Sally Ann Castagnetto, Suzie Sam, and Lucy Brown. An informative publication entitled *Guide to the Yosemite Valley Cemetery* is on sale at the Visitor Center. If you do visit the cemetery, remember that it is a sacred place for many and that proper respect should be shown.

Wheelchair Accessibility
Many programs, facilities, and trails in Yosemite Valley (and throughout the park) are suitable for visitors in wheelchairs, with assistance. Information on accessible park programs, facilities, and trails can be found in the *Yosemite Magazine* or at park entrance and information stations.

Q: How many rangers does it take to change a light bulb?
A: None. Rangers aren't afraid of the dark.

Visit the Wilderness Center
Located in the small building between The Ansel Adams Gallery and the post office, the Wilderness Center offers a number of informative displays, a great relief map of the entire park, information on planning your own trip into the wilderness, and maps, guidebooks, and selected backpacking items. It's also the place to pick up wilderness permits, make wilderness reservations (see page 16), and rent bear-resistant food canisters.

Pack a Picnic
There are a number of fine spots for a picnic in Yosemite Valley. In the eastern end of the valley, ride the shuttle bus to Happy Isles or take the walk to Mirror Lake. To the west try El Capitan picnic area (on the right side of Northside Drive about two miles west of Yosemite Lodge), Bridalveil Fall parking area (intersection of the Wawona Road and Southside Drive), Cathedral picnic area (on the left side of Southside Drive just past the El Cap crossover), Sentinel Beach picnic area (on the left a mile or so further along Southside Drive), or Swinging Bridge picnic area (less than half a mile further on the left). See the map on page 24-25 for locations.

Enjoy an Outdoor Adventure
Throughout the year, the Yosemite Association presents a series of outdoor seminars in Yosemite Valley and at other park locations. Some of the courses, covering such topics as botany, geology, natural history, photography, art, and backpacking, are offered for college credit. Programs have been designed for all levels of experience and for every type of Yosemite user. The instructional staff is excellent. For a catalog of classes or more information call (209) 379-2321, visit www.yosemite.org, or write: Outdoor Adventures, Box 230, El Portal, CA 95318.

Q: Where did the Mariposa Battalion camp on their first ever visit to Yosemite Valley in 1851?
A: In Bridalveil Meadow. There's a plaque commemorating this event on the edge of the meadow near the Merced River.

Three Easy Hikes on the Valley Floor

Mirror Lake. Take the free shuttle bus to the Mirror Lake Junction (bus stop #17). During the winter you'll have to walk from the Pines Campgrounds (bus stop #19). From this point it's a relaxing half-mile saunter over pavement to Mirror Lake. The trail beyond is also gentle as it follows Tenaya Creek eastward and then circles back. Walking up Tenaya Creek adds about 3 miles to the total distance. Views of Half Dome, Mt. Watkins, and Basket Dome are superb.

Vernal Fall Bridge. This special vantage point is reached from Happy Isles (stop #16 on the free shuttle bus route). You'll need to walk from Curry Village during the winter when the shuttles don't run this way. Undoubtedly the most popular and busiest hike in Yosemite (you'll be elbow to elbow with lots of other people), the Mist Trail leads seven-tenths of a mile to a bridge that allows a breathtaking view of Vernal Fall. The trail, while paved with asphalt, is not as easy as the other two hikes listed here.

There is a moderate slope most of the way to the bridge, and a few ups and downs. But its definitely worth the effort. If you're a strong hiker and still feeling hardy, the remaining hike to the top of the fall is about a half-mile. Be warned, however, that it's all straight uphill over a very steep trail and a large number of granite steps. It's called the Mist Trail because it leads along the right flank of Vernal Fall, which, particularly in spring, blows heavy mist over trail and hiker alike.

Lower Yosemite Fall. Walk, drive, bicycle, or ride the shuttle bus to the Lower Yosemite Fall parking area near Yosemite Lodge (bus stop #6). It's no more than a quarter-mile to the base of the lower fall and its boisterous, watery display (at least most of the year). This, too, is a very popular excursion. If you continue over the bridge and follow the trail, you will loop back to the parking area in less than a half-mile. On full-moon nights in April and May, take this walk and watch for beautiful "moon bows" in the lower fall—a phenomenon first written about by John Muir.

Note: The floor of Yosemite Valley is crisscrossed with many trails, and paths hug the base of both the north and south valley walls. From about any point, there's good hiking. Wherever you walk, be sure it's not on one of the main roadways. Get out of your car and explore some of Yosemite's less-developed locales. You'll be amply rewarded for your effort.

Further Reading

Easy Day Hikes in Yosemite by Deborah Durkee. Yosemite NP: Yosemite Association, 2000.

Map & Guide to Yosemite Valley by Dean Shenk. San Francisco: Rufus Graphics, 2001.

The Waterfalls of Yosemite by Steven P. Medley. Yosemite NP: Yosemite Association, 1999.

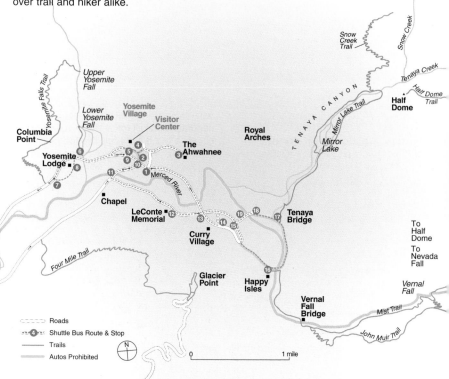

Four Classic Routes to Yosemite Valley's Rim

*E*ach of the major trails to the valley rim is very strenuous and requires an uphill hike of at least 3.5 miles over tens of switchbacks. Be sure you possess the requisite time, energy, and physical condition before you set off on any of these hikes.

1. Yosemite Falls Trail. This climb up the sheer north wall pays off with remarkable perspectives on both the falls and Yosemite Valley generally. The trail leaves from behind Sunnyside Campground across from Yosemite Lodge. The 3.6-mile route gains 2,700 feet in elevation as it passes Columbia Point, the top of Lower Yosemite Fall, and finally leads to the brink of Upper Yosemite Fall. When you reach the top, head back south toward the rim and find the walk down to the pipe railings. At this lookout, water leaps from the rock and braids itself into impressive patterns below you. Allow 6 to 8 hours for the round trip. Strong hikers should consider continuing on to Yosemite Point or Eagle Peak (see page 39).

2. The Four-Mile Trail to Glacier Point. Perhaps most disappointing to hikers on this route is that the Four-Mile Trail is almost 5 miles long (maybe somebody rounded off a little too liberally). It's also an awful lot of work carrying yourself up 3,200 feet only to be greeted by automobiles, lots of people, and a snack bar at your destination. But the views from Glacier Point are sensational and all the more satisfying for the exertion. The trailhead is below Sentinel Rock on Southside Drive about a mile from Yosemite Village at road marker V18. To drive to it you must make a loop on the valley's one-way road system, crossing over at El Capitan (watch for signs returning you to Yosemite Village). One of the earliest trails built in the valley, it is generally cooler than other routes to the rim given its location below and along the south wall. This hike requires from 6 to 8 hours up and back.

3. Tenaya Zigzags/Snow Creek Trail. This is a less-used 3.5-mile route to the rim that actually originates in Tenaya Canyon, just east of Mirror Lake about 2.5 miles from shuttle stop #17. It affords stunning views of the canyon including those of Clouds Rest and Quarter Dome, and directly across from you as you ascend, of Half Dome. Once you've hiked the 108 switchbacks to the rim, the closest promontory is North Dome, which is another 3 miles (see page 39). If North Dome is your destination, allow 8 to 10 hours round trip. The trailhead is Mirror Lake, reached by taking a shuttle bus to the Mirror Lake junction (bus stop #17) and hiking a half-mile to the east. From the lake the trail takes off to the north of the lake up the canyon for a mile and a half, then turns left up the cliff.

4. Vernal and Nevada Falls Trails. The walk to Vernal Fall over the Mist Trail is covered in the "Easy Hikes" section (page 32), but the trail continues on to Nevada Fall above. Describing the route is a bit difficult, because there are two different segments leading to the same place—one primarily for horses and one exclusively for people. The horse trail takes off just past the Vernal Fall Bridge and is less steep, though longer (3.5 miles to Nevada Fall). The Mist Trail (foot traffic only) continues on past the top of Vernal Fall about a mile and a half over switchbacks to the rim. Ascending a gully to its left, hikers are treated to the world-famous profile view of Nevada Fall. From the top of the fall, trails lead to Little Yosemite Valley and Half Dome, and to Glacier Point over the Panorama Trail. Depart from Happy Isles (bus stop #16) and give yourself 6 to 8 hours for the round trip.

Mist Trail

Half Dome: The Hike. For many the summit of Half Dome represents a hiking challenge they can't resist. For all its allure, the trip is long (about 17 miles round trip), steep (4,900 feet of elevation gain), and physically demanding. It's rewarding, too, particularly the incredible views both along the way and at the top. The last 200 yards up the back of the dome require the use of steel-cable handrails and will really make your adrenal gland active. If it sounds like too much of a grunt for one day, consider spending the night in Little Yosemite Valley (you'll need a wilderness permit) and make the ascent when you're fresh the next morning. This busy trail (someone estimated that about 700 people scale Half Dome daily during the summer) begins from Happy Isles (bus stop #16). Allow 10 to 12 hours minimum for the round trip.

Q: What was the preferred route of the Yosemite Indians to the north rim of Yosemite Valley?

A: They regularly used what we now call Indian Canyon, but no trail is maintained any longer up this very steep ravine.

Valley Camping

*Yosemite Valley for a home or camp,
the Grand Canyon for a spectacle.*
—John Burroughs

There are about 415 campsites in Yosemite Valley, most of them on the NPRS reservation system year-round. Despite the fact that many of the campgrounds are practically void of vegetation and that campers are closely packed, these campsites are immensely popular. After all, it's Yosemite Valley.

It was in response to this popularity that the strictly-structured reservation system was developed. While the need to reserve in advance does discourage spontaneity and acting on impulse, it allows visitors coming from all over the US and the rest of the world to expect, with some certainty, that they will find a place to camp when they arrive. From all appearances and reports, the system works well.

As indicated above, the campground reservation system is administered by NPRS, which has some fairly exact requirements. See page 12 for information on making an NPRS reservation.

For campers without reservations who find themselves in Yosemite Valley, there is an NPRS office at the north side of the parking area at Curry Village. Occasionally campsites become available due to cancellation, but to obtain one of them requires standing in line, sometimes for long periods of time. These sites are very limited and nearly impossible to obtain. You must put your name on a waiting list at the Curry Village campground reservation office as early in the day as possible.

Camping Regulations

Camping Limits: From May 1 through September 15, there is a seven-day camping limit in the valley. It extends to 30 days between September 16 and April 30. Thirty total camping days per calendar year are permitted in the park (the "no homsteading" rule). A maximum of six people is allowed in each campsite.

Check Out Time: Campsites must be vacated by 10 a.m. on the day of departure. Check-in time is also 10 a.m., and sites may not be occupied before that time.

Bears: Yosemite Valley and other park locations provide excellent bear habitat. Bears are attracted by the same foods many campers enjoy—marshmallows, hot dogs, watermelon, etc. You are foolish if you do not store your food properly in your campsite (it's also a federal law). All of the valley campgrounds feature bear-proof food lockers measuring 45"w x 18"h x 34"d

that are very effective. Keep your bear locker latched and secured with its clips at all times. Food is not allowed in any parked vehicle after dark. Remove all trash from your campsite and place it in animal-resistant trash cans or dumpsters.

Pets: You may camp with your pets only in designated campgrounds. Be sure to inform NPRS when you make your reservation that you'll be bringing Fido or Garfield. Pets must be on leashes (no longer than six feet) at all times, should never be left unattended, and are not permitted on trails off the floor of Yosemite Valley.

Hook-Ups: There are no recreational vehicle utility hookups in the park. Electrical extension cords may not be connected to campground restroom outlets. Sneaky, but no cigar.

Fires and Firewood: Collection of firewood of any kind (including dead and down wood) in Yosemite Valley is strictly prohibited. This regulation is the first step towards eliminating campfires that have contributed significantly to serious air quality problems in the valley. (It's also aimed at making people smell less smokey.) Campfires are permitted only between 5 p.m. and 10 p.m. At this time, firewood may still be purchased from the concessioner. Please use established fire rings and grates, and start your campfire with newspaper, not pine needles or cones. Use of chain saws is not permitted in the park.

Vehicle Parking: Only two vehicles are allowed per site. All of your vehicles including tent and utility trailers must be parked on the parking pads. You can't just drive into your campsite. If you have more than two vehicles, you must park any extras outside the campground. The maximum length for recreational vehicles is 40 feet.

Dump Stations: No wastewater of any kind should be drained onto the ground. That's gross. Use utility drains at campground restrooms for dishwater and other gray water. Use the dump station at Upper Pines Campground for RV and other septic tanks.

Quiet Hours: Campers are expected to maintain quiet between 10 p.m. and 6 a.m. Quiet generators may be used sparingly during the daytime. Or not at all if I'm camped next to you.

Showers: Try to stay clean during your visit. Unfortunately, there are no shower facilities in any park campgrounds. In Yosemite Valley, showers are available for a fee at Curry Village and at Housekeeping Camp.

Laundry: There is a public laundromat at Housekeeping Camp.

Valley Campgrounds

The following campgrounds are located at an elevation of 4,000 feet in the eastern end of Yosemite Valley. Most require NPRS reservations (see page 12) and have a nightly fee of $18 per site (unless otherwise indicated). Some creative person decided to include "pines" in the name of practically every valley campground, so be sure to take note of the location you've been assigned or you may spend hours trying to find your way home. As dates of operation are subject to variation, check with NPRS or the NPS for details.

North Pines: This set of 84 campsites is located adjacent to the stables and next to the Merced River. Both recreational vehicles and tents are accommodated here between April and September. Some pets allowed. NPRS reservations required.

Upper Pines: The easternmost campground and the largest in Yosemite Valley, Upper Pines is closest to Happy Isles and the trail to Vernal and Nevada Falls. There are 238 sites here, and some pets are permitted. Both RVs and tents are welcome, and a sanitary dump station is available. Open all year. NPRS reservations required.

Lower Pines: Across the river from North Pines with several campsites near the banks of the Merced. The 60 campsites are available for both recreational vehicle users and traditional tent campers. Open March to October. Some pets are allowed. NPRS reservations required.

Sunnyside Walk-in: This campground is primarily for climbers and backpackers; traditional family campers would feel out of place here. Climbing headquarters for Yosemite Valley, Sunnyside attracts mountaineers from all over the world. It's located across from Yosemite Lodge on Northside Drive. Parking spaces are provided outside the camping area, and users must carry their equipment and food to

their sites. The 35 campsites are communal in nature (six campers are assigned to each); the nightly fee is $5 per person. Operated on a first-come, first-served basis, Sunnyside is not on the NPRS system. Be sure to arrive early because the campground fills up by mid-morning practically every day of the summer. These campsites are not wheelchair accessible. Open for walk-in campers all year round; no pets are allowed.

Backpacker Walk-in: Designed for backpackers (be prepared to show your wilderness permit), bicyclists, and bus passengers, this area of 25 sites has no parking area. All access is by foot and there is a one-night maximum stay. Users should check in at North Pines Campground, where a ranger will provide directions to the area. Open from April to October in a typical year. Campers are charged $5 per person per night on a first-come, first-served basis (NPRS procedures do not apply). No pets are allowed.

Group Campground: Special campsites are available for organized groups in Yosemite Valley by prior arrangement; reservations can be made through NPRS starting five months in advance. The fee is $50 per site for no fewer than 13 and no more than 30 people. Parking is provided for up to five vehicles per group, and all equipment and gear must be carried to the campground. For information and reservations contact NPRS at the address on page 12 or visit the NPRS online site at www.reservations.nps.gov. The group campground is not wheelchair accessible and no pets are allowed.

Campfire Limits

From May 1 through October 15, campfires are permitted only between 5 p.m. and 10 p.m. in Yosemite Valley. This measure was implemented to protect the air quality in Yosemite National Park. You should plan to bring your own firewood (wood gathering is not permitted in Yosemite Valley), or buy firewood at one of the valley stores.

Gas Food & Lodging

Gas

There are no longer any service stations in Yosemite Valley and gas is not available. The nearest gas to be pumped is in El Portal on Highway 140 (13 miles). There are also stations at Crane Flat on the Big Oak Flat Road (15 miles), and in Wawona on the Wawona Road (27 miles). Plan ahead and be sure you have plenty of gas before you drive into the valley.

A repair garage is open all year behind the Yosemite Village Store. A towing service is available 24 hours a day by calling 372-8390.

Food: Restaurants

Though the cuisine is strictly American and waits can be considerable during the summer, there are plenty of places to eat in Yosemite Valley. The following is a location-by-location listing of valley eating establishments. Check the Yosemite Today *for hours of operation.*

Yosemite Lodge

Food Court: Open for breakfast, lunch, and dinner the year round. Quick and perfect for families. Many different choices, plus a good coffee bar. Inexpensive.*

The Mountain Room: Offering dinner only, daily from spring to fall, and on weekends and holidays in winter. This is Yosemite's "steak house," with other entrees including salmon and pasta. The remodeled facility is very impressive, and the room offers remarkable views of the Yosemite Falls area from many tables. And it's one of the only places to dine out-of-doors in the summer. Open from 5:30 to 8:30 p.m. Moderate to expensive.

The Mountain Room Bar & Lounge: Besides beer, wine, and cocktails, this facility offers a la carte continental breakfast, and lunch featuring gourmet coffee, sandwiches, salads, cold appetizer plates, and yogurt. Hours vary, but it's usually open from 6:30 a.m. to 10 p.m. Inexpensive to moderate.

Yosemite Village

Degnan's Deli: Open year round for sandwiches, snacks, salads, and picnic items. They will build a sandwich to your specifications, and you can piece together a nice lunch basket. There's limited outdoor seating so plan on making yours a moveable feast. Inexpensive to moderate.

Degnan's Fast Food & Ice Cream: Lunch and dinner selections, year around. Fare includes hamburgers, chicken, frozen yogurt, and ice cream. Limited indoor seating, but a fairly large patio. Inexpensive.

The Loft: Serving lunch and dinner, spring to fall. Located upstairs at the east end of the Degnan's building, The Loft offers pizza, salads, and appetizers from a cafeteria-style line, with plenty of indoor seating. Moderate.

The Village Grill: Fast food breakfasts, lunches, and dinners, spring to fall. Patterned roughly on a MacDonald's menu (look for the Royal Arches?), offerings include burgers, chicken strips, sandwiches, shakes, and fries, with a morning menu of breakfast sandwiches and entrees. Located next to the Village Store with outdoor seating only. Inexpensive.

Curry Village

Pavilion Buffet: For breakfast and dinner spring to fall. Breakfast items include yogurt, cereal, fruit, baked goods, and hot entrees. For dinner, there's soup, salad, pasta, hot entrees, stir-fry, taco bar, and desserts. A family favorite with inexpensive to moderate prices.

Hamburger Stand: Open spring to fall, this fast food outlet has about the same offerings as the Village Grill. Hamburgers, chicken, fish sandwiches, chicken nuggets, salad, and soft drinks to go for consumption on the deck outside. Inexpensive.

Pizza & Bar: Open daily from spring to fall, this facility offers pizza and salad from 4:30 p.m. to 10 p.m. on weekdays, and from noon to 10 p.m. on weekends. Tables are outdoors on the deck. Inexpensive to moderate.

Taqueria: Open daily from spring to fall, this new facility offers Mexican food from 11 a.m. to 5 p.m. Early and late in the season it only operates on weekends. Inexpensive to moderate.

Coffee Corner: For the caffeine-deprived; here you can find fresh ground coffees, espressos, lattes, cappuccinos, fruit, baked goods, and boxed lunches. Located within the Curry Pavilion. Inexpensive.

Ice Cream: Open spring to fall, this small outlet offers sweet treats. It's located inside the Curry Pavilion at the Coffee Corner. Inexpensive.

* Inexpensive: dinner for one adult might cost up to $10. Moderate: dinner for one adult might cost from $10 to $20. Expensive: dinner for one adult might cost over $20.

The Ahwahnee

The Ahwahnee
The Ahwahnee Dining Room:
Breakfast, lunch, and dinner, year round. This regal dining room is a true delight. It's a joy to behold with its beamed ceilings and impressive chandeliers. Perhaps breakfast is the most enjoyable meal here; casual attire is allowed and one experiences a feeling of relaxation and elegance as daylight filters through the massive windows. Dinner is the traditional, formal meal at The Ahwahnee (though the views are obscured by darkness). Men must wear jackets with ties preferred, and reservations are suggested. Call 372-1489. Moderate to expensive.

The Ahwahnee Bar: Light fare and appetizers are served in the bar from noon to 10 p.m daily. Moderate.

Food: Groceries
Yosemite Valley contains four outlets for groceries and camp supplies. They are open year round with the exception of the Housekeeping Camp Store which closes in winter. Check the Yosemite Today *for hours of operation, or call the indicated phone number.*

Village Store: If you can't find it anywhere else in Yosemite Valley, come here. Of particular note are the butcher shop and the fresh produce. Located at the east end of the Village Mall at bus stop #2. Open from 8 a.m. to 9 p.m. (and sometimes later). Phone 372-1253.

Degnan's Delicatessen: Included in the restaurant listings above, Degnan's Deli also has a decent selection of foodstuffs for picknicking and snacks. West of the Village Store and next to the U.S. Post Office on the mall. Open from 8 a.m. to 6 p.m. Phone 372-8454.

Curry Village Camp Store: A general store with convenience items and gifts. Located in the Pavilion building next to the Hamburger deck at Curry Village. Open from 8 a.m. to 7 p.m. Phone 372-8325.

Housekeeping Camp Store: This is a convenience store catering to campers. It's open from spring to fall only, usually between 8 a.m. and 6 p.m. (and sometimes later). Located at Housekeeping Camp near shuttle bus stop #12. Phone 372-8353.

Lodging
The following is a list of lodging facilities, ranging from rustic to luxurious, existing in Yosemite Valley. Quoted rates are approximate only, based on double occupancy, vary with the seasons, and are subject to change. Some rates are lower in winter. Some room rates were scheduled to be reviewed in April, 2004. To make reservations, see page 11.

Yosemite Lodge
Open all year, the lodge offers two types of accommodations: there are 229 lodge rooms ($156 plus tax in season) and 19 standard rooms ($109 plus tax in season). Special value-season rates (both weekend and mid-week) are available between November 1 and March 15. Yosemite Lodge is preferred to Curry Village in winter because of its warmer location. The Lodge is situated near and offers pleasant views of Yosemite Falls and the Merced River.

Besides the restaurants listed above, the following are available at Yosemite Lodge: gift shops, cocktail lounge, tour/activities desk, post office, outdoor amphitheater, swimming pool, bicycle rentals, and free shuttle service to various locations in the park.

Curry Village

Curry Village
Open from spring to fall and on holidays and weekends in winter. Originally designed to provide an economical lodging alternative in Yosemite Valley, Curry Village still features the least expensive accommodations. They are of four types: standard motel rooms with bath ($109 plus tax in season), cabins with bath ($87 plus tax in season), cabins without bath ($80 plus tax in season), and canvas tent cabins without bath ($64 plus tax in season). Special value-season rates (both weekend and mid-week) are available between November 1 and March 15. All cabins without bath utilize communal bathrooms.

Curry Village is cooler in summer than other valley locations and is known for its informality. Nearby attractions are Happy Isles, the campgrounds, and the riding stables.

Other amenities include gift shops, showers, a mountaineering shop, a climbing school, swimming pool, an outdoor amphitheater, tour/activities desk, free shuttle service to various locations in the park, and bicycle and raft rentals, plus an ice rink in winter.

The Ahwahnee

Ansel Adams called The Ahwahnee "one of the world's distinctive resort hotels." Open year-round, this grand and imposing hotel is definitely at the luxury end of the Yosemite lodging spectrum. Besides its regular rooms in the main building, The Ahwahnee features several cottages on the grounds. Rooms and cottages all have bathrooms and rent for $371 plus tax per night. Parlor rooms are $447 plus tax per night.

The hotel's Great Lounge is a study in high style (afternoon tea offers a relaxing respite), and the dining room (see page 37) is without parallel as an elegant setting for a meal. Located below the Royal Arches, The Ahwahnee offers fine views of Glacier Point and the valley's south wall.

Other guest services available at The Ahwahnee are gift shops, a cocktail lounge, and a swimming pool for guests of the hotel only.

Housekeeping Camp

The experience at Housekeeping Camp is somewhere between camping out and staying in a rustic cabin. Guests are provided a developed "campsite" that features a covered shelter, a cooking and dining area, cots, a table, and a fire ring. You must bring your own linen (or sleeping bags) and cookware. Call it luxury camping, if you prefer, which differs from staying in a Curry Village tent cabin because you are able to prepare your own meals. Each housekeeping unit rents for $64 plus tax (plus $5 per each person over 4), and the camp is open from spring through fall only. Housekeeping Camp is located near the public campgrounds, across from LeConte Lodge, and adjacent to the Merced River.

The camp offers public showers, a store, and a laundromat.

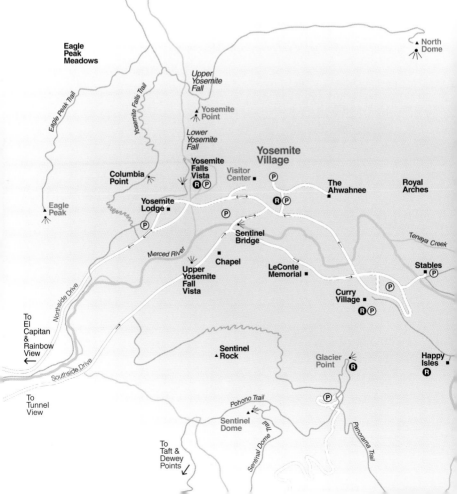

The Ten Best Views from Above

I can see for miles and miles.
— Galen Clark

Glacier Point: Not only does the point provide an overwhelming panorama, but it's accessible by car (for better or for worse). The commanding views of Yosemite's high country, Half Dome, Yosemite, Vernal and Nevada Falls, and the valley below are unequaled.

North Dome: This promontory allows the best view there is of Half Dome and Tenaya Canyon. Located on the north rim, it can be reached only by foot either from Yosemite Valley (via the Yosemite Falls or Snow Creek trails) or from the Tioga Road via the Porcupine Creek trailhead near Porcupine Flat Campground. All routes are very strenuous. See page 33.

Eagle Peak: This lookout is actually the highest rock of the Three Brothers formation. About three miles by trail from the top of Yosemite Falls, the peak offers impressive views of the entire Yosemite region, the Sierra foothills, and the Coast Range far beyond. See page 33.

Sentinel Dome: Lacking Glacier Point's glimpses of Yosemite Valley, this dome is almost a thousand feet higher. An unobscured, 360-degree vista presents itself to hikers who make the one-mile walk from the Glacier Point Road. Particularly spectacular under a full moon.

Tunnel View: While only part way up the southwestern rim of the valley, this viewpoint just below the Wawona Tunnel on the Wawona Road is a Yosemite classic. More film is used at this location than anywhere else in the park, and for good reason. El Capitan, Bridalveil Fall, and Half Dome couldn't be more photogenic.

Half Dome: The only drawback of a perch here is that the view doesn't include Half Dome! Something seems missing from the landscape when you're sitting on this enormous rock that has come to symbolize Yosemite more than any other landmark. The eight-and-a half-mile hike from Happy Isles is quite difficult, though hundreds of people a day undertake it each summer. See page 33.

Yosemite Point: About three-quarters of a mile to the east of the top of Yosemite Falls, the point is famous for its proximity to the Lost Arrow Spire, a remarkable free-standing shaft of granite. The view to the south rim is one of the best. See page 33.

Dewey Point: The series of viewpoints along the Pohono Trail on the south rim of Yosemite Valley is special. Dewey Point can be reached over the McGurk Meadow trail that heads north from the Glacier Point Road near Bridalveil Creek Campground. Both Dewey and Crocker (a half-mile to the west) Points allow unusual perspectives on El Capitan and Bridalveil Fall.

Rainbow View: This location is about a mile and a half up the rockslides trail that crosses the base of El Capitan. While the hike is a rough one over boulders, from the viewpoint roughly opposite the east end of the Wawona Tunnel one is sometimes treated to rainbow displays in Bridalveil Fall during mid-afternoons in summer.

Taft Point and the Fissures: Also on the Pohono Trail, these spots are accessed from the same trailhead on the Glacier Point Road that heads to Sentinel Dome. An easy walk leads to Taft Point with its view of the Cathedral Rocks and Spires and the north rim, and to the Fissures which are deep clefts in the rock which drop hundreds of feet towards Yosemite Valley. Check out the echo here.

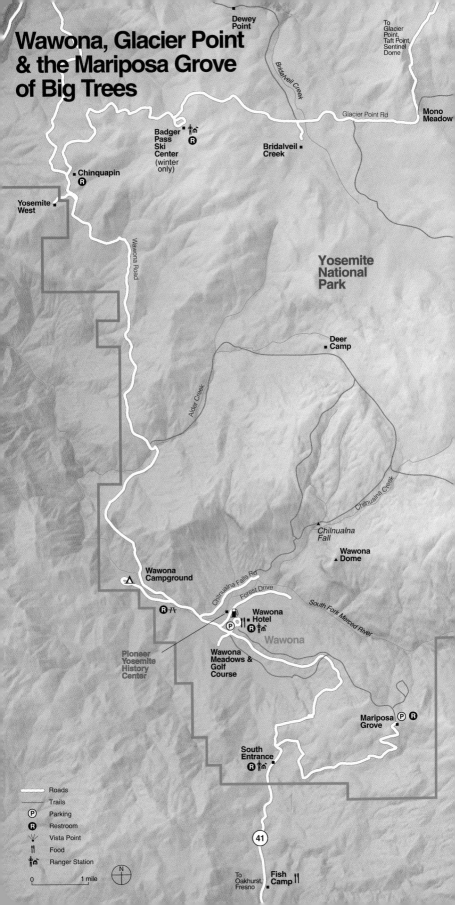

Wawona, Glacier Point & the Mariposa Grove of Big Trees

Dewey Point

To Glacier Point, Taft Point, Sentinel Dome

Bridalveil Creek

Glacier Point Rd

Mono Meadow

Badger Pass Ski Center (winter only)

Bridalveil Creek

Chinquapin

Yosemite West

Wawona Road

Yosemite National Park

Deer Camp

Alder Creek

Chilnualna Creek

Chilnualna Fall

Wawona Dome

Wawona Campground

Chilnualna Falls Rd

Forest Drive

South Fork Merced River

Wawona Hotel

Wawona

Pioneer Yosemite History Center

Wawona Meadows & Golf Course

Mariposa Grove

South Entrance

Roads

Trails

Ⓟ Parking

Ⓡ Restroom

Vista Point

Food

Ranger Station

0   1 mile

N

41

To Oakhurst, Fresno

Fish Camp

South of Yosemite Valley

To the south of Yosemite Valley lies a part of the park that is less busy and noticeably more quiet. Known as the "Wawona District," the south end includes historic Wawona, the world famous Mariposa Grove with its giant sequoias, and the road corridor that leads to Glacier Point. All of these locations are reached primarily by private automobile via the Wawona Road, as only limited, seasonal shuttle and commercial bus service is available.

Mt Clark

Illilouette Creek

Ottoway Lakes

Ostrander Ski Hut

Ostrander Lake

BUENA VISTA CREST

Buena Vista Peak

Crescent Lake

Johnson Lake

Buck Camp

To Chain Lakes

South Fork Merced River

Star Lakes

Mt Raymond

Sierra National Forest

Iron Mountain

Wawona

Wawona Meadows themselves might be called the Sleepy Hollow of the West. It is the most peaceful place that I know in America, and comes near being the most idyllic spot I have seen anywhere.
— Joseph Smeaton Chase

Wawona is a historic community nestled on a beautiful meadow near the South Fork of the Merced River about 25 miles south of Yosemite Valley. The area was settled very early in the park's history and became a stopover point on the stagecoach route to the park. Galen Clark, a significant figure in Yosemite's past (see page 107), built Clark's Station there, and that cabin later grew to become the Wawona Hotel we know today.

To the east of the main road on both sides of the river, a large number of private cabins and homes have been developed. This area, known as Section 35, was held privately for many years before it became part of Yosemite National Park. Known as an "inholding," the tract is still largely privately owned, although the National Park Service has purchased several homes and lots. Many of the residences are available as summer rentals (see the "Lodging" section on page 53).

If you need information, directions, or help, there is an information station in Wawona. To find it, turn off the Wawona Road into the Wawona Hotel grounds. The station is located within the Hill's Studio building that is to the left of the fountain as you face the main hotel section. If there's not parking available, park near the store (just past the gas station) and follow signs up the hill to Hill's Studio. The phone number at the Wawona information station is 375-1416.

The Wawona Shuttle Bus

During the summer (as funds permit), a free shuttle bus operates in the Wawona area. Generally, the system runs from Memorial Day to Labor Day on a daily basis with stops at the Wawona Campground, the Wawona Store, South Entrance, and the Mariposa Grove of Big Trees. Check the *Yosemite Today* for details, hours, and exact schedules.

Further Reading

Map & Guide to Wawona and the Mariposa Grove by Steven P. Medley. San Francisco, Rufus Graphics, 1997.

Q: Name the three U.S. Presidents who have stayed at the Wawona Hotel.

A: James Garfield, Ulysses S. Grant, and Rutherford Hayes.

The Wawona Hotel viewed from the golf course

Best Bets South of Yosemite Valley

The walk to Wawona Point. Quiet, little-visited, and offering a remarkable view, Wawona Point is the perfect destination for an excursion in the Mariposa Grove. See page 49.

The outdoor barbecue at the Wawona Hotel. Enjoy a delicious meal on the lawn under the pine trees at this fine old hotel. Red-checked table cloths in the wilds. See page 44.

The slopes at Badger Pass. Every winter, Badger Pass is transformed into a hot bed of skiing and snowboarding activity. Both downhill and cross-country opportunities abound. See page 20.

Stage coach rides at the Pioneer History Center. Hold on to your hat on this horse-drawn stage as it makes a short loop to the Wawona Hotel. See page 44.

The view from Glacier Point. From the railing at Glacier Point, you are lord (or lady) of all the Yosemite you survey. The view is unforgettable. See page 39.

A round at the Wawona Golf Course. Play nine holes at this exceptionally scenic course or just take a walk once it has closed for the day. See page 44.

Ostrander Ski Hut in winter. A nine-mile ski from Badger Pass south of the Glacier Point Road, the hut offers shelter and warmth to wilderness skiers. See page 21.

The Mariposa Grove of Big Trees. No one comes away unimpressed by these towering sequoias. A world class attraction. See page 48.

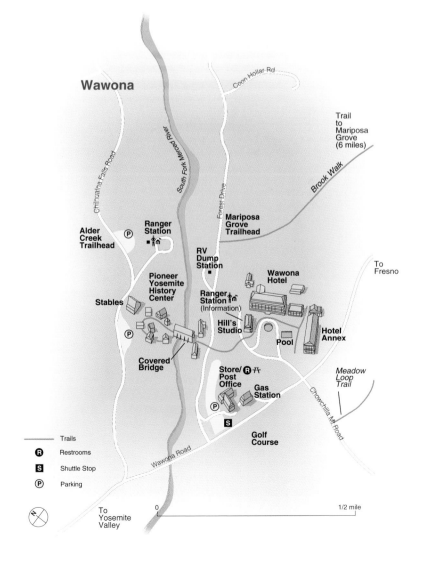

Activities at Wawona

Step Back in Time

The Pioneer Yosemite History Center is a collection of historic buildings that have been moved from other locations within the park. The center is located near the Wawona Hotel, just east of the gas station (prominent signs will direct you there). During the summer, park rangers and volunteers dress in period costume and populate the buildings. Each building represents a different time period in Yosemite's history, and the rangers engage in "living history," which means that they portray actual Yosemite residents from bygone days. You can try, but you'll have a hard time getting these old-timers to break character.

Interesting attractions are an exhibit of old horse-drawn vehicles, the covered bridge over the South Fork built in the 1870s that has been restored, and a blacksmith who actually practices his craft while you watch.

For a small fee, you can take a short ride on a horse-drawn stage to get a feel for what early trips to Yosemite must have been like. During parts of the year, regular ranger-led tours of the History Center are scheduled (consult the *Yosemite Today* for details).

The covered bridge, Wawona

Hit the Links

A conspicuous adjunct to the Wawona Hotel is its beautifully laid out golf course nearby. Whether you're a golfer or not, a stroll around the 9-hole circuit is both relaxing and replete with scenic vistas. (If you're a non-golfer, take your walk after the course is closed, please!)

The golf course was built in 1917 and features some of the most magnificent golfing holes anywhere. While the lay-out is not particularly long, it features lots of rough and water hazards, and is remarkably challenging. Watch out for deer grazing the fairways, particularly on the first hole.

Golf clubs and carts are available for rent at the Golf Shop, and reserving a tee time is recommended (phone 375-6572).

Enjoy an Outdoor Barbecue

Every Saturday night during the summer, an old-fashioned barbecue is served outdoors on the expansive lawn of the Wawona Hotel. Red-checked table cloths sport steaks, hamburgers, corn on the cob, western beans, and more. Check at the hotel desk for times and prices.

Get in the Swim

The South Fork of the Merced River as it runs through Wawona is dotted with swimming holes and beaches. Find a spot to put down your towel and cool off, or try your hand at fishing (see page 29 for general fishing information and regulations). Guests at the Wawona Hotel may use the small swimming pool on the grounds.

Horse Around a Little

A riding stable is maintained during the summer by DNC Parks & Resorts at Yosemite at the back side of the Pioneer Yosemite History Center on Chilnualna Falls Road (about 1/4 mile off the main highway). Guided horseback rides of varying lengths are offered. Stop by the stable for details or call 375-6502.

Hike Some More

A variety of hiking awaits you at Wawona, from easy and flat to steep and strenuous. The hiking rules outlined for Yosemite Valley (see page 30) apply in Wawona as well. Give yourself plenty of time and don't undertake more than you're capable of.

Range with a Ranger

Throughout the year, a program of ranger naturalist activities is presented free of charge to the public in the Wawona area. That program is expanded greatly during the summer. Check the *Yosemite Today* for listings and times.

Tour an Artist's Studio

The Thomas Hill Studio on the grounds of the Wawona Hotel is usually open in summer as an information station and often features exhibits of the work of Hill along with other art programs. Thomas Hill used the building as a summer studio from 1885 until his death in 1908, and his fine landscape paintings of Yosemite and elsewhere have gained critical acclaim. Check the *Yosemite Today* for hours of operation.

Q: What was the toll to use the Mariposa trail through Wawona to Yosemite Valley during the 1850s?

A: Man and horse each way, $2.00; pack mule or horse, each way, $2.00; foot man, $1.00.

Three Hikes from Wawona

The Meadow Loop. This pleasant walk begins directly across the Wawona Road from the entry road to the Wawona Hotel. Follow the gravel road about 50 yards across the golf course just into the trees and take the road that leads off to the left. This almost entirely flat route skirts the edge of the Wawona Meadow, then circles back, crosses the Wawona Road, and finishes up behind the Wawona Hotel. Approximately 3 miles total, the loop should take an hour and a half or less. The hike is easy, leisurely, and picturesque.

Chilnualna Fall. The trail to this delightful cascade is fairly strenuous, gaining almost 2,500 feet in approximately 4 miles. Start from the trailhead, which is located 1.7 miles east of the main road on Chilnaulna Falls Road. There's parking space on the right for 25 to 30 cars. If the road turns to dirt, you've gone too far. The route is an enjoyable one through manzanita, deer brush, and bear clover, and finally meets with Chilnualna Creek. The fall, instead of leaping and free-falling from some precipice, drops through a narrow chasm in a furious rush. Allow 6 to 8 hours for this 8-mile round trip. Carry lots of water in the summer when temperatures can be extreme.

The Mariposa Grove Museum

Mariposa Big Trees. Starting behind the Wawona Hotel is a long, uphill climb to the Mariposa Grove of giant sequoias. Passing through forest most of the way, the trail offers excellent views of the Wawona Basin and Wawona Dome as it nears the big trees. The trail ends at the Mariposa Grove Museum in the Upper Grove near the fallen Tunnel Tree. Because the elevation gain is 3,000 feet in 6.5 miles, this hike is for the well-conditioned only. For an easier alternative, take the summer shuttle bus to the Mariposa Grove and hike back to Wawona. Figure on spending 8 to 10 hours making the up-and-back trip of 13 miles.

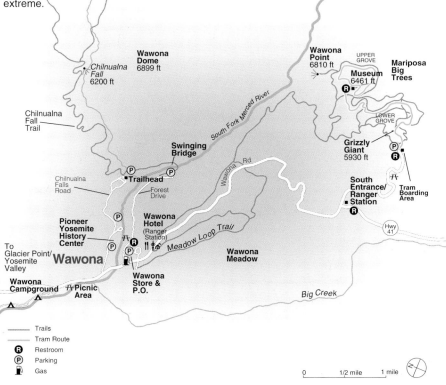

Activities Along the Glacier Point Road

The road to Glacier Point leaves the Wawona Road at Chinquapin junction, 9 miles south of Yosemite Valley and 12 miles north of Wawona. The route winds 16 miles to the amazing promontory at Glacier Point, passing a variety of sites and attractions along the way, most of them short hikes from the road.

The route is open to the point during the three milder seasons, but in winter the road is plowed of snow only as far as Badger Pass, the downhill ski area 6 miles from Chinquapin. Be sure to carry tire chains in your car if you're heading out the Glacier Point Road during the "off-season."

Stare at the Stars

During the summer, ranger naturalists maintain a large telescope at Glacier Point and schedule regular evening programs that make use of it. There aren't many better spots for gazing at the heavens, plus you'll have the help of knowledgeable astronomers. Check the *Yosemite Today* for dates and times and for the schedule of other ranger-led programs and hikes at Glacier Point and Bridalveil Creek Campground.

Hike, Hike, and More Hike

Given its proximity to the south rim of Yosemite Valley, the Glacier Point Road provides a series of natural trailheads for spectacular day hikes. And thanks to DNC, you have the option of walking all the way down to Yosemite Valley without needing to retrieve your car. During the summer, a "Hiker's Bus" is operated from the valley to spots along the road all the way to Glacier Point. Call 372-1240 for information.

Strap on Some Skis or a Board

Badger Pass, six miles from Chinquapin out the Glacier Point Road, is the center of Yosemite ski activity during the winter. Not only are there ski lifts, ski and snowboard rentals, and a lodge, but cross-country skiers are encouraged to utilize the groomed tracks out the Glacier Point Road (see page 20).

Q: Which landmark near the Glacier Point Road offers a 360 degree view of the park and is the location of a much-photographed Jeffrey pine?

A: Sentinel Dome (the Jeffrey pine died several years ago).

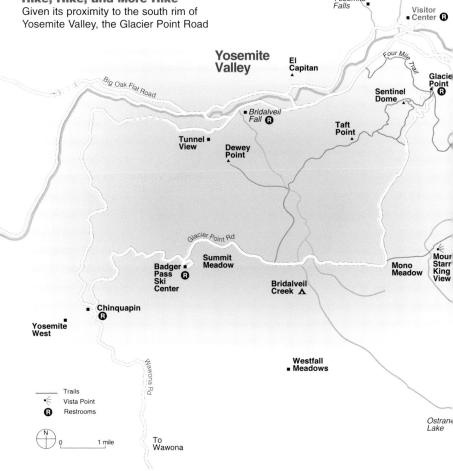

Five Great Hikes from the Glacier Point Road

Dewey Point. One of the most interesting perspectives on Bridalveil Fall and El Capitan is afforded by this commanding viewpoint (7,385 feet). The trail starts two-tenths of a mile west of (before you get to) Bridalveil Creek Campground on the Glacier Point Road. While there are trail markers on both sides of the road, you will want to head north. The route meanders through forest and meadows, intersects with the Pohono Trail (go left), then extends to the valley rim. While there's not much elevation gain or loss, the round trip is approximately 7 miles. Allow 4 to 6 hours for the out-and-back hike.

Mono Meadow and Mt. Starr King View. From the parking area 2.5 miles beyond Bridalveil Creek Campground on the Glacier Point Road, this trail leads to the east and to a terrific spot for admiring Mt. Starr King, Half Dome, and Clouds Rest. You will drop steeply for a half-mile to Mono Meadow, then continue a mile further to an unmarked clearing where the view is an obvious one. Stop short of the switchbacks down to Illilouette Creek. The three mile round trip (a little strenuous on the way back) should take about 3 hours.

Taft Point. Unusual rock formations and an overhanging lookout point reward hikers on this short route. Start at the parking lot on the Glacier Point Road about six miles past Bridalveil Creek Campground (it's on the left, when you first catch a glimpse of Sentinel Dome). The trail is mostly flat and slightly downhill to the Fissures (wide gaps in the rock hundreds of feet deep) and Taft Point, where you'll be standing on the only solid object between you and the valley floor leagues below you. Be thorough in your investigation of the point, which offers up several unique views. It's just over two miles round-trip; give yourself two hours.

Sentinel Dome. The trailheads for this hike and the one to Taft Point are the same. Park on the left about six miles past Bridalveil Creek Campground on the Glacier Point Road (it's about at the spot where you first eye Sentinel Dome). The 1.1 mile hike to the top is a small price to pay for the 360 degree panorama of Yosemite's unbelievable landscape. You'll be at 8,122 feet (more than 4,000 feet above the Yosemite Valley floor); it's a good idea to have a park map for landmark identification. Try this easy hike at sunrise or sunset or on the night of a full moon. The round trip requires about two hours.

Half
Dome ▲

Vernal
Fall ■

orama Cliffs Trail

Mount
Starr
King
▲

Illilouette Creek

View from Glacier Point

Yosemite Valley. Take the "Hiker's Bus" (see page 46) or have someone shuttle you to Glacier Point and walk back down to Yosemite Valley over the Four-Mile Trail (4.8 miles) or via the Panorama Cliffs Trail by way of Nevada and Vernal Falls (8.5 miles). The Four-Mile Trail begins to the left of Glacier Point and follows a series of switchbacks down the face of the south valley wall. It terminates about a mile west of Yosemite Village on Southside Drive. The Panorama Trail begins to the right of the point, heading south to the top of Illilouette Fall, then back north and east to Nevada Fall (see page 333). There are two routes to the valley (either the "horse trail" or the Mist Trail, see page 33) and trail's end at Happy Isles (shuttle bus stop # 16). Figure on 3 to 4 hours to hike the Four-MileTrail and allow 6 to 8 hours to travel the Panorama Cliffs route.

Activities at the Mariposa Grove of Big Trees

Located at the southernmost end of Yosemite, the Mariposa Grove is the largest stand of giant sequoias *(sequoiadendron giganteum)* in the park. These ancient monarchs are inadequately described with numbers, but how else do you do it? Some of the trees are 2,000 years old, others reach almost 300 feet into the sky, still others are more than 50 feet around. A typical mature sequoia weighs in at over 2 million pounds.

Notable trees here are the Grizzly Giant, almost three millennia old and 96 feet around at its base, the fallen Wawona Tunnel Tree, through which a hole was cut that allowed thousands of automobiles and other vehicles to pass through and be photographed before the tree toppled in 1969, and many others. There are over 500 sequoias here in two related groves, the Upper and Lower.

You may drive to the edge of the Lower Grove, where hiking trails lead out among the trees. The road to the Mariposa Grove is oftentimes closed in winter when the snow is deep.

Ride the Open-Air Tram
If you'd rather not hike into the Mariposa Grove, buy a ticket and board one of the open-air trams that will carry you out among these magnificent giants. In summer 2004, the fee was $11 for adults and $5.50 for children 4-12 (children under 4 ride free, and there is a discount for seniors 62 or over). The trams cover a 5-mile loop and leave about every 20 minutes.

The first tram departs at 9 a.m., and the last tram leaves at 4 p.m. The trip takes slightly less than an hour, but you'd be well-advised to get off the tram and spend a little time walking in the grove. The trams do not operate during the winter.

There are three regular stopping points along the route: the Grizzly Giant, the fallen Tunnel Tree, and the Mariposa Grove Museum. On your way back down, consider getting off at the Grizzly Giant and walking the eight-tenths of a mile back to the parking lot. It's all downhill and remarkably relaxing.

Be sure to visit the Mariposa Grove Museum where there are exhibits about

the giant sequoias and books and other literature for sale. Restrooms are located there, too.

Mariposa Grove of Big Trees

Walk in the Sequoia Forest
All trails into the Mariposa Grove of Big Trees are uphill. From the trailhead at the far end of the parking lot, there is an elevation gain of about 1,000 feet to the Upper Grove where the fallen Wawona Tunnel Tree is located, a distance of 2.5 miles. The going is gradual, however (22 children from Mrs. McDaniel's second grade class made it up and back!), and walking is the best way to appreciate the majesty and serenity of these stately trees. Be sure to check park hiking regulations before you take off (see page 30).

Notable Sequoias of the Mariposa Grove

Name	Diameter at Base	Height
Grizzly Giant	31 ft	209 ft.
California Tree	23 ft.	232 ft.
Faithful Couple	40 ft.	248 ft.
Columbia Tree	28 ft.	290 ft.
Clothespin Tree	22 ft.	266 ft.
General Grant Tree	29 ft.	290 ft.
Washington Tree	30 ft.	238 ft.
Lafayette Tree	31 ft.	267 ft.

Three Easier Hikes in the Mariposa Grove

The Grizzly Giant. From the parking lot it's only eight-tenths of a mile and a 400-foot climb to the Grizzly Giant, one of the largest trees in the Mariposa Grove. Along the way you'll encounter lots of other sequoias and get a personal perspective on the mammoth scale of these trees. Allow from 1 to 2 hours for the round trip.

Wawona Point. This excellent lookout on the entire Wawona basin is a short walk from the top of the Mariposa Grove. Get off the tram at the fallen Wawona Tunnel Tree and walk back to the north to the Galen Clark Tree, where the old road to Wawona Point branches off. Ask your tram driver for directions if you need them. The walk is only one-half mile, and you'll be able to see back to the Wawona Meadow and golf course, with views to the east of Wawona Dome. The round trip walk should take you less than an hour.

Mariposa Grove Parking Lot from the Wawona Tunnel Tree. It's always easier to hike downhill, so why not ride the tram to the top of the grove and get off at the Wawona Tunnel Tree? The hike down through the Upper and Lower Groves leads past the Mariposa Grove Museum and just about every significant sequoia in the area. It's only two and a half miles back to your car, and shouldn't require more than two to three hours to complete.

Q: When did the Wawona Tunnel Tree fall over and why?

A: In 1969 as a result of the tunnel cut through its base, enormous impact to its root system from cars and people, and a heavy snow load.

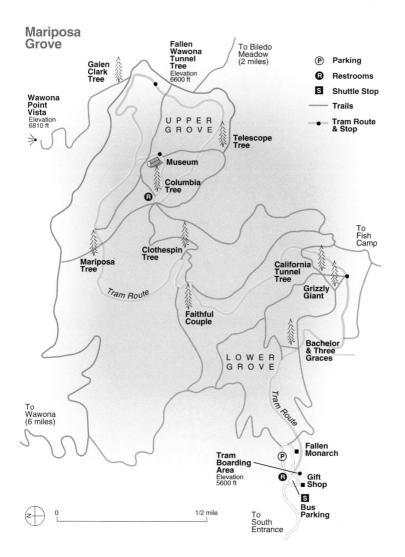

Mariposa Grove

Wawona History

The Wawona area was first settled by Yosemite pioneer Galen Clark (see page 107), who homesteaded 160 acres there in 1856. Though probably not deliberately, Clark selected a spot that was almost exactly half-way between Mariposa and Yosemite on the route that developed for visitors. Clark seized the opportunity and built a rustic lodging house for travelers that was known as "Clark's Station."

Though Galen Clark recognized the potential of his way station, he proved unable to fulfill it. His management of Clark's Station was poor, and he invested considerable funds in completing the Mariposa stage road to Wawona. Financial pressure forced Clark to take on Edwin Moore as a full partner in 1869, and all signs indicated that Clark's fortunes had turned.

But over the next five years, ill-advised investments in mining ventures and land purchases along with the completion of the Coulterville and Big Oak Flat Roads into Yosemite Valley spelled doom for Clark and Moore. They were forced to sell their lodging house and related properties to the Washburn Brothers in December of 1874.

U.S. Cavalry at Camp A. E. Wood

The Washburns were an enterprising group of three brothers, who came to California from Putney, Vermont. They undertook a number of ventures in the Mariposa area before purchasing Clark and Moore's. It was their New England background that led them to cover the existing bridge over the South Fork of the Merced; it's the same bridge that leads into the Pioneer Yosemite History Center today.

Contemporaneously with their acquisition of the Wawona traveler's stop, the Washburns began work on the completion of the stage road from Wawona to Yosemite Valley. In this way they hoped to compete with the other routes. They finished the job in June of 1875, and their plan began to meet with success.

In 1876 the Washburns put up the long white structure that stands just to the right of the main hotel building today. And when that building burnt in 1878, the two-story structure that is still used as the main hotel building went up the next year. Until 1882

the inn was known as Big Tree Station when it officially became the Wawona Hotel. Additional buildings went up over the years.

Congress established Yosemite National Park in 1890 and directed that the U.S. Army should be responsible for managing it. Because Yosemite Valley and the Mariposa Grove of Big Trees had already been granted to the State of California and were not part of the national park, locating park headquarters became a challenge. As Wawona was one of the few developed areas within the new park (though not part of it) and for other reasons, it was selected as the summer command for Army personnel.

Known as Camp A. E. Wood, headquarters were located on the site of the present Wawona Campground. For sixteen summers cavalry troops from the San Francisco area occupied the camp and engaged in caring for the new park. Among their many activities were exploring and mapping, trail building, fish planting, and enforcing anti-hunting and trespassing regulations. When the state grant and Yosemite National Park were combined in 1906, Camp A. E. Wood was abandoned and Army headquarters were relocated to Yosemite Valley.

Over the years, changes to Wawona generally came with changes in transportation. Following the completion of the Wawona Stage Road, the Washburn's stage company flourished and visitation grew. In 1914, automobiles first navigated the road between Wawona and Yosemite Valley. The Wawona Hotel management recognized that the automobile travelers preferred more recreational opportunities, and proceeded to build a dance floor, soda fountain, croquet court, swimming tank, and golf course over the next fifteen years.

As the Wawona Hotel prospered, so did the community in Section 35 (the number assigned to the plot of land in its legal description) that included several homesteads and housed workers for the hotel and for other support services. When most of the Wawona region was added to Yosemite National Park in 1932, only Section 35 remained in private ownership. It is this area of Wawona where many private homes, cabins, and visitor rentals are located today (see page 42).

Further Reading

Yosemite's Historic Wawona by Shirley Sargent. Yosemite: Flying Spur Press, 1979.

Galen Clark: Yosemite Guardian by Shirley Sargent. Yosemite: Flying Spur Press, 1981.

Camping South of Yosemite Valley

*T*he campgrounds in this part of the park tend to be less busy and crowded, though in summer they are full practically every night. Advance reservations are required for the Wawona Campground between May and September, but Bridalveil Creek Campground is operated on a first-come, first-served basis when it is open between July and September. In campgrounds where no reservations are allowed, visitors will benefit by arriving as early as possible to arrange for a camping spot, because check out time is 12 noon.

Camping regulations are roughly the same as those for Yosemite Valley (see page 34). Pets are allowed in designated sites in both the Wawona and Bridalveil Creek Campgrounds, and there are no showers in any park campground. The camping limit is 14 days in summer south of Yosemite Valley, and a 30-day limit applies the rest of the year. A total of 30 camping days per calendar year is permitted in the park.

Wawona Campground: This popular spot is located at the 4,000-foot elevation on the banks of the South Fork of the Merced River approximately 25 miles south of Yosemite Valley on the Wawona Road. The daily fee for the 93 sites here is $18, and the campground is open all year (prepare for extreme cold and snow in the winter, however).

Bridalveil Creek Campground: You'll find this group of 110 campsites nine miles out the Glacier Point Road from Chinquapin (about 25 miles from Yosemite Valley). Open from June or July through September, the campground is much cooler than Yosemite Valley or Wawona given its location at over 7,000 feet. The nightly fee is $12.

Group Campgrounds: Sections of the Wawona and Bridalveil Creek Campgrounds have been set aside for use by organized groups only. Reservations can be made through NPRS (see page 12); groups of between 13 and 30 people are allowed in each campsite, where only tent camping is allowed. Pets are not permitted in group sites. There are also horse camps at both the Wawona and Bridalveil Creek Campgrounds. For more information, call (209) 375-9520.

Q: How fast can a backpacker carrying a pack that's one-fifth his or her body weight expect to travel?

A: About two horizontal miles per hour. Add one hour for each 1,000 feet of elevation gain.

South Fork of the Merced River, Wawona

Gas, Food & Lodging South of Yosemite Valley

Gas

The only gas station in this part of the park is located in Wawona, just north of the Wawona Hotel on the main highway. The self-serve facility accepts major credit cards (it's a Chevron station), it's open year-round, and tire chains are available.

For towing services, call 372-8320 at any time of the day or night.

Food: Restaurants

For other than snacks and simple sandwiches, there's only one choice in the south end of the park—the Wawona Hotel Dining Room. If you're near the South Entrance, there are a number of good restaurants along Highway 41 between Fish Camp and Oakhurst, all within a half hour's drive. The following places to eat are open seasonally only; be sure to check the *Yosemite Today* for dates and hours of operation.

Wawona Hotel Dining Room:

Serving breakfast, lunch, and dinner from Easter week through October and on weekends and holidays in the fall and winter. Located in the Victorian main building at the hotel, the dining room has retained a historic feel. The sepiatone photographs by Carleton Watkins and the sequoia cone light fixtures are perfect touches in this charming, multi-windowed facility. The food is fine, the wine list good, and there's a full bar. In summer, there are a few tables on the porch for outdoor dining, and they also serve in the bar area. There's cocktail service on the verandas and in the lobby lounge. Lunch and Sunday brunch are served buffet style. On Saturdays in summer try the outdoor barbeque on the hotel lawn. Reservations are advised for groups of ten or more; call 375-1425 for more information. Moderate to expensive.

Wawona Golf Shop Snack Stand:

Open spring through fall inside the golf shop at the Wawona Hotel. Cold drinks, hot dogs, pre-packaged sandwiches, and other simple items are available if you're in a hurry or need a light meal or snack. Moderate prices.

Glacier Point Snack Stand: A summer and fall operation (10 a.m. to 5 p.m.) with a limited menu. Primarily providing munchies for visitors to Glacier Point. Moderate prices.

Food: Groceries

Campers, vacation home renters, and park visitors have the following two choices for groceries in the park south of Yosemite Valley. Check the *Yosemite Today* for operating hours, or call the indicated numbers.

Wawona Grocery Store: Located adjacent to the gas station just off the main highway and north of the Wawona Hotel. Phone 375-6574.

The Pine Tree Market: You'll find this store in the heart of the community of North Wawona. It's less than a mile east of the main highway on Chilnualna Falls Road. Phone 375-6343.

Inexpensive: dinner for one adult might cost up to $10. Moderate: dinner for one adult might cost from $10 to $20. Expensive: dinner for one adult might cost over $20.

Wawona Hotel

Lodging

Wawona is the only area in the park where the majority of the lodging facilities is not operated by DNC, the park's main concessioner. The Wawona Hotel is part of the DNC system, and to reserve a room there, you should follow the steps which are detailed on page 11. You must contact each of the other lodging providers directly to reserve from them.

The quoted rates for the following listed lodging facilities are approximate only, based on double occupancy, vary with the seasons, and are subject to change.

Wawona Dome

Wawona Hotel

Open from Easter week through October and on weekends and holidays through Christmas. This is the oldest resort hotel in California; the structure to the right of the main hotel building was built in 1879. The whitewashing, wide porches, well-kept grounds, and an old-fashioned bathing tank (we call them swimming pools now) all suggest another era in Yosemite's history. It's a remarkably peaceful and relaxing setting, but guests should keep in mind that some of the rooms are 100 years old. Rooms with bath rent for $166 in season ($149 in the off season), while rooms that utilize a community bath-room are priced at $113 in season ($92 in the off season). Rates are scheduled to increase in March, 2002.

Besides a dining room (described at left), the Wawona Hotel incorporates a golf course with pro shop and snack bar, tennis courts, and a cocktail lounge.

The Redwoods Guest Cottages

Open year around. This is a collection of about 130 privately-owned vacation homes and cabins available for rental on a daily or weekly basis. Located in the privately-held section of Wawona near the South Fork of the Merced (approximately 1 mile out Chilnualna Falls Road), the rentals vary in size from 1 to 6 bedrooms. Rates vary with the seasons and range from $143 to $643 plus tax per night for units that all have kitchens and fireplaces; there is a two-night minimum. For information call 375-6666, or write to PO Box 2085, Wawona, CA 95389. The web site address is www.redwoodsguestcottages.com.

Yosemite West Condominiums

Open year around. Just beyond the park boundary, but accessible only via park roads, these rental units are situated about half-way between Yosemite Valley and Wawona. Their proximity (8 miles) to the Badger Pass ski area has made the condos a favorite of winter visitors. But cool summer temperatures and the short drive to Yosemite Valley (about half an hour) make Yosemite West popular other parts of the year, as well. Rates start from $99 to $129 (peak season), depending on unit size. Information can be had by calling 1-888-296-7364, a toll-free number. The web site address is www.yosemitewest.com.

Yosemite West Lodging

Open all year. This company handles the rental of a collection of studios, apartments, townhouses, duplexes, individual cottages, vacation homes, and mountain homes, all in the Yosemite West development. These are located just west of the park less than one mile south of Chinquapin off the Wawona Road (only 15 miles from Yosemite Valley and 8 miles from Badger Pass). All units have televisions and kitchens. Rates range all the way from $85 to $345 per night, and discounts are available for longer stays. For reservations, etc., call (559) 642-2211, or write PO Box 36, Yosemite National Park, CA 95389. The web site address is also www.yosemitewest.com.

Q: What was the source of ice for the Wawona Hotel each winter from 1886 until 1934?

A: Ice was cut by hand at Stella Lake, which was created by damming and diverting the South Fork of the Merced River about a quarter mile upstream from the hotel. The lake froze to a depth of about six inches.

Q: What was the first public lodging house developed in the Wawona area?

A: Clark's Station, built by Galen Clark in 1856.

Hetch Hetchy, The Tioga Road & Tuloumne Meadows

Lake Vernon

Laurel Lake

Lake Eleanor

Tueeulala Falls ▲ Wapama Falls

Hetch Hetchy Reservoir

O'Shaughnessy Dam

Tuolumne River

△ **ℝ**

Hetch Hetchy Backpackers Campground
(Wilderness Permit - Required)

Hetch Hetchy Entrance
ℝ 🚻 ■

Hetch Hetchy Road

Harden Lake

To San Francisco

Evergreen Road

Bald Mountain
▲

White Wolf ■ △ ‖

Lukens Lake

Tioga Road

To San Francisco

Big Oak Flat Entrance

120

🚻 ■

Hodgdon Meadow
△

Tuolumne Grove ■

South Fork Tuolumne River

Yosemite Creek
△

road closed late fall - late spring

Merced Grove ■

Crane Flat △ ⛽

Tamarack Flat △

Yosemite Valley

Yosemite Falls ■

El Capitan ■

Big Oak Flat Road

Bridalveil Fall ■

Sentinel Dome ■

El Portal Rd

El Portal ■

Arch Rock Entrance
🚻 ■

Glacier Point Rd

To Merced

Merced River

140

To Fresno

Wawona Road

Roads
Trails
Ⓟ Parking
ℝ Restroom
↯ Vista Point
‖ Food

N

0   5 miles

North of Yosemite Valley

Over two-thirds of Yosemite National Park lie north of Yosemite Valley, much of that region being wilderness. The area is made accessible primarily by the Tioga Road, the only trans-Sierra crossing between Walker Pass in Kern County and Sonora Pass to the north. Spectacular high country terrain, brilliant blue lakes, and astounding granite peaks are reached via this route that leads through Tuolumne Meadows, the largest subalpine meadows in the Sierra Nevada. The road crests the range at 9,945-foot Tioga Pass.

Spiller Lake

Soldier Lake

McCabe Lakes

Roosevelt Lake

Mt Conness

Young Lakes

Glen Aulin High Sierra Camp

Tuolumne Meadows

Dog Lake

To Tioga Pass Entrance/ Lee Vining

Lembert Dome

Facilities along Tioga Road available summer only

Tuolumne Meadows Visitor Center

Tuolumne Meadows Campground

Lyell Fork

Grant Lakes

May Lake

Mt Hoffmann

Cathedral Peak

Elizabeth Lake

Tioga Road

120

Tenaya Lake

Porcupine Flat

Olmsted Point

Evelyn Lake

North Dome

Valley Visitor Center

Clouds Rest

Sunrise High Sierra Camp

Vogelsang High Sierra Camp

Bernice Lake

Tenaya Creek

Half Dome

Vernal Fall

Nevada Fall

Merced River

Merced Lake

Glacier Point

Washburn Lake

Illilouette Creek

Mt Clark

Ottoway Lakes

Edna Lake

Ostrander Lake

Best Bets North of Yosemite Valley

Mt. Hoffmann

The summit of Mount Hoffmann. This is the geographic center of Yosemite, with extraordinary views in every direction. See page 61.

The beach at Tenaya Lake. Unbelievably fine on a warm day, a terrific spot anytime. Enjoy a picnic, swim, or simply take a nap. See page 61.

The turnout at Olmsted Point. To see the vast expanse of glacier-carved granite is worth the stop alone. But there's much more, and marmots, too. See page 61.

The hike to the Merced Grove. Flat, easy, and quiet. Plus this is Yosemite's most remote and least-visited sequoia grove. See page 58.

A meal on the porch of White Wolf Lodge. Lunch and dinner are likely times to sit outside at this quaint spot and watch the White Wolf meadow do whatever meadows do. See page 70.

A visit to Hetch Hetchy Reservoir. This body of water occupies a valley which has been characterized as Yosemite Valley's little brother. It has retained much of its beauty, and offers great hiking. See page 57.

The trail into Lyell Canyon. The Lyell Fork of the Tuolumne River is one of the park's most peaceful and inspiring settings. The trail leads to and along its course. See page 67.

The High Sierra Camps. Whether you hike the full loop or visit just one of these five backcountry encampments, the experience will be unique. Stop for a mindblowing meal, or pamper yourself by staying over. See page 64.

Tenaya Lake

White Wolf Lodge

Hetch Hetchy

Whatever Hetch Hetchy means—grass, seeds, trees—it is no longer relevant; everything is covered by water.
—Peter Browning

The Hetch Hetchy area of Yosemite, as it is called in this book, includes the portion of the park that is found on its western boundary along the Big Oak Flat Road north of Crane Flat, and along the Evergreen and Hetch Hetchy Roads (see map). The region is best known for its two groves of giant sequoias (the Merced and Tuolumne Groves), and for the Hetch Hetchy Reservoir on the Tuolumne River.

National Park Service headquarters here are located at the Big Oak Flat Entrance where there is a ranger station (phone 379-1899), a NPRS reservation office, a small visitor center and book sales area, a wilderness permit and reservation office, and public restrooms. If you've entered the park from the west over Highway 120, this is a good place to orient yourself; Yosemite Valley is still a 25-mile drive. There's also an entrance station at Mather, about eight miles from the Big Oak Flat Entrance on the way to Hetch Hetchy.

The route to Hetch Hetchy Reservoir is over Evergreen Road, located just north of the park off Highway 120. If traveling from the south, leave the park through the Big Oak Flat Entrance. The right turn onto Evergreen Road is one mile past the entrance station. From the north, turn left on Evergreen Road one mile before you reach the park on Highway 120. Hetch Hetchy is 16 miles out this road which becomes Hetch Hetchy Road at Camp Mather (bear right at the intersection).

Hetch Hetchy: The Dam

Many wonder how a facility like Hetch Hetchy Reservoir came to be sited within the boundaries of a national park. It wasn't easy or quick, but when the political struggle ended, the scenic qualities of Hetch Hetchy Valley had been "submerged" for the good of the citizens of San Francisco and their thirsts.

The city had been looking for a dependable mountain water supply, when shortly after the turn of the century, Hetch Hetchy was proposed as the perfect location for a dam site. The notion of a reservoir in Yosemite was not universally attractive, however, and John Muir, the Sierra Club, and others opposed the project and fought it for many years. On several occasions the Hetch Hetchy project was outright rejected. But the city fathers were persistent, and in 1913, the Raker Bill granting San Francisco permission to dam the Tuolumne River at Hetch Hetchy was passed in Congress.

The loss of the fight to save Hetch Hetchy was devastating for Muir. Many believe that his efforts severely drained him, left him exhausted, and contributed greatly to his death about a year later. On the other hand, the reservoir proved an enormous success for the City of San Francisco, which still relies on the project for the bulk of its water and power.

The dam was constructed beginning in 1919 and took about four years to finish. The resulting reservoir is 8 miles long, has a capacity of 117,400,000 gallons, and covers 1,861 surface acres (3 square miles). The dam itself is 410 feet high, 910 feet long, and 308 feet thick at its base that tapers to 24 feet at the top. One interesting fact about the Hetch Hetchy project is that the water in system pipelines flows all the way to San Francisco by gravity!

Activities in the Hetch Hetchy Area

The Hetch Hetchy area is best enjoyed in spring and fall, though it's remarkably mild some winters. The habitat of this region is more foothill than montane, and there are lots of gray pines, manzanita, and lower-elevation wildflowers. Stop at the Big Oak Flat Visitor Center (at the park entrance) to get oriented.

Merced Grove

Walk Through the Merced Grove

Yosemite's quietest stand of sequoias is the Merced Grove, accessible only on foot. It's a two-mile hike into the grove from the trailhead on the Big Oak Flat Road. Located 3.5 miles north of Crane Flat or 4.5 miles south of the Big Oak Flat Entrance, the trailhead is marked by a post labeled B-10 and a road sign.

Follow the dirt road for about a mile, then take the left fork down into the grove. This is the park's smallest group of sequoias (about twenty trees), which was probably first discovered in 1833 by the Joseph Reddeford Walker party. Look for the old Merced Grove cabin that was built as a ranger/entrance station, but is no longer used for that purpose.

These sequoias convey the silent majesty that has characterized them for thousands of years. The absence of motorized vehicles and the solitude are a real treat for hikers to the Merced Grove. Allow 3 hours for the 4-mile round trip.

Hike the Tuolumne Grove

The former route of the Big Oak Flat Road leads downhill from Crane Flat into the Tuolumne Grove of Big Trees, a cluster of about forty-five sequoias. Open to traffic until 1993, this dirt road drops steeply for about a mile where the first big trees can be spotted. An interesting attraction in the grove is the "Dead Giant" tree, a lifeless but still-standing partial tree that has been driven through by thousands of wagons and automobiles since it was tunneled out in 1878 (but no longer). There's also a self-guiding nature trail in the grove, a half-mile in length, that should take about 30 minutes to walk.

The trail to the Tuolumne Grove takes off near Crane Flat. From the intersection of the Big Oak Flat Road and the Tioga Road, take the Tioga Road one mile to the east (towards Tuolumne Meadows). Turn left at road marker O-1 and park in the lot there. The route is obvious; the round trip of about two miles is relatively easy, though it's all uphill on the way back.

Let Them Entertain You

In summer, National Park Service rangers conduct a variety of walks, programs, and campfires. Activities are centered at Crane Flat Campground and in the Tuolumne Grove, though other locales are used from time to time. Check the *Yosemite Today* under White Wolf/Crane Flat/Big Oak Flat Visitor Activities for specific details and times.

Lookout for Fire

The Crane Flat Fire Lookout is staffed during the summer when the National Park Service watches the surrounding forests for signs of smoke. Visitors are welcome at the facility that can be reached over a primitive road leading off to the east less than one mile north of Crane Flat on the Big Oak Flat Road. The uphill trip to the lookout is one and a half miles.

Be sure to watch for fire and other emergency vehicles along the way. The view from the lookout is a special one with glimpses of the park in every direction. It's also fun to ski here in winter.

Q: Who was the first Euro-American to visit Hetch Hetchy Valley?

A: Joseph Screech in 1850.

Q: When and where were the Big Trees discovered by Euro-Americans?

A: It is probable that the Joseph Reddeford Walker party discovered the giant sequoias in either the Tuolumne or Merced Grove in 1833.

Hikers at Hetch Hetchy

Hike Hetch Hetchy

*T*hough the once beautiful valley of Hetch Hetchy might be lost forever, many of its scenic wonders can still be appreciated. Tueeulala and Wapama Falls still thunder from the north rim, Kolana Rock still rises imposingly from the reservoir's southern shore, and a remarkable variety of plant and animal life still populates the perimeter of the place.

While Hetch Hetchy is at roughly the same elevation as Yosemite Valley, it's a much warmer spot. In the middle of summer it's downright hot. Perfect months for day hiking here are October through May. You'd be amazed at how warm the north side of the reservoir can be in the dead of winter.

The main trail at Hetch Hetchy leads over the top of the dam, through a tunnel, and along the north edge. The undulating route passes Tueeulala Falls, Wapama Falls (about two miles from the dam), and eventually Rancheria Falls (six and a half miles out). Hike as far or as little as you like. In spring, be prepared at Wapama Falls for high water and heavy mist that sometimes force closure of the trail. Retrace your steps back to the dam.

Fishing is allowed in Hetch Hetchy Reservoir, but swimming and boating are not.

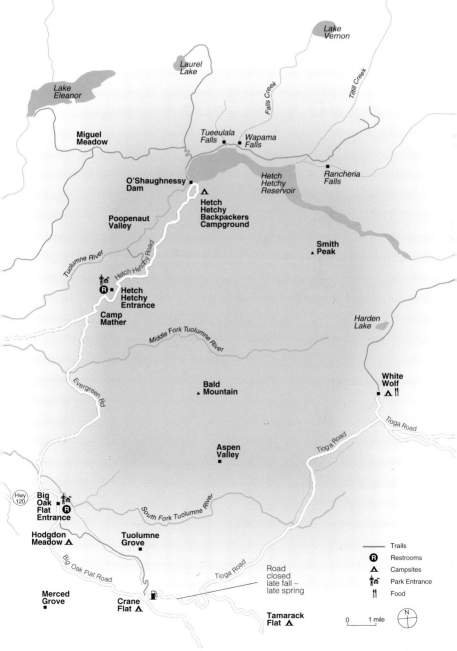

The Tioga Road

Originally a wagon road across Tioga Pass built by the Great Consolidated Silver Company in 1883, the Tioga Road literally splits Yosemite National Park in two. Improved to its present condition and alignment in 1961, the road opened up some of Yosemite's most stunning country and allowed access to previously remote high country destinations. Today the Tioga Road corridor is rife with scenic and recreational opportunities.

For the purposes of this book, the Tioga Road refers to the area of the park along the Tioga Road (which extends from Crane Flat to Tioga Pass some 46 miles east) except for the Tuolumne Meadows area.

Lembert Dome

Visitors should be aware that the Tioga Road is not open all year. Heavy snows require the National Park Service to close the road (from November until May or June, usually), though snow is a possibility in any season; be sure to carry tire chains when driving this route in spring or fall. Typically mild summer weather attracts both recreationists and travelers headed east in large numbers.

There are plenty of options for fun along the road, with multiple campgrounds, trailheads, lakes, streams, and scenic views to choose from. If you need information or assistance, there is a ranger station at Tioga Pass Entrance (as well as the Tuolumne Meadows Ranger Station described on page 65.)

The "Controversial" Tioga Road

In the 1950s, when the National Park Service made the decision to re-align and complete the "modern" Tioga Road, discussions ensued over whether the 21-mile central portion of the new road should be routed via the "high" or "scenic" line or along the general route of the old Tioga Road. Studies involving discussions with various cooperating groups, the Secretary of the Interior, and other interested parties became fraught with controversy.

Objections arose specifically from certain conservationists and the Bureau of Public Roads after it had been decided to proceed on the "high" route selected and approved years earlier. Changes to meet improved safety standards met resistance from such people as David Brower, executive secretary of the Sierra Club, and nature photographer Ansel Adams.

The Bureau of Public Roads believed that a wider road with wider shoulders was necessary so that cars could pull off the road in emergencies. The Park Service, meanwhile, wanted a safe width of road with narrow shoulders and with turnouts only where the terrain permitted to avoid scars from cuts and fills as much as possible plus higher costs.

The matter was finally settled in favor of the two-foot shoulders with few turnouts except for one section where the shoulder had to be widened to provide the necessary stability. Conservationists, however, continued to object to the blasting and gouging methods used and the resulting scars on the face of the glacially-polished granite surfaces at Olmsted Point.

Actual construction of the new central section began in 1957, and it officially opened in June 1961. Sections of the old Tioga Road were retained, such as that leaving the new road just east of the White Wolf intersection and winding down to the Yosemite Creek Campground; another short section climbs over Snow Flat to the May Lake Trail junction. Shorter sections still serve campgrounds along the old road.

from *Yosemite Historic Resource Study, Vol. 2,* by Linda Wedel Green.

Tioga Pass Entrance

Activities Along the Tioga Road

*W*hether you're just passing through or making a leisurely trip along the Tioga Road, your experience will be a better one if you know where you are and what you're seeing. A valuable aid in this regard is *The Yosemite Road Guide*, an informative book keyed to markers along the way. It's available at stores throughout the park or from the Yosemite Association. How else will you know about "Smoky Jack," the old Tioga Road, Siesta Lake, and the ghost forest?

Get in Over Your Head
The best place to have a swim along the Tioga Road is Tenaya Lake. The park's largest lake, it is located approximately 8 miles west of Tuolumne Meadows, or 30 miles east of Crane Flat. The inviting sandy beach on the eastern shore is a good bet, but be prepared for some cold water. Tenaya Lake is also a favorite of sailboarders, windsurfers, and sailboaters (check with a ranger for regulations). Use the dressing and bathrooms in the parking lot just east of the lake. If it's too cold to swim, have a picnic in this dramatic setting.

Be Programmed
During summer, ranger-naturalists offer free programs for visitors at various locations along theTioga Road. Likely meeting places are White Wolf and Tenaya Lake, but check the *Yosemite Today* for details.

Hike All You Like
The territory stretching out to the north and south of the Tioga Road is a veritable hiker's wonderland. From numerous points along the route trails lead into a landscape unequalled anywhere in the world. Hikes range from easy to very strenuous, and become more difficult with the increased elevation. Follow basic hiking precautions (see page 30), and in this high country setting, stay hydrated by drinking lots of liquids. The most common hiking-related ailment is altitude sickness; consider spending a day or so getting acclimatized before starting to hike.

For those hikers who travel to Yosemite without a car or who wish to leave their vehicle in Yosemite Valley, there's a hiker's bus operated by the DNC, traversing the length of the Tioga Road each day from July 1 to Labor Day. You can arrange to get off at trailheads along the way. The bus returns to Yosemite Valley every afternoon. For information, call 372-1240.

Wet A Line
Fishing can be amazingly good along the Tioga Road. Spots like Lukens Lake, Harden Lake, Tenaya Lake, and May Lake (all described in this chapter) are home to many feisty, if somewhat small, trout. Yosemite Creek and the Dana Fork of the Tuolumne River can also yield up a fish or two. The general park fishing regulations apply (see page 29); check with a park ranger for any special rules.

Check Out Half Dome's Back Side
One of Yosemite's most remarkable scenic overlooks is found at Olmsted Point, and it shouldn't be missed. This major pullout is located at road marker T-24 (2.5 miles west of Tenaya Lake and just slightly more than 2 miles east of the May Lake turnoff). Here the enormity of the granite walls of Tenaya Canyon is revealed, and unique views of Half Dome and Clouds Rest are allowed. To the east, the landscape includes Tenaya Lake and the many domes and peaks of the Tuolumne Meadows region. A short nature trail leads down from the point, and watch for fat and sassy marmots in the rocks (but please don't feed them).

Q: How did Gin Flat (about 5 miles west of Crane Flat on the Tioga Road) get its name?

A: Reportedly, a barrel of gin fell off a freight wagon, unmissed by the driver. It was found by a bunch of cowboys, sheepherders, and roadworkers who got "ginned up."

Seven Sensational Hikes from the Tioga Road

1. Harden Lake. This is a relatively flat three-mile walk to an attractive little lake that offers picnicking, swimming, and fishing. Start in front of the White Wolf Campground and head north on what was the original Tioga Road. You can follow the road all the way to the lake or catch a trail branching off about a mile from it. If you take the road, bear to the right when it forks. There's a good view of the Tuolumne River Canyon from the far side of the lake. The round trip is about 6 miles and should take about 4 hours.

2. Lukens Lake. It's mostly uphill, but this hike of less than a mile terminates at a lovely spot amid meadow flowers and grasses. Being so close to the road, Lukens Lake is perfect for families with young (but not infant) children. Take your fishing poles and a picnic lunch. The trailhead is found 1.8 miles to the east of the White Wolf intersection; it's also 3 miles west of the spot where the Tioga Road crosses Yosemite Creek. Head north up the hill, then drop down to the lake. This easy hike is not quite two miles up and back, and requires about an hour to cover (a little longer for families!). You can also reach Lukens Lake from White Wolf. Ask for trail directions at the lodge.

3. Yosemite Creek to Yosemite Valley. From the point on the Tioga Road where it crosses Yosemite Creek (about 5 miles east of the White Wolf turn-off), a trail leads southward over level and downhill terrain all the way to Yosemite Valley. Because it's a one-way hike of 13 miles, you'll have to arrange for a ride to the trail-head, plan on shuttling back to pick up your car on the Tioga Road, or use the "Hiker's Bus" mentioned on page 61. The trail follows Yosemite Creek down to Yosemite Creek Campground and eventually to the top of Yosemite Falls. Check out the spectacular view from the top (see page 33) before descending the final 3.5 miles to the Yosemite Valley floor. This is a strenuous hike for the physically fit. Allow at least 8 hours for this demanding but satisfying trip.

4. North Dome. This difficult hike to one of the best views of Yosemite Valley (see page 39) takes off to the south of the Tioga Road at road marker T-19, about 5 miles beyond the point where the road crosses Yosemite Creek (this is also 2 miles west of the May Lake turn-off and just east of Porcupine Flat Campground). The walk is mostly downhill and flat for 4.2 miles to the dome. Watch for the erratic boulders left by the glaciers here, and check out the impressive view of Half Dome directly across from you. Because the return trip to the Tioga Road is mostly uphill, this should be considered a strenuous hike. Give yourself 6 to 8 hours for the 8.5-mile trip out and back.

5. May Lake and Mount Hoffmann. For those who like to get in the middle of things, Mount Hoffmann is the geographic center of Yosemite National Park. It offers superb views of the park's high country from its 10,850-foot summit. The trail up

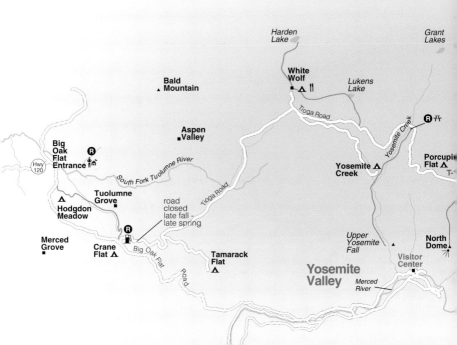

the mountain leads past idyllic May Lake, a beautiful spot and location of one of the High Sierra Camps (see page 64). Start your hike at the May Lake parking area. Turn north off the Tioga Road about 5 miles west of Tenaya Lake at road marker T-21 and drive 2 miles to the parking lot. It's an easy mile and a quarter to May Lake, and if you're adventurous, the 2 miles beyond to the top of Mount Hoffmann are considerably more strenuous but worth the effort (you will gain about 1,500 feet in elevation). Plan on 2 hours round trip for May Lake, and add 3 to 4 more for the ascent of Mount Hoffmann.

6. Mono Pass. This high elevation hike is a comparatively easy four miles with an elevation gain of only 1,000 feet. The route, however, begins at nearly 10,000 feet and almost reaches the 11,000-foot level (prepare for some heavy breathing). The trail begins 1.5 miles west of Tioga Pass at road marker T-37, and heads south along an old Indian trading route. At Mono Pass itself are the remains of several mining buildings and cabins that were used during the late 1800s. Views of Mt. Gibbs and Mt. Dana are extremely fine. This 8-mile round trip should take from 4 to 6 hours depending upon your level of conditioning.

7. Gaylor Lakes. Here's another trip for high-elevation freaks who love to huff and puff. The trail ascends steeply to the north from just a few feet west of the Tioga Pass Entrance Station that's 9,945 feet high. Middle Gaylor Lake is about a mile from the trailhead, but it's no easy climb. Follow the inflowing creek to Upper Gaylor Lake and the remnants of a stone shelter at the Great Sierra Mine 300 yards to its north. This is truly an alpine environment with few trees, strong winds, and often harsh weather. Allow 3 hours for this moderately difficult hike of 4 miles round trip.

Q: How should a hiker behave in a lightning storm?

A: Stay clear of open expanses of water, keep off open areas of rock and out of meadows, and stay away from prominent landmarks like lone, isolated trees. Seek shelter from the storm; a dense stand of trees of roughly the same height works well.

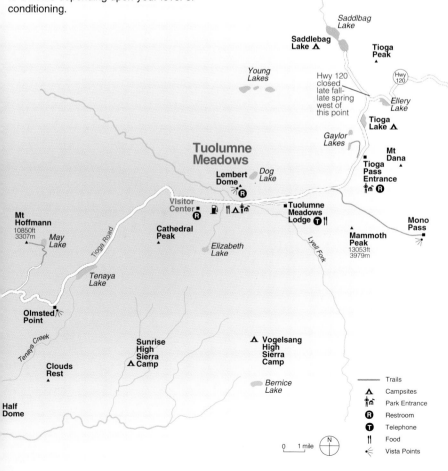

The High Sierra Camps

Six rustic colonies of tents in the park's loftier regions constitute an institution unique to Yosemite called the High Sierra Camps. Placed in a roughly circular pattern about one day's hike apart, the camps allow visitors to enjoy high-elevation backcountry in semi-luxury. The semi-luxury aspect of the operation includes wholesome hot meals prepared by the camp staff, and regulation beds with mattresses, pillows, woolen blankets, and comforters that await weary travelers. There are even showers!

The idea for the camps was that of Washington B. Lewis, Yosemite's first NPS Superintendent. He wanted hikers to enjoy Yosemite's high country free from the "irksome" load of equipment and food normally needed for a backcountry trip. In 1924, the first camps were installed at a number of locations (several of which already had unofficial "High Sierra Camps"), and the system was underway.

Over the years there have been as many as eight different camp sites (including Little Yosemite Valley, Boothe Lake, Lyell Canyon, and Tenaya Lake), but the present configuration of six has been set for quite some time. The camps are open for a very short season (roughly late June or early July to Labor Day), and are operated by DNC Parks & Resorts at Yosemite.

The only camp accessible by road is the Tuolumne Lodge (see page 71). Many people use it as a starting or ending point for the High Sierra Loop Trip. In a clockwise direction from Tuolumne Meadows the other camps are Vogelsang, Merced Lake, Sunrise, May Lake, and Glen Aulin. The distance between each averages nine miles.

Guests at the High Sierra Camps are accommodated in dormitory-style tents that sleep either four or six. The communal bathhouses offer running water, showers, and toilets. Guests must provide their own sheets or sleep-sacks and towels. Hearty breakfasts and dinners are served daily, and bag lunches can be ordered. Sizes of the camps vary, but about 35 people on average can be lodged.

A favorite of many High Sierra Camp users is the 7-day guided loop trip (there's also a 4-day option). A maximum of 14 persons is accompanied by a naturalist who provides ongoing interpretation of the geology and natural history of Yosemite's wilderness. Campfire programs occur nightly, and members of the group develop a real spirit of camaraderie and friendship.

The High Sierra Camps are tremendously popular. Despite the price ($109 plus tax per night, including breakfast and dinner), the camps are fully booked almost every night of the summer. Reservations are essential and are handled by lottery. Applications are accepted each year between October 15 and December 15 for the lottery that is held in mid-December. Applicants will be notified by February 28 as to their standing in the lottery. For an application or more information write to the High Sierra Desk, Yosemite Reservations, 5410 E. Home Avenue, Fresno, CA 93727, or call (559) 253-5674, Monday through Friday from 8 a.m. to 5 p.m., and Saturday and Sunday from 8 a.m. to 3 p.m. (Pacific time).

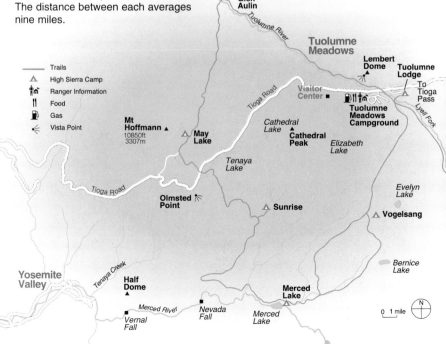

⛺	Trails
⛺	High Sierra Camp
⛺	Ranger Information
🍴	Food
⛽	Gas
⚲	Vista Point

Tuolumne Meadows

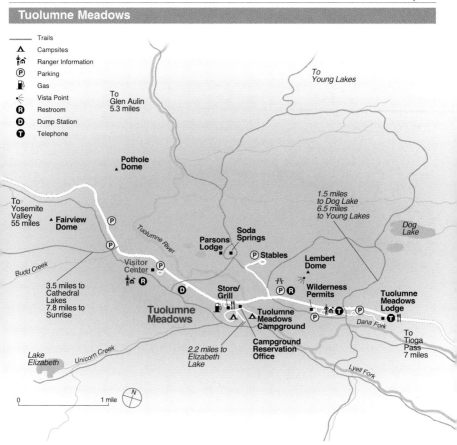

Trails
▲ Campsites
🏕 Ranger Information
Ⓟ Parking
⛽ Gas
🔭 Vista Point
Ⓡ Restroom
Ⓓ Dump Station
Ⓣ Telephone

To
Young Lakes

To
Glen Aulin
5.3 miles

Pothole
▲ Dome

To
Yosemite
Valley
55 miles

▲ Fairview
Dome

1.5 miles
to Dog Lake
6.5 miles
to Young Lakes

Dog
Lake

Tuolumne River

Parsons
Lodge

Soda
Springs

Ⓟ Stables

Lembert
Dome

Tuolumne
Meadows
Lodge

Budd Creek

Visitor
Center

3.5 miles to
Cathedral
Lakes
7.8 miles to
Sunrise

Wilderness
Permits

Store/
Grill

Tuolumne
Meadows

Tuolumne
Meadows
Campground

Dana Fork

To
Tioga
Pass
7 miles

Lake
Elizabeth

Unicorn Creek

2.2 miles to
Elizabeth
Lake

Campground
Reservation
Office

Lyell Fork

0   1 mile   N

The Tuolumne Meadow is a beautiful grassy plain of great extent, thickly enameled with flowers, and surrounded with the most magnificent scenery.
—Joseph LeConte

This stunningly picturesque region sits 8,600 feet up in the transparent sky of Yosemite's high country. Contained in a basin about 2.5 miles long, the meadow system may be the largest in the Sierra Nevada at the subalpine level. Tuolumne Meadows is only 55 miles by road from Yosemite Valley, but it's a world apart.

Called by some the "hub" or "heart" of the high country, Tuolumne is a seasonal phenomenon. It is closed by snow to visitation the bulk of year, but when summer comes, the action is impressive. Hikers flock here, both daytrippers and backpackers. Rock climbers who winter in Yosemite Valley adopt Tuolumne as a summer home. And visitors in their cars arrive to revel in the awesome beauty of the place, and to enjoy a less-developed part of the park.

There's plenty to gawk at, too. The Tuolumne River winds its way sinuously through the meadows, while an array of unusually-shaped domes rings the area. There are smooth-bottomed canyons and jagged peaks; delicate lakes and odorous springs. These multiple elements combine to create a landscape both wonderful and inspiring.

During the summer months there's a ranger station at Tuolumne Meadows operated by the National Park Service along with a small visitor's center. The ranger station is just off the Tioga Road along the road to Tuolumne Lodge, and the Visitor's Center is located near the half-way point of the meadows about a quarter-mile west of the gas station and store. For information or assistance call 372-0263 or 372-4450.

Further Reading
Map & Guide to Tuolumne Meadows by Steven P. Medley. San Francisco, Rufus Graphics, 1994.

Q: What is the final destination of the water in the Tuolumne River that flows through Tuolumne Meadows?

A: The water is captured at Hetch Hetchy Reservoir and eventually ends up in the domestic water system of the City of San Francisco.

Activities at Tuolumne

Climb A Dome

Scrambling to the top of one of Tuolumne's granite domes can be fun and exhilarating. It can also be hazardous to your health. Try one of the easier rocks like Lembert Dome (see the hiking section below) or Pothole Dome (adjacent to the road at the west end of the meadows). Wear proper footgear and don't go up anything you aren't sure you can get down. Climbing lessons are available from the Mountaineering School in Tuolumne Meadows. Call 372-8435 for details and rates.

Tuolumne River

Take A Swim

Because they are fed by the melting snow nearby, most of the streams, rivers, and lakes of the Tuolumne region are freezing cold. As the summer progresses, they warm a bit, but swimming is not for the weak of heart. There are plenty of good swimming holes along the Tuolumne River as it passes the campground, and on its fork that winds lazily through Lyell Canyon (see hiking section below). Lake swimmers should try Tenaya Lake, 7 miles to the west, Elizabeth Lake, or Dog Lake (both described below).

Become A Sheepwatcher

In 1986, a small herd of California big-horn sheep was transplanted to the park in the Tioga Pass region. The sheep are native to the park, but were eliminated here by disease and hunting before 1900. The introduced herd leads a precarious existence (the sheep are particularly vulnerable to mountain lion predation), but is still considered viable. In recent summers there have been reports of bighorn sightings in the Tuolumne Meadows area. Check at the Visitor's Center for information and directions.

Get Tall in the Saddle

Riding horses are stabled at Tuolumne Meadows by DNC Parks & Resorts at Yosemite each summer. As is the case throughout the park, they offer 2-hour, half-day, and all-day guided horseback

trips. The Tuolumne stables can be found by turning north at road marker T-32 that is just east of the bridge over the Tuolumne River near the campground. For more information and rates call (209) 372-8427.

Walk a Mile in Your Shoes

The hiking around Tuolumne Meadows is first-rate. The trails are varied, the scenery is exceptional, and the weather usually cooperative (but plan for afternoon thunder showers, particularly in August). A person staying at Tuolumne could take a different hike every day for a week and still not exhaust the possibilities. Be sure to follow normal hiking precautions (see page 30) and drink extra liquids to keep yourself hydrated at this high elevation

A free shuttle bus runs between Tuolumne Meadows and Tenaya Lake from July 1 through Labor Day. It's a good way to get to your trailhead and leave your car behind. Hours are posted on signs at bus stops throughout the Tuolumne area.

The DNC hiker's bus visits Tuolumne Meadows from Yosemite Valley once a day from July 1 through Labor Day. You can be dropped off at the trailhead of your choice and, if the timing works out, be picked up later. Call 372-1240 for information.

Get Centered

To learn more about the Tuolumne Meadows region, visit the Visitor Center located south of the Tioga Road a short ways west of the gas station. There you'll find exhibits, knowledgeable rangers, and books and maps for sale. It's also a good place to find out about free ranger walks and programs that will be happening during your visit (or check the *Yosemite Guide*).

Children can participate in the Junior Ranger program by purchasing a copy of the *Junior Ranger Handbook* (ages 3-6) or the *Little Cub Handbook* (for children ages 7-13) at the center. By completing the activities outlined in the handbook, they can earn certificates and badges while they learn lots more about the park. The handbooks are available at all park visitors centers; in Tuolumne call 372-0263.

Do Something Fishy

Tuolumne Meadows is loaded with family fishing opportunities. These high country trout seem to be plentiful, but they're small. Your kids will find the many rivers and lakes great places to practice their angling techniques. The Tuolumne River and its tributaries are excellent spots as are Dog Lake, Cathedral Lake, and Elizabeth Lake. Follow park fishing regulations (see page 29), and check at the Visitor Center for information or tips.

Seven Scintillating Hikes from Tuolumne Meadows

1. Cathedral Lakes. Taking off from the obvious parking at the west end of Tuolumne Meadows (south of the road), this trail is fairly strenuous gaining about 1,000 feet in under 4 miles. The route is uphill, then relatively flat for a ways, then uphill again before it drops into the Cathedral Lakes basin. Take the right fork in the trail to reach the lower lake, which is the larger of the two. Have a swim, enjoy your lunch, or fish a little. Your view of Cathedral Peak will be outstanding. The round-trip hike is less than 8 miles and should take 4 to 6 hours.

2. Elizabeth Lake. It's steep and short and well worth the effort. Elizabeth Lake is a lovely spot nestled against the base of Unicorn Peak, one of Tuolumne's most recognizable landmarks.The 2.3-mile hike begins at the back side of the Tuolumne Meadows Campground (across from the bathrooms for the group camp area), and is just about all uphill. Given the elevation (you climb to about 9,500 feet), it's a good idea to take your time and adopt a slow but steady pace. The water's cold though swimmable, and fishing is fair. Allow from 3 to 4 hours for the 4.6-mile round trip.

3. Soda Springs. Here's an easy hike that's flat and perfect for all ages. The trail leads out into the middle of Tuolumne Meadows and to a naturally-carbonated mineral spring that bubbles mysteriously to the surface. Park in the parking lot just north of the Tioga Road at marker T-32 (just east of the bridge over the Tuolumne River near the campground) adjacent to Lembert Dome. Follow the gravel road to the north, and where the road turns right, walk around the brown metal gate and continue north (if you get to the stables, you're off route). Besides the Soda Springs, you'll find Parsons Memorial Lodge (erected in 1914 by the Sierra Club), and the McCauley Cabin, a pioneer structure now used as a ranger residence. You'll be close to the river and will get a sense of the size and beauty of the meadows. You can make the mile and a half walk in an hour.

Iron deposits in Soda Springs

4. Glen Aulin. To reach this aspen-studded hollow along the Tuolumne River, walk to Soda Springs (see above for hike information). The trail continues past the springs and roughly follows the river 7 miles to a small campground and one of the High Sierra Camps (see page 64). The trail is slightly downhill all the way, and that makes the hike back a stiff one. Watch for Tuolumne Falls and White Cascade as you hike. If you are truly a glutton for hiking punishment, Waterwheel Falls, one of the park's most unusual cascades, is 3.3 miles past Glen Aulin. The trip to Glen Aulin is a very strenuous hike of 14 miles round trip; give yourself 8 to 10 hours to accomplish it.

5. Lembert Dome. From the top of this oddly-shaped dome the 360 degree panorama of Tuolumne Meadows is fantastic. Start at the parking lot at the rock's base located north of the Tioga Road at marker T-32 (just east of the Tuolumne River). Don't start climbing here; follow the nature trail and leave it at marker #2. Climb steeply up the back side of the formation and make your way to the top.Take your topo map for identification of the many peaks and mountains around you. Up and back is about 2.8 miles and should require 3 hours of your time.

6. Dog Lake. This easily-reached spot is perfect for swimming, but not for fishing (there is a rumor that no fish remain within it). The hardest part of this 1.5-mile hike is finding the trailhead. At the east end of Tuolumne Meadows turn onto the road that leads to Tuolumne Lodge. Past the ranger station but before the lodge is a parking lot on the left side of the road. Park there, walk up the bank to the north, carefully cross the main road, and begin your hike up the hill. The trail is steep at first, then levels off for a final gradual ascent to the lake. A moderate hike of three miles round trip; allow 4 hours.

7. Lyell Canyon. This hike is the proverbial stroll in the park. The trail follows the Lyell Fork of the Tuolumne River out through the beautiful canyon that shares its name.The trailhead is at the west end of the parking lot for Tuolumne Lodge, but park your car in the lot for the Dog Lake hike. Head into the forest, cross a bridge, then continue to double bridges over the Lyell Fork (less than half a mile out). You leave the river at this point and follow the trail, which rejoins the river further out the canyon. It's a flat hike the entire route and as scenic and relaxing as they come. Lyell Canyon is about 8 miles long and you can hike as little or as much as you like. Give yourself enough time to make it back before dark.

Camping North of Yosemite Valley

The campgrounds at the north end of the park can be characterized as more primitive and remote and generally smaller (with Tuolumne Meadows Campground being the main exception). Only a few are handled by the NPRS reservation system, and the balance are operated on a first-come, first-served basis. For campgrounds that can't be reserved in advance, remember that the check out time is noon; this is the perfect hour to attempt to secure a site.

Pets are not allowed in many campgrounds. Check the listings below to see if you can legally bring your pet, and always indicate that you'll be camping with a pet when you make your NPRS reservation. See page 12 for the specifics of dealing with NPRS and successfully arranging a campsite reservation.

There are also NPRS offices at the Big Oak Flat Entrance (where Highway 120 enters the park from the west) and in Tuolumne Meadows (at the entrance to the campground). At times campsites can be arranged at the last minute by stopping at one of these offices. Call 379-2123 for the Big Oak Flat NPRS and 372-0384 for the Tuolumne Office.

The summer camping limit is 14 days outside of Yosemite Valley, and most of the campgrounds are open only in the summer. The limit extends to 30 days the rest of the year, but you may only camp in Yosemite a total of 30 days in any one calendar year. For general park camping regulations, see page 34.

Hetch Hetchy Area Campgrounds

Crane Flat Campground: This camping area of 166 sites is situated at the 6,200-foot level where the Big Oak Flat and Tioga Roads meet. Of all the campgrounds located outside Yosemite Valley, it's the closest – only 17 miles away. The nightly fee is $18, and NPRS reservations are required. Normally open from June through September, Crane Flat is close to the Merced and Tuolumne Big Tree Groves and the Toga Road attractions. Pets are allowed.

Hodgdon Meadow Campground: Here is the first place to camp when you enter Yosemite from the west on Highway 120 (you'll be 25 miles from Yosemite Valley). All types of campers are welcome in this campground consisting of 105 sites. To reach Hodgdon Meadow, turn down the hill just south of the Big Oak Flat Entrance. It's less than a half-mile to the campground entrance. NPRS reservations are required between May and September ($18 per site); the rest of the year, it's a first-come, first-served facility ($12 per site). Pets are allowed.

Q: Where did Hodgdon Meadow get its name?

A: It's named for Jeremiah Hodgdon, a Vermont native, who homesteaded the area in 1865.

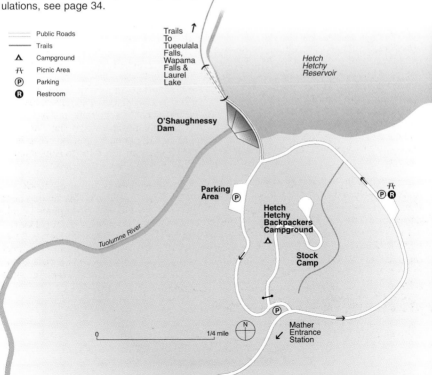

Hetch Hetchy Backpackers Campground:
This relatively new campground is exclusively for backpackers and other backcountry users (with wilderness permits) who are beginning their trips from the Hetch Hetchy trailhead. Stays are limited to one night at the beginning and end of wilderness outings. Located at Hetch Hetchy Reservoir, the campground features 19 backpacker sites (6 persons per site), 2 organized group sites (one accommodating 18 persons, the other 25), and 2 stock use sites (6 persons and 6 head of stock per site). Parking is provided near the campground, which has running water and flush toilets. No recreational vehicles, trailers, or pets are allowed. Prior arrangements should be made for the organized group and stock use sites. The fees are $5 per night for backpackers and $35 per site for the group and stock sites. Write to the Mather District Office, Star Route, Groveland, CA 95321 or call 372-0323.

Tioga Road Campgrounds

Tamarack Flat Campground: If you enjoy a more primitive camping experience (creek water that must be boiled and pit toilets), this campground fits the bill. It's located at 6,300 feet down a three-mile dirt road that takes off the Tioga Road about 4 miles east of Crane Flat (not suitable for large recreational vehicles or trailers). There are 52 campsites, the fee is $8 per night, and it's handled on a first-come, first-served basis. Usually open between June and September. No pets.

White Wolf Campground: A favorite of many high country campers, White Wolf is set on a beautiful meadow alongside a bubbling creek. Added amenities are the White Wolf Lodge with a small store and restaurant, and public showers for a fee. The 8,000-foot setting 14 miles east of Crane Flat makes for cold nights and brilliant days. There are 74 first-come, first-served sites which rent for $12 per night (not suitable for RVs over 27 feet long). The camping season here is approximately July through September. Pets are allowed.

Yosemite Creek Campground: Another primitive campground, the Yosemite Creek camping area is located 5 miles down a narrow dirt road to the south of the Tioga Road (the turnoff is less than a half-mile east of the White Wolf turn-off). Don't, repeat don't, even think about trying to take an RV or a trailer into this campground. The 75 sites utilize pit toilets and water from nearby Yosemite Creek (be sure to treat it). First-come, first-served, $8 per night, and open July through September only. Pets are allowed.

Porcupine Flat Campground: They call it a flat campground, but there are flatter campgrounds in the world. There is no running water and no flush toilets here, but Porcupine Creek wanders by and the lodgepole pines make a fine canopy. Because the roads in the campground are very bad, recreational vehicles are limited to a few campsites at the entry to the campground; there are 52 sites total. The fee is $8 per night for these first-come, first-served sites. Open usually from July through September; no pets are allowed.

Tuolumne Meadows Campgrounds

Tuolumne Meadows Campground: Here is the park's largest single campground with 304 sites. The road complex throughout the area is complicated and confusing, but once you get the hang of it, you'll love this campground. Families return here year after year for the camping, fishing, hiking, and scenery. NPRS reservations are required for half the camp sites, the balance are handled on a first-come, first-served basis. There's a store nearby, a restaurant and showers for a fee at Tuolumne Lodge, horseback riding at the stables, and fishing in the adjacent Tuolumne River. A sanitary dump station is also available. Backpackers and visitors without vehicles may take advantage of 25 walk-in sites for a fee of $5 per night, with a one night maximum stay. Regular sites rent for $18 per night, and the camp is kept open from July through September in a typical year. Pets are allowed.

Tuolumne Group Campground: Special campsites within this campground are available for organized groups by prior arrangement. Reservations should be in advance with NPRS (see page 12). Each site, for tent camping only, can accommodate no fewer than 13 and no more than 35 people. No pets are allowed. For more information, call 372-0402.

Gas, Food & Lodging North of Yosemite Valley

Gas

There are two Chevron gas stations in the north portion of Yosemite: one at Crane Flat and the other at Tuolumne Meadows. Only the Crane Flat station is open year round. If you are traveling the Tioga Road, be sure to check your gas gauge as it's a stretch of almost 40 miles where no services are provided. Major credit cards are accepted. Check the *Yosemite Today* for hours of operation. A repair garage is open all year in Yosemite Valley, and towing service can be arranged 24 hours a day by calling 372-8320.

Food: Restaurants

The north end of the park is relatively undeveloped. Visitors looking for fine restaurants and haute cuisine should try San Francisco or Los Angeles. While there are a few options for hearty meals in generally rustic facilities, you should plan on picnicking a lot and preparing your own food when you travel to Yosemite's north country. The following is a list of your choices (open only during the visitor season of June through October) should you choose to "dine out." Check the *Yosemite Today* for dates and hours of operation.

Evergreen Lodge: Not technically within the park, this old wooden lodge is 7 miles out Evergreen Road on the way to Hetch Hetchy. The simple dining room and unpretentious bar exude an unpolished charm, and at last check, the food was remarkably good. They serve dinner 7 nights a week and breakfast on weekends (lunch items are available at the small store on premises). The Evergreen Lodge is not listed in the *Yosemite Guide*, so call (209) 379-2606 for information on times of operation and to make a reservation. Their normal season is from April through October. Moderate to expensive prices.

White Wolf Lodge: With its covered porch and its low-key yet intimate dining room, the White Wolf Lodge, a whitewashed wooden structure, is an enjoyable spot to eat. Breakfast and dinner are served from a menu inside (grab a table on the porch if they're serving outdoors), and box lunches can be ordered and sandwiches and other items can be purchased from the adjacent store. There's a fine old fireplace, adequate food, and beer and wine. When you consider that the staff gets spread pretty thin with their multiple duties, the service is fine. Dinner reservations are recommended; call 372-8416. Moderate to expensive.

Tioga Pass Resort: Here's another spot that fails to qualify as a "park" establishment because it's two miles beyond the Tioga Pass Entrance on Forest Service land. But the place is a Yosemite institution and had to be included. They serve breakfast, lunch, and dinner in a room so small that many times you'll be asked to wait for long periods before you can be seated. The wait is worth it, however; try the homemade pies, delicious sandwiches, and substantial breakfasts. Get a load of the classic water spigot with rock-lined drain that's from some other era, and the wonderful curved counter. Recently they've added an outdoor coffee bar for those in quest of caffeine. For reservations, hours, or information, call (209) 372-4471. Moderate prices.

Tuolumne Lodge

Tuolumne Meadows Lodge: The lodge is one of the six High Sierra Camps in Yosemite (see page 64) and the only one accessible by automobile. The dining room is located in a canvas-sided tent-like structure that captures the feeling of roughing it in the high country. But the food will make you think you're someplace fancy. Breakfast and dinner are served from a menu family style; that is, you get seated with whomever happens to be present for mealtime when you are. It's good fun, and many fast friendships have been initiated in the lodge dining room. Beer and wine are served, and box lunches are available upon request. Dinner reservations are required and can be made by calling 372-8413. Moderate to expensive prices.

Tuolumne Meadows Grill: Located adjacent to theTuolumne store and post office, the grill is a great place for a hamburger. The service is as fast as you'll get anywhere, and they pour a big cup of coffee. Pull up a stool or stand and wolf. Fry-cooked meals are served at breakfast, lunch, and dinner (but the Lodge is preferred for breakfast if you're in no hurry). No reservations accepted (it's not that kind of place), and you can order menu items "to go." Inexpensive prices

Food: Groceries

The following outlets are basic convenience stores with limited selections. Check the *Yosemite Today* for operating hours.

Crane Flat Gas Station: Located in the main building of the Chevron station at the intersection of the Big Oak Flat and Tioga Roads. Phone 379-2349.

White Wolf Lodge: A very small camp store adjacent to the dining room at the lodge. Phone 372-8416.

Tuolumne Meadows Store: This facility offers the largest selection and variety north of Yosemite Valley. Phone 372-8428.

Lodging

As in the Wawona area, there are overnight accommodations in the north part of the park that are not operated by DNC Parks & Resorts at Yosemite. For reservations for DNC facilities, follow the steps outlined on page 11. You must deal directly with the other independent lodging providers to reserve with them.

The quoted rates for the following listed lodging facilities are approximate only, are based on double occupancy, vary with the seasons, and are subject to change.

Evergreen Lodge: Open April through October. Here are 18 rustic cabins on the road to Hetch Hetchy. One bedroom cabins are $99-139, one bedroom cottages are $139-159, and two bedroom family cabins are $159-189. Each cabin includes a private bath, but there are no kitchens. Other amenities are a restaurant, bar, and small convenience store. For reservations call directly to (800) 935-6343 or 379-2606. The web site address is www.evergreenlodge.com.

White Wolf Lodge: Open in summer only. These rustic accommodations are situated at delightful White Wolf, bordered by meadow and forest both. There are four cabins with private bath (about $87) featuring propane heating, a desk, chair, dresser, and two double beds. Limited electricity is provided for lighting and heat. The 24 canvas tent cabins share a com-

Tioga high country

munal bathroom and shower house (about $67). The canvas cabins are equipped with beds with linens, candles for lighting, a wood burning stove, and wood. There is no electricity. Special amenities include a dining room and store. Reservations should be made through DNC (see page 11).

Tioga Pass Resort: Open Memorial Day through mid-October. Nestled on the side of a hill at well over the 9,000-foot level, the resort consists of 10 housekeeping cabins, 4 motel-type rooms, and a central building with restaurant, store, and gas pumps. A new addition is the outdoor coffee bar. It's two miles beyond Tioga Pass Entrance and just outside of the park. Room rates vary from $100 to $175 per night. Weekly rates are offered. For reservations write PO Box 7, Lee Vining, CA 93541, or call 372-4471. The web site address is www.tiogapassresort.com.

Tuolumne Meadows Lodge: Open in summer only. Here are 69 canvas tent cabins set close by the Tuolumne River in a picture book setting. The tents are rustic and utilize wood stoves and candles (there's no electricity), but there are mattresses and linen on the beds. Bathrooms and showers are communal and anything but fancy. But that's part of the fun of the Tuolumne Lodge—it's roughing it easy. The tents rent for about $71 and will sleep up to 4. Reservations (which are much sought and highly coveted) should be made through DNC (see page 11).

Inexpensive: dinner for one adult might cost up to $10. Moderate: dinner for one adult might cost from $10 to $20. Expensive: dinner for one adult might cost over $20.

Hikers on Mt. Dana

Yosemite's Natural World

Yosemite is filled with living things of every description existing in a remarkable setting created by the various forces of nature. From its famous black bears and big trees to nocturnal owls, seldom-seen reptiles, pesky mosquitos, and mysterious fungi, the park is abundant with flora and fauna that are rich and varied. Because wildlife is protected in Yosemite, it has served as an "island" sanctuary of sorts, where natural processes have continued and biological diversity is still great. Other factors contributing to this favorable situation for animals and plants are the great range of elevations within the park (from 2,000 feet to 13,000 feet) and the corresponding variety of living conditions that change with the elevation.

Though inanimate, other natural objects and processes contribute to the ever-evolving Yosemite scene. Geological workings are constant, waterfalls ebb and flow, and meteorological forces add variety and life to the landscape. And because the setting has been so unchanged and undeveloped, Yosemite National Park is even more significant as a mountain laboratory of the natural world.

Yosemite Geology for Liberal Arts Majors

Most descriptions of Yosemite geology are rife with technical jargon, geological gobbledy gook, and scientific names. This is an attempt to make the processes that created Yosemite's landscape of granite and water more understandable for the layperson. And with it comes the promise that words like batholith, pyroclastic, and subduction will not be used.

Once upon a time about 500 million years ago, sediment was deposited in layers on the ocean floor at the west edge of what would later become the continent of North America. This sediment was consolidated into rocks like sandstone, chert, shale, and limestone. Neither the land mass of the developing continent nor the land mass covered by sedimentary rock under the ocean was stationary, however.

Time passed (about 300 million years or so) and the two land masses moved towards each other, met, and then some exciting geology took place. The rock beneath the ocean was forced under the continental land mass with interesting results. The process caused the rock of the ocean plate to become very hot and liquefy into magma (which is the molten rock that shoots out of volcanoes). This hot liquid rose up under the edge of the continent to form volcanoes, and where it cooled and hardened before making it to the surface, great areas of granite rock.

This process occurred in a series of pulses over a period of some 150 million years. When it was complete, a mountain range had been formed that ran in a rough line parallel to the west coast. Although it was largely covered by the continental crust (primarily sedimentary rock), this ancestral Sierra Nevada range was probably similar to the present Cascade Range of volcanoes. In some places the mountains may have been as high as 13,000 feet.

For approximately the next 55 million years, the main force at work in the ancestral Sierra was erosion (we all know what that is, right?). The volcanoes were worn away by wind and water as was the continental crust that sat on top of the great granite mass created by the molten rock as described above. The rock that eroded away was carried by rivers and streams into California's Central Valley. When this period of erosion was complete, what was to become the Sierra Nevada, now primarily exposed granite, stood only a few thousand feet high.

Everything was going along fine with the developing Sierra until one day about 25 million years ago, the land masses meeting along the present day San Andreas fault began to move again. The result was that the block upon which the Sierra sat was uplifted at its eastern edge and tilted towards the west. It is estimated that the tilt raised peaks on Yosemite's eastern edge as much as 11,000 feet.

Following uplift and tilt, river courses in the Yosemite region became steeper, and the erosive effect of their waters increased. The Merced River, for example, began to carve the granite much more sharply, and Yosemite Valley was deepened as a canyon. The Sierra Nevada began to show much greater surface relief, and started to take on the form we know today.

About 2 or 3 million years ago, the Earth's climate began to cool. Given its raised height, the Sierra Nevada became covered with glaciers and ice fields along its crest. At its most extensive, the ice covered over half of Yosemite, and sent glaciers down many of the valleys that had been created by the erosion of streams and rivers.

Glaciers tore loose large quantities of rock as they moved, carving U-shaped canyons and valleys, polishing rock faces, and breaking various rock formations like spires and domes along fractures or joints. The glaciers carried the broken rock as rubble and deposited it along the edges of its path.

This glacial period consisted of an unknown number of glaciations – perhaps as many as 10. The last glaciation reached its maximum between 20,000 and 15,000 years ago. At that point, the Earth's climate began to warm again, glaciers receded, and non-glacial erosion became the main geological force working in Yosemite once more.

Yosemite Valley is one location in the park that has changed its appearance considerably since glacial times. Because glaciers dumped enormous quantities of rock and rubble at its western end, the valley's outflow was stopped and its floor became covered with water. Lake Yosemite was formed. Over the intervening 10,000 years, the lake was filled with sediment and silt washed down from the park's higher regions, and the valley's flat, dry floor we know today was created.

Q: What is an erratic boulder?

A: A large rock that has been transported from a distant source by the action of glacial ice. (Look for erratics on Yosemite's peaks and ridges.)

Yosemite's landscape continues to change even now. While the geological processes are not dramatic (some changes take millions of years), erosion continues, avalanches occur, and rockslides are common. The geologic story goes on in Yosemite and provides us with a better understanding of the extraordinary scenery that has made the park famous.

Erratic boulders

Further Reading

The Geologic Story of Yosemite National Park by N. King Huber. Yosemite NP: Yosemite Associaton, 1989.

Domes, Cliffs & Waterfalls by William R. Jones. Yosemite NP: Yosemite Association, 1976.

The Geology of the Sierra Nevada by Mary Hill. Berkeley: University of California Press, 1975.

The Incomparable Valley by Francois E. Matthes. Berkeley: University of California Press, 1950

Geologists Disagree: Muir vs. Whitney

Nineteenth-century scientists were as puzzled by Yosemite Valley's origin as many first-time visitors are today. Their efforts to explain what they saw resulted in a variety of theories about the creation of the valley's sheer walls and spectacular waterfalls.

Josiah D. Whitney was the State Geologist for California and Director of the California Geological Survey and made many of the first studies of Yosemite during the 1860s. In his view, Yosemite Valley had not been formed by erosion or glaciation or any other traditional geologic force. He believed that a valley so deep could only have been created by a sudden, catastrophic collapse of that section of the earth below it. Because Whitney was an accomplished Harvard professor with quite a reputation as a scholar and scientist, his theory gained some acceptance.

At about the same time, mountain wanderer John Muir (see page 108) was making observations of his own. He, too, was fascinated with the geologic history of Yosemite Valley. Muir advanced the hypothesis that it was the action of glaciers, an "over-sweeping ice current," that had carved the Yosemite landscape. He worked to popularize the theory and it came to be known as "Muir's discovery."

Whitney was not impressed nor convinced. He characterized Muir's ideas as absurd, and passed them off as the ravings of a "mere shepherd." Doggedly, Whitney defended his "cataclysm" theory for some twenty years until his death.

While Muir was not correct in all the details of the work of the glaciers, he was remarkably close. Later studies proved the basic soundness of this theory and helped establish John Muir's reputation as a thoughtful and insightful student of the Sierra.

Joints Shaped the Rocks

The variety of rock shapes and formations that occur in Yosemite is impressive. From blocks to domes to spires to arches to sheets, there is tremendous diversity in the granitic terrain. How did these structures come to be?

All of Yosemite's unusual landmarks (with but a few exceptions) resulted from the existence of fractures within their original rock structures. These fractures, called joints, are the lines upon which the rocks have been broken. They create zones of weakness within the granite that yield to the action of glaciers and to the intrusion of water.

Joints occur both vertically and horizontally, and some are inclined (for example, the Three Brothers formation was created along inclined joints). Vertical jointing is most prevalent and produced features like the face of Half Dome and the Cathedral Spires. Where vertical and horizontal joints intersect, the result is rectangular blocks.

Half Dome and El Capitan are representative of rocks with very sparse jointing. Their resistance to erosion and glaciation has kept them practically unchanged for thousands of years. Incidentally, there probably is no other half of Half Dome. Geologists believe that only 20% of the dome's original size has been lost.

The type of jointing most dramatic in the evolution of the Yosemite landform is sheeting, that results in the concentric joints that lead to the creation of domes. How these joints form is fairly complicated, but they occur mainly with the unloading of the pressure from overlying rock. As relief is experienced, the granite expands upward and fractures result. The concentric fractures break off like the different layers of an onion in a process called exfoliation.

Yosemite Waterfalls

*T*he collection of waterfalls in Yosemite National Park is unequalled anywhere in the world. And nowhere else have so many spectacular waterfalls been concentrated in so small an area as Yosemite Valley. What's most remarkable is the number of park waterfalls that are free-leaping; they make their descent without being broken on intervening ledges or outcroppings. The park's glacial geology is directly responsible for this unique situation.

While the glaciers carved major water courses like Yosemite Valley very deeply, lateral tributary ice streams cut much more slowly and less effectively. The result was "hanging valleys," and streams and creeks which previously had fed directly into primary rivers became routed over the brinks of lofty precipices into the more deeply-carved canyons below them. These waters still leap into space over sheer walls as Yosemite's waterfalls today. Good examples of waterfalls originating from hanging valleys are Yosemite Falls and Bridalveil Fall.

Other waterfalls were created as the glaciers moved along and dislocated large blocks of granite from streambeds. The rock gave way along joints (pre-existing fractures where the rock was weak) and took on shapes like steps in a staircase. This was the process responsible for Vernal and Nevada Falls, which drop in two major steps from Little Yosemite Valley. Known as the "Giant Staircase," this landform is well viewed from Glacier Point.

Yosemite's waterfalls are at peak flow during the months of April, May, and June when 75% of the annual snow melt occurs. May is usually the best single month for waterfall watching. By July most of the surface runoff is gone, and many falls either dry up or are reduced to a trickle. Some falls rarely dry up because of watersheds with soils that are able to hold more water longer (for example, Bridalveil Fall).

Not all the waterfalls in the park are large, spectacular, or permanent. Many cascades exist where streambeds were resistant to the glaciers, but some gouging and polishing did occur. In those cases, channels were steepened, and now water spills

Q: What are ephemeral waterfalls?

A: They are minor waterfalls with small watersheds or falls created by stream flows originating in catch basins that have captured runoff or rainfall. They are characterized by their temporary duration. Examples in Yosemite Valley are Horsetail Fall (on El Capitan) and Staircase Fall below Glacier Point.

Tuolumne Falls

Upper Yosemite Fall

over irregularly-fractured granite or down gradual cliff faces. Other falls are ephemeral; they appear only during heavy thunder storms or at the peak of the spring runoff. As abruptly as the rain ends, so do these fleeting displays.

In winter, park waterfalls have a different beauty. Because the snow pack prevents soil moisture from freezing, water continues to flow in the falls. But they become edged with ice, and droplets of water actually freeze as they descend through space. When this freezing occurs in a large volume, frazil ice is the result. Streams at the base of the waterfalls become filled with ice crystals that create ice slush. As it moves, the frazil ice adheres to any object below freezing, and

Ice cone

can clog stream beds.

The most famous winter waterfall phenomenon is the ice cone that builds up at the base of Upper Yosemite Fall. As ice slabs that have frozen at the fall's edges fall and gently freezing spray collects, the ice cone grows, sometimes to a height of 300 feet covering some four acres. The cone usually melts away by April.

Further Reading

Granite, Water, and Light: Waterfalls of Yosemite Valley by Michael Osborne. Yosemite NP: Yosemite Association, 1983 (currently out of print).

The Waterfalls of Yosemite by Steven P. Medley. Yosemite NP: Yosemite Association, 1999.

The Spirits of Yosemite Falls - A Yosemite Miwok Legend

In the waters just below Cho'-lok (Yosemite Falls) live the Po'-loti, a group of dangerous spirit women. In the old days there was a village a short distance from the falls.

A maiden from this village went to the stream for a basket of water. She dipped the basket into the stream as usual, but brought it up full of snakes. She went further upstream and tried again, but with the same result. She tried repeatedly, each time a little farther upstream, but always drew a basketful of snakes.

Finally, she reached the pool at the foot of Cho'-lok, and a sudden, violent wind blew her into it.

During the night she gave birth to a child that she wrapped in a blanket and brought home the next morning. The girl's mother was very curious and soon took the blanket off the baby in order to see it.

Immediately a violent gale arose and blew the entire village and its inhabitants into the same pool. Nothing has ever been seen or heard of them since.

From *Legends of the Yosemite Miwok,* compiled by Frank LaPena, Craig D. Bates, and Steven P. Medley (Yosemite Association, 1993).

The Ten Highest Free-falling Waterfalls in the World

1.	Angel Falls	3,212 feet	Venezuela
2.	Tugela Falls	3,110 feet	South Africa
3.	Utigordsfossen	2,625 feet	Norway
4.	Mongefossen	2,540 feet	Norway
5.	**Yosemite Falls**	2,425 feet	Yosemite
6.	Espelandsfoss	2,307 feet	Norway
7	Ostre Mardalsfossen	2,149 feet	Norway
8.	**Sentinel Falls**	2,000 feet	Yosemite
	Cuquenan Falls	2,000 feet	Venezuela
9.	Sutherland Falls	1,904 feet	New Zealand
10.	Kjellfossen	1,841 feet	Norway

Waterfalls of Yosemite Valley

Yosemite Falls	2,425 feet	North wall, eastern end
Sentinel Falls	2,000 feet	South wall, west of Sentinel Rock
Ribbon Fall	1,612 feet.	North wall, west of El Capitan
Staircase Falls	1,300 feet	South wall, behind Curry Village
Royal Arch Cascade	1,250 feet	North wall, west of Washington Column
Silver Strand Falls	1,170 feet	South wall, far west end
El Capitan Falls	1,000 feet	North wall, east side of El Capitan
Lehamite Falls	uncertain	North wall, in Indian Canyon
Bridalveil Fall	620 feet	South wall, west end
The Cascades	uncertain	North wall, 2 miles west of Yosemite Valley
Nevada Fall	594 feet	Easternmost end of Merced River Canyon
Illilouette Fall	370 feet	Panorama Cliffs southeast of Glacier Point
Vernal Fall	317 feet	East of Happy Isles on Merced River

Natural Events

Fires

Fire has long played a role in Yosemite's natural world. It is a major ecological force, with impacts similar to those of other natural phenomena, such as floods, earthquakes, and hurricanes. Wildland fires, defined as all fires that burn in natural environments, greatly influence park ecosystems. Prior to the appearance of humans here, the ingredients for fire were largely controlled by climate. With the arrival of Native Americans and later Euro-American settlers, sources of fire and fuels were modified as people changed their environment.

Wildland fire fosters new plant growth, expands wildlife populations, and removes dead trees and litter from the forest floor. Also, shrubs and trees invading grasslands and meadows are killed by fires. Following fire, new healthy re-growth occurs. Accordingly, fire is recognized as an instrument of change and a catalyst for promoting biological diversity and healthy ecosystems.

On occasion, wildfires (unwanted fires in the natural environment) originating in national parks burn forests, towns, or homes, with devastating results. Because of these negative impacts, people often mistakenly consider all fires to be harmful, destructive forces. However, properly managed fire, referred to as prescribed fire, can be an effective natural resource management tool.

In Yosemite, fires usually are classified as either natural or human-induced. A natural fire is usually started by lightning. Natural fires may burn under prescribed conditions and are monitored. Wildfires are those that humans seek to extinguish.

A prescribed fire is initiated by humans under predetermined conditions and is used to manage certain types of landscapes. These uses include reducing fuel build-up around campground areas or providing proper soil conditions for the germination of such species as the giant sequoia. Among the other benefits of prescribed burning are:

- insect pest control;
- removal of undesirable plants that compete with wanted species for nutrients;
- addition of nutrients for trees and other vegetation provided by ashes that remain after a fire;
- removal of undergrowth, thereby allowing sunlight to reach the forest floor to encourage growth of desirable species; and
- clearing of congested forest areas to prevent the accumulation of fuels.

Note: For more information see the National Park Service FireNet web site. at www.fire.nps.gov.

The Fires of 1990

In August 1990, lightning from intense thunderstorms along the west side of Yosemite ignited about 40 different fires.

Because the fires threatened human life and property, park staff immediately began to suppress them.

But two of the fires, known as the A-Rock and the Steamboat, quickly grew to a size that was beyond control. A number of factors contributed to the severity of the fires, among them high winds, drought conditions, large amounts of available fuel, and steep terrain. The fires quickly advanced to become the most intense type, crown fires, which burn through the top layer of foliage on a tree, known as the canopy.

Containment and ultimate control of the two fires took some two weeks, more than 3,000 firefighters, and more than $13 million. The A-Rock fire eventually encompassed 18,100 acres, while the Steamboat fire covered about 5,280 acres. Damage was estimate at about $26 million, with the loss of homes (primarily in the park inholding known as Foresta) and concessioner and gateway community business income.

More than ten years later, the effects of the fires can still be seen. From the Big Oak Flat Road a few miles above Yosemite Valley, the Foresta region still appears starkly devoid of mature trees. While vegetation is slowly maturing, it will be many more years before some semblance of the area's previous coniferous forest returns. There are also stretches of the Wawona Road between Yosemite Valley and Chinquapin (the turn-off to Glacier Point) where many acres of burned forest are visible on both sides of the roadway.

Floods

Since Yosemite was first occupied by those who wrote about their experiences, its natural water courses have flooded periodically. In 1862, homesteader James Lamon was forced from his home by the rising Merced River, and in 1958 the Wawona Covered Bridge was damaged by the waters of the South Fork.

History has shown that flooding by the Merced is not uncommon - rather it should be expected. Specifically, floods in Yosemite Valley occurred in 1937, 1950, 1955, 1963, 1980, and 1982. Such events were the result of various factors, but the most common was warm winter rains falling on accumulated snow up to the highest elevations of the park. When such conditions occur, huge quantities of run-off cannot be accommodated by the existing river channels, and water flows into meadows, forests, and developed areas.

Because of the relative regularity with which flooding occurs in Yosemite Valley, its flood plain has been carefully mapped. That map is now an integral part of the Yosemite Valley Plan that guides all future development of the valley. From now on, no more structures will be built within the flood plain in hopes that harm occasioned by high water to humans and their property will be minimized.

The Flood of 1997

In the early morning hours of January 1, 1997, rain fell on packed snow in Yosemite at elevations up to 9,500 feet. The deluge from the storm combined with the huge amount of snow melted by the rain created a high volume of water rarely seen in the rivers and waterfalls of the park.

Run-off peaked in Yosemite Valley at about 11 p.m. on January 2, and streams and rivers there overflowed their banks and carved new channels. Over 2,000 people (employees and visitors alike) were initially stranded in the valley, when all three access highways were closed. After the water subsided, downed trees were removed, and road repairs were completed, evacuation was finally made.

The effects of the flood were wide-ranging. While the widening of water channels, scouring and erosion of riverbanks, and

uprooting of trees and shrubs did occur, the flood's impact on the natural scene was not major. On the other hand, human-made structures and systems were seriously affected. Electrical service was shut down, mud and rock slides blocked roads and damaged power poles, sewer lines broke, and campgrounds, buildings, and roads were flooded. In some cases, large sections of roadway were washed away or had their underlying roadbeds destroyed.

While initial repairs and recovery efforts were being made, Yosemite Valley was closed to the public for three months. For the next two and one-half years, repairs to the Arch Rock Road and Highway 140 continued, requiring regular road closures; unrestricted access to Yosemite Valley was finally achieved again in October, 2000.

1997 Flood Statistics

- More than 1.4 miles of riverbank and 550 acres of meadows were eroded in Yosemite Valley.

- About half of Yosemite Valley's 900 campsites were flooded. Many have since been eliminated and are not likely to be replaced.

- Nine road bridges in the valley suffered damage and required repair. The bridge at Happy Isles has been removed.

- A 300-foot section of the 14-inch sewer line located beneath the Arch Rock Road was destroyed, severing the valley sewer system and contaminating the Merced River.

- Over 350 motel and cabin units at Yosemite Lodge were flooded and removed.

- Over 200 concession employee quarters were flooded, and 439 employees were displaced.

- At least ten archeological sites sustained heavy damage, with total removal of some cultural features and artifacts.

- The estimated cost of recovering from the damage and effects of the flood is $178,053,000.

Yosemite Plantlife

*T*here are over 1,500 different types of plants in Yosemite. They range from the grand sequoias to tiny fungi and lichen. What follows is a brief overview of Yosemite flora with information on how to find out much more.

Trees

Both cone-bearing and broad-leaved trees appear in abundance within Yosemite National Park. The trees that bear cones (also known as conifers) do not shed all of their leaves or needles on an annual basis, and this has led to their designation as "evergreens." Most of the broad-leaved trees drop their leaves each year.

The Conifers: There are at least 18 different species of conifers that occur in the park. About half of them are pines. Most common at lower elevations are the ponderosa (or yellow) pine and the Jeffrey pine. The ponderosa is abundant in Yosemite Valley, has yellow-orange bark, needles in groups of three, bark scales that fit together like a jigsaw puzzle, and a trunk up to six feet in diameter. The Jeffrey pine looks much like the ponderosa but grows at higher elevations (Glacier Point is a typical locality). If in doubt, smell the bark. The Jeffrey exudes a sweet odor like vanilla or pineapple.

The two typical high-elevation pines are the lodgepole and the white bark. The lodgepole has needles in twos, yellowish bark, and small cones. The white bark features needles in bunches of five and purplish, pitchy cones, and tends to be dwarfed at tree line.

Other notable conifers are the red and white firs. Large forests of these trees can be seen along the Tioga and Glacier Point Roads. White firs occur between 3,500 and 8,000 feet and have 2-inch needles that twist off the branch and 3-to-5-inch cones. Red firs, in contrast, have shorter needles that curl upwards and larger cones (5 to 8 inches), and grow between 6,000 and 9,000 feet.

Broad-Leaved Trees: Almost without exception, these trees lose their leaves in the fall (they are deciduous). As the leaves die as part of this annual process, they take on different hues such as orange, yellow, and brown. It is the foliage of the broad-leaved trees, then, that provides us with sometimes spectacular "fall color." The deciduous trees are less varied than the conifers in the park.

There are many types of oaks in Yosemite. In the valley, the California black oak is distinctive. It grows to heights of 75 feet, has dark gray to black bark, and produces large acorns that the Yosemite Indians used as a staple in their diet. The other common oak is the canyon live oak, which has holly-like evergreen leaves.

Mountain dogwood

Other conspicuous broad-leaved trees are the mountain dogwood that produces beautiful and delicate whitish-green flowers each spring, and the quaking aspen known for its paper-thin white bark and the rustling of its often-colorful leaves with the slightest breeze.

Along streams and rivers, particularly at lower elevations, one will encounter cottonwoods (leaves are bright green on top and light below), willows (slender pointed leaves), and alders (dark green leaves with obvious veins and small teeth).

Q: What species are the large pine trees that sport long cones hanging from their upper branches like Christmas tree ornaments?

A: Sugar pine. Because the trees yield great quantities of even-grained, clear wood that is excellent for building, most of the forests of sugar pine in California were harvested during the nineteenth century.

Sugar pine

Ponderosa pine

Flowering Plants

The spectacular geography of Yosemite, with its elevations ranging from 2,000 to over 13,000 feet, supports a natural wildflower garden without equal, not to mention shrubs, grasses, sedges, rushes, ferns, and fungi. The differing temperatures, precipitation levels, and growing seasons ensure that a wide assortment of plants finds conditions to their liking at locations throughout the park.

The blooming season is a long one in Yosemite. It starts in the foothills in April and May and gradually moves upslope as the weather warms and the snow melts. It doesn't reach the park's highest elevations until August, when flowers appear for a brief two-month appearance. All told, the wildflower season in Yosemite lasts a full six months!

For the student of botany, Yosemite is indeed a remarkable classroom. Within the park is some of the most distinctive vegetation in the world. Because natural processes have been allowed to continue

Western azalea

and because little disruption of the physical environment has occurred, plant life is varied and rich.

Taking the time to learn about Yosemite's wildflowers (and other plants) can be amazingly rewarding. Being able to identify and learn something about the various flowers and plants you encounter will enrich your park experience.

Further Reading

Discovering Sierra Trees by Stephen F. Arno. Yosemite NP: Yosemite Association and Sequoia Natural History Association, 1973.

An Illustrated Flora of Yosemite National Park by Stephen J. Botti, illustrated by Walter Sydoriak. Yosemite NP: Yosemite Association, 2001.

Sierra Nevada Tree Identifier by Jim Paruk. Yosemite NP: Yosemite Association, 1997.

Wildflowers of Yosemite by Lynn and Jim Wilson and Jeff Nicholas. Yosemite NP: Sunrise Productions, 1987.

Q: What is the strange red plant (with no leaves or green of any kind) that is noticeable on the forest floor each spring?

A: Snow plant (*Sarcoides sanguinea*). A "saprophyte," it lives on decayed organic matter, appearing just after the snow melts each year.

Snow plant

Spice bush

The Giant Sequoias

*A mature sequoia tree is
3,125,000,000,000,000,000,000 times
larger than a single bacterium.*
—J. I. D. Hinds

After its granite cliffs and domes and its spectacular waterfalls, Yosemite is best known for its famous big trees, the giant sequoias. In fact, the 1864 Yosemite Grant set aside as a protected park only Yosemite Valley and the Mariposa Grove of Big Trees. These towering monarchs were recognized for their special qualities early in history, and they continue to inspire awe to this day.

The mature big trees can be recognized by their huge, columnar trunks that are free of branches for 100 to 150 feet. The foliage is blue-green and individual leaves create rounded sprays, unlike the flattened branchlets of the incense-cedar. The bark is quite fibrous, can be 4 to 24 inches thick, and is cinnamon-brown in color. This bark covering is non-resinous and very fire-resistant. Sequoia wood is pink when cut, then darkens to red. It is amazingly resistant to decay (many downed trees remain intact on the ground for years). Cones are quite small (2 or 3 inches), are abundant, and produce several hundred seeds each.

The giant sequoias *(Sequoiadendron giganteum)* grow from these tiny seeds that are no larger than flakes of oatmeal. You would have to amass over 90,000 seeds to produce a pound of them. Upon germination, a one-inch seedling results, and these seedlings grow into young trees through the years. These youngsters are characterized by a fairly symmetrical, cone-shaped appearance with sharply-pointed crowns.

Middle age is reached by sequoias when they are 700 or 800 years old. They are mature, have just about reached their maximum height, and have developed a rounded top. Some mature trees that have been burned are noted for their "snag tops." When fire damages the bases of the trees, water supply to their upper reaches is limited and the tops of the trees die. The trees remain healthy, but their appearance suggests the hazards and effects of age.

Scientists believe that the giant sequoia is the largest living thing in the world (though this is sometimes disputed). The trees stop growing upward at about 800 years of age, but they continue to add bulk. Maximum height seems to be about 320 feet, and diameters at the base vary depending on where the measurements are taken (there is quite a swelling at the base of each sequoia). Some trees at the base are over 35 feet in diameter, while at about 20 feet above the ground, that size drops to about 20 feet.

It is hard to grasp the enormity of the sequoias. One example that provides perspective is the largest branch on the Grizzly Giant tree in the Mariposa Grove. It is over 6 feet in diameter. At that size it is larger than the trunks of the largest specimens of most trees east of the Mississippi River. It is also larger than many of the conifers in Yosemite.

Despite their longevity, giant sequoias are not the oldest living things. That distinction is reserved for the bristlecone pines, which may live to be 5,000 years old. Sequoias are known to live at least 3,200 years, and John Muir reported finding an individual 4,000 years old.

Giant sequoias occur naturally only in the Sierra Nevada primarily at elevations between 5,000 and 7,000 feet. In Yosemite there are three big tree groves: the Mariposa Grove (see page 48), the Tuolumne Grove, and the Merced Grove (page 58). Any visit to Yosemite should include a trip to see these impressive trees.

Further Reading

The Sequoias of Yosemite National Park by H. Thomas Harvey. Yosemite NP: Yosemite Association, 1978.

A Guide to the Sequoia Groves of California by Dwight Willard. Yosemite NP: Yosemite Association, 2000.

The Enduring Giants by Joseph H. Engbeck, Jr. Sacramento: California Dept. of Parks and Recreation, 1973.

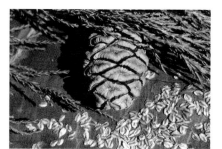

Sequoia cone and seeds

Sequoia seedling

Mammmals

Over 75 species of mammals have been recorded in Yosemite National Park. What follows are brief descriptions of some of those mammals, particularly those that are likely to be seen by visitors in the course of their stay in the park.

Mule Deer

Having experienced a life free of threat from humans, the mule deer in Yosemite seem almost tame. You are likely to spot one or more of these graceful creatures anywhere in the park, but they are especially obvious in Yosemite Valley and in the Wawona meadow area.

Despite the fact that they seem unconcerned by humans, mule deer should be treated as any other wild animal. These deer should be given a wide berth and not be fed (nor should any other park animal); many injuries have been caused to visitors who have disturbed these animals in the course of offering them human food. Even deaths have resulted from gorings and from the blows delivered by the surprisingly sharp hooves of the mule deer. In fact, more injuries occur in Yosemite inflicted by deer each year than those caused by black bears or any other park animal.

The mule deer takes its name from its large, mule-like ears. Weighing up to 200 pounds, it is primarily a browse animal eating leaves and tender twigs from trees, grass, and other herbs. The male mule deer (the buck) grows antlers each year for use in the mating season or "rut" each fall. Despite popular belief, the age of a given buck cannot be determined by counting the number of antler points he sports.

Mule deer are very common in Yosemite and are seen chiefly between 3,500 and 8,500 feet. They stay below the snow line in winter, often dropping into the foothills that border the west side of the park. Common predators of the mule deer are the mountain lion and the coyote.

Black Bear

The reaction of many people to the black bear is both fascination and fear. Because of the many stories that are told about bears throughout the national park system, there are plenty of misconceptions that exist about these largest of park mammals.

Yosemite's black bear is often confused with the grizzly bear, a species that no longer exists in the park. The grizzly once roamed the Sierra Nevada but was eliminated by hunters around the turn of the century. The last grizzly killing occurred in Yosemite in 1895, and the last authentic record of the killing of a grizzly in California was from 1922.

Grizzly bears are considerably more dangerous to humans than are black bears. Occasional black bear incidents do occur, but those mainly result from improper food storage by visitors. For information about storing your food properly see pages 17 & 85. Never feed the bears, and observe them at a distance (particularly when cubs are present)!

Despite their name, black bears can be brown, blonde, cinnamon, or black. There are no members of the brown bear species (or any other) in Yosemite. Individuals range in size from 250 to 500 pounds, although even bigger bears have been recorded.

These bears are omnivores – they will eat practically anything. Typical fare is insects, small rodents, berries, acorns, and seeds. But human food, from hot dogs to cookies, also appeals to park bears. Because dependence on a human-provided diet creates bears that become bold and are not afraid of people, the need to keep visitor food well-stored is even more acute.

Black bears can be observed throughout the park, particularly in the evenings. Many bears enter a den in winter for a period of sleep that is not true hibernation. Young are born in late winter and leave the den in spring to forage with their mother.

Black Bears & Human Food

Each year black bears are killed in Yosemite National Park as a direct result of human carelessness and improper food storage.

Driven by their excellent sense of smell and enormous appetite, black bears are drawn to human food. Once they have had a taste of it, they continue to seek it out from any possible source, including backpacks, picnic tables, ice chests, and cars. In the course of pursuing this new food, their natural fear of humans fades, and some bears may become aggressive.

When bears become too aggressive, they often have to be killed. In 2000, there were 654 incidents involving bears, resulting in over $120,000 in damage; five bears had to be killed. The only way to prevent the continuing loss of bears is to make sure that all food and trash are stored properly.

How to Store Food from Bears

"Food" includes any item with a scent, regardless of packaging. This includes items that you might not consider food such as canned goods, bottles, drinks, soaps, cosmetics, toiletries, perfumes, trash, empty ice chests, and unwashed food-preparation items.

What If You See a Bear?

Never approach a bear, regardless of its size. If you encounter a bear in a developed area of the park or on a hiking trail, act immediately: yell, clap hands, bang pots together, or throw small stones or sticks toward the bear from a safe distance with the goal of scaring the bear (you don't want to injure it). If others are with you, stand together to present a more intimidating figure, but do not make the bear feel surrounded - you want the bear to run away!

Use caution if you see cubs, as a mother may act aggressively to defend them. Never try to retrieve anything once a bear has it. If you follow these recommendations and act immediately, you should be successful in scaring bears away. Report all bear encounters to a park ranger as soon as possible.

Yosemite Wild Bear Project

A special group of "Keep Bears Wild" products, including t-shirts, enamel pins, and stuffed animal toys, have been developed for sale in Yosemite. Proceeds from the sales of these items directly benefit park bears through the Yosemite Wild Bear Project, a joint effort of the Yosemite Association, DNC Parks & Resorts at Yosemite, and the National Park Service. Among the many programs supported by the project is bear canister rentals for backpackers.

Donations are welcome to support the "Keep Bears Wild" effort (call 209 379-2646), and bear products can be seen and purchased online at www.yosemitestore.com.

Location	Bear-Aware Food Storage
Parking Areas	Place food in food storage lockers if available, or in your hotel room or cabin (but not your tent cabin). Food must not be stored in vehicles after dark. Don't forget to clear vehicles of food wrappers, crumbs, and baby wipes. Food may be stored in vehicles during daylight hours only.
Campgrounds	All food must be stored in food storage lockers without exception, day and night. Each campsite contains a food storage locker (bear box) measuring 33" x 45" x 19".
Tent Cabins	All food must be stored in food storage lockers, day and night. In Curry Village, coin-operated lockers are available for small items. Never leave items with an odor in your tent.
Hotel Rooms & Cabins	All food must be kept inside your room or cabin. If you are not in your room, the windows and doors must be closed.
Picnic Areas & On the Trail	Do not leave food unattended.
Backpacking	Bear-resistant food canisters are strongly recommended and are required above 9,600 feet (see page 17).

Mountain Lion

Terror-inducing stories abound about these large members of the cat family, but while they are present in Yosemite, they are almost never seen and rarely interact with humans. Also know as the cougar, panther, or puma, the mountain lion preys on other mammals, primarily deer. Individuals are wary of people, and go out of their way to avoid contact with park visitors; they are not a serious threat to human safety.

Besides deer, the mountain lion also will eat a number of small mammals including marmots, rabbits, foxes, coyotes, and raccoons, and even porcupines and skunks when the pickings are slim. Because they help to keep Yosemite's deer population in check, mountain lions are considered an important component of the park ecosystem.

Mountain lions can weigh from 75 to 275 pounds, and are 6 to 9 feet long including the tail. They are recognized by their size, solid tannish-brown color, and extended tail. Females give birth to a litter of 1 to 6 cubs in the middle of every other summer. Moutain lions produce a number of cat-like sounds, including hisses, growls, and yowls, and the mating call has been likened to the screams of a hysterical woman.

Humans and Mountain Lions

While mountain lion attacks on humans are extremely rare, they are possible. Generally, mountain lions are calm, quiet, and elusive. If you spot one, consider yourself privileged! The National Park Service offers the following safety recommendations:

- Do not leave pets or pet food outside and unattended, especially at dawn and dusk. Pets can attract mountain lions into developed areas.
- Avoid hiking alone. Watch children closely and never let them run ahead of you on the trail. Talk to children about mountain lions, and teach them what to do if they meet one (see below).
- Store food according to park regulations.

What If You See a Mountain Lion?

- Never approach a mountain lion, especially if it is feeding or with kittens. Most mountain lions will try to avoid a confrontation. Always give them a way to escape.
- Don't run. Stay calm. Hold your ground, or back away slowly. Face the lion and stand upright. Do all you can to appear larger. Raise your arms. If you have small children with you, pick them up.
- If the lion behaves aggressively, wave your arms, shout, and throw objects at it. The goal is to convince it that your are not prey and may be dangerous yourself. If attacked, fight back!

TRICKS FOR OBSERVING ANIMALS

Try strolling down a forest trail, or walk along the edge of a meadow. Avoid groups of people, as most animals are easily frightened. Consider the color of your clothing and don't wear white, it makes you too conspicuous. Darker shades are better. Walk slowly. When you see an animal, don't make quick movements. If you should come upon one, such as a deer or a squirrel, continue slowly so as not to alarm it. Stop to watch it when you are still some distance away. If you want to see an animal that has disappeared into a burrow – a marmot, ground squirrel or a mouse – find a comfortable place to sit and remain quiet. Usually it will reappear in a short time to see where you are and what you are doing. Watch for evidence of mammal activities, such as dens, trails in the grass, or piles of kitchen middens where squirrels have cut away the scales of pine cones. Watch, too, for holes dug where pine nuts or acorns have been buried. — from *Discovering Sierra Mammals*.

Coyote

Normally a very shy mammal, the Yosemite coyote has become accustomed to the human presence and is commonly seen here, particularly in Yosemite Valley. In winter, these dog-like creatures often can be viewed hunting in snow-covered meadows.

The coyote is one mammal that makes its presence known by its call. There is nothing more haunting (some would contend frightening) than the late-night howling and barking of a group of coyotes.

Weighing 25 to 30 pounds, coyotes live on small animals (primarily rodents), although fawns and an occasional adult mule deer are taken. Coyotes can be identified by their long, grayish fur (which is lighter on the underside) and a darkish tail.

Squirrels and Chipmunks

A variety of squirrels and chipmunks is present in Yosemite. Most visitors, particularly campers, will encounter one or more species of these active rodents.

The common squirrels are the California gray squirrel (all gray with a long bushy tail, often seen in trees), the Sierra chickaree (a reddish tree squirrel that chews on pine cones and squeaks a lot), Golden-mantled ground squirrel, and the California ground squirrel (a brown animal, speckled with white, which lives in burrows in the ground). At higher elevations, the common ground squirrel is the "picket pin" (or Belding ground squirrel), which seated in its erect posture looks like a stake driven into the ground.

There are at least 5 different species of chipmunks in the park. They are generally reddish-brown in color, smaller than the squirrels, and wear 4 light-colored stripes separated by dark on their backs. These chipmunks are remarkably animated and quick, and dig burrows in stumps or the ground that are very hard to find.

Marmot

A common sight in the park's higher elevations is the yellow-bellied marmot; watch for these rotund fellows at Olmsted Point on the Tioga Road. Actually members of the squirrel family, marmots resemble woodchucks for which they are sometimes mistaken. They regularly sun themselves on subalpine rocks, and behave tamely at certain roadside turnouts. Please do not feed them.

The marmots are about 15 to 18 inches long and have an average weight of about 5 pounds. They are yellowish-brown, live in dens under rock piles or tree roots, and hibernate during the winter. Their shrill warning note is distinctive.

Bighorn Sheep

Originally native to the Yosemite area, the Sierra Nevada bighorn sheep were eliminated here around 1900 as a result of hunting and the disease spread by domestic animals.

In 1986, a herd of bighorns was released in the Tioga Pass area of Yosemite in an effort by scientists and researchers to re-establish a viable population. To date the experiment has been a success. Additional transplants have augumented the herd, which has been able to reproduce and survive on its own.

Bighorn sheep are remarkable rock climbers able to ascend and descend amazingly steep terrain. Some sheep weigh up to 200 pounds and are 3 feet high at the shoulder. They are gray or buffy brown in color and grow hard, permanent horns. In the male, they spriral back sometimes into a full circle, while the females have small, slightly backward curving horns. Watch for these beautiful animals in the mountainous regions around Tioga Pass.

Other Mammals

These brief descriptions have touched on but a few of the numerous mammals native to Yosemite. To learn more, consult the following books that will provide greater depth and detail.

Further Reading

Discovering Sierra Mammals by Russell K. Grater. Yosemite NP: Yosemite Association and Sequoia Natural HistoryAssociation, 1978.

Sierra Nevada Natural History by Tracy I. Storer and Robert L. Usinger. Berkeley: University of California Press, 1963.

Yellow-bellied marmot

Birds

*B*ecause Yosemite plays host to over 240 different kinds of birds, it is not practical to provide an exhaustive and detailed bird list here. As was the case with the mammals, the following are highlights of the species one is likely to encounter in the course of a visit.

Steller's Jay

This is, undoubtedly, one bird that just about everybody notices in Yosemite. The jay is bright blue with a dark head and a very prominent crest. Unfazed by humans, it boldly alights on tables and other perches close to food, all the while screeching its disagreeable screech. Surprisingly, the Steller's jay also is capable of producing a soft, warbling song. When a group of jays encounters a hawk or owl, the raucous cacophony of shrieks and calls that goes up is almost overpowering.

Acorn Woodpecker

In Yosemite Valley, the acorn woodpecker is the woodpecker you are likely to see. Colored black and white with a red head marking (sometimes there's yellow also), these industrious birds drill holes in trees, telephone poles, and buildings and fill them with acorns that they eat later (along with the bugs that have entered the acorns). Their flight is a distinctive series of shallowly U-shaped glides, and they are exceptionally noisy, making a "wack-up, wack-up" call most often. Wherever you find oaks, you will find acorn woodpeckers.

Western Tanager

Here is a bird that is hard to miss. Though not common, the tanager is brilliant yellow with a bright orangish-red head. Likely to be seen in Yosemite Valley in spring and summer, this gaudy bird will sometimes come to your picnic table or the ground near you. This may be the only bird in Yosemite with "day-glo" feathers.

Belted Kingfisher

Along the Merced River and other bodies of water in the park, this striking blue bird can be seen flying low or perched on branches and snags, watching for fish and aquatic insects. If you're lucky, one will plunge into the water and emerge with dinner in its beak. There is a noticeable crest and a reddish band on the chest. You'll know its a kingfisher if you hear a loud rattling, clicking call.

American Dipper

Another water bird, the dipper is truly phenomenal. Though gray and non-descript, these acrobatic creatures are named for their habit of bobbing up and down almost constantly. What's so phenomenal about them is their ability to fly into a stream or river and walk upstream underwater along the bottom clinging to rocks as they search for food. As you stroll beside a stream or river, keep a close eye for the amazing dipper!

Clark's Nutcracker

The high country counterpart of the Steller's jay is the Clark's nutcracker. Also known as the "camp robber," this white, gray, and black bird with a prominent beak has a harsh, cawing voice. Very conspicuous in areas around Tuolumne Meadows, the Clark's nutcracker does crack and eat pine nuts, but is not averse to cleaning up around your campsite. You'll see these birds typically above 9,000 feet.

American dipper

Black-headed Grosbeak

While picnicking or camping, you may see this other common Yosemite Valley resident. The grosbeak is characterized by its black, white, and orange markings and by its "gross beak" that is used for opening seeds. Oftentimes woods echo with the grosbeak's delightfully lyrical song that has been called a rich warble. The black-headed grosbeak is a sure sign of spring.

Great Horned Owl

You may never get a glimpse of this bird, but chances are good you may hear one. This nocturnal dweller of most of the park's life zones is active from dusk until dawn. Most of that time it issues a series of deep, sonorous hoots. If you happen to hear the horned owl, see if you can locate its perch. These owls are excellent ventriloquists, so don't be surprised if you fail. Large ear tufts are sure signs that you're looking at the great horned owl.

Other Birds

There's a whole lot to be learned about Yosemite's birds, and plenty of ways to learn it. Try a ranger-led bird walk, or pick up a pair of binoculars and see what there is to see. The books listed are great guides and will make your bird education easier for you.

Yosemite's Ten "Most Wanted" Birds

Serious, sometimes fanatic, birdwatchers (or "birders") often keep a list of every bird known to occur in North America; its known as their personal "life list." When they see a bird they've never seen before, they will check it off the list. The goal is to see every single species on the list. There are several birds in Yosemite that are rarely seen anywhere else. These "most wanted" birds are feverishly sought by many zealous birdwatchers for their life lists.

1. Gray-crowned Rosy-finch
2. Great Gray Owl
3. Peregrine Falcon
4. Black-Backed Woodpecker
5. Flammulated Owl
6. Northern Goshawk
7. Pileated Woodpecker
8. Williamson's Sapsucker
9. Northern Pygmy Owl
10. Black Swift

Great horned owl   *Great gray owl*

Goshawk

Further Reading

The Sibley Guide to Birds by David Allen Sibley. New York: National Audubon Society, 2000.

Field Guide to the Birds of North America. Washington, DC: National Geographic Society, 1994.

Birds of Yosemite and the East Slope by David Gaines. Lee Vining, CA: Artemisia Press, 1988.

Reptiles & Amphibians

Lizards, frogs, and snakes are all members of this group of Yosemite wildlife. About 40 different species of amphibians and reptiles are known to have established populations in the Yosemite Sierra, and there are no doubt more.

All of the lizards in Yosemite are harmless reptiles. Because they prefer warm locations, they are found primarily in the lower elevations of the park (Yosemite Valley and below). Most commonly seen is the western fence lizard. He's black or blotched brownish-gray on top with a blue throat and belly.

At least 14 different types of snakes inhabit the park. With the exception of the western rattlesnake, they are all non-poisonous. The most regularly-seen species is the garter snake, which frequents meadows, ponds, streams, and lakes (it's a remarkably good swimmer). The garter snake is black, gray, or dark brown with a cream-colored strip down its back and usually red blotches on its sides.

The western rattlesnake is Yosemite's only venomous snake, but rarely bites people. The rattler varies from cream to black in color with a variety of blotches. The head is broad, flat, and triangular, and when surprised, the snake will coil and shake the rattles it sports at the end of its tail. The result is a buzzing sound that is a warning to stay away.

Frogs and toads are abundant in Yosemite; there are a minimum of 8 different kinds. You are more likely to hear from these denizens of the park than to see them. Most abundant is the Pacific tree frog, a small, green, gray, or brown fellow with a black mask and a constantly-heard year-round song. Recently it has been determined that the mountain yellow-

Pacific tree frog

legged frog, quite common 20 to 30 years ago, is in steep decline and possibly disappearing from the park.

The last of the amphibians are the salamanders and newts. These small, slimy creatures like it moist and dark. That's why they're rarely seen. Most likely to be discovered is the California newt, the brownish-orange newt that is often spotted after a heavy rain. Two species of salamander are found almost nowhere else but in the Yosemite region: the Mt. Lyell and the limestone salamanders.

Further Reading

Discovering Sierra Reptiles and Amphibians by Harold Basey. Yosemite NP: Yosemite Association and Sequoia Natural History Association, 1976.

California Amphibians and Reptiles by Robert C. Stebbins. Berkeley: University of California Press, 1972.

Q: Can rattlesnakes swim?

A: Yes, quite well. Their long right lungs provide increased buoyancy. They usually hold their rattles high and dry and may strike while in water.

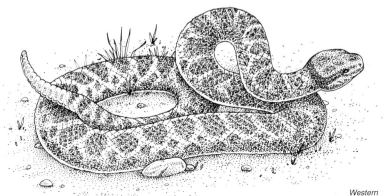

Western rattlesnake

Fishes

*D*espite the impression of many people that the Yosemite region is dotted with lakes and streams laden with native trout, there is only one game fish that naturally occurs in the park. That's the rainbow trout. There are five other native species, but they are relatively uncommon and are not game fishes (the Sacramento sucker, the Sacramento squawfish, the hardhead, the California roach, and the riffle sculpin).

When the glaciers moved through Yosemite during the last ice age, native fish populations were eliminated and most of the park's lakes and streams were left fish-less. One job of the U.S. Army in Yosemite National Park between 1890 and 1914 was to plant new fish species in the high country and provide greater opportunities for sport fisher-people. Non-native species that were introduced and now occur in the park are the cutthroat trout, the golden trout, the brown trout, and the brook trout. The brook and brown trout have adapted best.

For information about fishing in Yosemite, see page 29. For additional, more in-depth coverage of the park's fish family, see the sources at right.

Riffle sculpin

Q: What is the oldest record of trout planting in Yosemite Valley?

A: April 1, 1879, when the Yosemite Fish Commission began planting 20,000 young trout in the different streams of the valley.

A List of the Fishes of Yosemite National Park
("N" denotes a native species)

Trout
Brook trout *(Salvelinus fontinalis)*
Brown trout *(Salmo trutta)*
Cutthroat trout *(Salmo clarkii)*
Golden trout *(Salmo aguabonita)*
Rainbow trout *(Salmo gairdnerii)* N

Suckers
Sacramento sucker *(Catostomus occidentalis)* N

Mouth of Sacramento sucker

Minnows
California roach *(Hesperoleucus symmetricus)* N
Hardhead *(Mylopharodon conocephalus)* N
Sacramento squawfish *(Ptychocheilus grandis)* N

Sculpins
Riffle sculpin *(Cottus gulosus)* N

Further Reading
Fishes of Yosemite National Park by Willis A. Evans, Orthello Wallis, and Glenn D. Gallison. Yosemite NP: Yosemite Natural History Association, 1961. (Out of print).

Yosemite Trout Fishing by Hank Johnston. Yosemite NP: Flying Spur Press, 1985.

Sierra Trout Guide by Ralph Cutter. Portland: Frank Amato Publications, 1984.

Ranger plants fish in Yosemite lake, a practice now discontinued

The Poisonous, The Itchy & The Sickening

The relatively undeveloped landscape of Yosemite Valley and the vast regions of wilderness around it are home to plants, animals, and other organisms that may in one way or another be hazardous to your health. The threat from these sources is generally not serious, and there are a number of precautions you can take and signs to watch for to avoid problems. Whatever you do, don't become frightened by the following list.

Rattlesnakes

These wriggly reptiles are the only poisonous snakes in Yosemite. Out hiking, you will rarely encounter a rattler, and if you do it will almost always buzz its rattles when threatened. If you happen upon a rattlesnake, keep a safe distance and leave. Do not try to kill it or scare it away. It's always a good idea to watch carefully where you walk, where you put your hands, and where you sit.

Scorpions

In Yosemite's lower elevations, this threatening-looking insect hides by day and becomes active at night. The sting delivered by the scorpion is painful but not at all dangerous to humans. Scorpions hide under rocks and logs, so be cautious when you're lifting or rolling such objects.

Giardia Lamblia

This funny sounding creature is a protozoan that causes an intestinal disease called giardiasis. Its symptoms are chronic diarrhea, abdominal cramps, bloating, fatigue, and weight loss. Because giardia has been found to be present in park lakes and streams, you should purify any drinking water that is not from the tap. Either boil it for three minutes, use an iodine-based purifier, or use a giardia-rated water filter.

Mosquitos

These delightful insects have been characterized by one writer as the "most bothersome of the animal life in the High Sierra." Though relatively benign individually, roving bands of mosquitos can make the lives of visitors, particularly in certain areas of the wilderness, totally miserable. They breed in locations with standing water, so they are common wherever there is snow melt. Typically, that means 4,000 feet at the end of May advancing upwards to 10,000 feet by late July. What can be done about these pesky pests? Try repellents, long pants and long-sleeved shirts, and mosquito-net hats and tents. If you're backpacking, locate your camp to take advantge of any breeze and away from areas of moisture.

Ticks

Some park ticks, the small bugs that suck blood from a variety of mammals, carry an illness known as Lyme disease. Not every tick, however, is a carrier. Symptoms of the disease in its advanced form can include arthritis, meningitis, neurological problems, and cardiac symptoms, and the disease can be very serious. If it is detected early, treatment can cure or lessen the severity of the disease. If you think you might have been bitten by a tick, watch for a rash at the spot of the bite and for symptoms of the flu. If you contract Lyme disease and you believe its source was Yosemite, please call the Park Sanitarian at (209) 379-1033.

Poison oak

Poison Oak

This is one of the most widespread shrubs in California, and it's quite abundant in Yosemite's lower reaches. Fluids from the plant produce an irritating rash on the skin of humans and it can sometimes be very severe. Sufferers itch terrifically and can experience swelling. If you think you've been in poison oak, wash your body and clothes thoroughly to remove the oily fluid.

Spiders

There are a couple of interesting critters in this category. The single truly dangerous spider in Yosemite is the black widow. With its black, orb-shaped body featuring a red "hour glass" pattern on its underside, this arachnid is easy to identify. The black widow is not aggressive, but when disturbed can bite and inject a nerve poison that can cause severe symptoms and even death. If bitten, see a physician quickly. Much more fearsome in appearance is the tarantula, but this big, woolly fellow is fairly benign. Up to four inches across, tarantulas are active at night and don't bite unless provoked. The bite is painful but not dangerous.

Yosemite's Endangered Species

*W*hile Yosemite National Park is abundant with varied plant and animal life, several indigenous species have been lost to extinction over the years, and threats to park life forms persist despite the National Park Service's best efforts to protect them. Grizzly bears were once residents of the Yosemite Sierra, and other birds, mammals, and plants have been lost.

Some species of plants and animals, though still present, have undergone local, state, or national declines, raising concerns about their possible extinction if protective measures are not implemented. As a result, the U.S. Fish and Wildlife Service, California Department of Fish and Game, and Yosemite National Park have established categories for these species that reflect the urgency of their status, and the need for monitoring, protection, and implementation of recovery actions.

Not all threats to park wildlife are controllable at Yosemite. Take the peregrine falcon. These impressive flyers eat birds that migrate to Central and South America each winter. Use of pesticides is much more common in these wintering areas, and DDT has found its way into the systems of many Yosemite peregrines. The result is that the eggs they lay became thin-shelled and subject to breakage. Nesting success dropped dramatically, and park officials feared that peregrines might be lost for good.

But through a fairly complicated augmentation procedure, the National Park Service has seen a growth in peregrine numbers and nests. During the nesting season, climbers were employed to reach peregrine nests and remove the fragile eggs. They were replaced with plastic phonies. Captive-raised chicks were later placed in the nests, and the parents adopted the newcomers without hesitation. Work continues to encourage other countries to limit their use of harmful chemicals.

Other significant programs have involved the restoration of meadows, oak woodlands, and other park areas. As well, a number of revegetation efforts are underway to reclaim portions of Yosemite that have been over-used and stripped of any plant life. Watch for evidence of this important work as you travel throughout the park, and be sure your use of Yosemite is consistent with the protection of the plants and animals here.

Yosemite Species Listed as At Risk by the U.S. Government

Endangered
Sierra Nevada bighorn sheep

Threatened
Bald eagle
Red-legged frog
Valley elderberry longhorn beetle

Plant Species of Concern
Bolander's clover
Congdon's lomatium
Slender-stemmed monkeyflower
Three-bracted onion
Tiehm's rock-cress
Yosemite woolly sunflower

Yosemite Species Listed as At Risk by the State of California

Endangered
Bald eagle
Great gray owl
Peregrine falcon
Willow flycatcher

Threatened
California wolverine
Limestone salamander
Sierra Nevada red fox

Rare Plant Species
Congdon's lewisia
Congdon's woolly-sunflower
Tompkin's sedge
Yosemite onion

Source: Final Yosemite Valley Plan/Supplemental EIS

Bighorn sheep

Yosemite's History

U.S. Cavalry in Yosemite Valley, circa 1906

The recorded history of Yosemite National Park is as fascinating and important as it is short relative to that of other parts of our country and the world. While Native Americans were long-term residents, Yosemite Valley was not entered by European Americans until 1851, and not really occupied by them in any meaningful way until the last quarter of the nineteenth century.

These historical events are particularly significant because the actions of both men and governments in and relating to Yosemite proved to be pioneering efforts in the conservation of natural areas all around the globe. There is little question that at Yosemite the concept of national parks was born, and the park still serves as a model and symbol for the entire world.

Yosemite's Native People

*I*ndians resided in the Yosemite region for about 4,000 years before the Spaniards occupied California and the Gold Rush occurred. Anthropologists suggest that the earliest Indian inhabitants came from the east side of the Sierra Nevada looking for water and food in particularly dry years. Later, groups from the Central Valley (predominantly Miwok-speaking) invaded the foothills and greater Yosemite as Indian populations increased and competition for homeland grew. The Miwoks and the people from the east side came together and established permanent villages near the Merced River throughout Yosemite Valley.

Obviously, there is no recorded history of the Yosemite Miwoks until very recent times. Anthropologists believe that the Miwok culture evolved very slowly. Their simple lifestyle remained relatively unchanged, no doubt, for centuries. The Yosemites' basically primitive existence involved seed and plant gathering, hunting, and trading. Generally, they spent fall and winter in Yosemite Valley or the warmer foothills, then roamed into Yosemite's high country in spring and summer in quest of game and to barter with Mono Lake Paiutes and other people from east of the area.

Miwok bow

Indian people in California were brought in contact with Euro-Americans with the advent of the Spanish missions in the late 18th century. As the central and southern parts of the state became settled, white encroachment on traditional Indian territory increased. There is no evidence of this fact, but some believe that at the beginning of the 1800s the Indian people of Yosemite were struck with a "fatal black sickness," a plague of some type. Reportedly, the few survivors abandoned the valley and relocated to the eastern Sierra and were assimilated by other groups there. For a number of years (the exact number unknown), Yosemite Valley may have been uninhabited.

One of the offspring of the Yosemite people who grew up with the Mono Paiutes was Tenaya (see page 107). As a youth, Tenaya had heard stories of the beauty and bounty of Yosemite Valley. He finally visited the former home of his people quite late in his life. Being favorably impressed, he and 200 other Indians (some Yosemite Miwoks, some not) resettled the valley. Tenaya was named chief of the group.

These Indians lived in relative harmony in the valley they called "Ah-wah-nee" until the fateful Euro-American occupation of the Sierra foothills around 1850. Ahwahnee (as it is spelled now) probably means "place of a gaping mouth," although Lafayette Bunnell of the Mariposa Battalion reported that through hand signals the native people had indicated its meaning was "deep, grassy valley."

As friction between gold seekers and foothill Indians increased, anti-Indian sentiments blossomed. Groups from the Central Valley moved higher into the foothills, and conflict resulted both between Indians and whites and between rival Indian groups. As Tenaya and his fellows defiantly protected their mountain stronghold, violence did occur. The Mariposa Battalion was formed to locate, capture, and relocate to reservations the native residents, and the story of its discovery of Yosemite Valley and its removal of the Indian people is well known.

The white soldiers called the Indians the "Yosemites," from the Miwok word "uzumati" or grizzly bear. (The natives called themselves the Ahwahneechees.) Some consider this a corruption of the Ahwahneechee word "Yo-che-ma-te" which means "some among them are killers." Whatever the true meaning, the local Indians were known as fierce fighters who lived in an area where grizzly bears were fairly common.

Following Tenaya's death in 1853, what was left of the band of Yosemite Indians dispersed to other locations. Some went east to the Mono Lake area, while others joined neighboring peoples along the Tuolumne River. Never again did the remaining Yosemites gather together as a people.

Within twenty years, the number of native Indians living in the Yosemite area dwindled to below fifty. With white settlement of Yosemite Valley and ever increasing visita-

Obsidian arrow points

tion, the native Miwok culture was irrevocably corrupted.

Hotelkeepers and other concessioners employed some of the Indians for odd jobs and manual labor, but the Yosemites were only tolerated at best.

A Gentle Lifestyle

During their hundreds of years of occupation of Yosemite Valley, the Yosemite Miwoks were remarkably gentle in their use of the land. There were at least forty different camp spots on the floor of the valley. Most of them were summer encampments only. Because of heavy snow and extremely cold temperatures, the bulk of the valley residents moved to the El Portal area and the foothills below to pass the severe winter months.

The houses of the people were rude structures covered primarily by slabs of cedar bark. The typical house was a conical lean-to sporting three layers of bark and affording reasonable shelter from the elements. The Yosemite Miwoks also built earth-covered dance and sweat houses, and small elevated granaries for storing acorns and other edibles.

Native foodstuffs were hunted and gathered (very little cultivation was done).The staple of the Indian diet was acorn, which was elaborately prepared and eaten as mush. Other vegetation such as mushrooms, ferns, clover, and bulbs was also eaten. Fish and game included deer, squirrels, rabbits, rainbow trout, and the Sacramento sucker. Some insects like certain fly larvae, caterpillars, and grasshop-

Miwok basket

pers were considered delicacies.

Products of the Yosemite Indian culture included fairly coarse twined baskets and more fine-coiled baskets with elaborate patterns, as well as cradles, bows and arrows, obsidian tools and implements, bone awls and scrapers, and some ceremonial costumes.

Today the only noticeable evidence of the habitation of Yosemite Valley by native peoples is the occasional discovery of an obsidian flake or a granite grinding hole.

Q: What is the shiny black substance used by the Indians for making arrowheads and other implements?

A: Obsidian, a volcanic glass common on the east side of the Sierra Nevada. The Yosemites would trade acorns and other items with their eastern neighbors for obsidian.

Chief Lemee dressed for traditional Miwok dance

Maggie Howard places acorns in storage chuk-ah

The Euro-American Occupation

Yosemite Valley was sighted by Euro-Americans for the first time in 1833. A party of explorers headed by Joseph Rutherford Walker was crossing the Sierra Nevada that fall, and in their efforts to determine the best route, several of the group came upon the north rim of the valley. The cliffs were described as "more than a mile high," and after several efforts the mountaineers determined that they were "utterly impossible for a man to descend, to say nothing of our horses."

Some twenty years later, the valley was finally entered by someone other than Native Americans.

In response to actions by the Yosemite Indians and their neighbors in defense of their homeland, a group of men was organized as the Mariposa Battalion to kill Indians as necessary and to transport survivors to reservations in the Central Valley. A punitive expedition was mounted in March of 1851, and their quest for Indians led the battalion into Yosemite Valley, where they beheld what no other group of pioneers had seen before.

Yosemite Falls by artist Thomas Ayres, 1855

It wasn't long before the word began to spread about Yosemite's wonders. Letters from members of the Mariposa Battalion to San Francisco newspapers aroused the interest of James Mason Hutchings, who organized the first tourist party to Yosemite Valley in 1855. He brought the artist, Thomas Ayres, who made sketches of the geologic features, which sketches Hutchings used to disseminate Yosemite's fame even more widely.

An increasing stream of visitors arrived primarily on foot and horseback, but as the years passed, wagon roads were developed to permit yet greater visitation.

Hutchings became the chief entrepreneur and publicist for Yosemite, homesteading land and operating a hotel for early tourists. Other hotels and residences were built, livestock was grazed in the meadows, crops were planted, orchards were established, and Yosemite Valley was treated as no more than a resource to be exploited.

Clark's Station, circa 1860

The State Grant

Fortunately, not everyone viewed the valley as a capitalist's dream come true. Some amazingly farsighted persons took it upon themselves to work for the protection of Yosemite Valley for the public good. These early day conservationists, I. W. Raymond and Frederick Law Olmsted (the landscape architect who later designed New York's Central Park) prominent among them, appealed to Congress. Senator John Conness introduced a bill to grant Yosemite Valley and the Mariposa Grove of Big Trees to the State of California for preservation and protection. The bill was passed, and President Abraham Lincoln interrupted his preoccupation with the Civil War to sign the legislation on June 30, 1864.

It was a landmark event. Never before had a government set aside a piece of land for its inherent natural and scenic qualities to be preserved for the public use, resort and recreation "inalienable for all time." Yosemite became, in effect, the first state park and the first national park in the world. It unquestionably served as a model for the development of other parks and led to the birth of the U.S. National Park System as we know it today.

Public Management

Responsibility for management of the Yosemite Grant (as it came to be called) fell to a Board of Commissioners appointed by California's governor and to the "Guardian" that the board hired. Yosemite's first Guardian was Galen Clark (see page 107).

The 1860s and '70s saw improved access to the valley thanks to the completion of several wagon roads, and the Guardian

Cooke's Hotel, mid 1880s

had to contend with an astounding rise in visitation.

Many new hostelries were built including the extravagant Cosmopolitan Saloon and Bathhouse, Black's Hotel, Leidig's Hotel, La Casa Nevada Hotel, the Stoneman House, and others. Competition was fierce among the various operators, and unsuspecting visitors found themselves heavily lobbied by concessioners seeking their business.

Things in Yosemite were far from peaceful and quiet, however. Given the intense public interest in Yosemite as well as the disappointment of the original homesteaders who saw their opportunities to make a killing disappear, Yosemite politics were never boring. Several lawsuits were brought by individuals who were dispossessed by the Yosemite Grant (Hutchings foremost among them), and criticism was regularly leveled at the Board of Commissioners for its alleged poor management.

Greater Yosemite
While Yosemite Valley and the Big Trees had been recognized and protected, the thousands of acres of wilderness surrounding these relatively small park strongholds had not. Led by John Muir (see page 108) and by Easterner Robert Underwood Johnson (editor of the then influential *Century Magazine*), a group of preservationists began to focus attention on the need to protect the greater Yosemite area including the beautiful high country regions like Tuolumne Meadows.

As resource degradation in the form of mining, logging, and stock grazing increased, so did the efforts of Yosemite champions. Muir and Johnson did their

best to influence Congress and to inform the American people about the threats to the Yosemite. They derived important support from the Southern Pacific Railroad and its president, Edward Harriman, who were strongly interested in boosting tourism in the Sierra Nevada.

On October 1, 1890, the U.S. government acknowledged the preciousness of these wildlands by enacting the law that established Yosemite National Park. Interestingly, Yosemite National Park did not include Yosemite Valley or the Mariposa Grove, but encompassed an enormous area around them. The park was actually 30% larger than it is today.

Early visitors pose before Yosemite Falls

The Army Takes Control

The brand new national park needed management, and in 1890, the National Park Service had not yet been established. It was determined that the U.S. Army would assume the administration of Yosemite (as they had at other national parks), and members of the cavalry became a common sight in the park. Because much of the area was covered by a deep blanket of snow during the winter months, the Army limited its occupation of Yosemite to summers only. Usually soldiers from San Francisco would ride or march to and from their headquarters in Wawona each summer.

The duties of the cavalrymen were multiple and varied. They chased sheepherders from high country meadows, explored previously uncharted regions of the park blazing trails and preparing maps, surveyed boundaries, and prevented poachers from illegally taking park game. The work done by Army personnel was prodigious, and their mark on Yosemite's history was a major one.

During the Spanish-American War, when many U.S. troops were engaged, civilian rangers were hired by the Army to assist at the park. They were the first of their kind.

The existence of two different administrations, one for Yosemite Valley and the Mariposa Grove of Big Trees, the other for the greater Yosemite National Park, inevitably led to duplication, overlap, and conflict. Many individuals and organizations (including John Muir and the Sierra Club) began to push for a unification of all of Yosemite under the management of one entity.

Cavalry in Wawona Tunnel Tree

A Single Yosemite

The mood of the public was apparently shared by lawmakers and government officials. In 1906, the federal government formally accepted the "recession" of Yosemite Valley and the Mariposa Grove from the State of California, an action that obviated the Yosemite Grant once and for all. The price of the agreement was the reduction in overall size of the park to conform it to natural boundaries and to exclude private mining and timber holdings. But at last there was one Yosemite National Park with a single administration.

The U.S. Army continued its management of the park, moving its headquarters to Yosemite Valley (to a site near the present-day Yosemite Lodge). In 1914, a civilian administration was established, and the first "park rangers" were authorized and employed by the Department of the Interior.

The Army Years

The years between 1890 and 1914 were characterized by a transportation revolution. Regular stage lines began operation, and private wagons commonly made the trip to Yosemite. Visitation continued its remarkable expansion, and the completion of the Yosemite Valley Railroad from Merced to El Portal in 1907 effectively heralded the end of the stagecoach era in Yosemite. But more earthshaking changes in transportation were still to come.

In 1900, the first automobile entered Yosemite Valley (albeit illegally). The U.S. Army officially allowed automobiles into the park in 1913, and when they came, they came with a vengeance. Two years later, all horse-drawn stages connecting train passengers to Yosemite Valley were replaced by motor stages. By 1920, two-thirds of all visitors were coming to Yosemite via private automobile.

The period also witnessed growth and proliferation of concessioner facilities. Public campgrounds were initiated, Camp Curry was established, Best's Studio was founded, and Camp Ahwahnee was built at the base of Sentinel Rock. Competition remained hot and heavy, and considerable conflict resulted between concessioners.

A regrettable chapter in Yosemite's history was written during the Army years. The famous and bitter battle over the damming of the Hetch Hetchy Valley was settled in 1913 with the enactment of the Raker Act, and the resulting inundation of the area. See page 57 for more about the Hetch Hetchy controversy.

Q: Who was the first permanent Euro-American resident of Yosemite Valley?

A: James Lamon who took up a preemption claim in the Valley's east end in 1859 and built a cabin. Apple trees he planted still grow near Curry Village and the stables.

The National Park Service

A major change came about in the National Park System with the creation of the National Park Service in 1916. It had been recognized that administration of the parks required more than the part-time attention of the Army and that there was a war to be fought in Europe. The National Park Service was the Interior Department's chosen alternative.

It was Frederick Law Olmsted, Jr. (whose father had been influential in the establishment of the 1864 Yosemite Grant), who proposed that the purpose of the new agency should be "to conserve the scenery and the natural and historic objects and the wildlife therein, and to provide for the enjoyment of the same in such manner and by such means as will leave them unimpaired for the enjoyment of future generations." This phrase became the cornerstone of the act that created the N.P.S. and guides the agency still.

The years following 1916 were significant not only for Yosemite but also for all U.S. national parks because the basic policies of the agency were being developed and implemented. The process of interpreting the N.P.S. mandate to preserve the parks while allowing for their use was ongoing. Yosemite consistently was the park where new ideas were first tested and applied.

Yosemite's new National Park Service Superintendent was Washington B. "Dusty" Lewis, who was responsible for many innovations and changes at the park. During his twelve-year tenure the concessions were consolidated under one principal operating company (The Yosemite Park & Curry Company), roads including the Tioga Road were improved and tolls eliminated, new accommodations were built in Yosemite Valley (Yosemite Lodge and the Ahwahnee Hotel) and at Glacier Point, a new administrative center was constructed, and modernization of utilities, roads, and buildings was accomplished.

Interpretation

It was also shortly after the birth of the park service that Yosemite personnel inaugurated the educational program so familiar to park visitors today. Known as "interpretation," the original program was the inspiration of Dr. C. M. Goethe, and Harold Bryant and Loye Miller were hired as Yosemite's first "nature guides" in 1920. At the outset the interpretive program was pretty much limited to nature walks, but it has evolved to include visitor center displays, campfire programs, informal talks, multi-media presentations, and informational literature.

A logical extension of the interpretive program was the Yosemite Museum, plans for which were hatched about 1921. Several years later a permanent museum was completed in the park thanks to a gift from the Laura Spelman Rockefeller Memorial. At the same time a Field School of Natural History was established in Yosemite to provide for the training of future interpreters and nature guides.

These formative years of the N.P.S. reflected the realization that protection of the parks depended on a strong program of education designed to increase public awareness of the special values embodied by Yosemite and other outstanding natural areas. The Yosemite model has been emulated throughout the world and is still as vital as it was eighty years ago.

The Modern Years

The past seventy-five years in Yosemite have seen consistent management and burgeoning visitation. With scientific research and experience, resource policies have changed. Fire is no longer viewed as evil, wild animals are managed to be wild, and artificial attractions like the Fire Fall from Glacier Point have been eliminated.

The greatest challenge facing Yosemite today is its popularity. With visitation hovering around four million each year, the park sometimes suffers from overcrowding, congestion, and air pollution. Effects of these conditions are often resource degradation and a diminished experience for visitors. It can only be hoped that the coming years will provide solutions to these thorny problems and that Yosemite will long remain the preeminent national park in the world.

Further Reading

Discovery of the Yosemite by Lafayette H. Bunnell. First published in 1911. Yosemite NP: Yosemite Association, 1990.

One Hundred Years in Yosemite by Carl P. Russell. Omnibus edition. Yosemite NP: Yosemite Association, 1992.

The Yosemite Grant, 1864-1906: A Pictorial History by Hank Johnston. Yosemite NP: Yosemite Association, 1995

Yosemite Indians by Elizabeth Godfrey. Revised edition. Yosemite NP: Yosemite Association, 1977.

A Yosemite Chronology

1833—Yosemite Valley was first seen by Euro-Americans. The Joseph Walker party in crossing the Sierra encountered a valley with "precipices more than a mile high" that were "impossible for a man to descend."

1851—The Mariposa Battalion under the command of Major James Savage became the first group of pioneers to enter Yosemite Valley. They were pursuing "intransigent" Indians.

1852—The Mariposa Grove of Big Trees was discovered by a party of prospectors.

1855—The first tourist party visited Yosemite Valley with James Mason Hutchings as guide. Thomas Ayres, an artist with the group, made the first known sketches of Yosemite Valley.

1856—The first permanent structure, The Lower Hotel, was built in Yosemite Valley at the base of Sentinel Rock. The first trail into Yosemite Valley was completed by Milton and Houston Mann.

1859—The first photograph in Yosemite Valley was made by C. L. Weed. His subject was the Upper Hotel.

1864—Yosemite Valley and the Mariposa Grove of Big Trees were set aside by the federal government as the first state park in the world. Florence Hutchings was the first white child to be born in Yosemite Valley.

Cavalry in Mariposa Grove of Big Trees, circa 1890

1866—Galen Clark was named the first Yosemite Guardian.

1868—John Muir made his first trip to Yosemite.

1871—The first ascent of Mt. Lyell, Yosemite's highest peak, was accomplished by J. B. Tileston on August 29.

1874—The first road into Yosemite Valley, the Coulterville Road, was completed. The Big Oak Flat Road was finished a month later.

1875—George Anderson made the first ascent of Half Dome before the installation of ropes or cables. The first public school was opened in Yosemite Valley.

1876—John Muir's first article on the devastation of meadows in the Sierra Nevada by sheep was published.

1878—The first public campgrounds were opened in Yosemite Valley by A. Harris near the site of the present-day Ahwahnee Hotel.

Early campers in Yosemite Valley

1890—Yosemite National Park established. The park did not include Yosemite Valley or the Mariposa Big Trees, but encompassed a large region around them.

1891—The first telephones were installed in Yosemite Valley.

1892—Trout were first planted in Yosemite waters by the California Fish and Game Commission.

1896—Firearms were prohibited from the park.

1898—The first civilian park ranger, Archie Leonard, was employed at Yosemite.

1900—The first automobile (a Locomobile) was driven into Yosemite by Oliver Lippincott and Edward C. Russell.

1907—The first railway line to Yosemite, the Yosemite Valley Railroad, began operation.

1913—Automobiles were "officially" admitted to Yosemite.

1915—First appropriation for the construction of the John Muir Trail approved.

1916—The National Park Service was established. Washington B. Lewis was named the first N.P.S. Superintendent at Yosemite.

1917—The first High Sierra Camp, Tuolumne Meadows Lodge, was installed.

1919—The first airplane, piloted by Lt. J. S. Krull, landed in Yosemite Valley on May 27.

1921—The first installations in the Yosemite Museum were completed.

1926—The Yosemite Museum opened to the public.

1934—The first water from the Hetch Hetchy Reservoir flowed into San Francisco.

1935—Badger Pass Ski Area was developed.

1940—Ostrander Ski Hut was opened for winter use.

1946—The first ascent of the Lost Arrow Spire by four climbers was accomplished on September 2.

1949—The first use of a helicopter for rescue purposes was made at Benson Lake to fly an injured boy to safety.

1951—The first airplane planting of trout was done in Yosemite.

1954—Park visitation exceeded the one million level for the first time in history; 1,008,031 visitors were recorded.

1958—The first climb up the face of El Capitan was completed.

1961—Pioneer Yosemite History Center opened to the public.

1966—New Yosemite Valley Visitor Center built.

1967—For the first time over 2 million visitors were recorded.

1969—The "fire fall" from Glacier Point was discontinued. The famed "Wawona Tunnel Tree" toppled over from the weight of its winter snow load.

1970—The free shuttle bus system was initiated in Yosemite Valley.

1972—The first asphalt was removed from the parking lot in front of the Yosemite Valley Visitor Center. The area was converted to use as a pedestrian mall.

1974—Hang gliding was officially allowed from Glacier Point, and 170 flights were made.

1976—The Tioga Road opened April 10, its earliest opening on record.

1980—The Yosemite General Management Plan was completed and approved. It was the first systematically developed, long-range planning document for the park.

1981—Captive-born peregrine falcon chicks were successfully reared in a nest on El Capitan.

1983—The first-ever prescribed burn was accomplished in the Mariposa Grove of Big Trees.

Early ranger-naturalist program, probably in 1920s

1984—Yosemite was named to the World Heritage List. The California Wilderness Bill designated 94% of the park as wilderness.

1986—California bighorn sheep were reintroduced into Yosemite.

1987—Park visitation exceeded three million for the first time; 3,266,342 visitors were recorded.

1990—Yosemite celebrated its 100th birthday as a national park. Major forest fires raked the park during August.

1992—Delaware North Company was awarded the Yosemite concession contract by the National Park Service.

1995—The Yosemite Wilderness Center opened its doors, and the wilderness permit reservation system was initiated.

1996—A massive rockfall occurred in Yosemite Valley between Washburn and Glacier Points. The slide downed several hundred trees, damaged the Happy Isles Nature Center, and killed one visitor.

1997—In early January, major flooding occurred in Yosemite Valley; some 450 campsites, 350 motel and cabin units, and 200 concessioner housing units were lost. The estimated cost of repairing the damage was $178 million. Yosemite Valley remained closed to visitors for three months.

1999—Camp Curry celebrated its 100th anniversary.

2000—The Yosemite Valley Plan, the management document to guide future development, was completed.

Historical Sites in Yosemite Valley

The following locations have special historical significance or were the sites of early development in Yosemite Valley. They are listed in order of locale beginning at the west end of the valley, continuing to the east along Southside Drive, focusing on the east end of Yosemite Valley, then heading back to the west along Northside Drive. In your explorations, remember that all cultural resources should be left unimpaired, and that digging and use of metal detectors are not allowed. Marker references are to small wooden posts that have been placed along valley roads to indicate particular landmarks or attractions. See the map below for details.

Bridalveil Meadow (Marker V-13). This spot is where the Mariposa Battalion camped in March of 1851. The party was in search of Indians and was the first group of whites ever to enter Yosemite Valley. Around a campfire here, the group proposed and applied the name "Yo-semite" to this marvel of Nature's handiwork. It was also here that President Teddy Roosevelt and John Muir camped in 1903 and discussed the need to preserve our nation's wilderness areas.

Bridalveil Fall (Marker V-14 *that is just past the turnoff for Wawona).* This is roughly the place where the wagon road from Wawona entered Yosemite Valley. Towards the Merced River through the trees, a large sewer plant operated for many years. The sewer plant was removed in 1987, and over three acres were freed of development. Yosemite Valley sewage is now carried by pipeline to a new processing facility in El Portal.

El Capitan View (watch for Marker V-17 *in a parking area on the left where trees grow out of the asphalt).* Just upriver from here is the site of the bear feeding platform used in the 1920s and '30s. Garbage was dumped on the lighted platform that drew feeding bears and gawking tourists each night. Enlightened managers have long since dispensed with the spectacle.

Sentinel Rock View (Marker V-18 *about 1.4 miles past El Capitan View on the right and left).* Here was a portion of Lower Yosemite Village, which included the Yosemite Chapel (later moved to its present location east of here), Leidig's Hotel that operated from 1869 to 1888, and Camp Ahwahnee (1908-15). This is also the trailhead for James McCauley's Four-Mile Trail to Glacier Point, where for several years a tollhouse was maintained to collect fees from hikers and horseback riders. Watch for the locust trees that are the only remnants of this earlier occupation.

Swinging Bridge Turnout *(there is no marker here, but the turnout is about a quarter-mile past V-18 on the left).* The remainder of Lower Yosemite Village was located here. Black's Hotel stood from 1869 through 1888, photographer George Fiske's residence and studio were near the river to the west, Galen Clark had a residence here, and the Coffman & Kenney Stables operated for several years. As well, a boardwalk nearly a half-mile in length was constructed through the meadow to the east to connect the Upper and Lower Village areas.

Chapel Parking Area (Marker V-20 *about one-half mile beyond Swinging Bridge on the right).* This area was covered by extensive development from the 1860s until the 1950s. Here were the Upper Hotel (known at various times as Hutchings House, the Sentinel Hotel, and the Yosemite Falls Hotel), photographic studios (Boysen's, Foley's, and Pillsbury's), Best's Studio, Degnan's Store and Restaurant, the world-famous Cosmopolitan Saloon, the Village Store, and many other structures. In 1925, the "new" Yosemite Village site (the present location) was selected, and an administration building, museum, post office, and several artist studios were built. Slowly the Upper (old) Village was dismantled and razed. The Village Store was the last major building to go in 1959. The observant historian can still find plenty of evidence of Yosemite's yesteryears with a little exploring here.

Stoneman Meadow (Marker V-23

near Curry Village). This meadow has been the center of much activity over the years. Within it stood a large wooden hotel called the Stoneman House built by the State of California in 1886 that burned in 1896. James Lamon, a homesteader in the park's earliest days, built a cabin near here, and planted two apple orchards in 1859. One now serves as the Curry Village parking lot, the other is behind the Curry Stables (shuttle bus stop #18). Stoneman Meadow will also be remembered as the site of a riot in 1970 which pitted young people against N.PS. personnel in a clash over curfews, noise levels, and lifestyles.

The Ahwahnee Hotel *(Shuttle bus stop #3).* Before the present hotel was built, an active stable business was operated at this spot. Known as Kenneyville, the stable was extensive and there were horses, shops, barns, and houses mingled here. When automobile travel became popular, the need for such a large stable was eliminated. In 1926, to make way for The Ahwahnee, the stable was moved to its present location and the old buildings torn down. Many people are unaware that during World War II between 1943 and 1945 the Ahwahnee Hotel was closed to the public and converted to use as a Naval Convalescent Hospital. During that time almost 7,000 patients were rehabilitated.

Yosemite Cemetery *(Just west of and across the street from the Yosemite Museum in Yosemite Village).* This is the cemetery where, upon their deaths, local residents were buried between the 1870s and the 1950s. There's a wide variety of personalities interred here, from Native Americans like Indian Lucy and Sally Ann Castagnetto to pioneer settlers and innkeepers like Galen Clark and James Mason Hutchings. A guide to the cemetery is on sale at the Visitor Center.

Yosemite Falls (Marker V-3). In the forested area between the parking lot and Lower Yosemite Fall, James Mason Hutchings built a sawmill for preparation of lumber to upgrade his hotel. John Muir was employed to run the sawmill for a time, and constructed a cabin nearby to house himself. It featured running water: one strand of Yosemite Creek flowed right through it. Camp Yosemite, also known as Camp Lost Arrow, stood near the base of the fall and to its east from 1901 until 1915.

Yosemite Lodge (Marker V-4). The lodge area was first developed as Army headquarters for the park in 1906. The facility included two large barracks buildings, two bath houses and lavatories, 156 tent frames, and a parade ground. When the Army administration ended in 1914, so did the need for the headquarters, and they were converted to accommodate visitors in 1915.

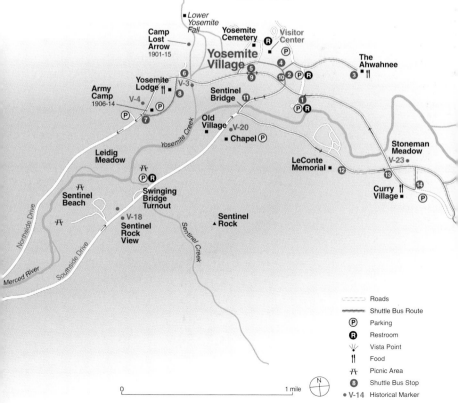

Yosemite's Future

A Plan for the 21st Century

For at least the past thirty years, National Park Service managers have worked to develop a plan to guide Yosemite's development in the coming century. In 1980, the "General Management Plan" was issued and approved. Since then, however, only a relatively few elements of that plan have been implemented.

In fall of 2000, a document that focused on Yosemite Valley was released to supplement the General Management Plan. The "Yosemite Valley Plan" incorporated a number of pending planning efforts including the Merced Wild and Scenic River Plan, the Concession Services Plan, the Yosemite Valley Housing Plan, the Yosemite Lodge Development Concept Plan, and the Yosemite Falls Project. The recovery program following the major flooding of 1997 also became tied up in the plan.

Needless to say, the planning process has been complicated and time-consuming. Further, several law suits have slowed the approval of various documents, which are still not okayed for final implementation. Once the Yosemite Valley Plan goes forward, there will be similar planning efforts for other parts of the park.

Details of the Yosemite Valley Plan

The Yosemite Valley Plan would restore approximately 176 developed and disturbed acres in Yosemite Valley to natural conditions. In addition, 173 acres of developed land would be developed to accommodate visitor and employee services such as campgrounds, day-visitor parking, and employee housing. There would be more campsites and fewer lodging units than there are now.

The plan would consolidate parking for day visitors at Yosemite Village, where a new Valley Visitor Center would be located, and in parking areas outside Yosemite Valley. There would be a major reduction in vehicle travel in the eastern portion of Yosemite Valley during periods of peak visitation.

The area of former Upper River and Lower River Campgrounds would be restored to a mosaic of meadow, riparian, and California black oak woodland communities. Roads would be removed from Ahwahnee and Stoneman Meadows, and parking and fruit trees would be removed from Curry Orchard and the area restored to natural conditions.

Southside Drive would be converted to two-way traffic from El Capitan crossover to Curry Village, and Northside Drive would be closed to motor vehicles and converted to a multi-use (bicycle and pedestrian) paved trail from El Capitan crossover to Yosemite Lodge.

There would be minimal new development west of Yosemite Lodge. The net effect of the plan would be to reduce development in Yosemite Valley by 71 acres.

Key Questions for Yosemite's Future

- As the population of the Central Valley of California continues to grow, how will park managers contend with 4 to 5 million people living within a two-hour drive of Yosemite?

- Should and will the National Park Service impose limits on access to the park to ensure the quality of each visitor's experience?

- Will a regional agency ever be put in place to monitor the effects on Yosemite of road construction, logging, suburbanization, global climate change, acid and nutrient rain, and other impacts that originate outside the park?

- Should and will the National Park Service eliminate motor vehicle use in Yosemite?

- Should an annual limit be placed on total number of visitors to Yosemite? Is the appropriate number 4 million, 6 million, 8 million, or more?

Yosemite's Original Management Plan

When Yosemite Valley and the Mariposa Grove were set aside as a public reserve by the federal government in 1864, the State of California was charged with creating a commission to administer the new grant. Noted landscape architect Frederick Law Olmsted was delegated the job of preparing a report and setting out the policy that should guide the management of the grant.

Olmsted's management plan was a visionary document. Among his key points was that: "The first requirement is to preserve the natural scenery and restrict within the narrowest limits the necessary accommodation of visitors." In elaborating, he stated: "Structures should not detract from the dignity of the scene. In preventing the sacrifice of anything that should be of the slightest value to visitors to the convenience, bad taste, playfulness, carelessness, or wanton destructiveness of present visitors, would probably yield in each case the interest of uncounted millions to the selfishness of a few."

When Yosemite's management plan is finally completed and approved, it will be interesting to see whether Olmsted's recommendations have been heeded.

The Yosemite Hall of Fame

Chief Tenaya

When Euro-Americans first visited Yosemite Valley in 1851, they encountered the Yosemite Indians. Their leader was Chief Tenaya. He has been called not only a brave warrior but an unusual personality who maintained his authority over his people by his native influence and the respect that he commanded.

Accounts have it that a tribal shaman warned Tenaya that "horsemen of the lowlands" (probably a reference to the Spaniards) represented the gravest threat to his people and should be guarded against. When in 1849 gold miners began entering the foothills and interacting with the native residents, Tenaya apparently felt threatened. He reportedly informed the invading whites that the Yosemites would be peaceable, but only if they could continue to occupy Yosemite Valley and not be disturbed.

Such an arrangement was obviously unacceptable to the new foothill residents. The Mariposa Battalion was dispatched to subdue the Yosemites, but met with only limited success. In May of 1851, the greatest portion of the band was rounded up and marched to a reservation in the Central Valley. Problems arose, the federal government never ratified a treaty, and by the end of the year, Tenaya and his people had either escaped or been permitted to return to Yosemite Valley.

The following year, Indians in the valley allegedly attacked a party of miners, and further efforts to remove them resulted. Tenaya's group fled to the high country of Yosemite and to the east side again. In 1853, they returned once more to Yosemite Valley, but their fate was practically sealed.

Despite his best efforts, Tenaya, the last chief of the Yosemites, was unable to protect his people and their homeland from the incursions of the whites. He was killed by stoning late in 1853. There are two versions of his death, but the most commonly accepted is that the Yosemites stole horses from their eastern Sierran neighbors, who attacked in retribution. Tenaya's name is common in the park today having been attached to a canyon, a lake, and other features.

Galen Clark

Known as the "Guardian of Yosemite," Galen Clark was as intimately involved in Yosemite's early history as any other person. He moved to the park in 1856 at the age of 42 suffering from a debilitating lung disease that doctors had indicated would quickly end his life. The Yosemite fresh air and inspiring scenery must have been therapeutic; Clark lived to be 95.

He first homesteaded at Wawona, developing his place as a stopping point on the stage route to Yosemite (Clark's Station). He visited the Mariposa Grove of Big Trees in 1857 with Milton Mann, then explored the trees and publicized them. He recognized the value and uniqueness of the sequoias and Yosemite Valley, and worked to bring about the enactment of the Yosemite Grant, the 1864 law that set aside the Yosemite Valley and Mariposa Big Trees as the world's first state park.

In 1866, Galen Clark became the first "Yosemite Guardian," employed by the State of California to oversee the grant. He continued in this job until the political winds changed in 1880 and a new Guardian was employed. He worked odd jobs for nine years and then was hired once again to be the Yosemite Guardian. His second term lasted seven years, and he closed out his life by guiding, writing books about the park, and helping wherever he could.

As Guardian, Clark made many needed improvements, worked to relocate homesteaders, and persevered in his efforts to protect Yosemite. John Muir called him "the best mountaineer I ever met . . . one of the most sincere tree-lovers I ever knew." Following his death, he was buried in the Yosemite Cemetery in a grave shaded by sequoias he planted himself and headed by a granite marker bearing his self-chiseled name.

James Mason Hutchings

James Hutchings will be remembered most for being Yosemite's first and best publicist. A native of England, he was attracted to Yosemite Valley very soon after its original entry by whites. In 1855, he organized and led the first "tourist" party to visit the valley, bringing with him the artist Thomas Ayres who sketched the first non-Indian illustrations of Yosemite's wonders. Hutchings published the sketches and paired them with his descriptions of the place, drawing national attention to a previously unknown scenic treasure.

When his health failed, he, too, chose to come to Yosemite, and in 1862 purchased an existing hotel that became known as Hutchings House. The hotel was very primitive; only sheets of muslin hung to separate the rooms. Hutchings built a sawmill along Yosemite Creek to prepare the lumber for more effective partitions, and for a time employed John Muir to run the mill.

When the Yosemite Grant was set aside in 1864, Hutchings became embroiled in lengthy and bitter litigation with the government as a property owner dispossessed. His political fortunes changed, however, in 1880 when he was named to succeed Galen Clark as Yosemite Guardian. He worked in that capacity for four years.

Hutchings' many writings will live after him. His *Hutchings California Magazine* is full of historical gems, and he published a series of handbooks entitled *Guide to the Yosemite Valley and the Big Trees*. His most famous work is *In the Heart of the Sierras*, which is representative of the best travel writing of that era.

Killed in a wagon accident on the Old Big Oak Flat Road in Yosemite Valley in 1902, Hutchings is buried in the Yosemite Cemetery.

John Muir

For his efforts on behalf of the park, John Muir has come to be recognized as the most significant individual in the history of Yosemite. This reputation is certainly deserved; Muir's contributions to the place through the years were considerable, particularly his efforts to create Yosemite National Park in 1890. He will also long be associated with the park thanks to his eloquent, loving writings.

John Muir first visited Yosemite in 1868 and returned the following summer to work as a shepherd in what would later become the park's high country. Late in 1869, he could no longer resist the lure of Yosemite Valley and found work doing odd jobs there for James Mason Hutchings. He built a small cabin on Yosemite Creek and began a long-term residence in his beloved Yosemite.

Muir roamed and studied the park, learning its aspects as intimately as he could. He became renowned as a guide, and entertained such visitors as Asa Gray, William Keith, Ralph Waldo Emerson, and other luminaries of the day. His marathon hikes with few or no provisions have become legendary. All along he recorded his experiences and documented the natural world around him in a series of journals.

In 1871, Muir published a newspaper article about Yosemite; it was the first of a series of articles and books he would write during his life. Topics of his writing included the glaciers, the forests, winter storms, and everything else about Yosemite that came to fascinate him. In the mid-'70s, he moved from Yosemite, married, and began a new life in Martinez.

In 1889, he returned to the park with Robert Underwood Johnson. It was during this visit that the two hatched a campaign to establish Yosemite National Park. Using articles, personal visits, and other lobbying efforts, the two saw the 1890 act to create the national park through to its successful passage.

Muir was later to write *My First Summer in the Sierra* and *The Yosemite* (among many others), both of which would become Yosemite classics. His tireless work in opposition to the damming of the park's Hetch Hetchy Valley (a fight that he lost), drained him physically and contributed to his death in 1914.

David and Jennie Curry

The Curry name is synonymous with the concession operation in Yosemite, and these lively people were pioneer innkeepers in the park. In 1899, they moved to California from Indiana and established a small camp in the eastern end of Yosemite Valley. Starting with seven tents for guests and a dining tent that seated twenty, the Currys initiated an enterprise that experienced immediate growth.

By the end of their first season, the camp size had increased to 25 tents, and almost 300 guests had been accommodated. The operation soon became known as Camp Curry, and thanks to their warm hospitality and outgoing personalities, the Currys prospered.

David Curry specialized in entertaining his guests with both disarming informality and brash showmanship. Every night at the campfire, people were encouraged to add wood to the fire, and while it burned, to tell stories or lead songs. Curry also revitalized the "Fire Fall," the spectacle that involved pushing burning embers from the brink of Glacier Point to create a stream of fire down the cliff face.

"Mother" Curry, as she was affectionately called, was considerably less flamboyant, but continued the Camp Curry tradition when David died in 1917. She was assisted by various family members and saw her camp grow to include lodging for 1,300 guests.

In 1925, the Curry Camping Company and the Yosemite National Park Company merged to form a single concession operation known as the Yosemite Park & Curry Co. that operated until 1993.

Ansel Adams

The man who best communicated the beauty of Yosemite through photography during the twentieth century was Ansel Adams, and his influence continues to be felt. His images have been a source of inspiration, delight, and enjoyment to millions of persons, and they have defined the Yosemite landscape for many. Further, he was a dogged conservationist who worked hard to protect the environment he photographed with such skill.

Interestingly, Ansel Adams was a gifted artist in two fields. He almost became a professional pianist, but the camera won out, particularly as Adams became more and more attached to Yosemite. He moved to the valley in 1920 to run the Sierra Club Lodge, and made the acquaintance of the proprietor of Best's Studio, painter Harry Best, who allowed Ansel the use of a piano. It brought Adams in contact with Best's daughter Virginia, whom he later married.

For several years, Adams worked as a "commercial" photographer doing publicity pictures for the Curry Co. and other such jobs. As the years passed, his promotional work gave way increasingly to his more "artistic" expression. His prints were offered for sale in gift shops and at Best's Studio, and before long he was gaining national recognition for his fine landscape work.

Many of his photographs were used to illustrate the beauty of natural areas that environmental groups hoped to have protected by Congress, and he undertook special assignments from the National Park Service to photograph the national parks. His landscapes became well-known for their detail, tonal ranges, unique composition, and fine printing. A multitude of awards were bestowed upon Adams for his photographic excellence.

He remained active as a photographer and conservationist until his death in 1984, teaching, lecturing, lobbying, and making new images all the while. Best's Studio is now operated as the Ansel Adams Gallery, and a peak on Yosemite's eastern boundary was named for him in 1985.

Selected Yosemite Place Names

Ahwahnee: The native Indians' name for both a large village near Yosemite Falls and for the greater Yosemite Valley. Those Indians were known as the Ahwahnechees. Lafayette Bunnell reported that the name meant deep, grassy valley, although this is unsubstantiated. Some linguists believe that "place of a gaping mouth" is a closer translation.

Big Oak Flat: A small town near Yosemite's northwestern boundary from which the Highway 120 route took its original name. The massive oak (reportedly ten feet in diameter) that inspired the name is long since dead, the victim of miners' axes in the 1860s.

Chilnualna: This name, common in the Wawona area, is of unknown origin and meaning. An unsupported theory suggests its meaning is leaping water.

Clark: Yosemite Valley's first guardian in 1864 and the discoverer of the Mariposa Grove of Big Trees was Galen Clark. His name now graces a mountain, a mountain range, and other features in Yosemite.

Conness: A senator from California in the 1860s, John Conness introduced the bill in Congress that set aside Yosemite Valley and the Mariposa Grove of Big Trees as a state preserve. Mount Conness is an imposing peak on the park boundary north of Tioga Pass.

Crane Flat: Most probably named for a group of sand hill cranes encountered there by Lafayette Bunnell (John Muir also noted cranes at the location), although some assert the origin was a man named Crean who at one time resided at the spot.

Curry: David and Jennie "Mother" Curry established a small tent camp for the public in Yosemite Valley in 1899. It grew to become Camp Curry and later Curry Village. The merger of their operation with the Yosemite Park Company resulted in the Yosemite Park & Curry Co., a longtime concessioner.

Dana: J. D. Whitney's California Geological Survey named a prominent peak east of Tuolumne Meadows for James Dwight Dana in 1863. Dana was a Yale professor and considered the foremost American geologist of his time.

El Capitan: This massive granite cliff was named by the Mariposa Battalion in 1851. It is the Spanish equivalent of the native Indian name Too-tok-ah-noo-lah meaning Rock Chief or Captain. Other names assigned the rock at one time or another were Crane Mountain and Giant's Tower (go Giants!).

El Portal: This is Spanish for gateway or entrance, and was used to name the terminus of the Yosemite Valley Railroad on the park's western doorstep. Now a small town on Highway 140, the site is slated to become the park's headquarters. Because of its searing summer heat, some have dubbed the place "Hell Portal."

Glen Aulin: James McCormick, at the behest of R. B. Marshall of the U.S.G.S., named this idyllic spot on the Tuolumne River with the Gaelic phrase for beautiful valley or glen in the early 1900s. A High Sierra Camp was built there in 1927.

Half Dome: Credit the Mariposa Battalion with describing this split mountain as a half dome. Of all the landmarks in Yosemite, Half Dome has worn the most names over the years, among them Rock of Ages, North Dome, South Dome, Sentinel Dome, Tis-sa-ack, Cleft Rock, Goddess of Liberty, Mt. Abraham Lincoln, and Spirit of the Valley. Somehow a t-shirt imprinted with the phrase "I climbed on top of the Goddess of Liberty" wouldn't quite work.

Happy Isles: One of Yosemite Valley's early Guardians named the three small islets on the Merced River for the emotions he enjoyed while exploring them ("no one can visit them without for the while forgetting the grinding strife of his world and being happy"). For years this was the site of a fish hatchery.

Hetch Hetchy: At one time a remarkably beautiful companion valley to Yosemite, Hetch Hetchy bears an Indian name that has been interpreted to have several meanings. The most popular is a kind of grass or plant with edible seeds that abounded in the valley, although some believe Hetchy means tree and Hetch Hetchy is descriptive of two yellow pine trees that grew at the entrance to the place. Hetch Hetchy was dammed by the damned City of San Francisco in the 1920s.

Illilouette: This French sounding name is actually an English translation (poor indeed!) of the Indian word Too-lool-a-we-ack. James Mason Hutchings opined that its meaning is "the place beyond which was the great rendezvous of the Yosemite Indians for hunting deer" (the great Miwok hunt club in the sky?).

Lembert: John Baptiste Lembert was an early settler in the Tuolumne Meadows region. He built a cabin at the soda springs in Tuolumne, and his name is attached to the granite dome nearby.

Lyell: Yosemite's highest peak (13,114 feet) was named for Sir Charles Lyell, an eminent English geologist, by the California Geological Survey in 1863.

Mariposa: The Spanish word for butterfly first applied to a land grant, later to the community, and then to the county. Because they occurred in Mariposa County when Galen Clark discovered them in 1857, the sequoias at the south end of Yosemite were called the Mariposa Grove of Big Trees.

Merced: The Spanish name given the river originating in Yosemite's high country when it was crossed in the San Joaquin Valley by the Moraga party. Formally known as El Rio de Nuestra Señora de la Merced (River of Our Lady of Mercy), the title was applied five days after the feast day of Our Lady of Mercy in 1806. All other names utilizing Merced in Yosemite are derived from the river's name.

Mono: Derived from the Yokuts Indian word monoi or monai meaning flies. At what is now known as Mono Lake, the resident Indians harvested, ate, and traded millions of the pupae of a fly—a favorite foodstuff of the native people of the region. The Shoshonean tribe grew to be known as the Mona or Mono Indians, and many landmarks east of Yosemite bear this name.

Nevada: Assigned as a name to the waterfall on the Merced River by the Mariposa Battalion in 1851. The word signifies snow in Spanish, and members of the battalion felt that the name was appropriate because the fall was so close to the Sierra Nevada and because the white, foaming water was reminiscent of a vast avalanche of snow.

Olmsted: A turnout with a remarkable view from the Tioga Road near Tenaya Lake was named for both Frederick Law Olmsted and his son, Frederick Law Olmsted, Jr. The senior Olmsted was involved in the earliest development of the 1864 Yosemite Grant, and served as Chairman of the first Board of Yosemite Valley Commissioners. His son worked as an N.P.S. planner in Yosemite and had a position on the Yosemite Advisory Board.

Sierra Nevada: This is the Spanish phrase for snowy mountain range. It was applied to California's greatest range of mountains by Father Pedro Font who glimpsed it from near Antioch in 1776. Because the word Sierra implies a series of mountains, it is both grammatically and politically incorrect to use the term "Sierras." If you do you will be castigated by self-righteous Yosemite word snobs.

Stoneman: A large hotel built by the State of California in 1885 once stood in the meadow just north of Curry Village. Known as the Stoneman House for then-Governor George Stoneman, it burned in 1896. The meadow and nearby bridge still bear the name.

Tenaya: The chief of the resident Indian tribe when the Mariposa Battalion entered Yosemite Valley in 1851 was named Tenieya. The battalion first encountered the Native Americans living near the banks of a lake near Tuolumne Meadows that they called Tenaya Lake.

Tioga: This in an Iroquois Indian word meaning where it forks, swift current, or gate. Miners at work on the Sierra crest near Yosemite established the Tioga Mining District in 1878, apparently importing the name from Pennsylvania or New York.

Tuolumne: An Indian tribe residing in the Sierra foothills near Knights Ferry was known as "Taulamne," reportedly pronounced Tu-ah-lum'-ne. The Indian name was applied to the river originating in Yosemite that flowed through their territory.

Vogelsang: Col. Benson, an Army officer and acting Superintendent of Yosemite National Park from 1905 to 1908, named a peak south of Tuolumne Meadows for either Alexander Vogelsang or his brother Charles Vogelsang, both of whom were affiliated with California Fish and Game. Vogelsang is German for meadow in which birds sing, an apt description of the site of the Vogelsang High Sierra Camp.

Wawona: The popular opinion is that the word is the Indian name for "big tree." The Indians viewed the trees as sacred and called them Woh-woh'-nah. The word is formed in imitation of the hooting of an owl, which bird to the native people was the guardian spirit and deity of the sequoias.

White Wolf: A meadow on the old route of the Tioga Road was named by John Meyer, who, while chasing Indians, came to the temporary camp of the band's chief. His name was White Wolf.

Yosemite: This name was assigned to the world's most beautiful valley by the Mariposa Battalion in 1851. They believed that the Yosemite people (as they were apparently known) who resided there should have their tribe's name perpetuated in the designation of the valley. The exact meaning of the name is disputed, but Lafayette Bunnell, a member of the battalion, later wrote that the term signified "grizzly bear." He was informed that because grizzly bears frequented the territory occupied by the Yosemites and because the Indian band was skilled at killing the bears, the name was taken as an appropriate one for the tribe.

Further Reading

Yosemite Place Names by Peter Browning. Lafayette, CA: Great West Books, 1988.

Place Names of the High Sierra by Francis Farquhar. San Francisco: Sierra Club, 1926 (out of print).

Getting to Yosemite

Most visitors to Yosemite arrive in private automobiles, but there are public transportation alternatives. Below are brief descriptions of those various alternatives. They are followed by detailed descriptions of the highway routes to Yosemite. If you need further information about transportation to Yosemite National Park, call (209) 372-0200.

By Air: The largest air terminal close to Yosemite served by a number of major airlines and several smaller ones is Fresno's. Formerly known as FAT (Fresno Air Terminal), the facility has been upgraded to the Fresno Yosemite International Airport (FYI). At this time there is no bus connection to the park, and a rental car (from several major car rental agencies in the terminal) is required for the two-hour trip to Yosemite Valley. A small airline also flies to Merced. Bus service is available from the Merced Airport on VIA/Gray Line daily. Call (209) 384-1315, or in California, 1-800-369-7275 (the web address is www.via-adventures.com). Rental cars also are available in Merced.

By Train: Train transportation is available to Yosemite from both Northern and Southern California. The Northern California AMTRAK train, originating in Emeryville, carries passengers to Merced daily. Connection to Yosemite is made via the VIA/Gray Line bus. For the return to Emeryville, an AMTRAK train departs Merced every afternoon.

There are Southern California trains from both Los Angeles and San Diego on AMTRAK. The trip requires bus inter-connects from Los Angeles to Bakersfield and from Merced to Yosemite. Return travelers can catch a VIA/Gray Line bus to Merced for the AMTRAK trip to Bakersfield and connections to Las Vegas and Southern California. For train and bus reservations call 1-800-USA-RAIL.

By Bus: For those staying in visitor accommodations surrounding the park, there is a car-free option. The Yosemite Area Regional Transportation System (YARTS) provides bus service from many of the communities outside Yosemite. Along the Highway 140 route, service is available from Merced, Catheys Valley, Mariposa, Midpines, and El Portal. From Highways 120 and 132, buses can be caught in Coulterville, Greeley Hill, Groveland, and Buck Meadows. Service also is available from Mammoth Lakes over Highway 120 during summer months only. For information, call toll free to (877) 989-2787, or visit www.yosemite.com/yarts.

As noted above, VIA/Gray Line offers routes from Merced on a daily basis.

Reservations should be made by calling (209) 384-1315, or in California, 1-800-369-7275 (the web address is www.via-adventures.com).

By Automobile: There are four major routes to Yosemite National Park. What follows are points of interest, restaurants, and motels along each route. The list is not meant to be complete or exhaustive; rather, it reflects the preferences of the author. Because motels and restaurants are often short-lived, be sure to call ahead to avoid disappointment. Note: All directions and orientations assume that one is traveling toward Yosemite.

HIGHWAY 41 FROM FRESNO

Oakhurst (45 miles north of Fresno):

Points of Interest

Yosemite Sierra Visitor Center: : On the right side of Highway 41 on the way out of town (just past El Cid restaurant). A great place to get oriented, ask for directions, and find books and maps about Yosemite.

Fresno Flats Historical Park: Turn right at the second Oakhurst stop light. Continue about half a mile to School Road (Road 427). Turn left and follow signs to this museum that includes a collection of old buildings depicting the lives of early settlers in the area. Hours are 1-3 p.m., Wednesday through Sunday.

Restaurants

Crab Cakes: 40278 Stagecoach Road (on the left, just past the second stop light, behind Subway), (559) 641-7667. Besides the namesake crab cakes, this small, well-run eatery serves fresh fish and shell fish, steak, chicken, and pasta. Meals include a bowl of delicious cole slaw and plenty of fresh bread. Patio seating is available.

Old Mexico Taqueria: Raley's Shopping Center (at the intersection of Highways 41 and 49), (559) 683-2777. This inexpensive outlet offers a lengthy menu of Mexican fare, and they prepare your choice as you wait in line. There are vegetarian options, and beer and wine are available.

Szechuan Restaurant: 40484 Highway 41 (on left, just south of the Best Western Motel), (559) 683-8328. Very acceptable Chinese food that's right off the highway and right on the price. "Spicy" alternatives are available throughout the menu, and they claim to use no MSG.

Erna's Elderberry House & Bistro: Highway 41 & Victoria Lane (on left on final descent into Oakhurst), (559) 683-6800. This is the proverbial diamond in the proverbial diamond in the foothill rough. One of the few 5-star rated restaurants in California, featuring old European cuisine with a California twist. Craig Claiborne of the *New York Times* spent three days here and wrote rave reviews. But beware, you must dress up and dinners run about $72 per person.

Oka Japanese Restaurant: 40291 Junction Drive (turn left onto Highway 49, turn right at first stop light), (559) 642-4850. Despite the walls painted with fish and other slightly odd bits of décor, this is a good place for sushi, and features first-rate, generally authentic food.

Motels

Oakhurst Lodge: 40302 Highway 41 (on the left just past Oakhurst's second stop light), 1-800-OK-LODGE. 60 units; rates for two are $45-50 in winter, $60-65 spring and fall, and $70-80 in summer. The web address is www.oklodge.com.

Shilo Inn: 40644 Highway 41 (on the left past Oakhurst's second stop light), (559) 683-3555. 80 mini-suite units, pool; rates for two are $49-$69 in winter (except holidays), $79-$129 in summer. The web address is www.shiloinns.com/California/oakhurst.html.

Yosemite Gateway Best Western: 40530 Highway 41 (on the left past Oakhurst's second stop light), (559) 683-2378. 122 units, indoor and outdoor pools and spas, restaurant; rates for two are $45-$80 in winter; $80-$100 in summer. The web address is http://www.bestwestern.com.

Holiday Inn Express: 40662 Highway 41 (on the left past Oakhurst's second stop light), (559) 642-2525. 42 units, pool; rates for two are $39-$69 in winter; $79-$125 in summer.

Chateau du Sureau: Highway 41 & Victoria Lane (on left on final descent into Oakhurst), (559) 683-6860. Affiliated with Erna's Elderberry House (see restaurants above), this is very expensive, luxury lodging. 10 rooms, pool; rates for two are $350-$550. The web address is www.chateaudusureau.com.

Mileages to Yosemite Valley	
Via Highway 41	
From Los Angeles	313 miles
From Bakersfield	201 miles
From Fresno	94 miles
From Oakhurst	50 miles
From Fish Camp	37 miles
Via Highway 140	
From Merced	81 miles
From Mariposa	43 miles
From El Portal	14 miles

Yosemite Falls

Fish Camp (15 miles north of Oakhurst):

Points of Interest

Yosemite Mountain-Sugar Pine Railroad: 56001 Highway 41 (one mile south of Fish Camp on the right), (559) 683-7273. Take time out for a ride on a historic logging train. Utilizing Shay steam locomotives and Model A powered railcars, the railroad covers a four-mile loop. Many special events (including dinner trips) are offered throughout the year. A fee is charged for the ride.

Restaurants

The Narrow Gauge Inn: 48571 Highway 41 (on the right just past the Yosemite Mt.-Sugar Pine Railroad, one mile south of Fish Camp), (559) 683-6446. A rustic but charming dining room with an excellent menu. Open April to October only.

The Sierra Restaurant (at Tenaya Lodge): 41122 Highway 41 (on the right as you enter Fish Camp), (559) 683-6555. Despite the p.r. department's claim that their "Sierra Alpine cuisine" borrows "heavily from the Native American and pioneering influences of the region," the food and service are actually pretty good.

Motels

Tenaya Lodge: 41122 Highway 41 (on the right as you enter Fish Camp), (559) 683-6555. 244 rooms, indoor and outdoor pools, fitness center, cocktail lounge, restaurants; rates for two are $153-$165 in winter, $175-$190 in summer.

Narrow Gauge Inn: 48571 Highway 41 (on the right just past the Yosemite Mt.-Sugar Pine Railroad, one mile south of Fish Camp), (559) 683-7720. 27 rooms, pool; rates for two are $75-$105. The motel is open April through October.

HIGHWAY 140 FROM MERCED

Mariposa (37 miles east of Merced):

Points of Interest

California State Mining & Mineral Museum: 5007 Fairgrounds Road (on the left side of Highway 49 at the Mariposa County Fairgrounds, about 1 mile south of town), (209) 742-7625. A well-exhibited collection of minerals plus a mine tunnel and gold displays. An entrance fee is charged.

Mariposa County Courthouse: Bullion Street (turn right on 8th Street near the middle of town, then left on Bullion), (209) 966-4056. This handsome wooden building (erected in 1854) is the oldest courthouse in continuous use west of the Mississippi. Self-guided tours Monday through Friday.

Mariposa History Center: 5116 Jesse Street (on the left side of Highway 140 towards the east end of town and next to the Bank of America), (209) 966-2924. Historic displays and reconstructions of early-day Mariposa environments. Call for hours of operation.

Restaurants

Castillo's: 4995 Fifth Street (one block off Highway 140; turn right at The Vault), (209) 742-4413. Castillo's is a good choice for regulation Mexican food. Outdoor seating available when weather permits.

Savoury's: 5027 Highway 140 (on the left side in the historic block downtown), (209) 966-7677. This small eatery has quickly become a favorite of the locals. A little cramped, but excellent food at moderate prices. Patio seating in summer.

Charles Street Dinner House: On the left of Highway 140 at Seventh Street downtown, (209) 966-2366. Good traditional food and plenty of it. A pretty sure bet.

Motels

Super 8 Motel: 5059 Highway 140 (on left about midway through town), (209) 966-4288. 46 rooms; rates for two are $45-$65 in winter; $65-$170 in summer.

Best Western Yosemite Way Station: 4999 Highway 140 (on left where the highway intersects with Highway 49 South); (209) 966-7545. 78 rooms, pool; rates for two are $59-$85.

Mariposa Lodge: 5052 Highway 140 (on right about midway through town), (209) 966-3607. 44 rooms, pool, pets are allowed; rates for two are $55-$65 in winter; $65-$85 in summer.

Mother Lode Lodge: 5051 Highway 140 (on left about midway through town), (209) 966-2521. 14 rooms, pool, one kitchenette; rates for two are $48-$112. The web address is www.mariposamotel.com.

Midpines (10 miles east of Mariposa)

Motels

Yosemite Bug Hostel: 6979 Highway 140 (on the left about two miles beyond "downtown" Midpines), (209) 966-6666. This alternative group of accommodations includes dorm cabins, family and private rooms with both shared and private baths, tent cabins, and campsites. The hostel is very popular with "backpacking" travelers and enjoys an international clientele. Rates vary by the season, and range from $16 plus tax for a dormitory bed to $115 plus tax for a private room. The Recovery Café offers inexpensive breakfasts and dinners, will pack a "trail lunch," and serves beer and wine. This establishment is affiliated with the American Youth Hostel program. The web address is www.yosemitebug.com.

El Capitan in winter

El Portal (29 miles east of Mariposa):

Points of Interest

Site of Savage's Trading Post: On the right side of Highway 140, 22 miles east of Mariposa, at the confluence of the South and Main Forks of the Merced River. This is the actual site of an early day trading post where the Indians and miners went for supplies and goods. There's a gift shop here now specializing in Indian arts and crafts. You'll also find the trailhead for a hike up the South Fork of the Merced that's ablaze with the colors of wildflowers in the spring. (209) 379-2301.

Yosemite Rail Exhibit: Turn left from Highway 140 onto El Portal Road and proceed one block to exhibit. Here are relics of early railroad activity in and around Yosemite, primarily old train cars and a locomotive. El Portal was the terminus of the Yosemite Valley Railroad.

Motels

Cedar Lodge: On the right side of Highway 140, 25 miles east of Mariposa, (209) 379-2612. 122 rooms, pool, restaurant, bar; rates for two are $85-$129.

Yosemite Redbud Lodge: At the site of Savage's Trading Post, on the right side of Highway 140, 22 miles east of Mariposa, (800) 321-5261. This establishment was being completely remodeled at the time this book was going to press. Its operators plan to offer multi-day rentals in the renovated units.

Yosemite View Lodge: On the right side of Highway 140 at the park boundary line, (209) 379-2681. 278 rooms, gift shop, pools, restaurant; rates for two are $99-$139.

HIGHWAY 120 FROM MANTECA

Oakdale (20 miles east of Manteca):

Points of Interest

Hershey Chocolate Company: 1400 S. Yosemite Avenue, (209) 847-0381. Free half-hour tours of the chocolate factory are conducted Monday through Friday from 8 a.m. until 3 p.m. See kisses wrapped and huge vats of chocolate, and you may even get a treat when you're done.

Jamestown (32 miles east of Oakdale on Highway 108, about 6 miles east off the main route):

Points of Interest

Railtown 1897: Fifth Avenue (just beyond town), (209) 984-4641. This is a State Historic Park featuring a 26-acre round-house and shop complex with steam locomotives and rolling passenger cars that have served the Sierra Railroad and Mother Lode since 1897. Open from 10 a.m. to 5 p.m. during summer and on weekends in winter.

Downtown Jamestown: Main Street Jamestown is lined with shops, restaurants, and galleries housed in restored historic buildings. The Gold Rush theme predominates in this thriving tourist attraction.

Restaurants

Jamestown Hotel: On Main Street, downtown, (209) 984-3902. Serving "continental California cuisine" from 5 to 9 daily, with a Sunday brunch. Outdoor cafe in summer.

Hotel Willow Restaurant: Main and Willow, downtown, (209) 984-3998. Food for the "California gourmet" at dinner nightly. Good for families.

Michelangelo: On Main Street, downtown, (209) 984-4830. An interesting new Italian option in a quaint location. Full bar available.

Bridalveil Fall

Moccasin (37 miles east of Oakdale on Highway 120):

Points of Interest

Moccasin Creek Fish Hatchery: On the left side of Highway 49 about 100 feet south of its intersection with Highway 120, (209) 989-2312. Take a self-guided tour of this facility (operated by the California Department of Fish and Game), where 1,000,000 catchable size rainbow trout are produced annually for Sierra foothill reservoirs, streams, and rivers. Open 7:30 a.m. to 3 p.m. daily, year round.

Groveland (9 miles east of Moccasin):

Restaurants

Hotel Charlotte: On the left side of Highway 120 in the center of downtown, (209) 962-6455. They characterize their food as hearty California country cuisine. Open for dinner from April through October only. The web address is www.hotelcharlotte.com.

Groveland Hotel Restaurant: 18767 Main Street - on the right side of Highway 120, (209) 962-4000. Serving a varied menu prepared from California seasonal ingredients with herbs from the hotel's garden, and featuring an award-winning wine list. The web address is www.groveland.com/rest.htm.

Motels

Groveland Hotel: 18767 Main Street - on the right side of Highway 120, (209) 962-4000. 17 rooms and suites; rates for two are $135-$210 (including breakfast). Mid-week and winter specials are available. The web address is www.groveland.com.

Buck Meadows (12 miles east of Groveland):

Restaurants

Buck Meadows Restaurant: 7647 Highway 120 (on the left where the road gets wide), (209) 962-5281. Offering classic American cuisine, a variety of beer and wines, and daily specials.

Motels

Best Value Yosemite Westgate Lodge: 7633 Highway 120, (209) 962-5281. 55 rooms; rates for two are $59-$139, depending on season.

Tioga Road view

HIGHWAY 120 FROM LEE VINING

Lee Vining (at intersection of Highways 120 and 395). A good web site for the area is www.monolake.org/chamber/.

Points of Interest

Mono Lake County Park: 5 miles north of Lee Vining on Highway 395. A great spot for a picnic with a trail down to the lakeshore.

Mono Lake Information Center: Downtown Lee Vining, (760) 647-6386. Operated by the Mono Lake Committee, the group primarily responsible for saving and restoring Mono Lake, this outlet offers free educational exhibits, slide shows, and movies to visitors, plus a good bookstore.

Mono Lake Visitor Center: Just north of town on the right side of Highway 395. This impressive multi-agency facility is replete with modern displays, exhibits, a bookstore, slide shows, and a great deck overlooking the lake. For the story of Mono Lake, this is a must visit. An admission fee is charged.

Restaurants

Mono Inn

The Mono Inn Restaurant: On Highway 395 five miles north of its junction with Highway 120, (760) 647-6581. This classic old inn overlooking the lake has been rehabilitated by the Ansel Adams family, and the food, décor, ambience, and view are terrific. Terrace dining is available in the summer. Open from April or May through October only. The web address is www.anseladams.com.

Mono Mike's Barbecue: Downtown Lee Vining, (760) 647-6432. Featuring ribs, chicken, burgers, and a front patio.

Tioga Pass Resort: Nine miles west of Lee Vining on Highway 120, (209) 372-4471. A local landmark, famous for its homemade pies (see page 70).

Whoa Nellie Deli: At intersection of Highways 120 and 395, (760) 647-1088. This somewhat strange establishment inside the Mobil Gas Mart features excellent food, including fish tacos, buffalo meatloaf, and lobster taquitos. You can even order a pitcher of margaritas.

Motels

Best Western Lakeview Lodge: On Highway 395 in downtown Lee Vining, (760) 647-6543 or (800) 528-1234. A nice motel run by even nicer people, the Banta's. 47 rooms, rates for 2 are $42-$112.

Murphey's Motel: On Highway 395 in downtown Lee Vining, (760) 647-6316. A decent motel with a AAA rating; one of the buildings is rustic, the other contemporary. 43 rooms, rates for two are $53-$108. The web address is www.murpheysyosemite.com.

Tioga Pass Resort: Nine miles west of Lee Vining on Highway 120, 372-4471. 10 housekeeping cabins and 4 motel-type units; rates for 2 are $100-175 per night, and $875-1075 per week.

Mileages to Yosemite Valley	
Via Highway 120 from the West	
From San Francisco	195 miles
From Sacramento	176 miles
From Stockton	127 miles
From Manteca	117 miles
From Oakdale	96 miles
From Groveland	49 miles
Via Highway 120 from the East	
From Reno	218 miles
From Carson City	188 miles
From Bishop	146 miles
From Mammoth Lakes	106 miles
From Lee Vining	74miles

Yosemite in Fiction

Since people started writing about it in the 1850s, Yosemite has figured as a grand locale for several works of fiction. From mass-appeal romances to beatnik epics to entangled mysteries, the array is an impressive one. The following is a list of some of the better and more unusual literary works with a Yosemite setting.

1. *The Forge of God* by Greg Bear. New York: Tom Doherty Associates, 1987. This science fiction novel is set in "futuristic" 1997 when there are profound changes to the solar system and the earth is threatened with destruction. People migrate to Yosemite to await their imminent demise. The book climaxes with an enormous cataclysm brought on by seismic disruptions. There's a great description of the collapse of the Royal Arches, the blockage of Yosemite Falls, the burial of Curry Village, and the destruction of Half Dome.

2. *Star Trek V: The Final Frontier* by J. M. Dillard. Based on the screenplay by David Loughery. New York: Pocket Books, 1989. Media spin-off in reverse. A book that grew out of the movie, part of which was filmed in the park. In one episode, McCoy, Spock, and Kirk are on "shore leave" in Yosemite. Captain Kirk attempts a free climb of El Capitan, apparently falls to his death, only to have Spock (wearing levitation boots) catch him by the ankles in mid-air.

3. *The Dharma Bums* by Jack Kerouac. New York: The Viking Press, 1958. The beat generation goes hiking! Here's a classic account of a 1955 climb of Yosemite's Matterhorn Peak by Kerouac, Gary Snyder, and John Montgomery, written as fiction. The description of two crazed beatniks bounding down the side of the Matterhorn, yodeling and laughing, is particularly joyful.

4. *The Affair of the Jade Monkey* by Clifford Knight. New York: Dodd, Mead & Co., 1943. A reprint edition was published by the Yosemite Association in 1993. Detective Huntoon Rogers tracks a suspicious character to Yosemite National Park. A body is found in the backcountry, so Rogers joins a 7-day hiking party. One of the hikers is murdered and a small jade monkey appears in another's pack. Can Huntoon solve the case and thwart an enemy plot directed against the nation?

5. *Angels of Light* by Jeffrey B. Long. New York: William Morrow & Co., 1987. Here's a Yosemite climbing novel with a twist. Its based loosely on the true story of the drug plane that crashed at Lower Merced Pass Lake in the park's backcountry. Before the rangers caught on, hundreds of pounds of marijuana were packed out by Yosemite climbers. The author characterizes it as the end of innocence for the park's climbing subculture.

6. *Images on Silver* by Rayanne Moore. Toronto: Harlequin Books, 1984. Believe it or not, a Harlequin Romance set in Yosemite. Christy Reilly is a highly-acclaimed wildlife photographer who meets Ranger Travis Jeffords. Travis keeps asking Christy why she has worked alone for so long. Christy's secret is something no man can understand.

7. *Fires of Innocence* by Jane Bonander. New York: St. Martin's Press, 1994. In a snowbound cabin in 1860s Yosemite Valley, Alex Golovin, a government attorney bent on buying up land for the national park, and Scotty MacDowell, daughter of a valley homesteader, come to know each other. Thrilling her with "searing kisses and teasing caresses," he will not let the "sensuous spitfire" stand in the way of his work. Steamy and far-fetched.

8. *Nurse in Yosemite* by Beatrice Warren. New York: Avalon Books, 1982. Nurse Doralee Dahlquist moves to Yosemite and takes a job at the medical clinic. All goes well until she falls for photographer Angus McGonigal. The conflict arises from fellow nurse Jan Stagnetto's claim that she will marry handsome Angus. Will Angus resist Jan's charms or will Doralee get dumped?

9. *A Body to Dye For* by Grant Michaels. New York: St. Martin's Press, 1990. Incredibly, this one's about a gay hairdresser/detective who finds the dead body of a Yosemite park ranger in the bed of one of his regular customers. In his efforts to solve the case, he follows leads back to Yosemite National Park, where his contacts in the gay world help him sort out a cast of colorful characters.

10. *High Sierra* by Nevada Barr. New York: Putnam & Sons, 2004. The famed national park mystery writer finally inserts her protagonist, Anna Pigeon, into Yosemite. She's working undercover as a waitress at The Ahwahnee, where her co-workers' odd behavior leads her into the backcountry and a showdown with some evil druggies. It's Yosemite as the "dark side."

Pacific tree frog

Yosemite on the Internet

T hanks to the amazing growth of the Internet, there are now lots of online resources available for Yosemite. Whether found on sites that are maintained by the government or on the personal pages of passionate Yosemite lovers, Yosemite information, photographs, maps, and stories are abundant. Here are some of the best available at this time.

Yosemite Online - The Web Site of the Yosemite Association (www.yosemite.org). This full-featured site is best known for its web cam view of Yosemite Valley from Turtleback Dome, its extensive news archives, a variety of diary accounts about Yosemite, and an area dedicated to natural history issues in the Sierra. There's also an extensive Yosemite Store and visitor information.

Yosemite National Park Home Page (www.nps.gov/yose). This is the official park web site maintained by the National Park Service. It has lots of visitor information, nuts and bolts data, official government press releases, a section about park planning and management issues, programs for students, and a park map.

DNC Parks & Resorts at Yosemite (www.yosemitepark.com). Operated by the park's chief concessioner, this site is most important for the information it provides about lodging options in Yosemite. Recently, the capability to make room reservations online has been added, and a certain number of lodging units can only be reserved this way. There's also information about special events, discount offers, and jobs in the park.

National Park Reservation System (reservations.nps.gov). This site provides an easy and convenient way to make camping reservations (using a credit card) for Yosemite and other national park campgrounds. It certainly beats trying to use their phone-in system. Options are available for individual, family, and group sites at all campgrounds that require reservations (see page 12).

Yosemite Trip Planning Online (www.nps.gov/yose/trip/index.htm). These pages are part of the official National Park Service site for Yosemite. They encompass a range of topics designed to help visitors make plans for their trip to the park. One particularly helpful feature is the Current Conditions page, with links to the *Yosemite Today* newspaper and info on what's open, weather data, etc.

Yosemite Wilderness Information (www.nps.gov/yose/wilderness). This National Park Service site provides extensive information for backpackers, including trip planning ideas, bear avoidance techniques, trail data, hiking conditions, and most important, an online wilderness permit reservation option. While the site sometimes goes long periods without updating, there's good solid material available here.

The Yosemite Fund (www.yosemitefund.org). This is the major fundraising organization for Yosemite, and its site reports on the status of projects being undertaken, discusses volunteer opportunities, describes the hugely successful Yosemite license plate program, and allows persons to make donations on-line.

The Yosemite Institute (www.yni.org/yi/). This organization offers environmental education in the park, and their site offers a program orientation slide show, information about the educational curriculum, organizational data, and teacher resources. For school groups interested in a high-quality learning experience in Yosemite, this is the place to check.

The Yosemite Store Online (www.yosemitestore.com). For visitors interested in information, books, maps, gifts, and other Yosemite-related products, this site is made to order. The collection of items available is extensive, all products are illustrated in color, and the ordering process (with a credit card) is efficiently handled through a secure server. Yosemite Association members can take advantage of a 15% discount on anything they order, too.

Yosemite Today Online (www.nps.gov/yose/now/today.htm). This site allows prospective visitors to download as Adobe Reader files (PDF format) the park visitor handout known as *Yosemite Today*. It contains a calendar of guided programs and park activities, as well as hours of operation for visitor centers and museums.

Tioga high country